DAWN OF A NEW WORLD ORDER

The CRANIO-GENESIS *Project*

TERENCE J. MURPHY

The Cranio-Genesis Project: Dawn of a New World Order by Terence J. Murphy

terencejmurphy.com

Acknowledgments

Thanks to my lovely wife, Tracey, for her love, encouragement, patience, support, editorial inputs, and transformative suggestions. Without her help, I could not have pulled this novel together. Additionally, I would like to thank my son Jared for his reading of my various cuts and keen insights into improving the content. Also, thanks to my daughter Lindsey for some essential Zeke quotes and Kirra for her tolerance as I progressed through the project. A shout-out to my long-time friend, Dan Hurst, for his critical suggestions that shaped vital elements of the novel. Lastly, a heartfelt note of appreciation for his critical review of this work to my former colleague and a great industrial leader, Jon Piatt.

Disclaimers

This novel is a work of fiction. The organizations and people described in the story are meant only as fictional references. They imply no actual likeness, similarity, or capability to a real person or referenced organization.

Table of Contents

Introduction: Introduction ....
Prologue: Prologue ....
Chapter 1: Setting the Trap 1
Chapter 2: Springing the Trap 19
Chapter 3: The Harrowing Aftermath 34
Chpater 4: Expanding Their Realm 43
Chapter 5: Revelation 50
Chapter 6: The Cranio-Genesis Secrets 60
Chapter 7: Meet the Children 82
Chapter 8: The Grand Unification 92
Chpater 9: From the Ashes, We'll Rise 101
Chapter 10: Backyard War Games 117
Chapter 11: Eliminate All Loose Ends 128
Chapter 12: You Earned Your Spot 150
Chapter 13: Strange Bedfellows 165
Chapter 14: Moving at Light Speed 179
Chapter 15: Uncertainty Under Pressure 204
Chapter 16: Ultimatum and Opportunity 223
Chapter 17: Training Days 240
Chapter 18: Fortitude Against All Odds 254
Chapter 19: Final Preparations and Farewells 267
Chapter 20: The Element of Surprise 304
Chapter 21: Chaos and Consequences 323
Chapter 22: One Nation Unwilling to Grovel 355

"The greatest thing that science teaches you is the law of unintended consequences."

- *Ann Druyan*

Introduction

We often marvel at today's most extraordinary technological wonders, such as a Space X rocket, the latest Apple iPhone, or a Japanese AI Robot. While pondering these modern feats, we often fail to reflect on the world's most significant piece of technology, the human brain.

The construct of the brain is both hardware and software and can complete tasks with unparalleled efficiency and speed. The simultaneous execution of billions of complex operations makes modern technology seem trivial compared to this human organ.

Supercomputers, the length of football fields, only achieve one percent of the processing speed of the human brain while requiring megawatts of electrical power to operate them. The human brain, weighing only three pounds, operates approximately one million times faster than the latest laptop processor and uses less than twenty-five Watts of power.

While such a remarkable piece of technology exists within us, today's science still provides a limited understanding of its workings and capabilities. However, research into its operation is achieving unprecedented breakthroughs daily. Feeding this research are global organizations delving further into the brain's inner workings with the hopes of one day availing themselves of its broader possibilities.

Scientists have long suggested that the brain is underutilized, and many have indicated that dormant powers remain hidden within it. As science continues to probe these boundaries, we must ensure our aspirations do not lead to dangerous ramifications. While untold opportunities for the betterment of humankind could result, scientists could also unleash, in an unintended manner, terrifying enhancements that could lead to untold supremacy for those who wield them.

Prologue

The Cranio-Genesis lab rushes to save two children tragically left brain-dead from a severe car accident, forcing the classified program office to obtain approvals to proceed with a new neuroscience technique on its first child patients.

"The project director and I have completed the final paperwork," said the deputy director of the Cranio-Genesis Project with a troubled expression to Dr. Heidi Davidson. "You are free to proceed with both children immediately."

"Thank you, Ken," was all he heard as the frightened scientist rushed into the medical lab.

A five-month-old boy and an eighteen-month-old girl lay on two tables with numerous electronic probes attached to their shaven heads. A flurry of people connected equipment and checked a large contingent of monitors. One of them was her husband and co-lead on the program, Dr. Peter Davidson, who positioned small antenna arrays around both children's heads.

"Peter, we have the okay to proceed," said Heidi.

"Just about ready," Peter responded. "Both are still stable on their life support, but still no brain activity. I'm ready to initiate both electromagnetic sequences if you are still comfortable with the two stimuli."

"I selected them based on our prior findings, their ages, and weights," responded Heidi. "It's my best guess from our data sets."

"I trust your judgment here," he replied, unsure what she expected him to say. "This is your area of expertise. I'm confident you got it right."

“I think we have to go with this,” she confirmed. “We can’t wait any longer.”

“I agree,” he said, turning to the computer in front of him.

Peter pushed a touchscreen icon, and the entire room watched in complete silence.

Beeps broke the room's hush as several monitors started flashing, screaming high-pitched alerts that filled the air.

“We have a start to brain activity in both of them,” said a technician to Davidsons’ right.

“We’ve been here before with the others,” Peter responded. “We have to see if the brain can maintain the restart.”

The team stared intently at the brain activity monitors, looking for the slightest decay in brain activity, a trait all ten prior adult patients encountered as their brains failed to retain operation after restarting.

“It seems to be holding,” said Peter. “Just like we projected.”

“This is the farthest we’ve gotten,” responded his wife. “Their brains seem to be taking back full body function. Heart operation appears normal in both, and they’re starting to breathe on their own. Shallow but stable.”

“Let’s wait a bit longer,” he said. “Let’s watch the brain sequencing and look for any anomalies.”

“Still looking strong and holding,” said the technician.

Peter reached over and hugged his wife. “Honey, I think it worked. All regions of the brain are operational and functioning. Look at those scans. Nothing seems out of the ordinary. We were correct in our assertions, you can restart the organ, and it recovers its full operation.”

The last part, he said as tears ran down his face.

As he pulled away from her, he saw she was also sobbing with tears of joy.

They both realized this was a moment beyond measure. However, it wasn't a time for emotional folly because the two patients had physical trauma that needed immediate attention from the awaiting physician.

"Please take them to the recovery room with Dr. Simons," said Heidi, hurriedly talking to one of the nurses. "Let us know if there is the slightest change in condition. We'll be in there in a few minutes."

"Honey, we did it," Peter said as the children rolled into the next room. "We saved them both and have now proven that a human brain can be revived. Not how we hoped to make our life's work come to fruition, but we did it."

"Peter, it's not over until we know they will make a full recovery," Heidi responded. "We don't know if there will be other complications, permanent brain damage, or other issues. I can't celebrate success until I know more."

"Fair enough," he replied apologetically. "But, I can tell from their brain activity that there doesn't seem to be any significant damage to either of them. I do, however, understand your concerns."

"They're just so little, Peter," she said, weeping uncontrollably. "Their whole lives in front of them. It's got to work. I need this to work."

"I know, and we just brought them back to us and the world," said her husband. "Let's remain optimistic. Their physical injuries seem manageable, and our optimism about their brain injuries is justified. After thoroughly checking them out, Dr. Simons will let us know what he thinks."

A knock caused them to separate from their embrace and turn to the glass door, where they saw the Cranio-Genesis program director smiling and excitedly waving.

Peter motioned for him to come in.

"My god, you two did it," said the program director. "You just implemented one of the most incredible medical breakthroughs in history. Maybe the greatest. I'm so happy for both of you."

"Thank you," replied Peter. "Not how any of us planned it."

"Indeed," said the program director. "But that makes it even more special. I'm going to begin the process of getting the work declassified. This breakthrough is too significant to all humanity and doesn't belong hidden in some top-secret program. It won't happen overnight, as you know. But, after a year of proven recovery and test results, we should be able to get it out into the public domain. Meanwhile, we can find other patients for you and replicate these results. Then you can rightfully accept the colossal accolades coming your way, including a Nobel Prize. The world will soon know your names."

"Let's not jump too far down the road," Peter responded. "Let's make sure the children recover fully and check out entirely. But thank you for your support, encouragement, and quick approval to move forward with these two. Once we know all is okay, we can move on to other patients and work with you to get this into the open literature. We know there are a lot of parents out there that would love to have this option available to them."

"Get into the recovery room and check into your patients," said the director. "Thank you both for making the Cranio-Genesis Project one of the most important in history. The results of your work are going to change the world."

Chapter 1

Setting the Trap

Recently elected U.S. President Paul Schmidt stares at the collection of artworks displayed in the Oval Office while taking a short break from his current meeting. He bristles as he scans the portraits and statues depicting the men and women who shaped the country he now leads. Secretly he wonders how he was elected to follow in their footsteps and whether he will measure up against such distinguished historical figures.

Paul Schmidt's unprecedented popularity led him to exceed the win margins of both Ronald Reagan and Barrack Obama, which still amazes the successful former businessman and son of an Indiana farming couple. So much work is required to execute his ambitious domestic agenda, but unexpected international issues with Iran, Russia, and China have consumed him. As one who grew up on a farm, he knows you have to often pick through the thorns to get to the flower, so he keeps an optimistic perspective about the future.

His Director of National Intelligence, Margaret Stoneman, busily shifts her briefing notes as she seeks the memorandum detailing the Iranian leader's quote. She is a seasoned intelligence leader, having served in senior positions at the CIA and on prior national security teams, including his predecessors. She is tough as nails, and a person, the new President, has quickly come to trust. Her briefing moments ago that Iran has stepped up its antagonizing of U.S. interests and buildup of troops along the border with Iraq left the group deeply concerned about Iran's ultimate objectives.

Alongside the Director sits Secretary of Defense Cassandra Edgard, who quietly peruses a short defense department briefing on the latest Russian testing of new hypersonic missiles. Cassandra Edgard was a former aerospace industry CEO. She cut her teeth for a decade and a half in the Department of Defense before being lured into an executive position at a prime contractor, where she blossomed, becoming an industry star. She knew the inner workings of the U.S. military and its capabilities, making her an ideal candidate to head the Defense Department. President Schmidt's timing was perfect as he lured her away from her CEO position just as she was planning to retire. The President's charisma and balanced perspective on military force convinced her to serve as the first female Defense Secretary.

The final meeting attendee, Vice President Alan McIlroy, reads an email from the U.S. ambassador in China on his phone. The Vice President developed a close bond with the President while on the campaign trail, and their relationship has strengthened over the first months of their term. Alan is a respected former multi-term Senator from North Carolina with strong senatorial ties on both sides of the aisle. The President selected him because they resonate with several common beliefs, and Alan will be a crucial asset to passing legislation through Congress needed to secure critical items on their agenda.

"Sorry for the delay, Mr. President," said the Director. "Here is the quote from the speech by the Iranian Supreme Leader. 'Shia Muslims had lived too long under the oppression of Sunni Islamic leaders across the world. It's time for the Islamic people to rise and unite under one true Islamic leader.' That's a dangerous limb, even for Iran."

"Almost like some broad jihad that Supreme Leader Nouri preached in the early days of his tenure," said the Vice President.

"I agree," said the President. "How does Iran think they can instigate something of that magnitude? And lining troops along Iraq's border makes no sense. It seems strange they would invade Iraq because Sunni leaders have treated Shia poorly there for years, but we have seen strange things out of Iran in the past. Keep me informed of any other incidents."

The Supreme Leader of the Islamic Republic of Iran holds the highest official political and religious position. In fact, he is unquestionably the head of the country. After his confirmation, the Supreme Leader executed most of his rivals for claims of heresy and treason. Ultimately, Supreme Leader Nouri believed he could lead a revolution in Islam to span the globe and unite all Muslims. The U.S. considers him far more dangerous than any leader except Russia's Alexei Kovalyov, only because he possesses far less firepower than Kovalyov.

"Concern is growing about Iran amongst our allies," said President Schmidt. "Most believe they are poking us because of our years of economic sanctions and efforts to derail their nuclear program. They still haven't gotten over our cyber-attack with Stuxnet that took their nuclear centrifuges offline, setting their nuclear program back years."

President Schmidt was not about to waste time further guessing Iran's intentions, so he moved on to his discussion with Israeli Prime Minister Oren Yaakv.

"As you know, I had a call with the Israeli Prime Minister a few days ago," continued the President. "The Prime Minister shared his concerns over Iran and informed me that Israel was aggressively preparing to retaliate for any military actions against them. We know Iran is a massive thorn in the region with Hezbollah, Hamas, and others, but Yaakv believes Iran is up to something more concerning. They just don't know what it's.

He confirmed to me that Iran has uncharacteristically avoided any direct hostilities with them, but he remains untrusting of them. Prime Minister Yaakv shared that the view in much of Israel is that if Iran successfully invades Iraq, their most dangerous enemy is far too close to their border, and Israel will need to act.

I confirmed our intentions to stay out of this unless Iran perpetrates a direct attack against us. He didn't seem concerned by this, nor did he request that we get involved. He sought assurances that we would continue to provide military equipment and asked if we could expedite some aircraft orders. I told him that we would meet our commitments and investigate accelerating some orders. My take on the entire conversation is that they wish to deal with Iran themselves and don't want us holding them back."

As the President was about to wrap up, his assistant knocked on the door and entered.

"Mr. President, the Secretary of State is outside and urgently needs to speak with you," she said with a quiver in her voice.

"Please tell him to come in," he said. "We were just wrapping up."

The Secretary of State quickly entered with a horrified look.

"Mr. President, we just had a terrible incident involving American civilians," he hastily said. "On its way to New York, a U.S. commercial airliner was flanked by Iranian military jets shortly after takeoff from Kuwait. It diverted to Tehran under the threat of being shot down. There are two hundred and seventy-eight passengers and crew on board, many of which are Americans. They've just landed in Tehran, and Iran is broadcasting it live. It's been picked up by all the international news networks."

They quickly turned on the television in the office, and a news station appeared.

On the tarmac, stood the crew and passengers facing Iranian soldiers with guns. Passengers were crying and shaking in fear as the soldiers paraded before them. The camera focused on a set of parents who held their children tightly beside them, trying to calm their fears. It panned then to the aircraft pilot intently screaming something at one of the Iranian military leaders, who quickly bashed him across the face with the butt of a rifle sending him to his knees as blood spurted from his nose.

The anchor said, 'Just in, the interpreter tells us the Iranian government claims the people are all spies and subject to immediate execution. I'm unsure what that means because this is a standard commercial flight.'

As the anchor finished, a figure to the side in the live video feed, dressed in religious garb, motioned to the military head. The military commander yelled an order to the Iranian soldiers, who raised their weapons and fired upon the crew and passengers.

"What the hell?" yelled the President. "What do they think they're doing?"

The Iranian soldiers marched up and down the line, firing at will on the helpless people. A few passengers took off running and were shot in the back. Others crouched over fallen passengers only to be shot themselves. Many passengers begged the soldiers, but their pleas were ignored, and the executions continued.

The anchor returned and said, 'This is senseless. A foreign military is executing innocent people. These murders are unprecedented. And they're broadcasting it for everyone to see. It's barbaric.'

An Iranian military leader came over, grabbed the aircraft pilot, and yanked him forward from the line. He motioned for a soldier to bring him his weapon.

As the pilot saw the soldier approaching with the gun, he struck the Iranian leader with his fist. Another soldier came up behind the pilot and used the back of his rifle to hit the pilot behind his knees, sending him down onto the tarmac. The military leader lifted the gun to the pilot's head and shot him point-blank.

The anchor, removing his glasses, started to weep.

The President, who consistently displayed calmness, now exuded an intense ferocity.

His voice vibrated with clear resolve as he said, "The Iranians have crossed a line, and for some reason, they are determined to draw us into their evil plans. Executing people like this will bring a response Iran will wish they never invited."

Pausing to digest the graphic display, he raced through the possibilities about why Iran would take such extreme actions. None of it made sense.

The slaughter continued on the tarmac as the station continued to show the scene televised by the Iranian network. They finally cut away when the last passenger was shot and lay still on the ground.

The anchor returned and sadly announced, 'We understand that two hundred seventy-eight passengers and crew were aboard the aircraft, and you just witnessed them massacred for all the world to see. I expect the President and other nations to respond swiftly to such heartless and cowardly actions.'

"And that I will," said the President through a clenched jaw. "I've wanted to avoid military conflict. We can't let this go without appropriate action. I want to meet with the full Cabinet and national security team to plan our response in the morning. I must brief the nation, so I need a few minutes to prepare. Please update me if any further actions occur."

Everyone scattered from the room. The President sat for a moment considering his address to the American people. He quickly realized that he would do as he'd done on the campaign trail, tell them the truth as he knew it. Keep to the simple facts and let them know the U.S. would assess how to proceed. He couldn't give them any more than that at this time, and it was best not to elaborate.

A meeting with the press was quickly assembled. Each reporter, trying to keep abreast of emerging details, was locked to their phone, waiting for President Schmidt to take the stage.

In walked the President. He decided to use a podium in the press room to do the briefing. President Schmidt felt he could channel his intensity by standing to deliver the speech.

"My fellow Americans, it's with great sadness that I address you today," began the President. "As many of you saw, an American passenger plane was flanked by Iranian military jets and directed to land in Tehran under the threat of being shot down. The plane diverted and landed at the airport. The Iranian government removed the passengers and crew of the aircraft and summarily executed them on the tarmac. This gruesome act was televised by Iran as if taking pride in their heinous act. Words do no justice for these horrors and the senseless loss of life. My sympathies go out to the families of these victims, but I assure them that we'll act with the force of this nation.

You elected me on my promise to avoid policing the world and focus internally on creating a better America. However, the execution of these helpless people, many of them Americans, is an act of war. History is littered with unchecked regimes inflicting atrocities. It's incumbent on others to stand up to these tyrants and hold them accountable. It's imperative that we now act."

The President paused, recomposed himself, and stared into the camera. As he stood there, the anger he suppressed was boiling up again. Clenching his teeth to gain control of his emotions, he took a deep breath.

Releasing his ire, he began again, "We tolerated Iran's buildup along Iraq's border and treated it as a regional conflict. We were clear with Iran and others that this was not our fight. Moreover, we chose to mute our response when Iran antagonized our interests so that we could maintain peace. Iran chose to meet those restrained acts by murdering innocent Americans abroad. I unambiguously tell Iran that if you wanted our attention, you now have it. To my fellow Americans, I say, we'll not sit idly. I have no further details at this time. My administration will keep you informed of any further developments. God Bless America!"

The President took no questions and promptly left the room.

When exiting, he told his chief of staff, "Please keep me updated on any further developments throughout the night. I'll be preparing for my morning meeting."

The next morning, President Schmidt, who slept little that night but was left to his thoughts without further Iranian actions, entered the briefing room. The assembled group sat in complete silence, understanding the gravity of the meeting's purpose.

He quickly sat down and looked contemplatively around the room, studying each face before him. The President appeared amazingly fresh, given his lack of sleep and the events of the last twenty-four hours. While his outward appearance may have suggested otherwise, he was exhausted.

President Schmidt took a large drink of coffee, which he sorely needed.

"I handpicked each of you for this team based on your expertise, intelligence, and work ethic," he began. "Your talents are numerous and far-reaching and cover a diverse spectrum of crucial talents fundamental to running this great country.

Today, we're facing a decision I hoped would never surface. I made it clear to the American people that we must act now. That decision will knowingly result in the loss of lives, cost taxpayers' dollars, and remove focus from essential items this country desperately needs. The notable men and women in history, faced with similar grave decisions, have always found the strength to face the treacherous and bring them to justice."

During his campaign, he thought little about the possibilities of war. He knew he would face typical global challenges but didn't foresee a major conflict. Paul Schmidt considered himself a constrained hawk, which he defined as one never looking for a fight, but if a foe crossed the line, the President wouldn't be afraid to hit them back with what he had at his disposal. Iran's murdering of innocent people was one of those times.

The President repositioned himself. He had been sitting up all night, and his aching muscles were screeching at him. Adrenaline kept him going, and it still flowed through him as he couldn't escape the images of the execution in Tehran from clawing their way back into his thoughts. President Schmidt knew that his burning anger would linger for quite some time.

"I understand this country entered some prior conflicts with unwinnable plans," he continued. "Those wars resulted in the careless loss of lives and poorly executed exits. While those facts are true, I also know that we staved off tyranny in some wars, freed countless people, and abolished evil tyrants. Iran's abhorrent acts demand our military response as they have chosen the United States as part of its gambit. As President and Commander in Chief of the United States of America, I wish to go to war with the Islamic Republic of Iran."

The President paused again, taking another long drink of his coffee. He wrestled with his emotions through the night and wanted to ensure they weren't driving his leap to war. His wish was for peace across the world more than anything. War was a waste for humanity, but he knew evil leaders would plunder if not stopped. Countries with the means to stop them shouldn't avoid war against them, or the price of that avoidance may be unimaginable crimes against humanity.

The President carefully considered his words.

"We need Congress to declare war, and there in Congress, we'll face some who will be against this action because they are against any war," he said. "Others will oppose me simply because I'm not from their party. Some will treat it as political sport and fight against me for no other reason than that.

Despite these fringe elements, most people in Congress possess a broader perspective and will support my arguments to declare war. At the start of World War II, Franklin Roosevelt said, 'There can be no appeasement with ruthlessness,' and that same conviction rings loudly today. I believe our colleagues in Congress will agree with my decision."

The President had not prepared the words he had just said. The words he spoke came from his heart. He was still troubled about why Iran would boldly bring the U.S. to war. It still made no sense to him, but he kept that to himself.

"Let's discuss the plans for this war," he said. "There is much to do across this nation. The effects of this incident will barrel through the streets of this great country, and we need to be prepared to manage the storm."

"I would like to begin with you, Alan," the President said as he looked at the Vice President. "We discussed it last evening, but I would like your additional thoughts."

The Vice President admired the President for his temperament and determination. Most leaders, he knew, would recklessly sprint full speed down the warpath, not bothering to look before they leaped. He could tell the President burned with the same desire, but his leadership skills took over, and he insisted on following a well-planned course of action.

Vice President McIlroy smiled warmly at the President, understanding the immense pressure he was under, and replied, "Mr. President, I thought about this all night, and the only path for what's transpired is to declare war. I don't see that we can properly respond to what they have done without military action, and we must position ourselves from Iraq. The Iraqi President will support us in moving our troops into their country, giving us the necessary base locations to fight them effectively. I find no reason we shouldn't do as you said."

The President thanked him and appreciated having such a strong partner for his VP. Alan, he knew, was the second in command any leader would hope to have. He had come to understand that if Alan disagreed with him, he wouldn't hesitate to let him know, and if he agreed with him, it was not due to any loyalty; it was due to the Vice President thoroughly believing it.

President Schmidt turned to face his Secretary of State, Jack Anderson. Jack had brought the news of the incident to the President yesterday. Jack was a tall, distinguished elder statesman whose hair was a venerable salt and pepper belying his actual age. Jack's facial lines exuded decades of foreign affairs experience, and he brought assured confidence to his Cabinet. However, Jack believed all problems were solved with diplomacy and that the President wasn't using it effectively with Iran.

"Jack, you are the most seasoned of my Cabinet in international affairs, and I would like you to share your thoughts," said the President.

As cautious as always, Jack looked at his colleagues as if absorbing their inner thoughts and measuring their mettle.

"Mr. President, I was mortified by the actions of Iran yesterday," he articulately began as he returned his gaze to the President. "Never did we suspect they would violate all boundaries of international law. I wish I had been allowed to explore broader diplomatic channels in advance, but unfortunately, we missed that opportunity. I believe we could have made Iran take a different path. Even now, we have a choice. Sending troops to Iraq separates us further from a peaceful solution and another blatant attack by the U.S. against an Islamic nation."

The President considered Jack's words for a moment. He knew Jack Anderson would choose war as the last item on a list of a hundred alternatives. International relations were the man's lifeblood, and the venerable diplomat figured most problems worked themselves out when leaders sat down together. President Schmidt also felt that his Secretary of State felt that failings in diplomacy were the fault of others who didn't understand how to engage other leaders properly.

"Jack, we used significant resources to engage Iran along multiple channels," said the President, indignant that the Secretary of State would suggest the actions were because of diplomatic failings. "We offered restrained responses to their constant harassment. To murder innocent people because of so-called failed diplomacy is a view I'm unwilling to accept. Please get with your team and refresh our broad network of contacts in Iraq as we prepare for war there. We should also begin tight coordination with others in the region. Turkey, Saudi, and Israel must be concerned about Iran's move.

Regarding your comment about an attack against an Islamic nation, we were very patient with Iran. Furthermore, our years of sanctions were an attempt to derail a dangerous plan for nuclear proliferation in the middle east. I have never decided a single decision based on religion, and my conviction, in this case, has nothing to do with Islam. It's only a response to the murder of our people and my belief in accountability."

Jack, deciding not to test the President further, offered, "We'll reestablish our contacts in Iraq and around the region, Mr.

President. I'll also continue to see if we can make some progress with Iran."

The President studied the Secretary of State, seeing the man's turmoil born from the guilt that none of his numerous contacts indicated Iran's intentions. Still, the President felt the Secretary was somewhat irrational, believing everything could be solved through negotiation. The President knew it didn't take too deep a study of world history to see numerous leaders who pursued evil courses feeding the pages of those texts. Those chapters often discussed war as the means to end these tyrants' reigns.

Not wishing to pursue the topic further, the President promptly looked to his Secretary of Defense.

"Cassandra, I want this done right. We go in there with the right assets and enough personnel to take this on. I want a war proposal with clear objectives, resource needs, and detailed plans."

The Defense Secretary was prepared for the topic because she knew she would be a focal point of today's discussion.

"You know we're ready to take any military action that you and this country require," she replied, looking up from her notes. "Admiral Lawton and the Joint Chiefs concur with that. We're familiar with Iraq and will reconstitute our numerous operational bases there. Then we can position a large contingent of our forces around the three areas of Iran's buildup. Naval assets will also move to the region, and the Army is already mobilizing brigades for deployment."

She hesitated because of what she was going to bring up.

"If I may, Mr. President, I would like to raise one concern on my part," the Defense Secretary said.

"Go ahead," the President responded, curious about what bothered her.

"Moving our troops back to Iraq and reinitiating another war is a huge distraction for the Defense Department. We're just now getting our budgets focused on the nation's long-term needs and driving the production of F-35s, shipbuilding, Space Command, and cyber defenses. China and Russia made great strides against our capabilities while we fought the wars in Afghanistan and Iraq for so many years. We're about to repeat the same mistake."

The President peered at her with a bit of amazement. She was playing the long game and considered this a distraction. Defense Secretary Edgard understood the DoD's pressures with years of war and hated having it derailed again. However, he knew she would strike fear in the enemy when the war started, regardless of how she felt about it.

He looked at her but wanted to respond to the entire group.

"I appreciate your concerns," he said, looking around the room. "They're valid. However, I won't avoid a war due to the distraction of money and resources. We'll choose war based solely on principle alone. Our principles must stand above all, and those who decide to fight for that distinguish themselves, even at their own peril. In the long run, a failure to put our values first and address the actions of Iran will bear a much greater cost to this nation."

A knock at the door interrupted the President just as he finished his response to the Defense Secretary. The door opened, and his chief of staff informed the President that Iran's Supreme Leader was getting set to provide a televised address. The President directed him to put it on the large screen in front of the room.

The Supreme Leader's much-anticipated speech was beginning when the screen came on. It was being translated into English by the network. The President hoped the Iranian leader would clarify what happened and display remorse.

"We have been at the mercy of the West for too long," said the Iranian leader. "The infidels push their objectives, beliefs, and will upon Iran and other Muslims worldwide. Allah has bestowed upon the Islamic people a capability so fearsome that we'll now emerge from the darkness created by these infidels and fight our holy war to banish them. Allah has chosen the Shia Islamic Republic of Iran to wield this power and unite all Islamic people in our jihad. You witnessed our first strike as we captured and executed Americans spying on our nation and sent them to their deserved fate. We'll no longer accept their treachery. The world will soon see Allah's true might as we unleash his gift and reign supreme over all nations. Shia Islam will then endure as the one true religion, and I now call for an end to the Shia-Sunni divide in Islam."

He stopped there without clarification of his claims, and the broadcast cut away to an anchor trying to interpret the undertones of his short speech.

The President felt the pit in his stomach, lingering from the previous day, growing. What were they missing? Was Iran stupid enough to use its newfound nuclear weapons capability? None of it made sense. One thing was clear, Iran had no remorse for what it did and appeared to have more extensive plans. The U.S. needed to strike now, was his only thought.

The President and Cabinet discussed the Supreme Leader's speech and garnered little insight into the message's meaning. They weren't sure if there was something lost in translation or just another unapologetic rant. Unwilling to speculate further, the President switched back to the discussion of war.

The recent events affected every aspect of the country, and their respective responsibilities would soon consume his Cabinet. Despite these pressures, the President asked each Cabinet member to share their input. One by one, they offered well-thought-out concerns and ideas about managing their areas of responsibility and concerns about a war with Iran. At the end of the meeting, the entire team, even the reluctant Secretary of State, unanimously agreed to send troops to Iraq and seek a declaration of war.

The President instructed his team to reach out to their congressional contacts and prepare to roll out their plan when the vote for the war declaration was approved. The meeting attendees quickly dispersed, and the President headed to the Oval Office to prepare for his address to Congress and the nation.

In his address, the President provided a vivid picture of the events leading up to that moment and reaffirmed that he, his Cabinet, and his national security team had considered all alternatives, but sending troops to Iraq was the only appropriate response. He told them that he had tried peace, avoided conflict with the Islamic republic, and was vehemently against the war until Iran executed the innocent Americans on the tarmac in Tehran.

No alternative path, he said, would provide the proper response to ensure the nation's security and protect the American people at home and abroad. The President shared that Iran was now a nation with nuclear weapons, a point the U.S. government had never publicly confirmed before. The President argued that Iran being a nuclear power made them far more dangerous and that this was no longer a suspicion but an established fact. Based on the facial expressions of those present in Congress, most already understood his point well.

He proposed an initial military strength of one hundred and fifty thousand soldiers and marines at three bases near the border sites where Iran's troops reside. Additionally, the U.S. would move significant naval and airborne assets to the Gulf region to provide combat support.

One unpopular point with the President's approach was that he wouldn't strike Iran first. He added this at the last minute, without counsel from anyone. With the U.S. sitting on their doorstep, he hoped Iran would seek a different path.

Many hawks in Congress thought that Iran had already struck the first blow and a retaliatory strike by the U.S. was overdue, but the President was unwavering in his approach.

By a modest majority, Congress supported the President's declaration of war. Small contingents of both parties withheld support, as he had expected. The ultimate win cost him significant political capital that he ultimately hoped to use on his domestic plan. Still, he convinced himself that he was making the right decision, and it was well spent.

Chapter 2

Springing the Trap

General Keith Jenkins, newly appointed to serve as the Commander of United States Central Command in Tampa, Florida, reviewed the latest intelligence from his recently deployed forces in Iraq.

General Jenkins, an imposing, battle-hardened West Point graduate with multiple deployments to both Iraq and Afghanistan, was an easy choice for the role. Commanding one hundred fifty thousand troops back in Iraq, with over sixty thousand of those embedded close to the Iranian forces, was not what he expected from his assignment. Iraq, he believed, was a war of the past.

He studied his troop locations and the positions of his naval assets in the region, including two carrier groups. This gave him a lot of firepower, and he still had additional Air Force assets he could utilize in Turkey. Convinced the U.S. was ready for what may come, he turned to a recent report from his Iraqi commander. He was due to brief the Army Vice Chief of Staff shortly, so he wanted to include all essential details. Unsatisfied that the information was half a day old, he scheduled a quick, secure video conference to ensure he had the latest.

General Jenkins entered the meeting, acknowledged the standing officers, and ordered them to be at ease and take their seats. His secure command room consisted of a large front wall with a matrix of video displays showing live footage from the region's airborne aircraft. At the same time, other screens showed maps identifying troop positions and critical asset locations.

"Brian, good evening to you there; I hope we can make this short," he said, seeing his in-country commander on screen. "I have a call with the Army Vice within the next hour, and I need the latest intel report to share. Any significant additions to the written brief I received from your morning report?"

Lieutenant General Collier had previously served under General Jenkins as a lieutenant colonel while deployed to Afghanistan. General Collier always found the general a sharp, balanced, and charismatic leader with a no-nonsense approach. The lieutenant general was not ecstatic about another deployment to Iraq but was happy to serve under General Jenkins. General Collier was laser-focused on the considerable responsibility he was assigned and operated from his headquarters at Camp Imperative, a large base just outside Baghdad.

"General, two incidents occurred within the last six hours that I need to update you on," he replied. "Our drones observed intense Iranian troop activity at all three border gates. That's out of character from what we've witnessed over the last thirty days."

"What do you think it was?" asked General Jenkins.

"We speculate that they are getting ready for something significant, but it's unclear from the video footage what that may be."

"And the other item?" inquired the General.

"The second item, also observed by the drones, involved helo transports arriving at each camp. We believe they carried high-priority personnel since there was a tremendous uproar when they landed. Dignitaries of some sort. They disembarked under covered passageways and were escorted into each location's headquarters by large security forces."

Things had been quiet since the U.S. arrival in Iraq. Something was afoot, and General Jenkins wondered if Iran decided to back down now that the military was there or play this out.

"Anything else?" he asked.

"No sir, you are up to date other than these two," responded Lieutenant General Collier crisply.

General Jenkins nodded, turned to his left, and said, "Scott, do we have any intel about dignitaries visiting these camps?"

Colonel Scott Marsden was a twenty-six-year veteran and Army intelligence officer. He coordinated General Jenkins' intelligence network at his command headquarters in Tampa.

The colonel frowned slightly and offered, "General, I'm sorry, but we have no intelligence about any military, political or religious leaders with plans to be in the region of any of those camps."

"I expected as much," replied General Jenkins. "Nothing I've seen or heard suggested it."

A subtle sigh of relief emanated from the Army colonel, relieved he hadn't missed something important that would have him catch the general's ire.

"Colonel, get on the phone. Find out if there is anything out there that may help us understand what's going on. The two events are the first real notable activity since we arrived there. Maybe the camp movements were simply to prepare for these dignitaries."

Lieutenant General Collier respectfully asked, "Sir, If I may clarify?"

"Absolutely. Go ahead."

"We believe the activity was more than housecleaning for dignitaries. The footage reflected preparation for troop movements. We can't tell whether they plan to retreat or invade, but I believe they are preparing to move. I'll include the videos in the report I send out shortly. It'll give you a better sense of what I'm saying."

"Roger that," the General responded. "Keep me posted on anything new, and I'll get back to you when I receive the intel follow-up from Colonel Marsden. CENTCOM out!"

The military aide disconnected the video conference, and General Jenkins headed to his office to prepare for his meeting with the Army Vice Chief.

In Iraq, Lieutenant General Collier was met by his aide as he exited the briefing tent at Camp Imperative.

The aide saluted.

"Sir, Brigadier General Hollins requested to speak with you while you were on with the general," the aide said. "He has some new intelligence captured from the drones. He didn't say what the intel entailed, but you needed to see it immediately."

Lieutenant General Collier offered a short, "and so it begins." He followed that with his usual terse order, "Send him over immediately."

Brigadier General Hollins' job was to consolidate all Iraqi intelligence for Lieutenant General Collier. What he had just seen across his desk was troubling, so he rushed to the general's office and entered.

"General Hollins, what do you have?" asked the Iraqi commander.

"Sir, something peculiar just happened at all three border points. Their forces cleared a swath outside each gate on the Iranian side. It formed a clear-out region in a semicircular radius of about thirty yards. Subsequently, two trucks with open cabins and attached trailers entered the cleared areas. The vehicles are about twenty feet apart, and the trailers contain what appear to be stacks of shiny metal discs in a pyramid arrangement. All three gates show the same thing."

He unfolded some printouts and laid them in front of the General.

"These images here show the discs," he said, pointing to a particular spot. "They appear approximately twelve inches in diameter and look like small flying saucers. Each stack has eight discs per side at the base, forming a pyramid as the next layer goes down one disc per side. So, if our math is correct, there are about two hundred discs in each stack. Drones of some type or maybe explosives? Hard to tell."

The Lieutenant-General studied the images and was puzzled by what he saw. Two trailers full of these at all three locations. What was Iran doing?

"Get me a short report on this, and I'll send it off to CENTCOM for further analysis," he ordered.

He dismissed the general and sat back at his desk to sift through the intel and drone images, deciphering what this meant.

After an hour, Iran made an opening move, sending the U.S. forces on high alert. General Jenkins returned to his command center at his Tampa headquarters to watch the emerging action while Lieutenant General Collier returned to his command tent. Each watched intently to see Iran's next moves.

As the U.S. military leaders looked on, Iranian soldiers set off explosives blasting the gates away at the three crossing points. Inexplicably, no weapons fire erupted from the Iranians afterward, and the U.S. forces maintained their positions, waiting for Iran to initiate some form of attack.

The U.S. scrambled F-35 jets to the region as a precaution. The U.S. already had Predator drones flying routine surveillance rotations, so they focused on the blasted gates and readied their Hellfire missiles to defend against any incoming attack. Sitting back from the gates were Apache attack helicopters circling the region to support embedded ground troops. Abrams tanks and Bradley fighting vehicles were strategically positioned to engage any entering forces and provide heavy support for the large contingent of bunkered forces behind them.

At the CENTCOM and Camp Imperative headquarters, the video feeds from Predator drones, and Apache helicopters were transmitted live from each of the three gates. Lt. General Collier used the video to keep a visual of his forces and the Iranian activities. Meanwhile, back in Tampa, General Jenkins watched patiently with his team. It remained unnervingly quiet. General Jenkins couldn't fathom a stranger beginning.

It had been half an hour since the gates were destroyed when six mysterious robed figures suddenly emerged. They were strange in appearance and looked exceptionally large in stature and broad at the shoulders. Watching video feeds made it difficult to discern detail under the cloaking robes. General Jenkins thought that a strange beginning just got a lot stranger.

Puzzled faces by U.S. military leaders abounded as they watched from their various locations. The robed figures made no gestures but climbed into the vehicles sitting in the cleared areas and faced forward.

The strange Iranians simultaneously started their vehicles as if being signaled by some remote source. Infrared video from the Predators confirmed it as they displayed the heated engine hoods and hot exhaust. The vehicles began to move forward, passing through the blown gates to the Iraq side of the border.

A serpentine configuration of concrete barriers stood in their way, having been placed there by the U.S. forces to slow any rapid influx of potential truck bombers. The six trucks proceeded slowly, making no sudden motions. The trucks stopped when they cleared the barriers, and the six mysterious figures exited their vehicles.

Lumbering forward with a wide gait, they stopped in front of the trucks and faced the U.S. forces.

"Get a close-up of those figures from the Predators," ordered Lieutenant General Collier while watching from the command room.

An order went out from a soldier at the front of the command room to his forces, and the predator videos at all three locations zoomed to the standing robed figures.

The video was crisp but not enough to reveal details of the people under those clothes at their current altitude. The figures appeared huge, a height that seemed unnatural. Their trunks, limbs, and necks were thick and broad, one of the few details discerned from their cloaked bodies. The mysterious nature of the whole display was disturbing.

"Not good enough to determine who or what is in those robes, but whomever or whatever it's, they sure are big," the general barked. "Tell the Apaches to approach the three gates, hover at half a klick back from the vehicles, and fully zoom their M-TADs system. I want the video from both their day and night sights."

Again, the order went out from the room, and the Apache video began to zoom on their screens. The Apache M-TADS system is one of the world's best day and night vision sights, with ultra-high-performance cameras in both visible and infrared. At half a kilometer, the general knew the detail should be as good as standing before the robed individuals and looking them directly in the face.

Unfortunately, even the zoomed video couldn't get a view under those hoods. The robes completely covered their faces, hands, and feet. None of them moved, but the brisk wind flapped their robes against their bodies. The outline reflected that of a person with hulking proportions.

Frustration lingered in the room as they couldn't tell what they were confronting.

The six figures raised their arms as if cued for their moment on television by some unknown director. As they moved their arms skyward, the discs on all six trailers lifted into the air. The discs soared overhead and spun like a raging whirlpool of metal, not in a chaotic pattern but in a coordinated formation of great exactness.

The robed figures, acting the part of maestros, orchestrated their arms which synchronized with movements from the discs, suggesting they were steering them somehow. However, it was unclear what mechanism they were using to control them.

Above the figures, the discs soared fifty feet into the air and formed a circular matrix of discs, about ten feet in radius. The group of discs began to spin with tremendous rotational velocity. The speeding discs blurred into a single solid circle due to an optical effect of the high rotational rate.

Abruptly and coordinated, the discs slowed and split into four smaller equal-sized circular groups and repeated the spinning wizardry. They quickly changed formation, and the discs aligned into a continuous stream, with each disc following another. They sped through the air in a series of helical and rotational patterns, each disc soaring like a flock of starlings zigzagging with pure grace.

The discs then returned to the front of the robed figures and organized into a circular ring with a radius of about forty feet. Spinning as if tracing the circumference of the giant circle, they raged until the sand from the desert began to swirl in the turbulent air generated by the revolving saucers.

The display was extraordinary. The synchronicity and precision of the discs at such enormous speed exceeded anything the U.S. military had ever witnessed. Fear flooded their faces as they quickly realized the vulnerability of their forces against such capability.

Great confusion filled the room at CENTCOM as a buzz of speculation about the discs took over the command center. Perceptions about the type of new drones, their propulsion, and how Iran obtained such leading-edge capability overwhelmed the usually stoic team.

The room silenced suddenly as each hooded figure's discs split into smaller groups shaped in outward-pointing V patterns like multiple arrows set to fire on their targets from a set of archers. Other discs moved into a defensive formation out front of each figure, providing a shield wall to protect them against an enemy's counterattack. An ominous feeling gripped those watching.

The arrows made of discs shot out from the six figures in various directions, racing across the Iraqi terrain. One group of discs from each robed person headed toward a respective Apache helicopter, positioned moments ago by the U.S. Iraqi commander and now the closest American target. Other groups split off and headed toward other airborne helicopters while the shielding discs maintained their tight formation in front of the robed figures.

The V-shaped sets approached the Apache helicopters with blazing speed. Unfortunately, the U.S. forces were under direct orders to hold fire until Iran opened the attack. As directed, the aircraft and personnel hovered in fixed positions, essentially sitting ducks.

The discs closed the distance in seconds. Sensing their doom at the last moment, the pilots took quick evasive maneuvers, but the discs were too fast. The approaching discs tracked their movements and split into three groups, one aimed at the center and the other two to each side.

The center group got there first and exploded through the windshield of each helicopter, shattering the glass windshield into thousands of shards, rocking the aircraft, and impaling the pilot and co-pilot, killing them instantly.

The other two groups, diverting at the last second to attack the aircraft's body, slammed into the helicopter's sides, puncturing the outer frame like a can opener and quickly rendering the vehicle inoperable.

Lieutenant General Collier watched as his Apache helicopters spun out of control, their tail rotors destroyed, in billowing spirals to the earth below. The Iraqi desert ignited into massive thundering fireballs as the helicopters slammed to the ground.

The Iraqi Commander couldn't believe what he was seeing. He saw crumpled heaps as he scanned the screens, burning furiously after only seconds into the fight. His eyes widened in horror as he saw the mysterious discs reconvening from the destroyed aircraft, unscathed by the attack they had just delivered on one of America's fiercest weapons. The War had begun!

"All units engage," the general screamed.

His message immediately went out to the troops.

The Iranians were only beginning their slaughter as their other discs set out new attack patterns against the remaining helicopters.

Meanwhile, the U.S. forces received their go-ahead to engage the robed figures and fire upon the discs. The American forces' weapons erupted from multiple regions of the battlefield. Hellfire missiles were launched, and powerful machine gun fire littered the sky. Anti-aircraft guns, positioned with the troops, aimed for the discs as they soared in all directions.

Effortlessly, the discs evaded the fire or angled themselves to deflect it. Their superior speed and precision allowed them to dip and twist through the barrage and pummel the U.S. missiles and aircraft. A bone pile of aircraft quickly littered the Iraqi battleground as the discs swept the skies to seek and destroy every airborne asset.

The pummeling continued to catch the U.S. forces off guard. However, they still possessed incredible capability in the air with the new F-35s flying high overhead and the hovering Predator drones loaded with their missiles. The discs, they expected, would be no match for the altitude and speed of the F-35s and their state-of-the-art weapon systems.

In witnessing the destruction of the helicopters, Lieutenant General Collier ordered the F-35s to engage the discs and his ground troops to fire upon the robed figures. The general was unsure what role the robed individuals played, but he wanted to remove any doubt if they controlled the discs.

The Iranians had their own plans as their discs headed up to meet the jets. The U.S. F-35s approached at attack speed as each faced incoming discs flying a V pattern. Dogfighting with a set of discs was never part of their Air Force training, so the pilots were unsure how to engage. The pilots quickly assessed that the discs were capable of independent movements and phenomenal maneuverability. It was less like dogfighting and more like countering an array of air-to-air missiles.

Unfortunately for the pilots, their training was against one, or at most, a few air-to-air missiles. In this case, they were simultaneously dealing with fifteen discs approaching them.

The jets and discs raced toward each other, and the F-35 pilots lit off their AIM-120 medium-range air-to-air missiles toward the incoming discs. The AIM-120 missiles possessed 'fire and forget' precision guidance and barreled toward the discs.

Unbelievably, the discs diverted into a twisting spiral providing the incoming missiles with no distinct target to track. The spiraling movements confused the air-to-air missiles with their fluidity, and the missiles were unable to lock.

As the missiles approached the discs, the discs adeptly sidestepped them and cut in at the last second on their vulnerable sides, exploding the missiles into fireballs.

Seeing their missiles dispatched so easily and the discs closing quickly, the F-35 pilots had limited options. They lit off their short-range sidewinder missiles and fired their 25mm Gatling guns in hopes that the discs would be overwhelmed by the high rate of ammunition and the blistering closing speed of the rockets. The Gatling guns, firing three thousand rounds per minute, were efficiently dealt with by the discs as they once again evaded the fire with uncanny agility. The short-range sidewinders proved no match, as the discs destroyed the heat-seeking missiles as they met one another in the sky above.

Such skill from the discs at avoiding the jets' weapons left the F-35 aircraft as easy marks. In less than a second, the discs closed the final distance on the jets and slammed into the aircraft, rocking the region with unprecedented explosions. Fire and metal rained from the sky as multiple burning jets cratered into the ground below. The F-35, one of the U.S.'s newest military technologies, was made obsolete in a few dreadful minutes.

The last airborne hopes were Predator drones and F-15s dispatched from the carriers. The Predators unleashed their missiles on the Iranian-robed figures hoping that this would somehow derail the onslaught from the discs. As each missile from the drone fired, a set of flying discs intercepted it. Interestingly, the Predators themselves were not engaged, allowing their video to stream for U.S. leadership to see. It was as if the Iranians wanted the American leaders to witness the unfolding events.

The F-15s, deployed from the carriers, were faster than their newer F-35 counterparts. Still, they proved no more fearsome for the Iranians as the discs made quick work of them and sent them to their demise with the litany of other aircraft on the Iraqi ground below.

Air superiority was won by the Iranians in less than twenty minutes, leaving the troops and their ground vehicles at the mercy of the flying discs.

Armored tanks and vehicles became the next targets. The combat vehicles used their arsenal of weapons on the hooded men and the flying discs, but they were less of a match for the elusive discs than their airborne counterparts. In desperation, troops sent fire streaming from their anti-aircraft guns and individual rifles. The sky was a swarm of ammunition, mortars, and missiles seeking to destroy the discs and kill the hooded individuals.

The robed figures remained safely behind their retained discs, shielding them from the incoming rounds. The clattering of the fire against the shielding discs pinged loudly, like golf ball-sized hail against a metal seam roof. Even armor-piercing Javelin missiles, fired by the troops at the robed figures, never concerned them as they met the incoming antitank rounds with their discs at a distance, ensuring their safety.

Unencumbered by the bombardment, the metal saucers deployed top attacks on the tanks, bludgeoning them with successive barrages. Their bashing of the armored hulls rang out like giant church bells in a town courtyard. They repeatedly struck as it announced the drumming of the day's battle until they pierced the U.S. armor and killed their crews. The discs made short order of the combat vehicles leaving smoking carcasses wherever they flew.

Now exposed with no airborne or armored ground support, thousands of vulnerable troops were left on the battlefield to face the menacing discs. They flew around the battlefield like murderous hornets wrested from a kicked nest, stinging every helpless soldier and marine with their deadly venom. There was no hiding from the discs as they hunted each person as if their position were programmed into a predetermined map for them to follow.

The gut-wrenching aftermath left the desert region in a bloody, fiery mess of death and destruction. The six hooded figures, untouched the entire ordeal, stood at the front of their vehicles. The discs collected themselves from the battle and restacked into their organized pyramids behind the robed figures on the trailers.

Devastation lay before the Iranians, yet their vehicles and robed figures appeared as if they were not part of any battle, let alone one of this magnitude. The Iranian flying discs destroyed six F-35s, nine Predator drones, twenty-two Apache attack helicopters, fifteen Blackhawk helicopters, eighteen dozen combat vehicles, and killed more than sixty-four thousand soldiers and marines in just fifty-four minutes. The loss marked the worst single defeat in American history. The U.S. military, simply no match for these Iranian discs, was shown they were no longer the world's leading military power.

Chapter 3

The Harrowing Aftermath

The world was stunned by the American defeat. The vivid videos that emerged showed the battle and its end. The President ordered an immediate and complete withdrawal of U.S. forces from the region, as the U.S. needed to regroup and assess what occurred. The Iranian government announced its intentions to let the infidels flee Iraq without further attack.

The Iranian military forces, which sat idly by at the gates while the discs destroyed the U.S. forces, marched into Iraq's major cities escorted by the robed warriors, a term the global media was now using. Their move into Iraq was a parade to show off their unrivaled discs and robed figures conducting aerial concerts for everyone to see. The triumphant march was unnerving, seemingly more to celebrate the mechanism and dominance of their defeat of the U.S. than to complete the invasion.

The Iranian President and the Supreme Leader openly gloated in public speeches about their new prowess. A blessing from Allah, they claimed. They reiterated to all Muslims that they would lead the charge to expunge the infidels. Their television networks ran constant videos and images of the aftermath of the destroyed American forces. They presented it as a badge of honor and a stern warning to other nations.

Furthermore, Iran likened the hasty withdrawal of the U.S. military to a mangy dog banished by a superior breed. It played out immensely well for them as they completed the assimilation of Iraq with little resistance from the Iraqi people. Shia law was quickly declared, and Iran designated Iraq as an additional province of their nation.

In the U.S., President Schmidt now led a nation whose pride was mangled and cast aside in Iraq. Devastated by Iran's unprecedented display of force, he now understood that Iran had planned this all along. They baited the President, and he stepped right into their trap. President Schmidt knew that taking down Goliath in front of the world gave Iran the distinction it craved.

The President wanted to tell himself that he had made a terrible mistake, but he had no choice with the intel he possessed. He took one element of comfort; the battle took place overseas, not on U.S. soil, where the ramifications would have been much worse.

The horrific defeat, however, rattled the American psyche. America always thought it could stand toe to toe with any nation and best that foe. However, Iran's stunning upset of the U.S. forces inflicted feelings on the American people they were unaccustomed to experiencing. Fear and insecurity now seethed in the minds of every citizen, most of whom had never faced that in their lifetimes.

President Schmidt's patriotism sparked as he reflected on the nation's situation. He knew his new role was to lead the country on a quest to reverse these fortunes and kick Iran back onto a level playing field. There was no way Paul Schmidt would let America settle for anything less than holding Iran accountable for its deeds.

The President called an emergency meeting with his Cabinet and national security team. He wanted answers to what occurred in Iraq. How could Iran possibly have such a capability, and the U.S. did not know?

President Schmidt entered the meeting with his team, who were already seated. Their faces and postures did not reflect the same group who sat with him a few months back and decided to go to war. His team looked lost.

"We witnessed the worst military defeat in our history, and the blood of our men and women is on my hands," he said, determined to get to the bottom of what transpired. "I decided to act on the facts as I knew them, but they were grossly incomplete. We need immediate answers on this new weaponry and how we allowed this to happen without any knowledge on our part. The U.S., the supposed leader of the Free World and greatest military superpower, was destroyed on a battlefield in under an hour. Iran possessed this power, yet we knew nothing about it. Our failures are too numerous to count. Cassandra, what the hell are those discs and robed figures?"

The Defense Secretary, pained by the previous day's events, responded without hesitation, "Mr. President, the department has no explanation for the technology behind those discs nor what role the hooded Iranians had in their usage or control. Our military, government, and industry personnel are reviewing all available details, and they are unsure what technology is behind them."

She paused for a moment. The President was listening intently, as were the rest of the attendees. They hoped she had more than to share than a rehash of the events.

"The discs evaded our 25mm rounds at full firing rate from the F-35's high-speed Gatling guns with the aircraft flying Mach two," she continued. "They could elude and destroy the jet's newest air-to-air missiles, and they outmaneuvered our various aircraft easily before pulverizing them with devastating force. It's simply unprecedented and far beyond our technology. Even our latest work in hypersonics can't remotely equal the combination of speed, control, and precision. China and Russia, from our intelligence, are behind us in these areas, so we don't see them at the center of this."

The Defense Secretary felt it was necessary to repeat what happened to ensure everyone was on the same page before she revealed some disturbing findings from her team. It was evident that the group, especially the President, was unsatisfied with her initial statements, but what she was about to reveal wasn't going to be more satisfying.

"We suspect the discs are tungsten carbide," she said, picking up where she left off. "It's an extremely hard, dense metal that can withstand elevated temperatures, allowing it to inflict damage and emerge from the fiery rubble, more or less unscathed, and fly to its next target. We use it for armor-piercing rounds, which is why the discs effectively penetrated our armored vehicles. We're looking into indications they have been buying or mining tungsten to confirm our suspicions."

Secretary Edgard hesitated again, but the President intended to hear her out and let her continue without interruption. She knew what she had to say next would be alarming to all, so she took a deep breath.

"We have to assume that they have numerous discs placed around their country for defensive reasons," she began again, seeing the President was impatiently waiting for more. "We saw their offensive prowess but believe they are equally devastating in a defensive role.

Our scientists calculated some of the maneuvering speeds they used against our F-35s, and those results indicate they can defeat our nuclear missiles, even the ICBMs, which travel at Mach 20. We can't even intercept ICBMs reliably at this point. Even stealthily bringing ballistic missile submarines to their shores, their discs could defeat the missiles shortly after launch. It's impossible to see how we could bring nuclear weapons to bear on them.

Summing all that up, our complete arsenal is questionable against such capability. I know you want more. I wish I could provide it. We're trying to get to the bottom of this, but right now, Mr. President, I have not heard one credible explanation. For that and more, I'm sorry and offer you my resignation."

Defense Secretary Edgard sat back with a defeated look on her face.

The President was not the least surprised. He had anticipated her doing this.

"Cassandra, I don't accept your resignation," he responded immediately. "You remain the best person for the job, and I need you. The failure in Iraq is not your fault, and I, nor anyone else, blame you. If you are at a loss for what they have, everyone else in this country is also. However, you're not off the hook. I need all resources focused on figuring this out. We lost as many people in fifty-four minutes as in Vietnam, Iraq, and Afghanistan combined. We sent those people to their graves. We must do better! I need insight now and don't leave any stone unturned. Push your department harder."

The President hesitated and added, "Are we absolutely sure the Russians or Chinese aren't behind this?"

Several team members attempted to answer that question, but the President looked to the entire team and said, "I understand there are lots of opinions on this topic, but I need facts."

"Margaret, I'm unaccepting of the lack of intelligence we had on the Iranian capabilities," said the President looking directly at his National Intelligence Director. "How did we miss this? So many assets across the world and a lot of money feeding it all. We must determine if this came from the Chinese, Russians, or other sources. If not, who else could develop this capability? I find it hard to believe that Iran developed it independently or that Allah bestowed it upon them. Like our Defense Department, our intelligence groups must be better than this."

"Mr. President, our teams are equally confused about our lack of intelligence," said the Director, taking the President's criticism without pushback. "We spent numerous resources trying to better understand Iran's intentions before sending troops to Iraq. There was not a single hint anywhere that they could unleash this capability. We know the Supreme Leader previewed this in his speech after executing the people on the tarmac, but it was too vague for us to garner what he meant. Our best guess is they learned from prior failures during their nuclear weapons development and tightened security protocols to keep it secret. They sensed how powerful the disc technology was and chose to keep it hidden until they mastered and proliferated it. Then they baited us into being their guinea pigs."

"Okay, but were the Russians or the Chinese behind it?" the President asked.

"Sorry that I didn't answer that part," she replied. "We don't believe that the Chinese or Russians are behind this capability for one simple reason: they would be using it themselves if they were. Plain and simple."

The room filled with low-level chatter on the last point, and all seemed to concur. The Chinese and Russians would love nothing more than to possess and exploit this capability. Several in the room also noted that their usual public ridicule of an American failure would typically have been extensive. However, both countries were reticent in this aftermath, likely implying they weren't sure what they witnessed either.

The President accepted the premise, but this did little to allay his concerns. He recognized that there was little else they could do while sitting in this meeting, so he decided to end the discussions.

"I need you and your teams to tirelessly work in your respective responsibilities to keep this nation afloat," directed the President. "Our people are devastated, the nation's morale is at an all-time low, our already frazzled economy is under further stress, our sudden weakness roils our allies, and we have little to offer any of them. Many people now believe that the American Empire has cratered overnight. I'm unaccepting of that notion. We do as Americans have always done. We get up, brush ourselves off, and fight. Before we do that, we need to calm our people and prepare ourselves against this new enemy."

The deaths of so many entered his thoughts again. He was genuinely disturbed by the murders on the tarmac, but that was nothing compared to the slaughter in the Iraqi desert.

"Iran, emboldened by their new status, ravenous in their thirst for retribution to the Western World, and fueled by the belief that these weapons are bestowed on them by their god, will likely seek to control the world," railed the President, focusing on the enemy. "This nation and the entire world, especially Israel, undoubtedly Iran's fiercest enemy, have never faced a more dangerous nemesis. I don't know their ultimate desires, but I suspect we'll hear much more from Iran. Their unrivaled advantage, as Cassandra suggests, could lead them to consider an attack on U.S. soil."

While the President recognized the U.S. surely had a prominent position in Iran's long-term plans, Israel faced a greater risk. Since the Iranian revolution installed the theocratic Islamic leaders in 1979, Iran's hatred for Israel has grown. President Schmidt recalled that the Iranian Ayatollah referred to the U.S. and Israel as the Great Satan and Little Satan when he took control. However, it was not hatred alone that would drive Iran toward Israel; control of Jerusalem was a big lure in and of itself.

"Leaders from other nations are reaching out, and I'll shortly follow up with our closest allies, seeking their help in our quest," said the President, trying to close out. "Once done, I'll address the nation early this afternoon. Thank you, and I need all of you to stay intricately connected with me and each other. I'll plan regular meetings to ensure tight communications of all relevant information."

The President stood and left for his office, following up with various U.S. allies, trading intelligence with them as appropriate. He talked with leaders from the U.K., France, Germany, Canada, Israel, Japan, and Korea before stopping the calls to prepare for his afternoon address to the American people. U.S. allies had no greater insight into Iran's new weapons. Each of them offered their support in intelligence sharing. They were quick to speculate what China and Russia may be up to, but each made it abundantly clear they weren't engaging in military efforts against Iran. President Schmidt couldn't secure their support before entering Iraq, so he knew he wouldn't get any military help now that they had witnessed Iran's new weapons and the U.S.'s quick destruction.

The President's address to the nation was short and without answers. He knew he couldn't address any fears or confusion about what occurred and determined that it was best not to speculate. President Schmidt merely told the American people that the U.S. military was regrouping and assessing its arsenal of military weapons and tactics to better combat any aggressions by Iran. He assured the American people that the U.S. would use any weapons it possessed to ensure the safety and protection of the country. Still, the American leader knew the citizens didn't understand how hollow that statement was.

Americans were always confident in their nuclear powers, assuming the deterrent benefits and offensive risks kept other nations at bay. It gave the country a sense of security that sanity would prevail over mutual destruction. He was not about to burst that bubble even though his Defense Secretary had done so for him.

The President affirmed to the American public that Iran had agreed to suspend any hostilities if the U.S. kept clear of Iran and its interests. He kept his concerns about the long-term veracity of that statement to himself.

Chapter 4

Expanding Their Realm

The assimilation of Iraq was only weeks old when intelligence reports emerged that the Iranian military was carrying out wicked retribution against all resistance they encountered in former Iraq. They expunged Sunni leaders from all positions, and stories of their disappearances were rampant.

Additional robed warriors, always surrounded by their flocks of discs, popped up throughout the former country to serve as security support for the embedded troops, answering the world's question of whether there were more of them. Iran did not mention the robed figures or the discs; they referred to it as the might bestowed on them by Allah. All indications were that resistance in Iraq became quickly muted, with only a few pockets willing to test the Iranian forces and risk the consequences.

While the leadership of Iran continued to boast of its newfound relevance on the world stage, its primary focus was on reconstituting Iraq in its mold. Most of the world suspected much more was in store for the region once Iran was comfortable that Iraq was stable.

Iranian leadership mentioned little about Europe or the United States. Both kept their distance from the regime, reeling from the Iraq aftermath. However, shortly after Iran invaded Iraq, it received large delegations from China and Russia. Both countries sent their representatives to fawn over Iran's political and religious leaders as they sought to ingratiate themselves with this newly established heavyweight. The display, while sickening to the Western world, was nonetheless expected.

China emerged quietly from its meetings with Iran with a subdued temperament. Their leaders openly discussed furthering economic opportunities but offered minor other talking points. Their public demeanors appeared cordial, but neither China nor Iran showed warmth for the other.

On the other hand, the Russians emerged from their meetings, emboldened by their discussions. Panic in Europe occurred as Russia quickly began a series of military exercises along its eastern border. Their leader, Alexei Kovalyov, always a thorn in the side of the West, displayed greater bravado in his speeches while spewing his incessant hatred for capitalism.

Suspicion grew in Europe that Kovalyov was up to something by the apparent change in behavior after talks in Iran. Russia was dangerous enough, but allying itself with the Iranian government created a disturbing union. Europe sensed they might be in trouble, not from the growing influence of Iran, but from their eastern nemesis, who openly coveted taking the whole continent.

The next phase of Iran's plan surfaced during a speech by the Supreme Leader from Baghdad, the former capital of Iraq.

Speaking from the banks of the Tigris River, he said, "Fellow brothers of Islam, Allah has bestowed upon us the power to assert our leadership over the world and take our intended place; however, we must first unite amongst ourselves. Our fractured Islamic leadership has left us without focus and purpose, weakening us against the infidels. We must join politically and religiously to succeed in what Allah has chosen for us. We must allow his guidance to drive us. Allah chose the Islamic Republic of Iran to lead this quest and assume responsibility for implementing his will. We shall bring forward his might and rejoice in his many blessings."

"Prophecies of Mohammed foretold Muslim conquests of nations and that Islam would spread the world over," he went on. "Many religious leaders and scholars have argued that previous historical occurrences satisfied those prophecies. I'm now sharing with you that these assertions were false. For you currently live in the time of the fulfillment of these prophecies. Allah planned for true conquest linking Islam into one massive state, not of nationalist borders but borders set by faith. Therefore, I announce that Iran was granted its warriors to execute this jihad and realized Mohammed's true prophecy.

While there have been hundreds of years of division amongst Muslims, I announce that today that will end. I extend a simple gesture of unity for all the faithful and allow you to join us and guide the spear to make it happen."

The undertones of his speech scared most leaders within the Muslim World, who have rarely aligned themselves with the Iranian leadership. Interpretations of his verbiage seemed to stop at no border.

In contrast to the leaders of the Islamic nations, the general Islamic population worldwide was whipped into hysteria over the concept. Most were quickly enamored with the thought of Islamic domination. The frenzy flowed into the streets in massive demonstrations far greater than the Arab Spring of the early part of the second decade.

Iran's idea of defeating the U.S. and calling for all Muslims to unite under them was the most masterful stoking of humanity's core desire to win while justifying their cause. Government leaders within Islamic nations feared dispelling the uprisings for fear of revolt from their inspired people or retaliation from Iran and its disc weapons.

The Supreme Leader quickly followed his speech with military movements in Iran and former Iraq. While supposedly not interested in nationalistic pursuits, Iranian forces positioned themselves along the border with Saudi Arabia and Turkey, seemingly becoming their two new targets. Both leaders of the Sunni nations clamored for support, but none emerged. Moreover, they both knew they were incapable of withstanding the new Iranian might.

The U.S. President was closely following the activities of Iran, trying to gauge their broader plans. After the Supreme Leader's speech, it wasn't difficult to see that Iran planned to use its new might to strongarm the Islamic world as its first course of action. At least, he thought, their focus was there first and not on the U.S. or Israel. Events were happening quickly, and he was due to receive an intelligence update from his National Intelligence Director.

Margaret Stoneman prepared for her scheduled update to President Schmidt. Information constantly flowed from Turkey and Saudi Arabia, so she jotted down some last-minute notes before heading out to the President.

She met the Defense Secretary outside the President's office. The President's assistant escorted the two inside. He greeted them both, and they took their seats.

"Iran invaded Turkey earlier today," said the Intelligence Director. "They headed across from their border and went straight into Ankara. The Turkish forces attempted to spread out around the city to avoid a single battle as we had in Iraq."

The Defense Secretary added, "We believe it was an attempt to spread Iran's forces and, more specifically, the fight against the robed Iranians and the discs."

The Director continued after the Defense Secretary finished.

"The technique slowed Iran a bit but was no more effective against them than we were. They took Ankara in a few hours. From there, they headed to Istanbul. Reports flowed to us that many Turkish forces, hearing the news from Ankara, surrendered to the sweeping Iranian forces even before reaching Istanbul. Istanbul fell even faster than Ankara as most forces had been purposely pushed forward to Ankara as a hope to save Istanbul from much of the brunt."

"And the Turkish leadership?" asked the President.

"Unknown, Mr. President," said the Director.

"If Iraq were any indication, it didn't turn out well," said the President.

"I suppose that it didn't," she concurred. "There isn't a lot of love for each other. Centuries of built-up animosity."

"What about Saudi Arabia?" the President inquired.

"Iran is using a completely different military tactic," answered the Defense Secretary. "I believe you know Iran shut down all air traffic into the country. They threatened to use their discs to take down any aircraft entering or leaving with their discs. We're not aware of anyone who has tested that decree. They then stationed a ring of military forces around the country and slowly swept inward. Tightening the noose around Riyadh and most likely the Royal Palace."

"I just received an update before I came over," said his National Intelligence Director. "They reached the Royal Palace an hour ago, and word is they executed the entire royal family. Supposedly, they spared no person with known royal blood."

The President rocked a bit in his chair. Bold steps continue from this regime, he thought. He could see Iran's plan continuing to materialize: invade powerful Islamic countries first, eliminate the leadership of those countries who had reasons not to participate in Iran's scheme, and welcome the masses for a grand Islamic crusade against the infidels.

The ploy followed fundamental tenets of manipulation and mind control that someone or some group had planned for a long time. He reasoned that each future step by the U.S. must be carefully and secretly planned, or the U.S. may step into yet another trap.

"These are quite astonishing events again for Iran," said the President. "Now Iran is in Europe with their control of Turkey. They now possess valuable Mediterranean coastline and control an old foe in taking the former seat of the Ottoman Empire. With Saudi Arabia, Iran now controls Medina and Mecca, important religious acquisitions for greater influence over the broad flock of Muslims."

"If we don't watch it, they may run the tables on all of Islam here shortly," said the Director of National Intelligence. "Sounds like that is what they're up to."

"Possibly," responded the President. "I guess that it won't end there. I suspect far grander plans than that."

"And their military strategy is working quite effectively," interjected the Defense Secretary. "That much power does not bode well for anyone attempting to stand in their way."

"Which brings me to another topic, Cassandra," said the President. "Any progress on understanding the disc technology?"

"Mr. President, I have several groups trying to ascertain the origins and basis for the technology," the Defense Secretary replied. "We have all industry and government experts digging into what is behind this. I'm sorry to report that no progress has been made on determining what is behind this."

"Keep at it," the President responded. "I, for one, believe that if they can do it, then so can we. Make sure we put a huge effort behind it, and let me worry about appropriations to cover it from Congress."

"Anything else on the invasions?" the President asked.

The Director and the Secretary of Defense answered no, so he concluded the meeting. The President knew he had to craft a comprehensive plan to get out front of what was emerging with Iran.

The annexation of Saudi Arabia and Turkey gave Iran immense influence over the remaining Islamic countries. Possessing Saudi Arabia and the critical cities of Mecca and Medina, Iran's Supreme Leader now folded two of Islam's holiest places under his control. Additionally, Iran picked up the nation's substantial oil reserves and infrastructure. Turkey provided geographical and economic benefits with its footprint in Europe and added greatly to Iran's obvious superpower intentions and regional influence.

Saudi Arabia and Turkey were quickly declared provinces and added to the growing Islamic republic. Iran established itself as the fifth-largest nation in the world by population in six short weeks. It positioned itself by land and sea as a powerhouse in economic and military influence. Speculation about Iran's long-term vision and who could inhibit or even squelch their progress became a media storm.

Chapter 5

Revelation

Defense Secretary Edgard requested an urgent meeting with the President and the national security team. She needed to inform the President of disturbing information concerning the Iranian conflict. The group quickly assembled in the secure briefing room.

Working in the Oval Office, the President received notification that his team was assembled and ready for him in his secure conference room. He quickly left his office and headed to the briefing room. The President always carried himself with a youthful demeanor, but the unbelievable pressures of the last six weeks began to show. The areas underneath his eyes were dark from lack of sleep, the gray in his hair seemed more pronounced, and deep lines of concern seemed to have overtaken his face.

Sitting down, he looked to his Defense Secretary, who had a beleaguered expression.

The President opened the meeting.

"I understand you have discovered some critical intel that is somehow relevant to the Iranian weapons," he said to the Defense Secretary.

Looking flustered about what she had to share, the Defense Secretary began with a hint of tentativeness.

"Mr. President, we've uncovered the mystery behind the discs and the hooded warriors," she replied. "We now understand the origin of the technology. I hate to tell you this, but it comes from us. By us, I mean the U.S. Department of Defense. We invented it, and we're the culprits."

Jaws fell open, and silence momentarily lingered in the secure room's air.

While always composed, the President's eyes betrayed his outward calmness. Fire leaped from them as he heard her news. He just sent thousands of American troops to their death at the hands of weapons the U.S. developed.

He sat up, looked squarely at the Defense Secretary, and uttered through a tightly clenched jaw, "Please continue."

Understanding the President's ire, the Defense Secretary furtively glanced at the Chairman of the Joint Chiefs and then back to the President.

She continued without hesitating further, "The Defense Department had a top-secret program run by the U.S. Air Force about a decade and a half ago. We believe the Iranians are deploying the technology from it."

Unable to contain himself, the President exclaimed, "Then why in damnation did we not deploy the same disc weapons against them and fight back? More importantly, why are we finding this out six weeks later? What your telling me makes no sense. After the battle in Iraq, you assured me that we had no idea what those discs were or how to defeat them."

Again, the Defense Secretary tried to maintain her composure.

"We never developed similar weapons because that was not the basis of the classified program's research. It had a different focus," she continued.

Given the current situation, the entire group was confounded by this and wanted to fire away at the Secretary. However, each member figured it best to let the President handle things.

"Cassandra, get to the point. Are we responsible for these weapons or not?" demanded the President.

"Mr. President, I think it best to begin from the top. I'll explain what I learned to the best of my abilities and ask Admiral Lawton to help me explain any details I miss. The technology behind their weapons most likely originated from a highly classified and tightly compartmentalized program called Cranio-Genesis.

I use the phrase more likely because we can't confirm how Iran got the information, but all indications are that they did.

The program explored neuroscience associated with the brain's response to electromagnetic radiation. Specifically, it was to determine if we could recover or restart the brain of military personnel injured in battle and found to be brain-dead. As you know, head trauma is one of the leading causes of death on the battlefield, and often the bodily injury is treatable, but there's no brain activity, so the person remains dead."

The President was frustrated that the U.S. was somehow responsible for the death of sixty-four thousand of its people. The convoluted explanation was not helping.

"Cassandra, how does a program trying to revive brain-dead soldiers result in high-speed, precision-controlled discs destroying the damn U.S. military?" he asked, interrupting her. "I'll be clear with you. I'm a bit frustrated, and we all have much on our plate."

Secretary Edgard understood his frustration. She felt the same way when she was informed.

"Sir, I know this doesn't make sense yet, but I promise to get there soon," she continued. "I need everyone to understand what this is about, and the details I'm about to share are important. I beg for your patience for just a bit longer. The details are shocking."

The President nodded that he'd stop interrupting.

"The research efforts focused on exposing traumatized brain-dead patients to varying electromagnetic pulses intended to stimulate the cerebral impulses within the brain and initiate a reboot," she said, getting more into the details.

She paused for a second, and Admiral Lawton added, "This is much like a defibrillator for the brain, but instead of current to the heart, it provides electromagnetic pulses at certain frequencies to the brain's cortex to shock it into a restart."

While still not understanding where this was going relative to the flying discs, the entire group was mesmerized by the possibilities of this work.

"The research was unsuccessful in the first trials, and no patients were able to be revived with the technique," she said when the admiral finished. "They tried a variety of pulses to no avail. Nothing seemed to revive the patients as they had hoped. The two distinguished neuroscientists who led the research effort speculated that the brain is completely developed in adulthood and may not sustain the electromagnetic restart once the brain is dead.

They proposed and were subsequently approved to experiment on children, unbeknownst to only a few senior Air Force personnel. They reasoned that the brain grows rapidly between birth and age two and is more likely to respond to electromagnetic stimulation, given its current active state of development. Furthermore, they argued that brain injuries in children were also prevalent and that research on children would prove equally beneficial to science. Their program head supported their theory and allowed the project to continue."

"Cassandra, you're telling me that the U.S. Air Force is running around exposing brain-dead children to electromagnetic pulses," interjected the Vice President, appalled they were using children. "Why don't we know about projects like these and provide the appropriate oversight?"

The entire room had the same question, but the Vice President voiced it first.

"Alan, I asked the same question, and I'm not happy with the response I received, but I was assured they followed protocol," answered the Defense Secretary immediately. "Maybe the protocols need to be reviewed, but they did, in fact, do as they were supposed to. No rules were broken. Many unique undertakings occur in highly classified programs that receive stealthy Congressional funding, and a small but trusted group of highly vetted individuals manage them. This work is critical to our military success as a nation."

The President stopped her in her tracks.

"We all know the benefits, Cassandra, but rogue projects like this are unacceptable," he cautioned. "We'll review the protocol and ensure something like this never happens again. Telling us that they didn't break any rules doesn't make it any less wrong from a moral standpoint. I still don't see how this has anything to do with Iran's weapons. Get to the point!"

The Defense Secretary was trying to get to the critical revelation but wanted to ensure they understood the background.

Sensing the President ready to explode, she quickly picked back up.

"They began their research on two children, injured in a serious car accident and left brain-dead," she said. "One child, a boy, was five months old, and the second, a girl, was eighteen months old. The pulse technique proved to be successful in both. The children's brains restarted with sustained functionality, then took over normal operation of their bodily functions. The results were miraculous and frankly a feat of modern science."

The audience was left awestruck at her recount of the research. You could see their heads spinning with the possibilities of what this research meant to thousands of children worldwide left dead due to head trauma each year.

Cassandra shifted in her chair, seeing the team engaged in thought, and sipped some water.

"An issue emerged from the two research subjects shortly after being revived," she added as she picked back up.

Her notion of an issue jerked the attendees from their thoughts. They focused back on what she was saying with renewed interest.

Secretary of the Interior, Mike Tindale, spoke up as he listened.

"Sorry to interrupt Cassandra, but did the children not survive long?" he asked with concern.

"No, Mike, they survived and are alive today. Furthermore, they're thriving," Cassandra responded.

"I now get to the crux of it all," she said, seeing no further questions. "The children went through some extraordinary changes after their revival. First, they began to grow at an alarming rate physically, almost ten times that of a typical child.

Additionally, they began to display strange capabilities, and I assure you it's no joke, but the missing link to the discs is that the children began to show abilities to move objects with their minds. They were developing telekinetic capabilities."

Simultaneously, the tie into the discs became apparent.

The President took the opportunity to say what the whole group was thinking.

"So the key to all this is that the discs are not the technology, the hooded people control those discs with their minds, and Iran is using them; as brutal weapons," he shouted.

"Exactly, Mr. President!" responded the Defense Secretary.

"Mr. President, if I may continue, there is more to hear," she said, knowing there was more to share. "They reached enormous size by age six, each about seven feet in height and weighing around six hundred pounds. The new brain functions needed a larger energy source, so their bodies altered in ways needed to support the changes in their brains, giving them the energy source they needed. I know this is hard to accept, but I assure you we verified all this before coming here today.

We've met with the two scientists that ran the program and reviewed all their program paperwork in detail," added Admiral Lawton. "It's real."

The President diverted off point to ask a question.

"Did we stop the program at that point, and what happened to these two children?"

From the Defense Secretary's facial expression, the President could see that research did not stop at the two children.

"No, it didn't," she replied, embarrassed the Defense Department didn't see the red flags. "They successfully repeated the same electromagnetic restart on ten other children. The team shuttered the program shortly afterward. Since the closure, all twelve children have been hidden away in secrecy. They live together under the care of the two neuroscientists, a husband-and-wife team, in rural Maryland, with security provided by Air Force special operations. All at the government's expense.

The children range in age from fourteen to sixteen, and all are in good health, per my discussion with the two neuroscientists. Doctors Peter and Heidi Davidson, the husband and wife, approached Admiral Lawton about the likelihood that the Iranians had somehow replicated their work and created an army trained with the discs to defeat our military. Knowing we would have picked up on the size, Iran kept them hidden under robes to conceal this from us and the rest of the world."

Mental fireworks raged as to what this all meant regarding the current situation with Iran. Grasping a future with beings that can move objects has been great movie fare, but its reality was far more terrifying. The stuff of science fiction was now punching them in the face.

"This explanation is a difficult pill to swallow, even for someone who considers himself a closet geek," said the President dismissively.

The Defense Secretary, carefully trying to stay on point, said confidently, "We have read the reports and met with the Davidsons, as Admiral Lawton told you. It all lines up, Mr. President. They can sense objects around them and move those objects with great force and speed. No other capabilities. At least we now understand what we're dealing with, and I hope it helps find us a way to defend ourselves."

The President couldn't help getting caught up in the possibilities of what she had just shared with them. Were they facing some Jedi-like warrior? It almost seemed like a joke, but no one was laughing. Time for those questions to be answered would come over the following days and weeks, but now he needed to conclude this meeting and decide where they were heading with this added information.

The President exited his wandering thoughts ad tried to focus on where to head with this news.

"Thank you for bringing this to us," he told her graciously. "I know you have experts already looking into Iran's capabilities, but we need to assemble a panel of experts to address what we learn from the neuroscientists. Find the best of the best in this country and get them cleared at the highest level because I want this all kept airtight, and I mean the most compartmentalized security level we have.

If someone has question marks that make them a risk in their background check, don't waste time sorting it out. Just drop them from consideration. Only accept the most highly trusted Americans into this group because it's too vital to our national security. I want scientists, weapons specialists, and other areas of expertise that you or the national security members think may be relevant.

I want to meet here with that group in three days and hear from these two researchers about the details of their work. I'm unsure what this means, but I need us to understand every detail. Then we can decide how to leverage it to formulate a plan for the future. Any other questions?"

The President was about to stand when the Treasury Secretary, Brian Walters, picked up on a critical point the group had missed.

"Based on what we have heard, are we to assume the Iran warriors that so easily destroyed our military are also children?" he asked.

The shocking details of the Defense Secretary's revelations had blinded the group, even the President, to this obvious point.

The President quickly turned back to Cassandra.

"Yes, I'm afraid it's true, given they surely leveraged our program," she uttered softly. "Our two researchers are convinced and are the best to judge. Depending on when they stole the project details, the Iranians are most likely younger than the Davidson children making them twelve years old or younger, depending on when the Iranians revived them."

The President gave one final command.

"Get the neuroscientists every item of intel we possess before we meet with them so they can assess everything we have on those Iranian warriors. I want there to be no question about where this originated. Meeting adjourned."

Chapter 6

The Cranio-Genesis Secrets

The President's meeting with Doctors Peter and Heidi Davidson was about to begin. The President's entire Cabinet, national security team, and thirty recently cleared experts in various fields attended the briefing by the two neuroscientists. The experts were hand-selected by the Defense Secretary. The President asked them to serve as advisors moving forward as he sought to counter the Iranian threat.

Per the President's direction at the last meeting, the Davidsons were provided a full briefing on every bit of intel the U.S. possessed on the Iranians. The two neuroscientists astute connection to their research led them to raise their concerns. Still, they were shocked to meet with the President and his team.

They sat nervously at a table set out for them at the front of a secure auditorium. The lights on the ceiling were pointed down to illuminate their faces but shone so brightly that it was difficult for them to make out the faces of the packed room sitting in front of them. The front two seats in the auditorium were unoccupied, as were two other unoccupied seats at the table where they sat, one to each side of them.

The door to the side of the room opened, and the President, Vice President, Secretary of Defense, and Chairman of the Joint Chiefs entered together. The President and Vice President took the two front seats with the audience, while the Defense Secretary and Chairman took the seats beside them.

President Schmidt opened the meeting, "Good morning, Doctor Davidson and Doctor Davidson. I appreciate you coming here today on short notice. We greatly appreciate you recognizing the correlation between your project and the robed Iranian individuals and their discs. We speculate they kept them hooded to conceal the exact details you picked up on, hoping the U.S. would not discover the truth.

I have assembled my Cabinet, national security team, and thirty top experts, all cleared at the highest levels. We fear the Iranians have grander plans for which we may need to defend ourselves or come to the aid of another ally at some point in our future.

I ask you to share as many details as possible so we may understand the ramifications of your work and help us in our endeavors to counter the Iranians. Additionally, based on your knowledge, please feel free to speculate about the unique capability of their warriors concerning us fighting them in the future. We have assembled a panel of scientists specifically chosen to address what we know about your results, and they will support our efforts moving forward. So please arm them with as much relevant information as you believe pertinent to this objective. Please feel free to begin."

Looking at her husband briefly and returning to the audience, Heidi Davidson began, "Thank you, President Schmidt and other distinguished guests. It's an honor to be here today, and I apologize if my husband and I seem slightly intimidated. Presenting our research to this renowned audience is quite overwhelming for us."

The President smiled at her, understanding why they would feel that way. For most people, it's intimidating to meet a

President, but to meet the President with his entire Cabinet and a host of other important people was a lot to ask. Toss in that it was about something that led to the loss of so many American lives due to your scientific work, and it had to be downright petrifying.

After taking the President's smile as a gesture of reassurance, she continued, "My husband and I are neuroscientists specializing in cognitive brain function. Our specific area of research involves understanding brain function and how it generates and reacts to electromagnetic activity. As you're all likely aware, there's been tremendous progress in detecting and measuring electromagnetic signals generated by the brain.

One well-known example is work done by scientists extracting images formed in people's minds and recreating them on a computer display. Another instance is sensors placed on the head to pick up brain signals to control prosthetics. Both have been discussed extensively in various magazines and newspapers in the open literature.

While the work is in its infancy, it holds tremendous promise as we learn to tap into the brain's signals. One day, as we continue to explore, we hope to probe the brain's inner workings and interpret what we see, feel, and think in great detail. Furthermore, it's practical to expect that we can link them to machines and computers once we understand those signals, thus allowing for a seamless connection between a person's brain and external systems. You can imagine that the possibilities are endless once we achieve that level of integration.

However, the examples I mentioned focused on extracting signals and mapping the complex electromagnetic processing of the human brain into functions and images for the outside world. We can also do the reverse, inject signals into the brain, and let the brain react to the various stimuli we input. Once we attain that understanding, we can produce a bidirectional connection between humans and machines. Fascinating work with still so much to learn."

Dr. Davidson stopped there and switched the pages of her notes. She was very well-spoken, and her delivery allowed the group to grasp her complex research in understandable terms.

Once synced with her notes, the neuroscientist continued, "My husband and I were experimenting in this second area of research. Our specialty is introducing electromagnetic radiation into the brain and studying its effects on our cognitive abilities and other functions. We were particularly interested in what effects certain electromagnetic stimuli had on the overall processing capability of the brain. For instance, had it slowed down, sped up, retained more, or retained less were key areas of our research.

The effects on our brains due to certain chemical influencers like alcohol and drugs are common knowledge. Yet electromagnetic excitation of certain frequencies, pulse rates, and bandwidths provide far more possibilities for specific responses within the brain and likely with more control. One could liken this area of research to the endless opportunities we see as we peer out into deep space on a clear night, virtually limitless.

Humans have suspected, and scientists have shown for years, that the brain offers far greater powers than we garner from it today. It remains an underutilized organ. Additionally, many researchers have suggested dormant genetic capabilities are hidden in the brain, waiting to be unlocked by the proper triggers. Unlocking them could result in an accelerated state of evolution."

Heidi paused to catch her breath, and her husband reached over and gently squeezed her hand. She was trying to carefully present the complexities of their work in ways that everyone could understand, and he wanted her to know she was doing an excellent job. The blinding lights made it difficult for her to see the entire audience, but of the ones she could see, they were locked in deep thought about what she was saying.

Needing to get to the more essential aspects of their work, Heidi began again, "Peter and I were working at a classified facility in Maryland, near Johns Hopkins University, where we both received our doctorate degrees. The U.S. Air Force employed us under a project focused on impacts on cognitive function due to various electromagnetic sources a pilot or astronaut is exposed to during their missions at high altitudes.

During our research, we discovered a series of resonances in the human brain when exposed to specific electromagnetic frequencies. When injected into the brain stem at these frequencies, the brain seemed to experience some form of reboot where the patient would temporarily blackout, and the brain would restore their last memories before the excitation. It was as if the brain went through a complete reset.

We saw unprecedented neurochemical activity in the brain during these restarts. We experimented with numerous frequencies, bandwidths, and pulse rates to gain more insight and determine the optimum responses that initiated the reboot.

As we experimented, we came up with the idea that we could potentially restart the brain of a severely injured individual through the excitation of the nonfunctioning brain, thus resurrecting a brain-dead person.

Suppose you consider the defibrillator for a moment. When a person's heart stops pumping, the individual is considered dead. However, we now know that the heart can still operate but needs an excitation to restart the pumping. In the simplest case, chest compressions can accomplish that, but in more severe cases, it requires excitation to jolt it back into pumping, hence the invention of the defibrillator.

So now consider the brain, which we believe is no different from the heart under some circumstances. The brain function ceases under extreme trauma and needs an excitation to jolt it back into operation. Like the heart, just because the accident causes the organ to cease functioning, the organ is not dead; it just needs the right stimulus to restart it.

It was far-reaching work, but based on what we observed in our experiments, we believed this research held great promise and would be relevant and welcomed within the Air Force.

We made our proposal for this new research soon after completing the project we were on at the time. We created the name the Cranio-Genesis to reflect the intent, a rebirth of a dead brain. The Air Force approved the research, but only under strict classification, given that the project would involve experimentation on military personnel. The challenge was we needed the patient brought to us within a short period of becoming brain-dead and their bodily injuries manageable. We didn't want to risk the skewing of the results by severe injuries complicating the patients' responses to our excitations."

A hand went up in the audience, and a person stood up and said, "If I may ask a question? I'm Dr. Christopher Tomkin, a medical researcher working on military injuries at UCLA. I'm fascinated by your work and have a thousand questions, but most can wait. I would like to know, how long could you wait before trying your excitation on a patient, and how did you get access to patients like that in Maryland?"

The UCLA researcher sat down, and Peter Davidson responded, "We surmised that as long as the body remained on life support and depending on the degree of trauma to the brain, we could wait as long as seventy-two hours. We were unsure about the exact timeframe but decided to start with that criterion. Still, given the limited access to patients nearby, we agreed to try all patients received within the seventy-two-hour window, regardless of the complications of their injuries. There was no exact science here because each patient had unique trauma, so it was all uncharted territory."

After Peter's explanation and no other hands went up, Heidi felt like the context of their briefing was at the appropriate level for all to follow.

"The brain is the most complex organ in the body," she continued. "It uses tremendous interconnectivity to tie together its four main lobes. The frontal lobe is for our cognitive functions. The parietal lobe is for our sensory functions except for vision. The occipital lobe, our third lobe, controls our vision. Finally, there is the temporal lobe, which combines our memories with other brain functions. Additional support pieces within the brain control voluntary and involuntary functions throughout the body, long-term memories, motivational behaviors, etc. These lobes and support pieces are wired together with a highly dense fabric comprised of neurons and synapses.

A traumatic injury to the head can damage or destroy one or more of these functions, disrupting the complex structure and impeding connectivity, thus resulting in a brain-dead state. We proposed that we could kickstart the brain from its shutdown state by reinitiating a startup at the brain stem with these resonant frequencies."

Another hand went up in the audience, and a woman stood up.

"I'm Dr. Beverly Cardell, a physicist with a background in studying electromagnetic energy in the cosmos," the woman said. "I can see the possibilities with this would be expansive in medical science. How did you know which electromagnetic pulses to use since you never applied it to a brain-dead individual?"

"For many years, we studied the effects of energy level, frequency, pulse rate, and bandwidth on many patients," Peter replied. "We learned what responses resulted from which pulses in functioning brains. Heidi and I mapped that into a large matrix of test results, extracting what we believed to be the best resonance candidates from that. The two of us based our selection on solid experimental data, but we would still require experimentation to see which excitations worked with a brain-dead individual."

A person with their hand in the back had patiently waited for Peter to finish.

"I'm David Lee, a Professor of Computer Engineering at Stanford University studying computer architectures that mimic the brain," said the man. "If you failed to revive a patient through your excitations, how did you know whether it was due to the brain injury or the wrong set of electromagnetic pulses?"

Once he sat back down, Peter answered, "Great question. We didn't. We knew there would be trial and error, but we never understood why the patient did not respond. We exposed each patient to a fixed set of impulses and watched for their response. There were twenty-four different pulses used, all derived from our matrix. We could see the expected reboot of the brain occurred, but their brains could not sustain normal operation afterward."

Peter wanted to make a point for the group about ethical concerns. The audience knew the program stopped for unspecified reasons. He wanted to ensure the audience knew it had nothing to do with excitations on brain-dead patients.

"One important aspect to remember is that the patients were already brain-dead, so a failure on our part was not detrimental to the patient's health. I'm not trying to be flippant in any way. I'm just pointing out that failure didn't result in loss of life since the person was already technically dead; thus, there were no ethical concerns due to our methods."

Peter stopped, and no other hands came up from the group as they pondered his statement.

"Let me continue, and I think we can clear up a few things along this line of questioning," Heidi stated. "We worked on ten patients, all military personnel ages twenty-two to forty-four. All suffered head traumas and were brain-dead but had manageable bodily injuries. We received our patients from six to sixty-four hours after being declared brain-dead, but all were kept on life support and delivered within our defined window.

All of these patients responded to the excitations as we had hoped, but none of them could sustain the reboot cycle, and all, unfortunately, remained brain-dead. We became discouraged and began to ask ourselves similar questions to those asked a moment ago. Were we using the correct excitation pulses? Did the patients' injuries inhibit the sustained restart? And a host of other questions.

Our Air Force project lead began questioning whether we should continue the program. We argued that there were other pulse sets to try, and we needed a larger sample size to see if they may allow their brains to sustain neural activity.

While our project lead considered extending our work, Peter and I realized that our subjects may be limiting our work. The human brain rapidly grows from birth until about two years old. The growth of the brain after age three is less than fifteen percent and very little after age five. It's quite different from the rest of the body, which takes several more years to complete its growth cycle.

We surmised that the revival of a child's brain under the age of two when the brain is in an active growth period might result in a more reliable restart of the brain activity and therefore be able to sustain brain activity after the reboot.

The two of us made our proposal, and our project lead saw the merit in our updated submission, but it was unclear how we would find children available for the experiment. Moreover, there was the question of approaching them at such a traumatic moment. Unsure how to proceed, we were stalled while considering our next steps.

Sadly, two children whose parents were cleared on the program became available. The parents consented to the experimentation in hopes of saving their children. One child, a boy, was five months old; the other, a girl, was eighteen months old."

Heidi stopped for a second to compose herself. She looked to Peter with a lingering stare and then turned back.

"Both children suffered serious head trauma in a car accident and lay brain-dead, but their bodily injuries were more manageable," she continued. "They were perfect candidates for the project."

Several hands flew up in the audience, but the President interjected first.

"I'm sure many of you are asking how a military program uses children in their experimentation," he said to the broader audience. "We're reviewing this and plan to fix it."

Turning to the Davidsons, the President asked them to please proceed.

"The results from the excitations revived the first child, the younger of the two, immediately and sustained neural activity," continued Heidi Davidson. "Our hypothesis was confirmed, and we had the first revived brain-dead person, a medical breakthrough.

However, due to the age difference and limited data on children, we decided to re-tune to a slightly different set of electromagnetic pulses on the second child, the older child of the two. We quickly proceeded with that excitation, and she also revived immediately, the second successful confirmation of our approach."

Heidi paused and looked to the audience expecting a flood of questions. She wasn't surprised when a chorus of hands went up in the room, many waiting to see if the President would preempt them again.

Interestingly there were no questions from the President, Vice President, Cabinet members, or others on his national security team. The Davidsons surmised they were briefed by the Defense Secretary and were already aware of this revelation.

Peter Davidson pointed to the first audience member who raised his hand.

"Your results are astounding," said the man. "You did this work a decade and a half ago. Why don't we have this available in our hospitals today?"

Looking to his wife and choosing not to get ahead of her presentation, Peter Davidson stated, "There were complications that arose, and my wife will get to that in a moment. Undoubtedly, our work was revolutionary, but the project was terminated shortly afterward with our concurrences and placed under a tight seal of top-level compartmentalization."

Several hands went down with that response, some deciding to wait and some with a similar question.

A middle-aged woman on the far left kept her hand raised.

Peter kindly pointed to her.

"Not to take us off track from your presentation, but as a mother myself, I would like to ask how the children are?" she asked.

Peter responded with a smile.

"Both children are healthy and living secretly with us in rural Maryland."

He stopped and turned to another man in the center with his hand raised.

"You mentioned tuning the electromagnetic radiation for the two children differently, but in both instances, they revived them.," he said. "Do you believe you need to tune the excitation for each individual?"

Peter answered the gentleman.

"Both worked and now we understand that while they revived the children, they created unique differences in their outcomes.

The remaining ten children were all excited with a common excitation which we later derived as a combination of the first two excitations."

Peter recognized that his wife had not yet mentioned the other ten children and saw the surprise on some audience members' faces. With no other hands up, he quickly turned back to his wife so she could proceed.

Heidi picked up his signal and restarted promptly.

"Let me stay on the first two children for the moment," she stated, knowing they wanted to probe about the others. "I realize Peter revealed the other ten, but I want to stay on the first two. They quickly recovered from their injuries. We were both excited beyond belief, and our project office was discussing a Nobel Prize if we could get the results declassified.

However, things quickly changed. Both patients developed enormous appetites and unusual growth patterns. Their brain scans began to show abnormal changes, including pituitary gland enlargement. They were consuming over ten thousand calories a day. As you might expect, their physical size swiftly grew, like certain other larger mammal species.

Multiple changes occurred within their bodies also. Their tissue, bone, and muscle structure seemed to transform rapidly, becoming denser than you see in humans. Scans of their brains showed indications of continued additional growth, as well. Outgrowths in the lower region of the brain seemed to show the formation of two new lobes, one on the lower left and the other on the lower right side of the brain. They both wrapped around an enlarged hypothalamus and pituitary gland. Interestingly, their four main lobes seemed to remain normal in size and function.

After one month, when their weights had more than tripled, and their heights had increased thirty percent, they started displaying strange abilities. It began with subtle things like a toy they wanted. We could feel what appeared to be a slight tug on the item they desired, but they weren't physically touching it. Then it progressed to seeing objects move inside the room toward them as they seemingly called for it. Within a couple more weeks, they were moving objects around with ease. We realized then that they were developing telekinetic abilities.

Also, at that point, we recognized that the changes they were experiencing in their bodies were symbiotic alterations to support the needs of the new brain. The genetic programming we unlocked was multi-faceted with a complex interdependence."

She stopped and looked at the skepticism on the faces.

Heidi decided to address that head-on and said with a poised air, "I can see the disbelief on your faces as I say that. I assure you, we were disbelieving for an initial period until the evidence became overwhelming. Even as scientists, we wondered if we had unlocked some horror movie scenario. The children's overall demeanors and behavior remained typical for their age, so there was no concern that they had developed any terrifying traits. We focused on the science and immediately started charting their growth, brain activity, and documenting their telekinetic abilities.

Peter and I also started to notice another ability, sensing objects around them, and it was also rapidly progressing. Initially, we thought that maybe it was some type of echolocation tracking. The two of us quickly eliminated that when we tested them inside an anechoic chamber where they couldn't hear anything outside. Even under those conditions, they could sense objects outside the chamber that were neither visible nor audible to them.

As they matured, which continued at an unprecedented rate, their language skills blossomed. We could communicate more effectively with them and learn what they saw, felt, and were purposefully doing. Putting together the complicated picture of their radar mapping inside their brain gave us insight into how the sensing of an object interacted with their ability to move that same object. It was an uncanny combination of force and precision, working together seamlessly. Frankly, their ability to move objects is remarkable, but their sensing is even more extraordinary.

We could never fully understand the physics behind their powers because it's not our field of study. However, through some research and our reasonable grasp of physics, we believed that both new lobes somehow interact with graviton waves.

As they continued to grow, their telekinetic abilities increased and enhanced until age four. The number of objects they could interact with grew over that period, peaking at around two hundred.

Their two new brain lobes matured, and each lobe ended up about twice the size of the frontal lobe, the largest of the typical human brain. The first lobe we named the telekinetic lobe. It allows them to move objects about themselves. The second lobe, which we call the positional lobe, allows them to sense things and track them in a three-dimensional mental map.

One tiny hint from the Iranians we picked up on was their use of a few hundred discs. Similar to our children and likely not a coincidence. The other is their physical size. While the Iranians were robed to conceal themselves, we could identify these two features along with their telekinetic powers. It immediately made us believe Iran somehow stole our research and created their telekinetic army."

Heidi decided to continue without pause, recognizing that there would be a thousand questions, but she needed to give them a complete picture before Peter, or she would answer more questions. She asked that they hold them a bit longer.

"Our research shows they can control a few hundred objects simultaneously without losing force or precision. Once they exceed that limit, they somehow saturate their telekinetic lobe and quickly lose precision and force.

I also mentioned the size of the Iranians - our children are approximately seven feet tall and weigh roughly six hundred pounds. They reached full maturity by age six. Their bodies comprise a healthy, dense muscle and bone structure with unique fibrous arrays meshed throughout their bodies and limbs. These fibrous structures contain high concentrations of metallics and connect in a bundle at the brain stem. We perceive this to be some intertwined structure that feeds the two lobes and enables their powers to interact with objects.

As for their physical size, their two new lobes demand high power for operation. The unique abilities we unlocked in the brain with our excitation also unleashed changes to their biological makeup, giving them the necessary battery, which is a crucial function of our bodies, and the self-sustainability for the demands of these additional brain functions."

Heidi had the group ablaze in thought, from revived brain-dead children to telekinetic evolutionary states. Too bad, she thought, misguided leaders had snatched all the possibilities of their work for war.

As she paused for the audience to ask questions, the President had picked up on something the Davidsons avoided, purposefully, he guessed.

"You mentioned that the first two children were used on the project because cleared parents under the program allowed for this. Do you two happen to be the parents?"

The marvel of the Davidsons' revelations caught the audience in a swirl of fascination. Few, if any, put two and two together like the President.

Peter answered with a reserved, "Quite perceptive, Mr. President. They're our two children by birth and were injured in a severe car accident outside Baltimore-Washington International airport. Heidi and I were heading off for a vacation to Italy. My parents, who were watching the kids for the week, drove us to the airport. Before we even took off, we received a call from the police about a serious accident involving my parents, who had passed away at the crash site not far outside the airport, and our children, who were on the way to the hospital with significant head traumas during the rollover.

Heidi and I hurried to the hospital, where we discovered that our children were on life support and lay there brain-dead. Mortified by the events and recognizing that no available medical procedure would reverse their current conditions, we sought our own recourse to save our children.

We phoned our program head seeking permission to use them on the Cranio-Genesis Project. Applying our excitations to our children was not how we imagined our research to play out, but it saved our two children, Alan and Beatrice.

We did not tell you this upfront because we wanted everyone to focus on the project and the results, not the patients or their parents.

I'll tell you this, Mr. President, while the Cranio-Genesis Project was canceled with our concurrence as we recognized that the world might not be ready for what resulted. We would do it again for a child if we needed to and not regret it for a second. They are both wonderful children, as are the other ten.

The other ten, which we've yet to discuss, were orphaned children living in foster homes before their injuries with no known or living parents. As you might imagine, it took two-and-a-half years for the government network to find appropriate patients meeting the criteria. The protracted period benefited the overall research because it allowed us to document the development of the children before the program was shuttered.

Once the program terminated, we adopted the other ten children. We have kept all twelve of them hidden from the world to allow them to grow up and become adults before deciding how to move forward. Today may be an important milestone on that path ahead as they, for the first time, are now revealed to a broader group of people."

The President smiled at them and replied, "I can only imagine your joy when you revived your children. I'm happy to hear that all twelve of them are doing well, and we'll support your efforts to introduce them into society when you deem it appropriate. I offer whatever resources and help that you need."

Peter then pointed to a man who patiently stood during the exchange with the President.

The man snickered a bit as if the question he was about to ask was silly.

"If they can move objects, can they move themselves and fly, so to speak?"

Peter knew the question was well-founded and didn't laugh.

"Great question again," Peter replied. "The answer is no. They can move objects relative to their body but not their body relative to other objects like the Earth. We don't completely understand the phenomenology. We hypothesize that it has to do with the reference of the telekinetic lobe originating from within themselves. Regardless of the science, we're certain they cannot do this. They can, however, move each other relative to themselves. So, as you might imagine, with twelve children possessing this capability, it can create some parental challenges from time to time."

Despite the seriousness of the meeting's purpose, the audience laughed at his comment as they all pictured children horseplaying by lifting one another into the air.

Peter then pointed to another woman who said, "The Iranian warriors were controlling a few hundred discs at once with astounding precision. You mentioned that your children could do that as well. Does every child possess the same power and the same control limits?"

Peter was waiting for this question.

"No, there are two exceptions," he answered. "It's due to their unique excitations. Alan possesses three times the strength of the other eleven, but he can still only control the same number of objects. Beatrice, the other unique child, can handle a thousand objects simultaneously, but her strength is consistent with the other ten.

Suppose the Iranians did somehow steal our work. In that case, they only know the excitation we used on the final ten and don't understand that there may be increased capability if the excitations were tuned differently.

Due to the emergency circumstances with Alan and Beatrice, we never documented the unique signals we used on those two. We only recorded the excitations used on the last ten children in our project documentation. As such, the Iranians match the abilities of our last ten children, but Alan and Beatrice possess some more extensive abilities beyond theirs.

We don't expect that Iranian scientists would be able to recreate the deviations we used because they don't possess the preliminary work. Still, we prefer they don't realize there may be more to gain here by changing excitations."

Once Peter finished, a man stood and said, "Hello. I'm Dr. Nicholas Carter. I wonder if you could elaborate on their positional lobe mapping. You mentioned that you hadn't seen a saturation limit. How far out does the sensing reach?"

Peter explained, "We haven't seen a saturation limit. As for the reach, the map extends large distances, but they can move within the map and focus in and out as needed, much like we do with our optical vision. You see many things with your eyes, but you can focus on a specific area and gather more detail.

Same with their positional lobe. They can focus this sense and peer closer at an object within that map. Items with a large mass or high speed show further and brighter within the map. For example, small things with high speed are intense, as are large objects with low velocity, while large objects at high speed are ablaze within the map.

The Iranians used this to assess the battlefield around them constantly. Our military weapons are either fast, large, or both. These characteristics are how success has been historically won on the battlefield. These weapons shine brightly in their senses, and their telekinetic capabilities are equally suited to defeat them."

The group was putting together a solid foundation of what they faced with the Iranian warriors. The questioning went on for another three hours. Audience members probed the Davidsons about the specific capabilities of the children and how they measured their abilities. They asked whether they trained for warfare, their diet, emotional maturity, physical maturity, unique emotional issues, behaviors, and even the games they played.

Peter Davidson answered them all and assured the group that the children were like any other child except for being more mature physically and emotionally for their age. Like most children, he clarified that they still had much to learn. They could be impulsive, rebellious, and temperamental at one moment while loving, inquisitive, and caring the next. Most of the audience resonated with these descriptions as if referring to their own children.

Although the meeting had been insightful, it was still unclear what it meant for the path forward, but it provided a clearer picture of what they were against with this foe.

As the President was about to thank the Davidsons and dismiss the assembled experts, Peter Davidson asked, "Would you like to meet Alan and Beatrice? We brought them here today after receiving the Defense Secretary's approval. They are waiting outside the room in one of the neighboring offices."

The room became a sea of bright eyes as the President looked at the Defense Secretary and said, "You brought them here?"

She gave him a devious grin and said, "I figured it was easier for you to believe if you could see them firsthand."

The President, exhibiting a bit of eagerness, said, "Bring them in!"

Chapter 7

Meet the Children

Into the room walked two enormous human beings with astonishing brawn. Hard to fathom that these two giants were, in fact, children. They reflected every bit of their seven-foot, six-hundred-pound bodies as they paraded in.

Their frame and heads were large but proportionate to their size and other features. Each of their faces was soft and reflected their youth, and both were quite attractive. Similarities to their parents shone through even in their immense stature.

Beatrice had brown hair like her mother's, with elegant facial lines contradicting her immense size. She carried herself with an assured stride and a sparkle in her bright eyes that oozed self-confidence.

The young man, Alan, had chiseled facial features and a strength reflected in his squared chin that bore similarity to his father's. He looked more the part of a massive football star, a prospect that would make any NFL team drool, as he moved with an athletic gait and a powerful step. While not childlike in his mannerisms, he did reflect a demeanor more his age than his sister.

They approached their parents' table and turned to face the group.

"Mr. President, if I may, I would like to introduce all of you to our children, Alan and Beatrice," said Peter Davidson. "Al and Beatrice would like to give everyone a quick display of their capabilities. Is that okay? It will provide you with a stronger assurance that the Iranian warriors are a replica of our children."

President Schmidt, without hesitation, replied, "Please do."

Peter then asked Beatrice to take out the objects she carried in a small bag on her side.

Beatrice promptly opened the bag, and twenty balls emerged and floated into the air in front of her. The balls moved above her and spun as a group in a singular rotating circle about three feet in diameter. She rotated them at such high speed that they blurred into a single circle, just as the Iranian warriors had. The whirring became deafening, and the wind they generated blasted the audience and sent the papers flying in all directions.

After wowing them for a few minutes, Beatrice separated them into four groups and repeated a similar rotational display. Next, she showed a variety of controlled formations, exercising the balls through a series of progressions just as the Iranians had done in Iraq. The group was familiar with the Iranian exhibition, so it was easy for her to show that she could perform similar skills.

Beatrice smiled at the sea of heads moving with the spectacle. Putting her unique touch on things, she sent the balls flying like a string of beads, each following one another through the air in a sequence of acrobatic movements. She exhibited extraordinary precision and control as she weaved them up and down throughout the room while zipping in and around various objects and people.

Heads spun as they were all left amazed. The adage, seeing was believing, indeed proved true. Beatrice returned the balls to her side and dropped them back into her bag one by one.

Peter and Heidi Davidson saw the amazement on their faces. Their decision to bring the two children drove home the capabilities of these two and made it clear that the Iranians had gotten ahold of their research. Beatrice's demonstration left them with no doubt.

Al then stepped forward.

Peter prompted the group before his son began, "I'll have Al show some of their ability to lift and move an object of significant weight."

Al wasn't sure what to do because he didn't have an object to use, unlike Beatrice. His parents hadn't coordinated with him their intentions, so he looked around the room and got the idea to lift Beatrice. Al figured he might have to live with her scorn for quite a while, so he figured it best to choose someone else.

Going with the next best thing, he turned to Admiral Lawton, who looked confused and uncomfortable at Al's stare.

The admiral and his chair quickly floated out front of the audience.

First, Al moved the admiral forward toward the President but stopped a few yards in front of him. Admiral Lawton, clearly unprepared for what was happening, let out a brief 'whoa' as Al stopped him midair. The admiral quickly quieted himself, realizing his outburst, as a few snickers erupted from the audience.

Al then moved him back and forth in front of the crowd in a side-to-side motion for all to see. With a quick move backward, he brought Admiral Lawton directly in front of him and began to spin the admiral in a side-to-side tumble. Al kept the spin rate slow and then moved the twirling admiral around the room in various motions before safely returning him to his initial spot on the ground behind the table next to his parents.

The admiral seemed relieved to have landed safely back on solid ground.

Admiral Lawton offered Al a quick, "Thank you for putting me down! That was, um..., quite interesting. I could feel a force exerted on my body as you moved and rotated me. But it wasn't like a weightless feeling. It was more like being held by some invisible hand. It was quite unnerving, yet very impressive."

Al smiled back and replied, with a deep voice one would expect from someone his size, "You're welcome, sir. I hope I didn't scare you too badly."

The admiral offered a smile and a terse, "Not at all."

However, the audience, not convinced of his sincerity, let out a hearty laugh.

Peter then opened the floor to questions for the children. He explained that they would let the children give their accounts instead of answering themselves.

The room became a wave of rising hands popping into the air.

Peter let the children handle the questions by themselves, confident they were comfortable doing so.

However, the first question came from the President, which surprised both children. Their large faces turned bright red.

Noticing their blush, the President took a soft tact with them.

"Thank you both for coming here today," he said warmly. "We've heard a lot about both of you and had the opportunity to meet your wonderful parents. I appreciated the display of your skills a few moments ago, and I couldn't help getting a laugh out of Admiral Lawton spinning in the air!"

"On a serious note, is there anything you've seen from the Iranians that you don't think you can do?"

Beatrice looked at Al and gave him a look telling him that she would answer the question.

Al nodded, and she answered, "We've seen the videos on television and the internet. Our parents were initially reluctant to show us the footage. Yet as they became suspicious of the hooded Iranians, they allowed us to watch several videos and provide them our feedback."

"We can do everything they did. We've never trained to fight or use weapons, but we've tested our skills in various manners. I'm sure we could match their abilities, even exceed them in some cases. However, we haven't done so because our parents have rules about using our capabilities or powers, as our brother, Zeke, likes to call them."

Beatrice was very composed, and the group hung on her every word. Her confidence in what she described went well beyond her years. All couldn't help being impressed.

"We play several games where we move objects for force, speed, and precision to build and test our skills, but never with the intent to hurt anyone," she proceeded to tell them. "One game we play, which we call obstacle dash, pits two of us against each other in a race over an aerial obstacle course we created outside our home. The game's object is to get your thirty balls through the course ahead of your opponent while completing a series of gates. The difficulty comes in playing both offense and defense against your opponent, using your balls to deflect, divert or block your competitor's balls as you move through the course.

You saw the Iranians use similar skills with the discs in various offensive and defensive maneuvers. The force and precision they also demonstrated line up with our abilities."

Beatrice smiled at the President and waited to see if he was satisfied with her answer.

Before responding, the President considered that while her voice was deep and reflective of her size, it came across with an elegance that contradicted her immense size. Still, it reinforced the assuredness he witnessed as she strode into the room with her brother.

President Schmidt smiled and said, "Thank you, and you're an impressive young lady."

The President then turned to the parents.

"You should both be very proud of these two," he said, complimenting them.

When the President didn't add anything further, Beatrice scanned the audience and pointed to a man in the front row with his hand raised.

"Can you tell me what you feel and see of objects in motion around you?" he asked. "I have spent my whole career working on inertial sensing, and your abilities are so extraordinary."

Beatrice thought for a minute.

"I would describe it as an add-on to our normal consciousness where people sense and process touch, taste, sound, and vision," she answered. "Your brain weaves them together seamlessly. This sense is merely another sense rolled into that. Imagine a 3D map in black and white that's all around you for several kilometers. You can sweep through the map and focus on any object or several simultaneously. Large and high-speed objects show brighter. We can move within the map and choose objects to focus on for greater acuity. Similar to focusing on an object with our eyes. This view melds into our consciousness to give us a secondary vision, if you will, but with greater fidelity."

"Consider the Iranians," she continued, trying to draw some relevance to the battle. "They could see and track the bullets, missiles, aircraft, and objects and choose which ones to target, evade, or deflect. The discs were the ultimate tool for those three purposes. Their size and material choice gave them destructive force, armor-piercing, and reusability. There was no need to reload. They just recalled them and used them again.

Furthermore, they were large enough to damage or block most things. Subtle and simple, but nevertheless, ingenious. They had thought this through and were well prepared to fight our forces."

This last note was ominous, coming from someone with the same powers. Everyone in the room was keenly aware of the annihilation by the Iranian warriors and how fast they accomplished it. It was clear that no one in the room felt better about America's current situation from what they had just heard.

A rugged man to the far right raised his hand, and Beatrice called on him. He stood up and straightened his uniform.

"If I may, this is a question for your brother," he said. "I'm General Nunez from the U.S. Air Force, and your parents said that you possess greater strength than the others; how strong are your powers?"

Al stood up and answered with a tinge of boastfulness.

"I've lifted as much as thirty-five thousand pounds," he replied. "While I've never been able to demonstrate it, my parents believe, based on their test estimates, that I could move a thirty-pound object at six thousand miles per hour if it could stand up to that velocity. The other children would only be able to attain a speed of three thousand miles per hour for the same object."

"Call me skeptical, but I still find it hard to believe we created Jedi warriors," the general contemptuously said.

Al didn't know how to respond and looked at his dad.

Peter Davidson stood up. The haughty tone lobbed at his son by the general put him off.

Peter snarled a bit in his own tone as he said, "I appreciate your skepticism, General Nunez. The reference to Jedi, however, is misleading. These children are real and the result of a genetic transformation. It was a mutation excited by electromagnetic radiation, which caused their brains and bodies to move to another state of evolution.

I assure you no mysterious living creatures inside them give them this power like in the movies. There are no lightsabers or mind control, just object sensing and the ability to apply a telekinetic force to go along with it. As an Air Force general, I know you can appreciate they're no laughing matter after what happened in Iraq, and none of this is a joke or fairy tale."

The general and Peter stared each other down for a few moments.

President Schmidt stopped the general from further comments, wishing to move on from the contentious moment.

"We know it's no joke," said the President. "We believe everything you told us, which has enlightened us to how they adeptly defeated our forces."

The President encouraged the session to continue for another hour to ensure his team of experts garnered enough to help guide him forward. He stopped the meeting at that time and thanked everyone for coming.

"Thank you both for coming here today," he said, having learned much from the briefing. "We appreciate your insight and candor. Individuals having these powers is new to us, something from a science fiction movie. So, excuse some of our questions. Your demonstrations and answers helped us visualize what we're facing with Iran. You gave us much to consider, and we need to determine how we'll proceed from here, as we remain suspicious of the long-term intentions of Iran."

"Heidi and Peter," he said, turning to the parents. "Your children are very well-spoken and well-mannered. Quite impressive for their age."

"Well, they've only lived their lives around two neuroscientists, elite security forces, and each other," responded Peter. "So, they possess a more mature demeanor than most kids. At least most of them do."

The President didn't know what to make of the last comment but chose not to probe further. He knew they must be exhausted from the intense meeting.

"You have done a masterful job considering the circumstances," responded President Schmidt. "Also, I want to thank you for putting the puzzle pieces together for all of us. Your astute recognition of who the Iranians had under those robes answered how those devastating discs were powered. We may have continued to wander blindly for months without your help. And if we had, we would've given Iran a considerable period to execute what appears to be a large-scale plan.

At least we now understand what we're dealing with and the basis against what we must protect. No one, and I mean no one outside this room, is to know about our former program or these children until I decide it's time for that knowledge to come to light. Iran hid their warriors from the world to obscure the truth and give themselves time, so we must continue to let them believe they have us fooled.

We're investigating how Iran extracted the Cranio-Genesis data. We won't know how long they've had to build their army until we find out how they extracted the information. It's been long enough to make a small set of these warriors, but they may have many more, and no doubt they're producing more as we speak.

I guess their lie about it being a gift from Allah is fundamental to their plan. If exposed that we're the source, it could derail their grip on the Muslim world. They're focused today on religious unification, so let's continue to have them believing they fooled us.

Everyone, thank you for your participation. Your insight and ideas will be critical as we decide on our strategy in the coming weeks. We have a lot of work ahead of us, and I fear our nation and the rest of the world need our help."

Chapter 8

The Grand Unification

Iran's takeover of Iraq, Turkey, and Saudi Arabia was impressive and left little doubt that Iran desired more of the Muslim world. The ruthless manner they dealt with the resistance in those countries, albeit muted as the opposition was, was well known worldwide. They utilized television and social media as effective tools for their new republic to spread fear and promote their unifying movement.

Iran's Supreme Leader delivered the next phase of his plan in a public address in Tehran.

He announced his wish to unify all Islamic-majority countries under one nation. Once completed, the new nation would be known as the United Islamic Republic of Iran. As the spiritual leader of the unified country, he would lead all Muslims into their rightful place of global importance. He offered, without threat, for the remaining Muslim countries to join them. It was clear to these countries and the rest of the world that the invitation was actually a demand.

They announced a decision deadline of three months for each country to decide their allegiance to the United Iran but provided no details of the consequences should they choose not to join.

International media speculated that Iran needed three months to solidify control of Turkey and Saudi Arabia. While breaking any resistance in those former countries was initially paramount, they also needed to establish government control with their laws and an enforcement arm. Governing was never easy, regardless of whether the people resisted or not.

Whether recognizing their fate or relishing to be part of a new Islamic superpower, Egypt, Indonesia, Pakistan, Algeria, Sudan, and Bangladesh announced their intentions to join within the first week. The willingness of such varied cultures to accept Iran's offer indicated how much momentum their crusade was obtaining. One would have thought that the vibrancy of the cause would instill concern in Iran's new allies, Russia and China, but neither indicated that.

On hearing this news, the President called a meeting with his Vice President, Secretary of State, and Director of National Intelligence to discuss the latest updates from the U.S.'s varied sources in the region.

They met in the Oval Office, where the President quickly got down to business.

"Margaret, I've read the latest reports on the countries that have already agreed to join the United Iran. Who else are you hearing may join?"

"Right now, our intelligence reports think they may all join," answered Director Stoneman. "Iran has been quite savvy with its propaganda on unifying Islam and fortifying the force of Allah. The centuries-old divide between Sunni and Shia is gone in most Muslims' eyes. Iran's masterful spin that Allah settled the debate by giving Iran his mighty warriors is starting to take hold across the Muslim world. In addition, human nature makes people want to jump aboard the winning bus, which helps explain why so many are hopping aboard to be part of the winning team.

Afghanistan is the only one showing any reluctance. Despite having inferior weapons, Afghanistan mentions its successful resistance to the U.S. and Russia. They speak of the discs and robed warriors from Iran as the latest version of an aggressor trying to rule their nation. The Taliban leaders seem confident they can settle into their mountain caves and resist them as they did us. Why would Iran and its new weapons be any different? They boasted that their network of mountain caves withstood huge bombs, so why would they be vulnerable to little Iranian discs."

The President nodded his head, understanding the mentality of the Afghans. They were only a tiny piece to a vast unification demand, but he liked seeing some defiance from a country. Iran was rallying the Islamic people to a cause formed of false pretenses. Their grip on Islam would be much different if the people knew the truth behind the warriors.

Unwilling to overthink one country's participation in Iran's consolidation, President Schmidt said, "Not sure it matters much, but it will be an interesting test for the Iranian leadership. This will be the first opportunity for Iran to deal with hardcore defiance of their offer, which we know is a veiled edict. Iran has become accustomed to the Islamic populations quickly falling in line as they enter their countries.

Conversely, Afghanistan might discover these discs are not your typical weapon. It's not our problem, but it could help slow Iran's march. Let's do everything to encourage it."

"What about some of the smaller African countries?" asked the President, shifting topics. "We understand there are some attempts to overthrow the leadership of some countries with small Islamic populations and jump on the Iranian bandwagon."

"Yes, Mr. President. Islamic radicals in Cameroon and Ethiopia, with their minority Islamic populations, are working to overthrow their governments and join the United Iran," responded the Intelligence Director. "If successful, it may encourage others to follow suit. Some experts are worried that Iran could run the tables on the whole continent of Africa, including South Africa, which is starting to voice significant concerns.

It's already stunning what Iran has accomplished in five short months. Considering current facts, Iran will add eight hundred million people to its population once these new nations join the republic. They will add enormous land and coastline, several in key trading lanes. Iran will be entrenched on three continents, and they will only trail China and India in population with their estimated one billion two hundred million people. They will dwarf us who sit next on that list. To say they will be formidable is an understatement. They will be the largest in total landmass and most powerful empire ever established on Earth."

The group wore grim faces as they considered what was occurring. Iran somehow became the big bully who moved into not one but three neighborhoods simultaneously. The bully was starting to flex his muscle with demands on everyone around.

"Jack, we knew this was coming with Iran demanding inclusion on the U.N. National Security Council," said President Schmidt, shifting topics again. "Iran's demand that the council not grow in size and France or the U.K. be removed can't sit well with Europe in general. I don't trust Russia or China not to go along with this. What do you hear from France and the U.K. on this?"

The ever-composed Secretary frowned at the President's question while pulling his left cufflink. He was an old-school diplomat, and the new tactics of Iran shifted diplomacy protocols in ways that made the gentleman uncomfortable.

"Mr. President, it's not sitting well with either of them, as you suggest," Jack replied. "The consensus around the U.N. is that France should be the one to go, but the European Union countries are adamant that France stay. It will be a tough vote, but in the end, we can't hold Iran back from being voted in, and I expect France to be the one removed.

It's infuriating to Europeans that Iran stated that Europe has become less relevant on the world stage, and the need for both to participate was no longer required. Although, the dagger that hurt the most was that many nations outside of Europe agreed. With their two new allies, Russia and China, Iran is recentering all the power to Asia, with North America and Europe languishing on the sidelines. The clout of Iran is growing as fast as its empire, and its coattails are carrying two willing and dangerous tagalongs.

I'm trying to keep diplomatic ties open and get Iran to open discussions with us. A dialogue with you and their leadership is still my objective. Maybe even with Russia in the same accord."

President Schmidt knew Iran wanted no discussions with the U.S., and Alexei Kovalyov was the last person he wanted in the middle of that discussion if it even happened.

"I'm apprehensive about the relationship between Russia and Iran," stated the President. "Iran is fearsome enough on its own; however, their growing alliance spells trouble for everyone. Even before his budding relationship with Iran, Kovalyov was hard to deal with in international affairs. Now that he has a powerful cohort, his rants are more extreme and remind me of when Khrushchev tried to put nuclear missiles in Cuba.

His speech the other day had him pontificating about the irrelevance of the U.S. and other Western nations. He spewed his communist rhetoric in which he called us fat, weak, and lazy capitalists who are increasingly shrinking into irrelevance every day due to our gluttonous ways. Yet, he rules like a greedy king.

I always find it interesting when so-called communist countries like Russia and China criticize capitalist ideals like private property, profits, and free enterprise. Yet, they are the most significant users of it when it serves their interests and lines the pockets of their leaders. The hypocrisy is humorous, if not sickening.

I know one thing, Kovalyov's version of communism has nothing to do with the changing landscape and Iran's emergence. But Alexei Kovalyov will never miss an opportunity to jump aboard a train that serves him best. He is extremely dangerous at this point, and we must keep an unusually closer eye on what he is up to."

The President was irritated with his Secretary of State for continuing to insist there was a reason or a path to diplomacy. The Secretary continued to turn a blind eye to what these leaders were all about and their true natures. Not all situations or all people can be dealt with through diplomacy. Bullies needed to be punched to get their attention.

President Schmidt disliked the Russian President from the moment they first met. The man was a thug and tyrant dressed as a national leader. Kovalyov's KGB history and cagey ways made him more dangerous than any post-WWII Russian leader.

"Jack, what are you hearing from our Korean and Japanese friends?" asked President Schmidt, moving on to Asia.

After being sworn in, the President worked hard to keep solid relations with the leaders of both Asian countries. They were tremendous allies to the U.S. in many aspects, and he trusted them as much as any other nation to be faithful friends.

"Mr. President, both are worried about China but have seen no acts of aggression from them," responded the Secretary of State. "They keep constant diplomatic communications and see no aggressive activity like Europe is experiencing with Russia. They are both open with us about their attempts to work with Iran on economic opportunities, but they are quietly concerned by Iran's growing influence in the region.

South Korea keeps mentioning North Korea is trying to poke itself into relevance, acting as if Iran is an ally, but they know Iran is showing North Korea zero attention. I expect Korea and Japan to keep low profiles with Iran but will work on economic opportunities as they become available and attempt to maintain neutrality. Here is a great example where diplomacy is prevailing."

When his Secretary of State finished, the President ignored the last barb and wished to hear more about China.

"What's your take on China and its intentions?" he asked. "I see they continue to align themselves with Iran publicly and in every international discussion. They must be worried about Iran's influence over their Silk Road trade routes. In a blink, China has a new master over one of its largest economic initiatives, which can't sit well with its leadership. Moreover, they just moved down a rung to fourth place in their military relevance after heavily investing in bringing parity with us and Russia during the last decade."

Before the Secretary could respond, the Vice President interjected, "China should also be concerned about their treatment of Muslims in their country. It could come back to bite them. Iran can't ignore that China sent Muslims in the Xinjiang region into camps for reprogramming and the numerous atrocities that took place."

The Secretary shook his head in agreement with the Vice President's point.

"Mr. President, I think China is playing this very carefully," said the Secretary of State. " They see that Iran now controls several assets important to China, but they also see an opportunity. They are happy to pull back on their former initiatives to serve their self-interests and optimize what is available in the new world landscape. They are adapting their long-term plans as this unfolds.

As to Alan's point, it may be why their relationship with Iran is not quite as cozy as it's with Russia. They are undoubtedly cooperating but aren't getting the same warm public support from Iran. Regardless, we should expect China to continue taking outward jabs at us at every opportunity. It will keep them in Iran's good graces and serve their economic interests."

"Thank you all for this," said the President, drawing the meeting to an end. "Undoubtedly, every nation is discussing what is happening with Iran and its new allies. We must work to maintain our tight relationships across the globe. Many of our friends are afraid to show their allegiance to us for fear of retribution. I understand their rationale, but we must keep reminding them of their vulnerability as this plays out. Fear can cause leaders to avoid doing what they must, often to their own detriment. We can only keep reminding them of the risks while we work to find a means to neutralize Iran's robed warriors."

President Schmidt saw nothing but a deep conviction on the face of his team. He knew that America would need his team to be at its best as events worldwide became more perilous.

Chapter 9

From the Ashes, We'll Rise

President Schmidt was sure Iran had yet to satisfy their appetite for greater power, influence, and conquest. The President was determined to solve the Iranian imbalance of power. He knew this was an essential element of peace, bringing the aggressor into check.

Further exacerbating the situation for the U.S. and its allies was the growing alliance of Iran, Russia, and China. The President realized that the coalition made the present situation more difficult, but the solution to the ordeal began by countering the Iranian warriors. Once they could do that, the litany of weapons the U.S. possessed would again prove effective.

Unfortunately, the U.S. had no current solution to neutralize Iran's warriors. He wouldn't risk nuclear, chemical, or biological war, and he wouldn't violate the rules of the Geneva Convention nor risk global ruination. The U.S. President hoped the Iranian alliance recognized those principles but was unsure they'd play by any rules.

The President needed a solution quickly. He expected time was limited before Iran and the others decided to act again with an eye toward Israel or the West. Using history as a guiding tool, he leveraged an effective past endeavor and created a new program similar to the Manhattan Project used during World War II.

Considering where he felt the U.S. currently stood, he called it the Phoenix Project with the hope of America rising from the ashes. He placed the program under the highest security classification, focusing solely on developing weapons capable of destroying the Iranian warriors and their discs. The project's goal would not expand beyond that simple tenet, and he sought no broader means of mass destruction. President Schmidt aimed to neutralize their warriors and regain a global balance of power.

The President selected Nicholas Carter, an M.I.T. physicist, to lead the project. Dr. Carter was one of the greatest minds in the world and participated in the briefing by the Davidsons. He received his Ph.D. at twenty-three from Harvard and is versed in a broad spectrum of emerging technologies such as next-generation rocketry, lasers, particle physics, and nanoelectronics. Dr. Carter refers to himself as a pacifist hawk who believes powerful weapons are needed to ensure peace and keep tyrants in check but should only be used when absolutely required.

Along with his scientific credentials, Dr. Carter shared several core convictions with the President, such as realizing that world leadership starts with compassion for those less fortunate. Therefore, wealthy nations must share and use their resources to help those nations.

Likewise, as you engage with other countries, start with an appreciation for their culture and religion, not expecting that you can bend them to your ways or beliefs just as you would expect them to treat you.

Lastly, they both recognize that pockets of the world will always spin out new leaders seeking power and wealth while choosing evil means to obtain it. Countries like the U.S. must be willing to hold those leaders accountable for their aggression and cruel treatment of people.

As the Davidsons explained in the meeting with the President, defeating the Iranian warriors would be impossible without developing new weapons and tactics. No one was better for that task than Nicholas Carter.

Western intelligence sources had yet to establish how many warriors Iran possessed, so the extent of the challenge faced by the U.S. was unclear. At every turn, new Iranian warriors were emerging across their growing empire for use with their security forces, showing they had an ample supply of them in their arsenal. Hence, the challenge of a new weapon to counter them grew more daunting. Defeating one warrior would be no easy task, but taking down an army of them seemed impossible.

To succeed, the Phoenix Project would require a high probability of kill and a fast-acting weapon to overcome multiple warriors with uncanny sensing and swift retaliation with their fierce discs. The President knew if they fell short of achieving that when the U.S. attacked, the retribution from Iran would likely entail an attack on the U.S. home front, something he wanted to avoid.

The President clarified to Dr. Carter that he should not consider biological, chemical, or nuclear weapons unless there was no alternative. He had yet to explain what he meant explicitly by no alternative.

Unfortunately, the Iranian government had determined that this President would also likely avoid these weapons. They knew the standards by which the U.S. would operate would forbid their use. Dr. Carter recognized that the President's decision came from personal conviction, not Geneva Convention rules.

The headquarters for the Phoenix Project was established in a remote area south of Boise, Idaho. The facility was a little-used, cavernous, underground area built soon after Russia launched Sputnik. The U.S. government at the time was ultra-paranoid, suspecting Russia could now see all U.S. weapons development. So, they decided to secretly construct an immense structure, three times the volume of NASA's vaunted Vertical Assembly Building at its Kennedy Space Center.

The facility supported weapons evaluations requiring long distances and moderate altitude but kept it hidden from prying Russian satellites. The numerous open rooms and test facilities, enormous in size, were perfect for the Phoenix Project. The Defense Department utilized strict protocols for access in and around the area to ensure the tightest security.

Dr. Carter considered the insights he took away from the meeting with the Davidsons and a thorough review of the intelligence on the Iranian warriors before mapping the needs of his project team.

The children's ability to move objects enamored most of the scientists who attended the Davidsons' briefing, but Dr. Carter realized their sensing capabilities were the more challenging to overcome. His conclusion from the Davidsons' briefing and his review of the intelligence on the Iranians was that their sensory abilities would immediately detect any weapon they developed. Once sensed, the warriors would swiftly strike at the weapon system with their discs to destroy it. Speed was their hope, but he was still concerned about dealing with large groups of warriors simultaneously.

Intelligence had identified tens of these warriors, and they had to expect more of them to be hidden away by Iran. Based on what he knew today, he believed the only weapons the President had at his disposal with a chance for a successful attack were those banned by the President. He knew his job was to generate new ideas or advance current technologies in development.

Utilizing his vast understanding of available technologies, he considered candidates from various disciplines he felt gave the program the most extensive breadth of ideas and knowledge. He was aware of several technologies being experimented with under classified development programs. Still, his team needed to accelerate their maturity and expand their capabilities to defeat the Iranians.

The President committed to Dr. Carter that all necessary military and scientific resources would be available to the project, essentially giving him a blank check.

Dr. Carter then handpicked a team of experts after passing security background checks. The DoD trained the personnel on the stringent protocols to shroud the program from the world.

After completing his team roster, Dr. Carter decided to focus the project team on two technologies: laser cannons and short-range hypersonic missiles. Both would give an Iranian warrior less than a few seconds to react and respond. He hoped the team would identify more possibilities but wanted the group to start working on those two.

The Secretary of Defense assigned the Phoenix Project a military deputy to support Dr. Carter. Air Force Major General Frank Nunez was a seasoned military weapons expert with a Ph.D. in aerospace engineering from Georgia Tech.

General Nunez was a trained F-22 pilot but spent most of his career working at the forefront of advanced high-speed rockets.

His work involved a new missile technology using scramjet propulsion to achieve Mach 6 and higher speeds.

The general came to the project with a hardened edge and dismissive opinion about the Iranian warriors. He believed the Iranian warriors were hardly unstoppable and the U.S. used the wrong tactics against them in Iraq.

The briefings from the Davidsons did little to change his opinion, even after he had a contentious argument with the Davidsons after their briefing. His snide remark about Jedis during their briefing led to an encounter when the presentation ended.

During the argument, Peter Davidson implored the general to consider what his children told them about their capabilities being too much for current U.S. weapons. General Nunez doubted the children understood what the U.S. did and didn't have for weapons, nor how they might use them against the Iranians. His dismissive attitude insulted the Davidsons, who knew that any hope of success in defeating the Iranian warriors required open-minded thinking.

To make matters worse for both parties, Dr. Carter selected the Davidsons as his last two additions to the Phoenix team and assigned them to work with the General on tactics, given their in-depth knowledge of the children's capabilities. The Davidsons shared their concerns about the general's open-mindedness with Dr. Carter, who told them that was part of the general's role on the team.

Work began expeditiously in Idaho, understanding the urgency of the project and the uncertainty of when the President would need to deploy it. The team would remain resident at the facilities, except for the Davidsons, who were allowed to travel back home to Maryland each weekend.

Kerwin Templeton, a noted authority on ultra-high-speed rocketry, led the hypersonics team. He knew that short-range hypersonic weapons were not useable today as fieldable weapons but were promising for the future.

The current efforts in hypersonic weapons were still struggling with the extreme heat these rockets experience due to friction and how to control them properly at blinding speeds. Kerwin, a man whose career was made by fast-moving weapons, was enamored by the maneuverability of the discs at very high speed.

Kerwin invited the Davidsons to sit with his team and discuss their perspectives on potential hypersonic weapons they were considering. Besides the technical challenges of making a hypersonic weapon, he and the team needed more insight into how the Iranian warriors could sense the incoming missiles and subsequently destroy them, a point Dr. Carter had asked him to consider more closely.

After a quick introduction of the Davidsons, Kerwin explained that their insight into their children's capabilities could prove helpful to their mission. Without broaching it with the Davidsons first, he mentioned that the parents could obtain insights from their children should a question arise from the team that they couldn't answer themselves. The Davidsons didn't protest and figured; they could surely do that within reason.

He opened the floor to his team.

A young gentleman from the group stood up first.

"On the battlefield in Iraq, the Iranians allowed the Apache helicopters and numerous ground vehicles within half of a kilometer of themselves. If we could put a hypersonic weapon at that distance traveling Mach 6, north of four thousand miles per hour, the warriors would have less than a second to intercept it with their discs. Would they be able to do that?"

The Davidsons considered his question for a moment. They had some recent discussions with their children on this very topic.

"Based on our experiments, they would not use the discs against such a weapon but would use their telekinetic lobe to instantly nudge the rocket sideways and deflect it out of their path," answered Heidi. "Beatrice recently considered high-speed weapons and what tactics she would use, and she shared this insight with us."

Nodding as if accepting the defeat, the man commented, "At those speeds, a force sideways would probably make the rocket crumple and explode under the combined force. That's going to be a hard challenge to overcome."

The next question came from an older woman whom the Davidsons recognized from the national news a few years back when she won a Nobel Prize for her work in scramjet technology, a core element of hypersonic weapons.

She said, "I'm Dr. Neandra Shah, and I'm extremely pleased to meet you. I have read the details of your research with the children and would like to kindly offer you my Nobel Prize."

The Davidsons squirmed a bit in their seats. Completely caught off guard, they blushed but politely kept quiet.

Dr. Shah continued, "Due to the nature of your work and its classification, I know you will never get the credit you deserve. It was quite challenging for my colleagues and me to have our work published in a declassified manner. I can only imagine what it will take to bring yours into the open literature. Your results didn't yield the intended outcome, but they saved those children's lives and opened a new area of science. I commend you both on such a magnificent discovery and please consider my offer. It's not made in jest.

Now, on to our work here. Can we overwhelm the warriors with a massive barrage of hypersonic weapons hoping they can't deflect all of them if we deliver them one after the other in a short timeframe? I'm unsure how we provide one, let alone several, but one step at a time."

After Dr. Shah finished, the entire group rose to their feet and gave the Davidsons a standing ovation as she finished. None of them wanted Dr. Shah to hand over her Nobel Prize, but they agreed that the Davidsons deserved recognition they would likely never receive for their extraordinary work.

Heidi and Peter were embarrassed by the spectacle but were honored by her kindness. They believed their work was magnificent in its own right, but they cared little for the notoriety. Obscurity was essential for the parenting job they had over the last decade.

"Your gesture and the applause truly humble us," replied as the applause stopped. "Dr. Shah, we appreciate your sentiment more than you can imagine, but your work was astounding in its own right and won on its own merits.

We're proud of our accomplishments, but the restored lives of our children, all twelve of them, are rewarding enough. While our work was not allowed to continue, we do see merit in further exploration at a future time. As you said, there is a whole field of study as we learn to unlock and interact with the brain's potential.

Regarding your question, the children can exert force on a few hundred objects simultaneously. We believe that is why Iran's warriors used that number of discs. We don't see limitations from a sensory ability, but there may be one at a much higher level.

To get to your specific inquiry, I guess that you will find it impossible to launch enough at one time to overwhelm them, but if you are fast enough, with a large enough quantity, it may be impossible for them to counter all of them. It would take a lot, though. Hundreds, probably."

Heidi and Peter could see the looks of defeat on the team members, but the two could see the value they brought to the Phoenix team. These scientists knew little about what they were up against with the Iranian warriors. The Phoenix Project's success required no wrong assumptions, and the Davidsons possessed the broadest knowledge, outside of those in Iran, of what the telekinetic powers could do.

"I guess this would also be true if we sent the rockets from different directions," asked Kerwin, following up on the last question. "I guess they have the same spatial view in all directions."

"It makes no difference where or how they are located within their three-dimensional map as they have equal acuity in all directions," Peter answered. "The capability of this sensor is why the element of surprise is so difficult."

A stout gentleman from the group stood up.

"Would it be possible for a person with their capabilities to work with a hypersonic weapon and aid the weapon to reach its target by counteracting the force applied by one of their warriors?"

The group seemed enamored with this thought and listened attentively to the Davidsons' response.

Peter was unsure where the question might head, so he hesitated. Asking about helping a weapon seemed like a dangerous extrapolation that made him uncomfortable about where the individual was going with it.

"I suppose that is possible," replied Peter. "I'm unsure whether the opposing force would destroy the weapon or counteract the other applied force. I'll ask the children and get their insight. If they don't already know, I'll take them to the backyard, and we can try it with one of their balls for confirmation."

You could see the team perk up with his response. There was a new sense that all ideas wouldn't prove useless.

A little tentative in his follow-up, the gentleman asked, "Would it be possible for our team to work with one or two of your children as we assess the utility of our ideas and experiments?"

Stunned by the request, the Davidsons looked back and forth at each other, uncertain how to respond. Peter was afraid there had been more behind the man's previous question.

General Nunez, who had just walked up behind the team, interjected, "This military program's objective is to defeat the Iranian warriors in military battle. The Phoenix Project is not a place for children, nor do we need children working amongst our weapons. Our efforts here are dangerous and serious. It's time we all begin to respect that."

Not intimidated by the general, Kerwin said, "We're the experts here, and I'll remind you, General Nunez, that I report to Dr. Carter, so please don't provide direction to my team. I'd also remind you that the warriors you seek to defeat are children too."

With a spark of anger, the General said, "Kerwin, need I remind you that I'm the Military Deputy overseeing all tactics? I'm responsible for how the output of this program gets deployed. I'll discuss this with Dr. Carter and ensure he understands my concerns. As for the Iranians being children, we haven't yet actually confirmed the Davidsons' hypothesis that they're children resulting from their former research."

The General turned and headed out of the room. Heidi and Peter Davidson ignored his dismissive attitude. They were convinced they were right, and it was only a matter of time before it was confirmed.

Kerwin waited until the General exited, turned to the Davidsons, and hesitantly said, "Would you consider having the children support our team as we evaluate different ideas? They could also be a huge help on our test range."

"Frankly, I hate to agree with the General," responded Peter. "We're reluctant to put our children in danger. This program will require significant experimentation against realistic scenarios; our children have never trained like the Iranian warriors. We're happy to seek their guidance when answering some of your questions, but we're unwilling to put them in the middle of this project. It's simply out of the question."

Heidi nodded at the group to show her agreement with her husband.

Kerwin chose not to push the matter further.

Meanwhile, working at the other end of the facility, the laser team felt like they had the most viable shot at defeating the Iranian warriors. Light travels so fast that the warriors are no match, regardless of their abilities.

The team was confident that sufficiently powered lasers could blast their way through their discs and destroy the warriors in a fraction of a second. While the warriors could interact with gravitons, their powers weren't strong enough to deflect light in any measurable amount. Einstein's Theory of Relativity could prove that. So, if they could point the laser at the warrior, they had a real opportunity to meet the President's objective.

For years, the U.S. and other nations had high-energy laser cannons in development to shift away from traditional ammunition and take advantage of light's speed. The current drawback of a laser weapon is keeping its size small while providing sufficiently high power to destroy the intended target.

On top of that challenge, you must cool the laser and its power unit. Lastly, you must package that onto a mobile platform with an appropriate fuel source. Those elements were in development at various institutions, but none had successfully pulled the entire package together. The Phoenix Project planned to be the first to accomplish that.

However, if the Phoenix Project could eliminate those challenges, an additional issue would need to be addressed. Smoke and other atmospheric obscurants could render a laser useless since its energy can't propagate to its target. Long seen as a weakness of laser weapons, countries like the U.S., China, and Russia worked on battlefield obscurants to combat emerging lasers. Each knew the time was coming soon when this ultimate next-generation weapon would be a reality, and if they weren't first, it was best to have alternatives to render it useless.

While lasers were undoubtedly the best option, Dr. Carter wanted the team to focus on one issue at a time. He kept telling them to get the laser solution to the level that it could handle the warrior and the discs, and then they'd address the smoke.

Dr. Hans Stolton, a chief technologist at Lawrence Livermore National Laboratory, led the group. He was the leading expert in the U.S. on advanced, high-power lasers and firmly believed that a laser cannon was the weapon of choice for the future, especially against the Iranians.

The laser scientist viewed his team's objective to pull together the work of many institutions and turn it into a final product. Achieve that and achieve success. Dr. Stolton knew of several top-secret developments that would increase the probability of success. He always wanted to pursue them but didn't possess the team or the financial resources to make that happen. The President's Phoenix Project was that opportunity, and the scientist was excited to pursue what he knew was a dream laser that would otherwise take years to create.

Dr. Stolton, addressing his team, stated, "This team has a host of possibilities in our laser-based approach, but we must focus on a laser weapon that will target, kill and then race to the next target. We learned from the Davidsons that the Iranian warriors can quickly counterattack anything they sense. All indications are they will likely perceive the ionization of the air around the laser beam once fired. Luckily for us, even if they sense the beam, the speed of light is our friend, and the laser light arrives instantaneously for all intents and purposes.

Our job is to ensure that when it comes, it eliminates the warrior before the warrior or another warrior can destroy the laser. Therefore, our task is to get through their discs quickly, which we know is no easy feat. I'm making this our top objective.

Otherwise, the laser won't last long, and we haven't accomplished anything.

My calculations suggest we need a MegaWatt of power. That should blast through tungsten carbide discs at reasonable engagement distances and strike the warriors. We must maintain each pulse for a few seconds, and the power system must reload quickly to fire repeated blasts.

Lots of challenges, but there have been numerous advances that we can seize on and bring them together in some form of compact structure. We have lots to do to make this something we can field in a real battle."

Dr. Stolton was well aware that battlefield lasers faced an enormous problem.

"As we all know, we'll have to address the issue of smoke and obscurants," said Dr. Stolton, addressing the issue upfront. "We know Russia and China possess smoke devices with high absorption at the wavelengths we'll most likely use in our lasers. We must assume that Iran will have access to them and try to cloud the battlefield once they see we have lasers. I know there has been some work to counter those effects, but Dr. Carter has asked us to concentrate on getting the laser to a usable level and consider obscurants. Not to be discouraging, but our work is cut out for us. Questions?"

"I'm a former colleague of Kerwin Templeton, who heads the hyper-sonics team," said one of his team members. "We have remained friends over the years, and he told me over coffee this morning that his team requested the participation of the Davidsons' children in their efforts, but the parents rebuffed him. I believe that we could also use their help to assess our efforts. Kerwin and I discussed that we should try and convince the parents that their participation will significantly improve the likelihood of the Phoenix Project's success and that we can ensure their safety when we use them in our experimentation."

Dr. Stolton could see the heads nodding in agreement amongst his team. The laser scientist had been so focused on the technology that he hadn't considered using the children to aid their weapon development. He saw its logic but also understood the parents' reluctance. Dr. Stolton agreed to discuss the topic with Kerwin and bring it to Dr. Carter if the two felt it was crucial enough to the success of the Project.

Over in a conference room, General Nunez had the tactics team debating new approaches with current weaponry and some modifications they thought may help their effectiveness. The general remained convinced that changing tactics with current weapons was a viable solution against the Iranians. He knew that using current weapons with new tactics would lead to the fastest deployment. The Phoenix Project, he believed, may not have time to develop a new weapon if Iran moved quickly.

The general's team members relied heavily on the input of the Davidsons, an issue that was a constant annoyance for him. He continued to scoff at the parents' incessant discarding of the team's idea and insistence on how easily the Iranians would defeat their approaches.

Heidi and Peter Davidson were not being difficult. They were only sharing what they knew and what their children explained. Unlike the other two teams, the tactics group never suggested bringing the Davidson children aboard to help. Not because the members didn't see the value but because General Nunez disliked everything mentioned about the children.

Chapter 10

Backyard War Games

While the Davidson parents secretly worked on the President's new project in Idaho, a government security team watched the children. The kids were well-behaved and old enough to do their schoolwork and behaved appropriately for those in charge while the parents were away working. Trust was never an issue, as the parents had taken numerous trips without any problems.

The U.S. Air Force rotated security details every two years, and the teams quickly became familiar with the parents and children. It's hard not to become close with the family when you have responsibility for their safety around the clock and see them daily.

Before recent events, it was the only outlet to the outside world for the Davidson children other than electronic means, which were highly controlled, so they often engaged the personnel and welcomed them as a part of their family. On the other hand, the security detail recognized the uniqueness of the children and took their security responsibilities very seriously.

The Davidson children were ecstatic that their secret was known to someone outside their parents and security team. They couldn't wait to hear from their two siblings about the meeting with the President. The ten children who stayed home wished they would have had a chance to visit the President and wondered whether that would happen soon.

The other children begged Al and Beatrice for details about what went down in the meeting. The two promised to share every tidbit once they finished their studies that day. They were eager to hear about how the President, his Cabinet, and the group of scientists reacted to seeing giant children with strange powers. All had difficulty focusing on their studies. Still, they slogged through the day's lessons, eager to hear the specifics.

As school finished, Beatrice and Al spent the next few hours talking with the group about their demonstrations and some of their questions.

All the children listened intently. They were excited to know they were no longer hidden from the world. You could see the sparkle in their eyes as Al and Beatrice described the interactions of the meeting.

Thad, one of the middle children in age, which seems strange to differentiate the twelve by age since only thirty-two months separate them all, said to Al, "You actually spun a navy admiral in the air, and mom and dad didn't kill you. That's awesome. I wish I could've done that."

"I didn't think about it. I just looked around to find something heavy that I could lift," said Al, laughing. "I wanted to do it to Beatrice, but I knew she'd get angry, and I didn't want to deal with that. So, I saw the admiral, and I just went with it. Dad said nothing afterward, but mom gave me a good going-over. Beatrice piled on like she always does and kept mom spun up for a bit. Imagine if I'd spun her, I would have never heard the end of it."

Beatrice snatched one of the pillows off the couch with her mind and flung it at Al, but he was too strong for her and sent it directly back at her plucking her in the back.

Al smiled and said, "You deserved that, and don't bring that weak stuff at me."

She could have shot fire from her eyes briefly but let it drop.

Kai, one of the youngest children, was intrigued by the discussion.

"Let's get out in the backyard and start training," she told the group. "These people seem interested in what we can and can't do. Let's train like the Iranians and see if we can help them. What do you think?"

Ever the domineering child, Beatrice felt compelled to comment.

"I'm not sure mom would like us doing that," she warned. "They're interested in our insight, but I don't think she'd approve of us training like the Iranians."

Zeke, the consummate smart aleck of the group, retorted, "There you go again. You're acting like a junior mom. You can't do this, and you can't do that. You're not in charge of us. We play games all the time in the backyard without your approval. Training like them with balls will be fun, and I'm heading out to do it right now."

The group agreed with Zeke and hopped up to head out to the back.

Beatrice snapped at Al when he started to get up, "You're no help! Could've used some support there, brother."

Al smirked and offered a sly grin, saying, "You've got to be kidding me, sis. I can't wait to get out there and do this. Don't be your usual spoilsport, and come play with us."

Beatrice was just as excited as the rest of the kids but wanted to take a stance against it if their mom was unhappy when she found out. In fact, after the meeting with the President, Beatrice was eager to experiment more with their capabilities and see what limits they possessed. Her parents had never before shared why she and Al differed from the others, but now she understood. She turned and headed out back with the others.

There weren't enough balls to allow everyone to have a set of two hundred like the Iranian warriors, so they set out across the large acreage to collect large rocks spread throughout the farm. It took them about an hour to accumulate enough so that all twelve had their set of two hundred. Some bickering about what rocks each got in their collection erupted, but everyone settled down after a few minor tussles.

They started by performing the same opening display they saw on television that the Iranian warriors performed before attacking the U.S. military in Iraq.

Rocks and balls flew in the air as twelve groups of two hundred objects whizzed around their yard. Beatrice, ever in charge, was barking directions to the group. She told them when and what to do, and they all followed. It was going well until Zeke took his two hundred rocks and started targeting the objects of his two neighbors, Del and Irene.

It didn't take long before the others joined in, and a frenzy erupted. The play ended when Beatrice began yelling at them to stop.

"This is serious business," she barked. "We haven't been asked to use our powers for anything other than mom and dad's data experiments and to have fun, but this is important. The President of the United States asked mom and dad to help, so we've got to help. Please settle down, and let's train and see what we can learn about the Iranians."

Marian, the last of the twelve to be revived, uttered, looking down at the ground, "Sorry, Beatrice. We're just having a little fun. We'll behave. Promise."

The group settled down, got back to Beatrice's exercises, and began performing some movements they had witnessed from the television coverage released from the battle. It wasn't long before they were all quite skilled at the exercises and began to discuss new ways to evaluate the limits of their powers.

Ephrem, wanting to add more excitement to the exercises, asked the group, "What if we fought against each other? Instead of replicating what the Iranians did, why don't we consider going against each other? Wouldn't that be a lot of fun?"

All talking stopped, and everyone looked at Beatrice, waiting to see how she would respond. She was trying to process what Ephrem said and was torn about how to react. The eldest sister wanted to issue a motherly warning to the group but saw the merit in his idea.

"I don't know," she said after a bit. "I'm not sure mom and dad would want us to do that."

Al jumped in, ignoring Beatrice's prior admonishment, and said, "Pretty sure they wouldn't want us doing any of this, but we still did it."

Not liking Al's reminder, she snidely said, "Thanks, Al. Let's pair off and give it a try. No one can hit the other, but you win if you can get one object within two feet of your opponent. Got it?"

Gabriel and Lacey blurted out that they got to go first. Beatrice nodded, and the two lined up against each other.

Lacey had all balls, and Gabriel had about half balls and the other half rocks. Each lifted their objects into the air.

Not understanding what may work best, they began moving them around in the air dodging in and out with fake attacks on the other. It looked more like their objects were dancing with each other rather than fighting.

Lacey pulled her balls back suddenly, broke them into twenty sets of ten, and surrounded Gabriel with her objects about ten yards out from him.

Gabriel broke his set into four groups of fifty, creating shields at his front, back, and two flanks.

She raced her objects at him, weaving them in different directions to avoid his shields. Lacey timed her groups to give her multiple shots to penetrate his defenses.

He flexed his four shields to meet her attacks with great success.

However, she was sly and diverted a group for a top attack where he had no shield.

Gabriel was not having any of it and sent some pieces overhead to meet the attack. He smiled at his accomplishment but looked down and realized that Lacey had slowly snuck a single ball in along the ground at a snail's speed and won the battle.

She glowed over her accomplishment, and Gabriel looked down and booted the ball in anger forty yards out into the field.

They quickly realized that fighting against an inanimate object like a jet or helicopter was utterly different from fighting someone with their capabilities. From their parent's briefing with the President, they learned that their force was identical to the Iranians, so they figured what they were doing was relevant to the President's project.

Physics dictates that two equal and opposite forces merely neutralize each other, so fighting against someone with the same strength requires entirely different tactics. Since they all possessed equal power except Al, no one had a distinct advantage.

There was much to learn.

They continued to pair off and spent the next two hours fighting each other.

Al was only allowed to play once, and it was against Eve. He never lifted his rocks during the battle. Al took Eve's objects, forced all two hundred right back toward her, and made a cage with them all around her. His superior force was too much for them in a one-on-one competition.

They also didn't want to fight against Beatrice since she could control far more objects than any of them, so they told her she could play against Al. Beatrice wasn't sure how it would turn out, but she agreed.

Al said, "Hey, big sister. You better watch what's coming your way. I don't think you want any of this."

"Bring it on, little man!" she retorted.

Beatrice quickly used hers, Thad's, Eve's, and Lacey's objects in the battle. She lifted them into the air. She was spinning them around in intricate patterns.

"I know you can't handle this many, so you may want to give up now since you can't pull the same trick you used on Eve," she yelled to Al.

"Ha," he snorted as he lifted his two hundred balls into the air. "You know it's a race, and you won't be able to stop my objects. I see you only picked up four sets of objects so that you can resist my two hundred, but it won't help. Thad just told me that I'd win. Let's see if he's right, and you better not touch me with one of those rocks when I send you to the loser's bracket."

"On your mark," she answered. "Get set! Go!"

He sent his balls flying at her, and she sent her mixture of eight hundred rocks and balls hurtling toward him. The race was on. Both sets closed quickly, but Al's objects made it there first.

He screamed, "Winner! Winner! Chicken Dinner!"

Beatrice let one of her balls pluck him in the chest out of spite, and he shot her an angry look.

"Serves you right," she growled at him.

Unfortunately for Beatrice, as Thad predicted, Al's superior force against her countering force still allowed him to get there twice as fast. She was the victim of simple physics. Her pushing more objects at him paid no dividend.

Beatrice took some solace in knowing that while Al could do this to her, none of the others would be able to do that.

She knew they had learned a lot today and gained a lot of insight into fighting against other objects like the Iranians and fighting against themselves or someone with the same capabilities.

Later that night, Beatrice began to ponder what advantages she and Al possessed against the Iranians. Could they defeat them with Al's strength and her ability to command a more significant number of devices? Would they be difference makers for the U.S. efforts.? Beatrice cleared those thoughts from her mind since she knew her parents would not be happy with their exercises, let alone support any notions of them joining the fight.

Interestingly, Beatrice heard a light knock at her door after they went to bed. She shared a room with Irene and Lacey, but neither moved at the sound.

The children each shared large rooms with two others. The parents had selected the house for its remoteness and because the bedrooms were all enormous, which is critical when you have twelve children about seven feet tall.

They slept on unique beds made by their father in the farm's large woodshop. The construction of the beds relied on huge trusses that looked more like roof supports than children's bed frames. Some unique design features were required for furniture throughout the house to support their size and weight. Luckily for the family, their father was a capable carpenter, and he had a great helper in his handy son Thad who was always trying to build something.

The door slowly opened, and Al walked into the room.

He said quietly, "Beatrice, are you awake?"

She sat up in her bed, and he sat down beside her, causing the bed supports to creak at their combined weight.

Their dad had constructed the beds with these children in mind, knowing there would be times when more than one simultaneously ended up on the bed. Although every time that occurred, his design was put to the test.

Quietly Al asked, "Are the others awake?"

Beatrice shook her head no.

He lowered his voice, "I wanted to talk to you about this afternoon. It got me thinking when I overpowered Eve in today's game. I asked myself: Can I do this to the Iranians? Can I fight these people and win? Then I started thinking about you and me, working as a team, combining our skills. We'd be a powerful force if we trained together and most likely be unmatched. What a huge asset that'd be to fighting Iran. We would be the equivalent of six or eight Iranians."

His sister didn't share that she had similar thoughts earlier in the day and pondered his teaming idea. The concept was intriguing, but she did see one flaw.

She responded, "Al, your idea has some merit. However, Iran appears to have hundreds of these warriors. They could overwhelm us with their numbers if we tried to fight."

He considered what she said and replied with a devious snicker, "Not if they don't know we're coming. They'd have to have ten or more of them in one area to fight us. The Iranians haven't been working that way to this point. They seem very confident in their superiority, so they probably don't feel they need to. Likely we'd surprise them."

Beatrice was doubtful and said, "You think mom and dad would ever let us do that? They don't like us pinging each other with pillows, let alone fighting with the military. I told mom on the phone tonight about our backyard mischief, and she wasn't pleased. It was funny; she asked me several questions about what we had discovered. Mom didn't want to admit it, but she seemed intrigued by what I shared."

Al figured she would tell their mom. They had that special type of relationship where they talked about everything. The kids all knew that if they wanted anything approved by their mom, there was no better representative to get it sold than Beatrice.

Al said, "That's why you must ask mom and dad. You're always the overcautious one and mom's favorite. If you ask, it'll be our best shot."

"I'll think about it," she said, yawning. "Go get some sleep. We'll talk more about it tomorrow."

Al stood up, and the bed creaked loudly as the stress of his additional weight was relieved from the structure. He looked to see if the noise woke the other two; when it didn't, he quickly exited the bedroom.

The following day, the kids returned to the backyard to play with their rocks and balls. They quickly saw the benefits of training as their skills honed and their creativity in their one-on-one contests grew. Excitement swelled as they explored different ways to test their powers.

Al approached his sister again about talking with their mom and dad as they completed their matches. After seeing the children's growing skills, she agreed they could make a difference. Beatrice was also intrigued by Al's idea that they train together to optimize their abilities. She agreed to talk with their parents over the upcoming weekend.

Chapter 11

Eliminate All Loose Ends

The President was busy managing the chaos around the nation as the economy, people, and politics were in complete turmoil. The stock market experienced a sixty-two percent drop after the defeat in Iraq. It was continuing to experience colossal pressure and volatility. Crushing petroleum maneuvers by Iran and Russia severely limited industrial production in the U.S. and created widespread shortages, and the country was on the brink of a depression.

The President maintained some sense of unity and a strong spirit for supporting fellow Americans, but managing such broad-based issues was proving arduous. Unfortunately, numerous attacks against Muslim Americans were a daily occurrence. Terrorist incidents with Muslim claimants in Europe were fueling the backlash. In the U.S., the fringes of the political spectrum were finding their voices receiving more attention as the unrest in the country pressed on.

Tremendous strain rested on the President's shoulders. He and the nation's leaders were being pushed to act, including using military measures to attack Iran. President Schmidt's refusal to strike with weapons of mass destruction also alienated some portions of the population who felt there was plenty of justification to do so.

Consequently, the President recognized that the nation needed the secret Phoenix Project to bear fruit, or the current troubles were just the tip of the iceberg.

Upon the President's return from a short trip where he visited the sailors aboard the Navy's newest aircraft carrier in Norfolk, the Secretary of Defense requested an emergency meeting with him, the Vice President, and the National Intelligence Director.

The three entered the Oval Office, where the President sat behind his desk. He invited them to sit at the front of his desk in the chairs already positioned for them.

The Defense Secretary said, "Mr. President, we discovered the source of the leak of the Cranio-Genesis Project. The NSA and the CIA have tied out the loose ends, and we believe we now possess the full laydown of what transpired.

As you know, our computer networks and platforms had inferior defenses a decade ago, a problem that existed everywhere. It turns out that after the Stuxnet incident, where we infiltrated Iran's nuclear enrichment equipment in two thousand and seven and disabled their centrifuges, they hired Mikhail Federov, a noted Russian freelance cyber hacker, to steal our military secrets. He was contracted through an Iranian sleeper cell in Paris and operated out of that location for a few months.

The NSA has been able to track the extraction of the breach from the Cranio-Genesis Project's systems back to that sleeper cell. Interestingly, Federov and all known sleeper cell members were found dead in Paris shortly after the extraction. Word in France was that Federov uncovered something big for Iran, and they wanted to ensure there were no security leaks. Per French intelligence sources, nothing ever emerged from it, and France was happy to see the elimination of the cell and pursued it no further. The facts we've gathered align completely and explain how Iran ended up with this knowledge."

The Defense Secretary continued, seeing they were waiting to hear it all, "Someone in Iran had the foresight to see the results of Cranio-Genesis and figure out how to put them to military use. They wanted to ensure this never got out, so they executed the entire team. Once they had everyone involved in the extraction out of the way, they put tight security around it and conjured a plan for its use.

The challenge for us, Mr. President, is that Iran has been working on this for a decade. It has given them plenty of time to devise the discs as the best tool to fight, spend years training with them, and create numerous warriors. They likely have a sizeable, well-trained army at this point."

The President did not react in any outward manner. At least they knew it was true, and the Davidsons were correct. He also recognized that the U.S. had twelve children by which to judge Iran's warriors' abilities as they sought to create a new weapon. The advantage of the knowledge would prove instrumental in reducing the odds that the Phoenix Project would move forward with a weapon that wasn't effective.

He responded with an air of satisfaction, "Well, our worst fears have been recognized, but we're not any worse off for knowing this. We may be better off. Per the Davidsons, we now understand their capabilities, so we're no longer guessing over the true capabilities of Iran's warriors.

We know they likely have large numbers, but it's better to know than be surprised. Also, the Phoenix Project is better off designing with the assumption. All in all, a lot of guesswork is over. I'm going to look at this as a win.

A more critical question is whether Russia, France, or anyone else could pick up the extracted data?"

The Defense Secretary had also asked the NSA this, and the National Intelligence Director responded, "Mr. President, the NSA was able to verify there was only a single extraction of data that went to this French group. The NSA can't determine what they did with it from there, but we would expect the executions and post-clean-up were to ensure it never moved beyond that point. The argument that if anyone else possessed the capability, they would have indeed stepped forward to claim they have it seems to hold.

I'm still willing to accept that premise, but I wish we knew for sure. Please get a full briefing on this delivered to the Phoenix Project. I always want them to work off the latest intelligence. Anything else?"

"I would add that the Phoenix Project is working diligently to find a solution," replied the Defense Secretary. "No specific design has been identified, but several promising approaches exist. Dr. Carter believes we ultimately need a laser solution to defeat the warriors. He keeps telling me that the speed of light may be our only friend against their sensory capabilities. Light takes only five microseconds to travel one mile, which Dr. Carter assured me that even they can't react that fast, nor will their telekinetic lobe allow them to push it aside."

"Sounds good," said the President. "Tell Dr. Carter to keep driving, and good work on tracking down the extraction."

They all left the President's office. A clearer picture was emerging. President Schmidt hoped they could use these pieces to reinstill hope for the people.

The Defense Secretary did as the President asked. She told Dr. Carter that they confirmed the data extraction of Cranio-Genesis and let the Davidsons know they were correct. She then told Dr. Carter the bad news: Iran had it for a decade, and they likely had significant numbers of warriors.

Dr. Carter felt like the revelation was a win, just as the President had. His two project heads just asked him to bring the Davidson children on board to help. Now that he knew the Iranians possessed similar capabilities, the kids would be excellent additions to baseline the weapons in testing. The fact that Iran likely had numerous warriors was always his concern, and he was glad he made it an objective for the Phoenix team to assume that in their designs.

Back in Idaho, Dr. Carter had the Phoenix team brainstorming and testing several approaches to attack the robed warriors. As expected, the laser team seemed to progress most, but the others had some excellent ideas under evaluation. Work was advancing, but he knew they needed to step it up, so he invited the Davidsons to his office that afternoon to discuss the possibility of their children joining the effort. He hoped to convince the parents but refused to pressure them, respecting their concerns and wishes.

When the neuroscientists arrived at his office, he said, "Kerwin and Hans approached me to request your children's participation with their development teams. They would like to use them to evaluate and test their designs. I know you already expressed reluctance to Kerwin's team, but I would like to discuss it myself.

Before I present my thoughts, I would like to share that your suspicions on Cranio-Genesis being the source for the Iranian warriors was correct. The NSA confirmed a cyber extraction from the project systems just after the project closure. A Russian cyber specialist working for Iran extracted the data, and shortly afterward, he was executed along with the Iranian cell that hired him.

Your work is now confirmed to be the source of their robed warriors. The bad part is that Iran has possessed this information for a decade. Now we know for certain that your suppositions were correct."

The Davidsons seemed satisfied that their suspicions were confirmed. Given this finding, they hoped General Nunez would listen more to their input.

"Now, on to the point of this meeting, you can see that we're at a considerable disadvantage in evaluating our project ideas because there are no defined parameters against which to design. That usually leads to bad outcomes. Even with your extensive testing of the children, the details you possess are beneficial but incomplete and provide little quantification in determining the effectiveness of anything we ultimately develop.

I'll stop beating around the bush. We'd like to use them in our experiments, and I can guarantee that they will not be harmed. You two and I'll sign off on every test plan. I fear their participation is the only way to ensure we develop an effective weapon. We need to test every prototype against their abilities or risk missing something. There is too much at stake."

Dr. Carter saw that the parents were listening and considering his request.

"I propose the children be assigned directly to the teams," the project head continued. "We'll build them each a set of discs. A team is already doing that, even if you decide they can only use them at home. If you allow them to join, we can continue their studies with a tutor here."

"Thoughts?" he added. "And please be candid."

Peter looked at Heidi as if encouraging her to speak.

She took his cue, looked back at Dr. Carter, and said, "We see the logic of your arguments. We agree that our inputs about what they can and can't do are assumptions.

Peter and I can talk to the children and get their feedback, but it will never be absolute or quantitative. Both of us are reluctant to put them in harm's way, but if you can guarantee their safety and we get to sign off on all testing, we may consider this.

It would be outstanding for the children to be here with us. Besides that, it would also allow us to work here all week as the others. Let Peter and I discuss this tonight, and if we agree, we'll approach the children about it when we get home tonight."

Peter nodded his agreement.

Dr. Carter smiled at them both and marveled at how wonderful these two were, not just as scientists but as parents. Deep down, he felt the kids might make or break their chances of success, so he hoped the parents and twelve children would agree.

Heidi and Peter arrived home late that evening and realized how much they missed their children after doing the back and forth for only a month. The kids, who felt the same way, got off to bed shortly after the parents arrived home, given it was well past midnight due to the time change from Idaho.

Beatrice stayed back when the others went to their bedrooms and asked her parents, "Can I talk to you two for a few minutes?"

"Absolutely, honey," said her father. "What's up?"

Beatrice was prepared before uttering a word for a hard no answer but just went ahead and said, “We’ve been experimenting in the backyard with rocks and balls, training as if we were the Iranian warriors. We’re even battling against ourselves and testing our skills in new ways. None of us are hurting each other, so don’t worry about that. It’s been very eye-opening to us all.”

The parents looked at each other, not sure what to say.

“The other night, Al approached me with an idea that made sense,” she continued. “He suggested that the two of us train to work as a team and fight with the U.S. military. You’ve said our capabilities are beyond the Iranians, and Al’s idea is that he and I work together to maximize each of our unique advantages. We feel like we’d be difference-makers. We’ve already demonstrated this in the backyard when we paired off in mock battles against each other. We both want to help.”

The Davidson parents looked at each other, stunned by what she was proposing. They came home to suggest the kids help evaluate the new weapons on the Phoenix Project, and now their two children were asking to become warriors themselves. Horror was their first thought, and it shone brightly on their faces.

Beatrice saw this and turned red, expecting to be blasted with verbal outrage.

Instead, her father calmly said, “Beatrice, that is so brave of you and Al. You make your mom and me so proud to be your parents. You have grown into fine teenagers, but remember, you are still not adults and cannot fight in the military. We won’t let you, and I expect the President won’t allow you either.

Strangely, you raised this topic because your mom and I planned to sit down with all twelve of you this weekend and see if you would like to join us in our project out west. We can’t tell you the details until you are at the facility, but the project leader has asked that the twelve of you help the team in our work. There would be no further separation from us, and we would be all together again."

Beatrice was excited at the proposal and tried to contain her joy. She never expected her parents to agree, and while she wanted to argue that the Iranian warriors were probably their age, she let it drop.

She responded with a smile, "I think we'll like that. Everyone's going to be so excited."

Her mom chimed in with, "Go get some sleep. We'll talk as a family tomorrow about this. Before you go to sleep, they are making each of you tungsten carbide metal discs for use on the project. Sorry, but no more balls and rocks in the backyard."

Beatrice laughed but couldn't help showing the sparkle in her eyes as she considered having her own set of discs.

She had to add one more comment before shooting off to her room, "Could they make me five sets? It would be good to experiment with my additional spatial capabilities and fully utilize them. You may want to tell them to make Al's a little stronger too. Who knows what he could do to those discs?"

The parents chuckled at her response and headed off to bed, tired from a long week and a long flight home. They couldn't help but look forward to not doing the up-and-back flights every week. It would be a nice relief, and having the kids with them in Idaho would be icing on the cake.

After the parent's door closed, Beatrice headed to Al's room to share the news. She knocked softly, as softly as a seven-foot, six-hundred-pound person could, on Al's door. Al shared a room with Zeke and Gabriel. Al opened the door, and she came into the room. They both looked over at the other two tucked away in their beds.

Al said, "Don't keep me in suspense. What'd they say?"

Beatrice smiled and said, "What do you think they said? Of course, they said no."

She didn't initially let on the second part of her discussion with the parents.

"Shoot. I knew they wouldn't let us," he said grumpily. "Even with you doing the asking, they still said no. I still think we can make a difference. Did you tell them my idea about us working together?"

"Absolutely," she said. "Still didn't change their mind."

"Did they yell at you for suggesting it?" he inquired.

She decided it was time to tell him the second part.

Beatrice tried to speak softly and said, "They didn't yell. Better yet, we get to go out west with them and work on their project. They asked mom and dad to bring us on board to help. We'll get our own discs to use as we test their new weapons."

Both turned to the side as Zeke and Gabriel shot up in their beds, and Zeke blurted out, "That's so cool. We're going to have so much fun. Our discs are the bomb. Maybe I shouldn't use that word, but it's Da Bomb. Wait until they see my special triple spiral tornado loop that I've been working on with my rocks. The discs will be better than the rocks, so my tornado will be even more spectacular. They'll be super impressed, and I bet the President will probably want to meet me when he hears about it. Let's go tell the others."

Beatrice sharply gave one of her motherly looks at them, and their eagerness toned down a bit.

She grumbled, "Mom and dad will handle that tomorrow. You weren't supposed to know about this, so get to sleep and forget I came in here. Got it, both of you!"

Two big sighs came out as they plopped back down in their beds.

Beatrice headed out the door, and Al headed back to his bed.

When he laid back down, he tilted his head and said to the other two, "Can you believe we'll be legit? Our own metallic discs and helping the scientists figure out how to build a weapon to help our country. Tomorrow's going to be a good day for all of us. Beatrice didn't say it, but I bet we should act surprised when they tell us tomorrow."

The other two boys had lifted their heads to look at Al. Gabriel was smiling and nodding in agreement. Zeke was mumbling something about how his triple-loop tornado would make him famous. They settled back down after Al stopped talking and fell quickly to sleep.

Not long after they fell asleep, gunfire erupted outside the Davidson house. The noise came from all four sides of the enormous property, and the family could hear their security forces scrambling outside while the house alarm system blared.

Major Clemens, stationed outside the front door, burst into the house and yelled for the family to wake up and move to the secure room the Defense Department had built in a basement bunker.

As the family hustled downstairs, they heard the major's communication link broadcast, 'Multiple personnel down. There are attacking forces from all sides. They've evaded our security sensors, so this is a skilled unit. Unable to ascertain numbers."

"I sense ten men approaching from all directions," yelled Beatrice to the major as she scrambled down the stairs. "Three to the north, three to the east, two to the south, and two to the west."

"How'd you know that?" he responded.

"We can sense motion," she said back. "You know about our capabilities."

"I think you need to stay out of this and let them do their job," said their mother, coming down behind her on the stairs.

"Mom, we lost three security folks," said Al.

"Major, let us help you deal with these people," said Beatrice.

"I guess I never thought of your capabilities in that context," he responded. "How can you help?"

As the major finished, a call came over his communication link, "Alpha one here. I took out a man on the west side of the property. I got a close-up of him; he looks like Russian special forces. I don't know if he's working for their government or a mercenary."

"Why would Russian special forces attack us?" said the Davidsons' daughter, Eve.

"Quiet," said the major, not in a mean tone but in a manner of concern for dealing with the risky situation. "Beatrice, how can you help?"

More machine gunfire came from the north side of the home. The forces were converging from all directions toward the house.

"We can do several things," said Beatrice. "Depends on what you want. We can lift them and move them. We can attack them in a variety of manners. We can flush them out in the open for you. Tell me what you would like us to do."

"I'm not having you attack them or move them; too much risk," said the major. "We don't know what weapons they have at their disposal. Can you tell us the Russians' exact positions, and then we may have you help us flush them out in the open when my teams are in a position to engage."

"I've got north," Beatrice said. "Al, you take west. Eve, you have east, and ...."

Before she could finish, Zeke talked over her.

"I've got the south," he said. " I've been itching to show some of my tricks."

"Sure," said Beatrice dismissively.

"Shield his team from attacks with your powers," she added, looking to Al, Eve, and Zeke.

"Let's start with the north," said the major.

"I sense three Russians about thirty feet up to the north and east of your two security people," said Beatrice. "They're moving slowly in toward your men."

The major said over his radio, "Team Alpha. Three Russians thirty feet north and east of you and slowly closing on your position."

"Roger that," came the response.

"Do you want me to try and flush them out?" asked Beatrice.

"How?" asked the major back.

"I have an idea. Tell your men to be ready," she countered.

"Alpha, we'll flush the Russians in your direction," the major relayed to the team. "Stay down and be ready to engage."

The Russians were hunkered down in a densely wooded area of the property. The Air Force security team alpha was located outside a small clearing opposite the Russians.

Beatrice began to rustle the branches and leaves in the trees around the Russians. She could sense them respond by turning toward the rustling, and gunfire erupted at the motion. Beatrice increased the force, and the Russians unknowingly sprinted away from the commotion into the clearing, where team alpha engaged them and took them out.

"Alpha team here. Three eliminated. They appear to be Russian special forces. One has some government insignia, so I guess they aren't mercenaries. What created that ruckus and made them sprint into the clearing?"

"One of D12 made it happen," responded the major.

D12 was the nickname the Air Force security team gave the Davidson kids when they started providing security. The Defense Department loved its short acronyms, and the kids quickly received their unique moniker.

"Next up, the east side," said Major Clemens to Eve.

"Got it," Eve said. "Three more Russians. They're separated from each other by about ten yards. They're only fifteen yards out from your men."

"Can you get them to come toward my men, one at a time?"

"I think so," said Eve.

The piles of rocks they had been practicing were sitting on that side of the house. She lifted a hundred stones into the air and sent them toward one of the Russians.

"Going to send the first Russian straight at your men from the north and east. Tell them to be ready."

Major Clemens barked on the radio, "Bravo Team, three Russians are located fifteen yards from you. Due east. Spread about ten yards from each other along a north-south line. We're sending the one from the north straight at you first."

After he finished, Eve brought her rocks in at the Russian. She could have taken him out but was under orders to let the security team handle that. A barrage from behind knocked the Russian to the ground. The man got up, momentarily hesitated as he was hit again by a second barrage, and then ran ahead, only to be taken out by the Air Force security team.

"The Russians down," said Beatrice.

The major nodded and told Eve to send the next one.

"Bravo team, sending the next one your way next," said the major on the commlink.

Eve sent her rocks in behind the second Russian. She hit him hard enough to knock him to the ground. He stumbled forward and tried to run in the opposite direction, but Eve's rocks kept coming at him from that direction. Realizing he couldn't fight off the rocks, he headed just as the other had done, only to be taken out by the Air Force security team.

"He's down as well," said Beatrice.

"Get me the third one," he commanded to Eve.

She nodded that she had it.

"Bravo team, sending the last one your way," said the major on the commlink.

Eve sent her rocks back again for another attack on the man.

He was also knocked to the ground but laid still and didn't get up.

Eve was a little confused and unsure of what to do.

Beatrice said, "Eve, he's still moving. I don't know if this is a tactic to stop you from attacking him or if he's hurt badly enough that he can't move. Start slamming your rocks on the ground around him and see if he reacts."

"Will do," Eve responded.

She brought her rocks up high and began to drive them full force into the ground around the Russian.

It was a ploy. As the rocks began thudding around him, the Russian got up and ran in the opposite direction his comrades had done, sensing his doom if he repeated their failure.

Eve was having none of it. She quickly formed her rocks into a large basket configuration, scooped him into it, and dumped him into the clearing in front of the Bravo Team, where he was quickly neutralized.

"Nice work, sis," said Beatrice.

The commlink chattered, "Bravo team has eliminated the third Russian."

"Roger that," said Major Clemens.

"You're up, Al," said Major Clemens to the Davidsons.

"What do you need me to do?" Al asked.

"How many are there?" said the major.

"Two of them have surrounded your lone security man," responded Al. "They are less than ten yards from him."

Heavy fire erupted from that direction.

"I protected your man from their fire," said Beatrice to the major.

"Al, get those men out of there," said Beatrice. "I'll protect our guy, but they are too close to him."

Al lifted the two Russians into the air.

They began firing as they swiftly floated into the air.

Al sent them back away from the security person.

"What do you want me to do with them?" yelled Al.

"Team Alpha, two Russians coming your way from above," said Major Clemens over the commlink. "Special delivery from D12."

Al knew what he was supposed to do.

"On it," said Al.

The two Russians lifted even higher into the night sky, and Al bashed them together. He then spun them in a high-speed rotation that would disorient the best pilots. He then delivered them to the clearing, where Team Alpha eliminated them.

"There's only one remaining," said Beatrice to Major Clemens.

"Zeke, he's on your south side," she said.

"I need him alive, so bring him out front," said the major.

"Zeke, remember your rain barrel trick," said the dad.

"Where I lifted the water column and dumped it on Lacey?" asked Zeke, unsure what his dad was getting at with his comment.

"Yes, the man won't be able to fire or breathe if you surround him with the water, but it won't kill him," responded the dad. "It's the perfect ploy. This time put the man in the column and bring him out front, wrapped in the water."

"Got it," said Zeke. "I always knew one of my tricks would come in handy."

Zeke lifted the water column out of the rain barrel by the barn. He moved it out toward the lone remaining Russian. The Russian didn't know what hit him as the water suddenly encapsulated him.

"Got him," said Zeke.

"Team Delta, delivery is coming out the front. I want the Russian captured alive. Do not fire at him. I repeat, do not fire at him."

Zeke moved the entrapped Russian outside the front of the house. The Russian was panicked inside the water column and desperate to breathe.

Three Air Force security personnel surrounded the Russian as the water column landed out front.

"I need you to stay here," barked Major Clemens. "Let me handle this. When I give you the verbal signal, Zeke, release the man from the water."

"Roger that," responded Zeke. He loved being able to use military jargon.

The major and his three men surrounded the Russian, who was now about to lose consciousness from lack of oxygen.

"Now," screamed the major, and the water collapsed around the Russian.

He fell to his knees, gasping for air. Two of the Air Force security personnel quickly subdued the Russian.

"What is your mission here?" said Major Clemens to the man in Russian.

Major Clemens spent two years at the Russian Embassy in Moscow working on security detail. He spoke Russian well then but was a bit rusty without practice the last few years.

"What strange magic have you Americans used here?" responded the scared Russian in his native language, obviously terrified about what had happened to him.

"Don't make me use it again," said the major back in Russian.

There was fear in the Russian's eyes. Seeing a Russian special forces operative so shaken reminded the major of Navy Seal training he had once witnessed. Drowning is one of the most horrifying sensations that any person can feel. It obviously shook this Russian.

"Zeke, bring another water column," yelled the major back into the house.

"Did he say he wanted another one?" asked Zeke to his father.

"I think he is using it for his interrogation," said the father. "Just do it but hold off from inserting him into the middle."

"Got it, dad," said Zeke.

Zeke moved a second batch from one of the other rain barrels beside the Russian. Major Clemons saw the fear grow in the Russian as he saw the water column moving in the air toward him.

"You Americans are some type of demons," said the Russian.

"Not demons, but we're impatient," said the major back to him in Russian. "Give me your mission or face the water; this time, there will be no relinquishing its hold."

The Russian looked carefully at the floating water column and then turned back to the major. The soldier bowed his head in defeat.

"We were to kill the two scientists," said the Russian. "They were our target, part of a special mission supporting our Russian partnership with Iran. That is all I know."

"What about the children?" asked the major.

"What children?" replied the Russian, with a confused look. "No mention of children."

"Get him out of here," said the major to his men. "Additional security team is already on their way. Meet them out at the gate for transport."

The team secured the Russian and hauled him off toward the main entrance, where several military vehicles were arriving.

The lead vehicle continued down the driveway to the front of the house, where an Air Force colonel exited the car.

"I'm Colonel Abramson. The Pentagon has dispatched me to assess the situation."

"There were ten Russian special forces who attacked us from all directions," said Major Clemens. "I have two men lost and another severely injured. We have eliminated nine Russians. The tenth one you passed at the gate. I interrogated him in Russian, and he told me the mission was to kill the Davidson parents. He did not appear to know about the children."

"Status of the parents and the children?" questioned the colonel.

"All safe and secure inside. The children helped us take down the Russians."

"They did what?" said the astonished colonel.

"They helped our team flush them out with their capabilities," the major replied. "You wouldn't be here if you didn't understand their powers, so I assume you might know a bit about how that could play out."

"I didn't expect them to be involved in their own security," the colonel answered.

"I didn't either, but they were the difference, including securing the last Russian and making his interrogation successful."

"I would like to speak with the family," said the colonel.

"This way, sir," he responded, escorting him into the house.

The Davidson family stood together as they entered the door, discussing what had occurred.

Major Clemens addressed the parents.

"We've secured the compound, and the Russians have been dealt with," said Major Clemens. "This is Colonel Abramson from the Pentagon."

“Secretary Edgard has sent me,” said the colonel. “Your safety and the safety of your children are paramount to national security.”

“We get that,” said Peter Davidson. “But what’s going on with Russians coming to our home?”

“I used Zeke’s water column to get the Russian to divulge their mission,” said Major Clemens. “It was to eliminate you and your wife in support of Iran. They didn't appear to know anything about the children. I’m convinced that was true.”

Peter and Heidi immediately understood that Iran was trying to conceal the secret of their warriors under the robes long enough to terminate the two scientists who possessed the knowledge to help others match the linkage to Cranio-Genesis. The Russians were just their muscle in the attempt. It was a bold move, indicating their broad-reaching, nefarious plans.

“Your position is compromised, and we need to get you to a safe house immediately,” said the colonel. “It’s possible that other Russian forces may be on their way. We have a military evacuation team on its way.”

“Helicopters,” said Beatrice. “I can sense them.”

“Indeed,” said the colonel. “The transport group will land in the field over there momentarily. Please go inside and quickly gather some clothing and necessary items that you will need. Once we get you to the secure base, I’ll receive further orders.”

“We must be back to Idaho on Monday,” Peter Davidson told the colonel.

“Understood. That will surely be part of the orders. Please get your things so we can get you out immediately.”

The family dispersed and did as they were asked. They boarded a Chinook helicopter and took off for their unknown destination, escorted by four Apache helicopters. They flew for about an hour before landing at a small military compound. As the aircraft landed, they could see a few barracks and heavy armaments around the perimeter as they peered out the windows. Truly a fortress was their thoughts.

Upon landing, they were escorted to one of the barracks, which would serve as their lodgings for their short stay. They were told they would be briefed in the morning and get some sleep. That was quite a challenge for the family that had just dealt with an attack from Russian special forces at their home. The sophisticated attack on them by a foreign nation further added to the gravity of their situation. Nevertheless, they all settled down, including the children, and got some sleep at their parents' urging.

Chapter 12

You Earned Your Spot

The next morning came quickly after the excitement of the previous night. Breakfast of eggs and pancakes awaited them in the small base's mess hall. The parents struggled to get the children moving before they stopped providing breakfast. Colonel Abramson had informed the parents that he needed to speak with them at ten to update them on his orders.

The small base appeared to be in a remote spot and contained only a small contingent of soldiers. The location was heavily fortified with advanced weaponry and an exterior perimeter of thick concrete. It exuded heavy defense, and one would imagine the facility being used to house important people who require protection. The attack by the Russian special forces thrust the Davidsons into that category. Furthermore, the secrecy about the children was essential to the President's plan, so the remote location, which limited their exposure, was of utmost importance.

The parents saw the chairs and tables weren't going to support the children's enormous size, so they gathered the family outside under a large tree after collecting their breakfasts from the limited chow line.

Their dad initiated the conversation by saying, "Iran was trying to terminate your mother and me before we could link the Cranio-Genesis Project to their warriors. They hope to protect their treachery and disrupt anyone else from trying to build an army to match their own."

None of them ever considered their lives critical to national security before the incident. Now that they had been attacked at home, they understood the dangerous circumstances and lengths Iran would go to carry out their devious plans.

"We hoped to discuss something important with you this morning, but it's even more imperative now that we have this conversation," their father continued. "Originally, we were concerned about your well-being and were unwilling to consider what I'm about to discuss, but you twelve proved yourselves to be far more capable than your mom, and I think of you.

Dr. Carter, our project lead, asked if we would allow you twelve to participate in our program to assess and test our new weapons. They will provide you each with a set of tungsten carbide discs to train and work with on the project. The project team needs your abilities to verify what they are attempting to provide, an ability to defeat the Iranian warriors. After last night, we may need to protect the Phoenix team rather than the other way around."

"Peter, knock that off," said Heidi. "You're encouraging bad behavior."

"Alright. Alright. I wouldn't want to do that," said the dad, with a big wink to the children. "Your mom and I would like to hear from all of you whether you are willing to do this."

Shouts emerged as they all embraced the notion of taking their backyard activities to another level. No one seemed intimidated by the offer, and their eager chatter filled the air.

Everything was joyful until Zeke said, "Yeah, I like that. Before the Russians came last night, I thought about my triple-loop tornado with my own discs and how having discs would make it even better. I think people are going to think my tornado is phenomenal. My water column was awesome too, but the tornado takes that to another level."

A hush fell over the group as everyone turned to look at Zeke.

Zeke was lucky Al and Beatrice didn't combine their powers and launch him across the base. However, their looks implied that they might be considering it.

Realizing what he did, he tried to backtrack with, "Did I say before the Russians came? Uh, no, I meant just the last few minutes I've been thinking about it."

He let out a sheepish laugh and then shut up.

Their mom eased the disdain for Zeke by telling them, "It's ok. We talked with Beatrice last night about it before all the turmoil, and at least some of you heard about it after we went to bed. It's not a problem. So, I guess there is no opposition."

The group was unanimously nodding their approval.

She added, "It will be nice for us all to be together and not endure each week's separations. Your father and I were hesitant to have you involved, but how you handled yourself in the heat of the moment last night showed you are more ready than we care to admit. The work on the project could be dangerous, but they guarantee your safety. Still, we expect you not to be on your best behavior and not get into trouble! Also, they are providing tutors, so you continue your studies and work with the team only after your classes."

Groans came from the group as at least some thought they were getting out of schoolwork.

Eve raised her hand very politely and, after a head nod from her mom, asked, "Do you think this is a first step for us to become normal kids where we don't have to live in hiding?"

The mom and dad looked at each other for a second, and their mom gave her a big smile and said, "You know, it may very well be. Probably not too far from now, your secret will be known worldwide. Living out in the open will be much easier for you twelve when that happens. Until that time, we still have to keep you under wraps."

It was indeed a great day for D12. Joining the project was the first step in a new future for them. So much had changed for them in the last forty-five days. Now they were involved in national security and were fresh off fighting a band of Russian special forces.

The parents met with Colonel Abramson after the family discussion. The Secretary of Defense had already decided that the entire family would move to Idaho, regardless of the parent's willingness to have the children join the Phoenix Project. Secretary Edgard knew that the extensive security set up for the project best protected the family and the nation.

They flew to Idaho that evening under cover of darkness. Dr. Carter had the Idaho facilities prepared to house the twelve children. He leveraged a discussion with Peter a few weeks before to have some furniture outfitted for them.

As the children exited the plane and headed below ground to the facility below, they couldn't believe their eyes as they submerged into the immense secret facility.

Dr. Carter met them on their arrival with his three team leads.

Peter Davidson introduced their children to the group.

Dr. Carter explained, "We have discs constructed and available for each of you. There are pyramids containing two hundred and four discs, matching what we witnessed the Iranians using, except for one pyramid for Beatrice, which has one thousand and fifteen. They are stacked inside the underground test range and ready for use.

I have assigned three sets of four of you to each of our three teams. Team one is Del, Lacey, Eve, and Gabriel. You will be working with our hypersonics team led by Kerwin Templeton."

Kerwin raised his hand and smiled at the parents, appreciating their support for the children's participation.

"Next is team two: Marian, Thad, Kai, and Zeke. You will work with Dr. Hans Stolton, who heads our laser weapons team."

Zeke, unable to contain himself, yelled, "The laser team probably requested me. They must've heard what I can do. You know, with me defeating the Russians and all."

His brother Ephrem stopped him in his tracks by saying, "You were nothing but the waterboy in that endeavor."

Zeke looked at Beatrice, who was sneering at him. He saw that the embellishment of his role in the occurrence was not appreciated.

Looking at Zeke over his reading glasses, Dr. Carter smiled and poignantly said to Dr. Stolton, "Looks like you have your hands full with that one."

Marian couldn't believe Dr. Carter had selected Zeke to work with her.

She grumbled, "You better behave, or I'll surely let mom and dad know your every misstep."

Zeke looked down at his feet, afraid to look up at his mom and dad after his outburst and Marian calling him out.

Dr. Stolton raised his hand for the kids to see and peered intently at Zeke, who looked up briefly to catch his stare and quickly looked back down at his feet.

Dr. Carter said, "Our last team is Ephrem, Irene, Beatrice, and Al, who will work with our tactics team. Our head for that group is General Nunez. Al and Beatrice, you can help us push the limits in our experiments with your unique abilities to ensure we have a margin against the Iranians.

With the twelve of you on board, I plan to use your parents more broadly across all three teams.

Lastly, I read the briefing from your security team in Maryland. I see they referred to you twelve as D12. It seems like a great name, so I plan to use it whenever I reference the collective. I'll also pass it along to the rest of the team."

General Nunez didn't bother to raise his hand to identify himself to the four kids, nor did he smile. He figured his military uniform identified him, and he wasn't going to pretend to be happy the children were on board.

D12 spent the first few days settling in with their new tutors and playing with their discs in the expansive indoor test facility. The range stretched thousands of yards in length and width, giving them plenty of space to try their new toys.

The scientists gathered when the children started working out with their discs for the first time, and they couldn't help but be enamored with their incredible abilities. None of these kids had ever used the discs before they arrived, but seeing them now, you would have thought they had been playing with them for years.

It led to a bit of dread as they witnessed firsthand how difficult their challenge was and how terrifying these children could be with the discs.

The hypersonics team was making substantial progress in advancing some initial concepts from other DoD programs. The team was happy to have D12 on board because they needed some realistic evaluation of their progress.

The team had been itching to try one of their newly devised missiles. The prototype relied on integrating several concepts used on other classified projects. It was meant for short-range, on the order of ten kilometers or less. Using refined scramjet technology, it travels Mach six, or about forty-six hundred miles per hour, thus covering one mile in 0.78 seconds.

Kerwin's team believed they could defeat the Iranians with this type of missile because it moves so fast their warriors won't have time to respond, even though Heidi and Peter suggested otherwise.

The team built two prototypes for separate tests on the facility's range. Their goal was a realistic reenactment of a battlefield situation. The test plan was simple: one kid would stand downrange from the missile.

For their safety and the test's realism, a surrogate target for an Iranian warrior was designated by a post off to the child's side, one mile from the launch point. Once the missile fired, the children could use their discs to defend the target and attack the missile.

The scientists planned two tests and used two children for each run to check for their tactics and response time variability. No countdown would be provided to the child, so the reaction to the missile would be of their own making.

After Dr. Carter assured them the child would sit safely behind a safety wall if the missile flew erratically, both parents agreed to the test.

They selected Del to go first with his discs. He whirled his discs in the air, making acrobatic moves and keeping them sailing in the air around him. He patiently waited for the missile to fire while floating his discs back and forth by the target he was protecting. The scientists purposefully waited an extended period to inhibit any anticipation on his part.

Dr. Carter asked all three teams, including the children, to attend and see the experiment. Seeing how these tests fared, he figured there was much to gain from them.

Everything was eerily quiet as Del continued to wait for the missile to launch. Finally, in a loud blast erupting from the missile launcher, it fired and raced downrange in the blink of an eye.

Del sent only one of his discs, zipping for an angular missile intercept as if in complete sync with the launch. A massive explosion rocked the range about two hundred yards before the target.

The test was so fast that some attendees blinked and missed the whole experiment, while the others who watched couldn't make heads or tails about what had occurred because it was too fast. Everyone only knew there was an explosion, and the target was untouched.

Luckily, high-speed cameras were filming the whole event, and everyone would be able to see a slow-motion playback to determine what happened. Dr. Carter played the video on the large screen in the test site viewing room.

All eagerly watched to see what had occurred with Del's disc. They were stunned when the slow-motion video captured Del's one disc breaking its pattern from his aerial group and heading out to meet the missile. It nailed the side of the missile dead-on and crushed it mid-flight, causing it to explode into a fireball.

Unable to contain himself, Zeke yelled loudly, "Booyah to that missile. We're pretty awesome with these discs. Wait until you people see what I'll do to those lasers."

Zeke would have liked to crawl under the table when he looked up and saw General Nunez's disturbed look.

Dr. Stolton, keeping it to himself, thought that Zeke's optimism against his lasers might not be so well-founded, but they would save that for their tests.

Dr. Carter, trying to keep the mood upbeat, interjected a cheerful, "That's why we're here, folks, and that's why these kids are so important. There's no better way to learn than through experimentation. Great work, everyone, especially you, Del."

Del appreciated the congratulations, and everyone smiled except General Nunez.

The team selected Lacey for the second test, and she stepped onto the test range. Lacey hurled her discs in the air and spun them in four groups of circles. She looked down toward the missile, waiting for something to happen.

The scientists were being patient, seeking the element of surprise once again. Things lingered for several minutes, far longer than Del waited, and she thought there might be some trouble because nothing was happening.

Suddenly, the missile fired just as she looked to the viewing room to see if someone wanted to clue her into a problem. It exploded almost as it left the firing stand, an instant after it ignited. Everyone in attendance thought it was a dud missile since it didn't travel any distance.

Lacey trotted back to the viewing room to join them and stood quietly. The team gathered again for the slow-motion replay. The video showed the missile diverting noticeably to the left and disintegrating into a fireball only a few hundred feet from launching.

Puzzled looks and discussions about what may have been wrong with the missile ensued until Lacey perked up and said embarrassingly, "you told me I could attack it once it launched. You didn't say I had to use my discs. So, when it fired, I just shoved it sideways."

Everyone looked flabbergasted, realizing it wasn't a dud after all. Lacey crushed it by applying a force to its side shortly after takeoff.

Concerned she had done something wrong, she apologetically said, "I thought that's what I was supposed to do."

Dr. Carter made her feel better when he said, "You did what you were supposed to do. Excellent work."

Even the other children were impressed by her tactic. Her reaction was more instinctive than planned. The hypersonics team was confident that their missiles were too fast, yet the two children easily defeated them with unique tactics.

It was a harsh reckoning for all the scientists who were beginning to finally understand how the Iranian warriors quickly inflicted so much harm on the U.S. military. Even General Nunez, so doubtful of the children's capabilities, was becoming concerned about his prospects with conventional weapons.

The laser team stayed quiet and tempered their optimism after the display. However, they knew D12 would not be faster than the speed of light as their beams were over one hundred thousand times faster than the two missiles they had just defeated.

Dr. Stolton had the team furiously working as they held a glimmer of hope that they had the best prospects of defeating the Iranians. Two prototype lasers were quickly finished, which they hoped to test soon against the children on the test range. At this point, neither laser was at the power they hoped to achieve ultimately, but the test would nevertheless indicate whether they were on the right path.

The range setup was similar to the missile tests. Dr. Stolton told the children to shield the target, or the laser would hit it before they could react. He wanted the test to be as realistic as possible, not to cause doubt in their results.

Unlike the missile test, where it was acceptable for Del and Lacey to destroy the missile, Dr. Stolton created a surrogate target on the laser end for the experiment. Hit the surrogate, not the laser; he instructed since he wanted elements of the laser for future prototypes and testing.

They selected Zeke and Marian to go against the lasers, and both were free to use their discs as a shield to protect their target and for an attack on the surrogate laser target. The only stipulation was that they had to keep the discs close to themselves, and once the laser fired, they could attack with their discs. This requirement, Dr. Stolton figured, was an element of realism.

Zeke begged to go first, and Marian was happy to let him do it.

He placed forty discs in front of the target and another forty just behind them as a second shielding layer. Just for good measure, he thought. Per the test plan, he kept his other discs in the air and close to himself, flying conical loop configurations.

With little delay, the laser fired, and Zeke was caught off guard. His initial set of shield discs held firm for a few seconds, but suddenly one popped and blew apart. He became concerned and panicked just as another one exploded. Zeke tried to recover and focus, but he completely forgot about attacking the laser surrogate downrange and concentrated only on his shield.

His front discs continued to pop under the laser's blasts, and he continued to recenter those in his first layer to close the hole created by the blasted ones. Unfortunately, after several repetitions of that maneuver, he was getting short of discs in the front shield.

Still oblivious that he hadn't gone after the laser surrogate, he tried to fold his second shield in two to reestablish two-layer protection, each containing half the number.

Zeke couldn't help thinking they were destroying his precious discs and whether he could get more. He was so overwhelmed by the notion that he failed to recognize the laser destroying his shield layers and striking the target.

The laser had won, and Zeke hung his head in defeat and sulked as he slowly walked to the viewing station.

Once Zeke arrived in the viewing room, the Phoenix team watched the replay with renewed optimism. They recognized that Zeke could have ended the whole thing by sending his other discs to hit the surrogate and take out the laser. However, he didn't, and this was a small victory for the laser team as the early prototype showed promise. More power would bring greater success.

No one seemed happier with the result than General Nunez as he stood watching the video with a smug grin.

They decided to move to the second test with Marian, who was busy reminding herself to attack the laser.

She was about to head out to the test range when Beatrice approached her and whispered something in her ear.

Marian smiled at her and sped out to the test range.

Marian sent her discs in the air and set up a dual shield as Zeke had done. Once again, the laser team quickly fired the laser, seeing no benefit in delaying.

As soon as the laser fired up, she spun her front disc shield in a circular pattern at a very high rate while moving it from side to side. Her technique cleverly inhibited the laser from focusing its energy on a single disc. Likewise, the spinning of the discs kept them from overheating as they rotated through the cooling air.

Surprisingly, Marian didn't initially send her discs down range to hit the designated laser target. She made the same mistake Zeke had. Marian kept her shield spinning, waiting to see if the laser would make it through the first shield. Allowing a few more minutes to pass, she sent a single disc down range to ping the surrogate and end the test.

Marian was ecstatic at her accomplishment and ran back to the viewing station to watch the replay. She hugged Beatrice as she walked in the door and high-fived a few of the other kids. Her mom and dad warmly embraced her while she looked around the room to see only Zeke and General Nunez as the unhappy ones.

Dr. Stolton complimented Marian, saying, "Very astute of you to recognize the need to avoid the concentrated laser energy and keep the discs cool. We hadn't considered that technique as a defense. Impressive, to say the least, and you've proved we have more work to do."

Embarrassed by the compliment, Marian said, "It was Beatrice's idea. She figured it out while watching Zeke get beat."

Zeke turned bright red.

"I didn't get beat, Marian," he said. "I wanted to help them test their laser and see how well it worked. I could have hit that target right away."

No one heard Zeke's retort because everyone was looking at Beatrice, who smiled back at them. D12's value to the team grew, and they had only been there a short time. Even General Nunez was beginning to appreciate that there may be some goodness to their participation.

Overall, the laser team was encouraged but knew that much work was still needed.

Meanwhile, the tactics team tested the children in quantifiable experiments to measure their discs' speed, force, and accuracy. Detailed measurements would help the scientists better understand the options and effectiveness of their designs, and the experiments would provide confirmation.

At the current state of things, General Nunez had given up that the kids wouldn't be able to counter current military weapons using different tactics as the four children gave repeated demonstrations of defeating his team's approaches.

D12 kept practicing with their discs and refining their control and skills. Once Dr. Carter replenished his discs, Zeke remained enamored with his triple tornado loop. He formed them by separating his discs into three groups, spinning them in the air like tornados, and moving them around the test range. The others had to admit it looked amazing, and the scientists were stunned at how much force he achieved with his twisters, believing his circling discs could inflict damage without ever needing to bludgeon anything.

The two stars, however, remained Al and Beatrice. One of the measurements involved forcing each child to strike a single disc onto an impact measurement setup. Al broke the measurement device with his discs three times until General Nunez said enough was enough. The thud from his strike was so forceful scientists came out of their offices wondering what was causing the ground to shake.

While Al was wowing them with his power, Beatrice became quite adept at using her extended cache of discs. Watching the other children control their few hundred discs was impressive, but her use of a thousand at one time seemed far more spectacular.

She weaved them about gracefully and effortlessly, doing things with them that the other eleven seemed incapable of mastering. Beatrice showed her prowess with exciting spins and twists as if performing ballet, yet the speed and force she generated were just as fearsome as any other, except Al.

The training and experiments with the children continued for weeks. They were settling into a routine of improving designs and tests, but D12 continued learning and becoming more formidable. Dr. Carter was becoming extremely concerned about the prospects of success as time passed, and he could see his team of scientists was feeling the same way.

Chapter 13

Strange Bedfellows

Six months passed across the globe with little turmoil as Iran concentrated on shoring up its massive new republic and implementing its rigid government control. Integrating one billion two hundred million people into a single entity stretched across three continents proved challenging for the newly formed United Iran.

Their newfound importance emboldened many Muslims on the world stage, but that didn't make them more accommodating subjects for an overarching government. Different cultures, now relying on new government processes, forced bureaucracy on top of bureaucracy to make things work. Once again, history would show the strange fact that conquering is most often easier than governing.

While facing difficulties managing its acquisitions, Iran was flexing its might in trade negotiations, global leadership discussions, and military exercises while aggressively spreading its religious teachings into every pocket of the world.

Their constant religious calls for jihad led many non-Muslim countries to experience uprisings and terrorist events at the hands of Muslim extremists residing in their countries. Most of the incidents resulted in claims of support for Iran, and the governments of those countries brought muted responses in fear of Iran's wrath.

France and Greece suffered the largest number of these incidents. France had a history of Islamic terror incidents in recent years and had many Iranian-based cells within its borders. At the same time, Greece suspected Turkish influence as the source of their problems.

The United Kingdom, Germany, and the United States were experiencing fewer issues than most western countries as nationalist militias within the three countries threatened Muslim populations with brutal consequences. Many pundits argued that the militias forced some terrorist cells in those countries to act more cautiously.

The leaders of those nations were diligently trying to police these rogue militia, but as one popped up and was dealt with by government agents, another group emerged. Whether the nationalists or the sophistication of the government agencies were the cause, terror incidents were lower in those countries. However, their leaders faced juggling a concerned population inflicting human rights violations versus the risk of terrorist incidents destabilizing their country.

President Schmidt had made it clear to Americans that he was intolerant of vigilante behavior, and the federal government had a zero-tolerance policy for human rights violations. Yet, he overtly worked to quell any terrorists from creating unrest in the U.S., as he knew the nation had a fragile frame of mind.

Iran's takeover of the Muslim countries was now several months old. Military action worldwide had been limited, leading to a broader feeling that further war was avoidable. Just as those feelings sank in, the Iranian Supreme Leader and the Russian President disclosed that they had reached a new military pact, shattering the prospects of peace.

The pact details included a statement by Alexei Kovalyov that Russia planned to retake their former Soviet states, at least those that were not Muslim and had already become part of United Iran. As a part of the pact, Iran announced it would support Russia in its efforts and help them regain the elements of its rightful territories extracted from them by the meddling infidels in the West. Tremendous unease flared globally, but nowhere more than in Europe and North America.

The Supreme Leader announced his commitment of ten robed warriors with their discs to support the Russian effort. Russian President Kovalyov had planned this from the beginning as he cozied up to the Iranian leadership only days after their takeover of Iraq. It was apparent that Iran was allowing him to take on Europe while they continued their assimilation of the Islamic World.

Concern grew in the East as countries wondered whether China had similar thoughts. There were no similar announcements, and China was not present when Russia and Iran announced their pact. China quickly announced support for Iran and its endeavors but avoided advocacy for Russia and its intentions. Communications from U.S. allies, Japan and Korea, showed China quietly reassuring them that they had no similar intentions.

Kovalyov began moving Russian troops along his western border with Ukraine, Latvia, Belarus, and Estonia. Using a page from Iran's playbook, Kovalyov announced that Russia wanted a peaceful reunification with its former states. He argued they should willingly comply as he was saving them from crumbling along with the rest of Europe under their failed capitalist ideals. Kovalyov offered the former states three months to confirm their allegiance and rejoin the new Supreme Union of Soviet Socialist Republics. However, his threat about lack of compliance was far less veiled than Iran's, as he emphasized that ten Iranian-robed warriors would ensure efficient unification.

In response to the development, the European leaders of Germany, France, the United Kingdom, Italy, Norway, Finland, and Poland called a summit. Poland, a NATO member, had been selected by the former Soviet states to be their representative. They invited President Schmidt from the U.S., who accepted, to participate in the Summit to be held in Rome the following week.

The President expected the former Soviet states, including several NATO members, Poland being one of them, to call into play Article 5 of the NATO pact, which required members to support the others militarily if attacked. He expected the summit to result in the pact's demise, as he expected most countries would be unwilling to commit military action against the combined power of Iran and Russia.

The President flew to Rome the following week. Italy hosted the summit at the Quirinal Palace, located on the highest of Rome's seven hills. Each leader arrived with heavy security forces as everyone was suspicious of terrorists and Russian subterfuge. The leaders gathered for the private closed-door meeting in the ornate 16th-century building Napoleon selected to be his residence during his occupation of Italy before his defeat in 1814.

As the host, the Italian Prime Minister, Lorenzo Caponero, welcomed the attendees and opened the meeting for discussion.

Polish President Jakob Kaminski took the floor first and said, "I'm here representing all former non-Islamic Soviet republics except Belarus, which plans to accept Kovalyov's declaration.

The Muslim states are already unified under Iran and have cut all ties with our former states. As most of you know, they can only communicate through Iran under their new government directives.

Everything I'm about to tell you is unknown to any country outside our alliance. The rest of the former Soviet states unanimously agree that we'll never willingly join Russia. We'll fight as one in opposition to Russia.

We know the risks of swift defeat are high, but we all believe that fighting is better than rejoining their failed government. We've tasted our freedom again after the fall of the USSR, and most of us have thrived during the last three decades. We refuse to surrender it to Kovalyov without a fight. I'm here to secure the support of each NATO nation in their Article 5 responsibilities to support us in these efforts as many of us are partner nations in this alliance."

The Polish leader stopped there, seeing nothing but reluctance on the face of every single attendee.

President Schmidt had figured this would happen, but he was unsure what justifications would follow. The initial response was a silence that filled the room as each leader looked for the right words to answer the Polish President. They all knew it was coming but violating the tenets of their treaty in person was not easy.

French President, Jean Louis Corbin, responded first with, "President Kaminski, the threat against the former Soviet republics is not a threat against all of Europe or all of NATO. I know Article 5 does not require that, and you are within your rights to demand our participation. However, these are dangerous and unique times, and we believe this is a Russian ploy to take back more than they think they won after World War II. We perceive that Russia hopes that NATO applies Article 5 so they may take the whole of Europe with Iran's aid.

I cannot and will not risk the security of France, particularly given their support from Iran, in such a war. It would be fruitless, and we'll end up handing Kovalyov precisely what he wants: all of Europe. We need more time to find appropriate defenses before we can wage war against these Iranian warriors. President Schmidt can surely enlighten you on the perils of that endeavor. If we act as one today, we invite Russia with Iran's support to attack us all, and thus France will not support Article 5."

German Chancellor, Leon Kruger, spoke next.

"President Kaminski, Germany feels the same as France," he stated. "We play into his hands if we invite Kovalyov to fight all of Europe. We'll not support your fight with our troops, but we'll provide as much economic aid as possible in your efforts."

The Polish President expected no less and disliked the German's tone.

Unable to contain his anger, President Kaminski fired back, "Chancellor Kruger, are you sure that Kovalyov is not coming for you in all this? How long do you think Kovalyov will take to claim that Germany is his since East Germany was a part of the USSR? Do you listen to Kovalyov's rhetoric? He even suggests that all of Germany should be his since you were the aggressors in World War II and killed twenty-seven million of his comrades.

Did you miss his speech where he claims Germany never suffered appropriately for the atrocities against so many people? Please believe they are coming for Germany and likely all of you one day."

The last part, he said while looking every one of the leaders straight in the eye.

President Schmidt was more apologetic in his tone as he addressed the Polish President, "President Kaminski, I think you knew that we would not support Article 5 when you agreed to come to the summit. We all realize that one day, maybe not too long from now, the group of Russia, Iran, and maybe even China will make some military move against each of us."

Heads began shaking in agreement around the table.

The American President continued, "President Corbin is correct. We play right into their hands if we join you in the fight. Kovalyov is hoping that is what we do. We can't give them a reason to accelerate their perverse intentions. Quite the opposite, we must find a way to slow them down. It's crucial to bide time to find an answer to these Iranian warriors that doesn't involve nuclear, biological, or chemical destruction of the entire planet.

It would be best to spend our time here working on accomplishing that. Many people will die in the former Soviet republics if you resist. Still, far more will die if we join you under Article 5, and the former Soviet states will likely suffer more as the entire European front will concentrate in your countries. We beg you to understand and try and help us bide time. I know it's a lot to ask, but we're working hard to find an answer that saves us all."

The Polish President appeared somber and looked at the American President.

"I appreciate your directness and honesty. You are correct; we knew there would be no support, but my fellow leaders still wished me to make the demand.

Interestingly, you ask us to try and stall them in their efforts. We have decided, as a group, to fight the Russians and the Iranian warriors with guerilla tactics for that exact purpose. We know they will destroy us with their military and whip through us in no time with the Iranian warriors if we fight them conventionally as you did in Iraq. We're not entirely defenseless, but let's be truthful and acknowledge we're no match for the Russians, with or without the Iranian warriors aiding them.

Our only hope is to draw out the conflict and prevent them from moving too swiftly into our countries. Kovalyov is not a patient man; it's not beyond him to slaughter millions. We'll make him earn every death. Our plan is to move our women and children into Croatia and Slovenia, as far from the Russian border as we can locate them.

We'll then spread out across the former states, fight in a dispersed manner, and use the element of surprise to limit their use of the Iranian warriors. I believe our approach may provide what you are asking us to do.

I came here today, knowing you would not support the Article 5 obligation, but I did hope to get the support of our NATO allies for supplies and weapons from the rear of the conflict. Spreading out may be an effective military strategy to slow them, but maintaining supplies is more complicated.

We need your support in shoring up that element of the plan. Russia will be sure to try and keep those lines cut off, but I hope you can effectively create and maintain secret conduits into our efforts."

He stopped hoping to see support come from the attendees.

U.K. Prime Minister David Carrington quickly chimed in, "Jakob, the U.K. is prepared to make our resources available to supply your forces secretly. I think your plan is bloody brilliant, and we couldn't ask anything more of any of you. It's not cowardice that makes us refuse to comply with Article 5 but common sense. I hope you and your fellow leaders can see that.

The U.K. and I suspect everyone here is developing new weapons to counter the Iranians, the Russians, and even the Chinese if they are in cahoots too. Cheers to you and your mates for leading the front and giving us hope and time."

Italian Prime Minister Caponero offered, "We'll happily provide supplies for your forces, and Italy can do that through Croatia and Slovenia."

He smiled and continued, "I'll use the best smugglers in the world, our Italian Mafia, the Cosa Nostra, to help us in this. Other countries can funnel their goods into us, acting as your conduit. I'm sure the mafia has many inroads into your lands.

Meanwhile, as Prime Minister Carrington said, we're also looking into fighting the Iranian warriors and their discs, but we need to address another problem: petroleum resources. Without them, too many of our efforts will be compromised. Iran and Russia now control much of global production. We must increase our production in North America and Norway to operate our economies. If we don't solve this quickly, we won't be of much help to ourselves, let alone keeping supply lines going."

Prime Minister Jorgen Nilsen of Norway did not hesitate to respond, "We have been increasing our production over the last four months to support European needs. We'll continue to increase our output, but when Russia and Iran try to embargo us, which they will at some point, we need the U.S. and Canada carrying a large portion of that load."

He looked to the American President, and President Schmidt gave him a quick nod to affirm his agreement.

The Finnish President, Eero Lehtinen, was the last to speak amongst those assembled. Finland borders Russia for a long stretch to its east. Several former Soviet republics are accessible from Finland by sea over a short distance, so they have numerous options to supply the war activities secretly.

President Lehtinen said, "Thank you for inviting my country to participate in these discussions. Our location is unique, given our border with Russia and proximity to the other Soviet states. Given what you are trying to accomplish, we could quickly establish a reliable passageway into Estonia, Latvia, and Lithuania. Additionally, we could be a robust operating base for our nations to watch over Russia.

I assure you, Finland understands that Russia reclaiming their former Soviet republics is only the first bite to fill Kovalyov's agonizingly large appetite. Jakob, we'll proudly support Poland and the other former states, but like the others, if we don't have to fight today, we choose not to. So far, Russia has positioned no new troops on our borders."

British Prime Minister Carrington shifted the discussion from the support of the former states to a lingering question for all.

"Has anyone discovered the technology behind the discs or the strange characters cloaked in those robes?" he asked. "Our media, which can be creative in their ideas, believe that aliens are behind it. My best people can't make anything of it. And how does Iran come to possess this?"

He scanned the room, looking for anyone with better insight or an inkling they knew more. He detected nothing suspicious on any of the faces.

The French President was the first to respond. He said, "We believe the robed warriors are tied to the discs. They somehow control where they go, but we haven't determined their control method or how the discs are propelled. It has baffled our scientists, who find no indication of any exhaust. We would agree to share our insights with other countries willing to share theirs. We'd like to know how many they possess. It's frightful that they seem to pop up wherever they need them."

President Schmidt kept quiet about his knowledge of the origins of the robed warriors and the Cranio-Genesis Project. He also didn't let on that he started the Phoenix Project. The President trusted these allies, but the stakes were too high to have any information leaks, so he kept it all under wraps.

The group was looking for him to comment, so he cautiously stated, "We don't have any better answers on the discs or their numbers. They have been able to deploy new sets across their growing empire to support their forces, and now they are supplying a set to Russia. We expect they hold several in reserve to protect against an unexpected attack. Also, they are assuredly making more discs each day."

He chose to phrase his last statements coyly, emphasizing the discs versus the warriors to maintain the guise that the discs were the weapon of concern.

President Schmidt hated not sharing the whole truth. It went against his core, but he knew he had to stop and not reveal too much. The President learned that you never know whose hands secrets may appear when you allow too many spokes on the information wheel.

Once he became President, it took him only one CIA briefing to appreciate the perils in the world of global espionage. He chose not to answer the French prime minister's request to share information, forcing him to end up down a path he didn't want to travel.

The French President eyed the U.S. President suspiciously as he finished. President Schmidt chose not to look at him, hoping it wasn't apparent he was holding back.

The Norwegian prime minister added fuel to the fire by asking, "Should we consider regular summits to share intelligence and progress with our weapons efforts?"

The Polish President thankfully diverted the discussion by saying, "Once the fighting begins, it will be tough for us to participate in formal meetings. You'll want to hide any support for us, but we hope to maintain secret contact. Our Bulgarian compatriots developed special encryption to obscure our messaging. Here is the key for each of you. Please contain it under the highest security control. Our Bulgarian friends claim your best organizations can't decrypt it without the key.

I want to share a few more details of our plan. We'll feign our consideration of Russia's proposal to join until the last day. During the next eleven weeks leading up to their deadline, all the former states will announce an extensive holiday during what we'll start calling 'The Consideration Period.'

We would appreciate your countries offering abundant opportunities for our people to visit. This will give us cover to move our women and children to safe areas away from the front, maybe even having them stay in your own countries, should you be willing. Additionally, we'll use this holiday period to spread our military equipment and supplies around our countries.

By the time the Russians invade, we hope to have our cities nearly vacated and our guerilla teams organized throughout our lands. It's not a foolproof plan and has a tremendous risk that the Russians will catch on, but it's the best plan we can develop on short notice.

Many of our citizens remember how to keep secrets from Russia. While thirty years of freedom has eroded some of that, many of us still have not forgotten.

Our young people have never lived under their rule, so they know nothing of this, but we'll train them, and interestingly enough, they are the most committed to their freedom since it's all they have experienced. They have no tolerance for Russia's demand and scoff at it without consideration. Please don't fail us with your supply lines; we shall try to hold off the Russians for as long as possible."

Prime Minister Caponero spoke for the whole group, "We shall not fail you because it means we have failed ourselves. I want to discuss one more topic before we adjourn. Why is China not being more aggressive like Russia? All indications show they are allied with Iran as well. It's puzzling why China is holding back and not playing a similar game plan."

Chancellor Kruger concurred with his sentiments by adding, "Germany feels the same way. China is working diligently with Iran on economic opportunities and maintaining strong diplomatic ties, but they don't appear to have the same level of relationship as Kovalyov. We're also at a loss."

Their thoughts were similar to his team's. President Schmidt figured he would share the same plausible argument his team gave him.

The American President said, "We feel that China's past issues with Muslims in their country may limit their alliance's closeness. Russia has a horrible track record with Muslims, but they never rounded up huge Muslim populations and tried reprogramming them. For that reason alone, Iran may be far more cautious with the Chinese than with the Russians."

Everyone seemed to agree with the U.S. President's argument and dropped the topic. They continued to talk in small groups and one-on-one for another two hours. At that point, the meeting reached the pre-agreed length, and the Italian prime minister, as host, called the meeting to an end.

Chapter 14

Moving at Light Speed

Upon returning from Rome, the President called a meeting with his Vice President, Secretary of Defense, and Director of National Intelligence. The team had several agenda items to discuss. He wanted to share the details of his discussions in Rome, receive the latest intelligence from around the globe, check on the Davidsons, and learn about the progress of the Phoenix Project.

The President was in the Oval Office when the three were escorted into the room.

He opened the meeting, "Cassandra, how are the Davidsons?"

"Mr. President, they were quickly moved to Idaho and have settled in nicely as an important part of the team," she answered.

"Good," he responded. "We should have considered that Iran may go after the parents and the children."

"Yes, Mr. President," she answered with a frown. "We missed that. We learned that the children appear to be unknown to the Iranians and the Russians."

"Good," the President responded. "So, the Iranians believed what we learned from the parents about the closeout documentation listing all subjects as terminated. This secret remains a key advantage in our Phoenix Project work."

The Iranians believed they possessed the only warriors with telekinetic capabilities. Targeting the Davidsons was just another attempt to try and remove personnel who may realize what Iran had stolen and accomplished. It fit perfectly with cloaking their warriors and the rest of their intricate plans.

"Speaking of the Phoenix Project and my number one priority," said the President. "Are we making progress on Phoenix? Fate has been kind to us thus far and given us some time, but Russia and Iran's move last week just signaled an alarm for all of us. The Phoenix Project must be successful soon, or we may find ourselves in their collective crosshairs without an answer. I hope the Davidson children are helping us find a solution faster."

The Defense Secretary answered, "D12 are making a huge difference, but unfortunately, they keep proving that we don't possess an answer. They continue to trounce our hypersonic missiles, and our best hope, laser cannons, continue to show promise but don't have enough power to blast through their discs before they can destroy the laser.

Dr. Carter pushes the team as hard and fast as he's comfortable, but they struggle to find a solution. I sense the team is getting frustrated with their lack of progress. A visit by you may help to improve their spirits. The one Davidson child, Zeke, keeps asking Dr. Carter when you will come to see him. I'm unsure what that is all about, but a visit could help raise the team's spirits."

Sensing her firm belief that it would make an impact, he said, "I do love the name D12. Somehow the moniker seems so fitting. It might do us all some good to see their progress. Set up a visit in the next few weeks. Tell this Zeke that the President is interested in seeing his work and let Dr. Carter know there is to be no fanfare. Just show us what they are up to and where things stand. I promise to give the team a pep talk about the importance of their work to this country."

The part about Zeke, he said with a laugh. He had never met the ten other children, but he figured that if they were anything like the other two, they were indeed something special. Little did he know, this Zeke was a one-of-a-kind child.

The President said, "Margaret, I hear Iran is positioning to move against Afghanistan. We know they are still struggling to get their government functioning in many of these places, but they must feel comfortable enough with their progress to attack Afghanistan. When do we expect that to happen?"

The Director of National Intelligence responded confidently, "All indications they will invade Afghanistan within the next few weeks. Tehran's leadership is quite unhappy with Afghanistan's refusal to relent after all other Islamic-majority nations have joined the union. They've positioned troops along their border with Afghanistan, but there are fewer troops than in the other invasions of Turkey, Saudi, and Iraq. It appears they are going into the country with a different strategy.

Iran now has the advantage of controlling Pakistan, which the Russians and we did not. Afghans can't hide their leadership under Pakistan's protection as they did against us, and Iran has a large contingent of warriors sitting along their border watching for any movements.

Intelligence sources inform us that the Russians plan to aid Iran by supplying details of Afghan cave structures acquired during their war there and by airlifting Iranian resources, most likely their warriors with discs, into those mountains. Not sure how they use the robed warriors and discs in those caves, but sources tell us they are a central part of the plan."

The Defense Secretary added to the national security Director's last piece, "Russians may help get them to the fight, but as the Russians and we both learned, it becomes one big cave hunt to find where they are hiding. The Iranians haven't misstepped to this point, so I bet they have thought this out carefully."

The President considering her comment, said, "Ask the kids on the Phoenix Project to think about hunting people out in caves. Could they do it, and how easy would it be? Their response may give us insight into how long this may take."

The Defense Secretary answered, "Yes, Mr. President. Their insight will be helpful."

The President said, "I talked to Israeli Prime Minister Yaakv the other day. His numerous intelligence sources confirm Iran's frustration at the persistent governing difficulties they are experiencing across their new nation.

The Prime Minister also knew they would turn next to Afghanistan. His take was more to show they would not tolerate defiance than a desire to have Afghanistan in their united republic. Israel believes that Tehran thinks little of Afghanistan and the Taliban and wants only to show the final piece of its Islamic domination to its people and the world.

Israel, he shared, believes that once they finish with Afghanistan, Iran begins the second phase of their conquest, and they become the next target. Israel is the final holy jewel as Iran finally reunites Jerusalem under Islamic control.

He assures me that they have been quickly developing new capabilities to fight Iran, no doubt their Phoenix-like project. Unfortunately, they don't have the benefit of D12. I'm still not prepared to share that information with him."

The National Intelligence Director turned to the Vice President and said, "You heard an interesting rumor from one of your friends. He told you that Israel has some new high-powered lasers in development itself. It sounds like they see things similar to the Phoenix Project."

The Vice President said apologetically, "I received this from a friend with several high-level Israeli connections while you were in Rome. I haven't had a chance to share it with you."

"Not a problem," said the President. "A lot is going on. That's why these meetings are so important."

The Vice President continued, "They supposedly matured one of their development lasers and feel confident about its prospects of defeating the Iranians. They figured Iran would invade them to gain control of Israel, ultimately seeking to preserve Jerusalem without damage.

My source tells me they are busily manufacturing multiple copies of these weapons and positioning them throughout Israel, with heavy concentrations in Tel Aviv, Haifa, and Jerusalem.

He also informed me that Israel doesn't see the Russians involved in the Israeli invasion since they firmly believe that Iran wants to keep all the glory of the conquest for themselves.

They hear that the Supreme Leader wants to showcase the assimilation of Israel as the next step in their religious saga. Frightening perspective, but it seems to follow the narrative."

President Schmidt pondered what the Vice President said. He could see Iran wishing to deal with Israel independently, just as Israel wanted to deal with Iran without U.S. intervention.

The President responded, "No doubt Russia is focused on Europe. Europe is convinced Kovalyov wants the whole continent, which may have already been negotiated with Iran. We also know that Iran is coming for Israel, and taking it as another banner along their jihad makes complete sense. I have suspected they have grand plans since they destroyed our military in Iraq.

Given this, our best opportunity may be to attack Iran when they attack Israel. Iran will surely go into Israel with a large contingent of forces. It will consume Iran's leaders, who will be frothing over the idea of ridding the region of the Jews and taking Jerusalem. There is too much hatred built up between them over the years.

This diversion presents our best opportunity to strike Iran when it least expects it and is least prepared. I hope Israel has a few tricks up its sleeves to deal with Iran, and the fight is not as short as ours in Iraq.

Prime Minister Yaakv didn't ask for or desire our help, but when our forces attack Iran and, at a minimum, divert some of their attention, he will be greatly appreciative. The attack on Israel is coming soon. Iran won't let it go on too long. They have been waiting for this for years. We need results from the Phoenix Project soon, so our visit to Idaho is timely."

"Mr. President, we must remember this is a motivational visit," said the smiling Defense Secretary. "Can't add to their pressure by telling them we need it now. Any chance we want to reconsider chemical, biological, or nuclear weapons down the road?"

The President couldn't help being a little glib and responded, "Cassandra, are you telling the President what to do? I can accomplish being motivational and pressing while there, but Dr. Carter needs to see the risks we face. As for alternative weapons, nothing has changed for me. I can't fathom going down a path that leaves us ruining the Earth and destroying millions when I believe there must be alternatives. There is a reason the term 'assured mutual destruction' was coined. It ends badly for everyone. No one wins that war. I'll stop there and refuse to say never, but today I won't entertain it regardless of what some of these beltway groups around Washington think."

She responded, "I wasn't trying to be disrespectful, Mr. President."

"Cassandra, I know that. You're just keeping me on my toes. Before we end here, I want to give you three a run down from Rome.

It was an interesting meeting, and there are some key details that I want you to understand. As you know, Poland represented the former Soviet republics, except for Belarus, which had already accepted Kovalyov's demand.

Polish Prime Minister Kaminski recognized he wouldn't get Article 5 support, but he asked for it nevertheless. He received a no from everyone, as he expected. His real purpose in attending the meeting was to obtain our commitments to supply his forces.

They will pretend to be leaning toward rejoining during the next eleven weeks until the last day of Kovalyov's decree. During the eleven-week moratorium, they plan to holiday around Europe. They will use the guise to move their women and children away from the front and disperse their military resources away from the cities.

Once they reject Kovalyov's decree, they plan to fight with dispersed guerilla forces to avoid confrontation with the Russian might and the Iranian warriors. We asked them to stall as long as possible to give us time to find answers to Iran. They agreed, and then we decided to keep supplying them in their fight from behind.

Not sure how much success they will have, but I give them credit for doing what they can under the circumstances. One thing was clear; they had no intentions of submitting to the Russians without a fight. We must ensure their bravery is not in vain and do everything we can to support their efforts clandestinely."

The Defense Secretary was astonished.

"That is amazingly courageous for these countries to take on Russia with the Iranian soldiers," she responded. "We shall do everything we can to keep them fed with supplies."

"Please see that we do," said the President. "Finland and Italy will lead in creating supply lines for them. Kaminski also shared an encryption key we'll use for secure communications between our alliance and their resistance leadership. Bulgarian cyber experts developed it. Kaminski told me that the Russians, Chinese, or our NSA couldn't decrypt it without this key. We need to keep it under the control of the Phoenix Project so that we have one single point of failure. It's much easier to manage that way."

The President shared several other details from the meeting, including some of his side discussions and a desire to have regular meetings. He hoped that time would continue to be a friend to the U.S., but he wasn't counting on it.

A week and a half later, the President headed to Idaho to meet with the Phoenix Project team.

When his plane arrived, he exited the plane, and a military aide escorted him into the main underground test range, where the group had decided to show him some of the latest experiments firsthand. Inside the cavernous room, he saw the scientists hovering together and a lineup of twelve giant teens standing beside them.

He recognized Al and Beatrice, whom he had met before, but seeing the string of these children standing shoulder to shoulder brought to mind some adventure movie or video game created with computer-generated images. What physical specimens was his first thought.

A bit of awe passed over him for a second, as if for the first time, it hit him at what a remarkable discovery the Davidsons truly made. They rescued these twelve children from death and created a new human capability. As President, he would push for a national celebration if it weren't for the Iranians and their allies. He snapped out of his musings and reminded himself that he was there with intent.

A sadness fell over him as he focused back on the topic at hand. He realized how much destruction happens when governments twist science and engineering for wicked purposes. He had hoped to give Americans so much more when he was elected President.

On that notion, the President became invigorated that there was great purpose in what they were trying to accomplish with the Phoenix Project. He sought no advantage for the project, only an ability to restore the balance of power.

The President headed over to Dr. Carter and vigorously shook his hand while placing his other on Dr. Carter's shoulder. He appreciated a man of such talents taking on a critical role for his nation. During his life, Paul Schmidt grew to know there were many layers to heroes, those who fight and those who support them in various capacities. All are equally important to the cause.

The President then shook the hand of every scientist finishing with Peter and Heidi Davidson. A short discussion about the Russian attack ensued between himself and the neuroscientists, and he listened intently to their description of the events and how the children played a role. President Schmidt shared that the Defense Secretary shared how invaluable they were in defeating the Russian operatives and how important they had become to the Phoenix Project.

He saved the twelve children for last. The President had failed to rise and shake the hands of Al and Beatrice when they briefed him in Washington. He felt ashamed but was genuinely awed by the spectacle at the time. As a leader, he knew that was no excuse for him, but even the President of the United States could be caught dumbfounded.

President Schmidt started with Al, whose giant hand engulfed the President's strong hand. The President had a firm grip forged by years of hard work on an Indiana farm. Still, he could feel the power in Al's handshake, appreciating better Heidi Davidson's description of their dense muscle and tissue structure.

He said warmly to Al, "Good to see you again. I still haven't forgotten your spinning of the good admiral. I don't think he has either."

The President gave him a sly grin as he said it.

Al gave him a big grin and thought again that maybe he should've chosen Beatrice.

The President moved over to Beatrice and said, "Nice to see you again. I understand you beat Dr. Stolton's laser. Very creative thinking. Keep up the good work."

Being careful how she corrected the President, Beatrice said, "Marian did that. I just gave her a bit of advice."

The President appreciated her humility and willingness to give credit to her sister, but he knew she was the one who figured it out.

He decided not to make more of it and said, "Ah yes, you're right. Give credit where credit's due."

President Schmidt said the last part with a slight nod that he still appreciated her cunning.

Next in line was Gabriel, who already had his hand out. The President said, "very nice to meet you. Your name is?"

Gabriel stuttered and apologetically said, "Oh, sorry, Mr. President. I forgot to say that. I'm Gabriel, the third of D12. We're supposed to introduce ourselves and shake your hand while making sure not to crush it. I was so focused on not crushing your hand that I forgot the rest. Hope I got that right."

"You did fine, son," said the President as he smiled and moved to the next one in line.

He reached out and shook the next large hand. "Very nice to meet you, Mr. President. I'm Del, the fourth child of the Davidsons. I went a little easy on the shake myself. I tend to be a little rough on things, mom says."

The President was grinning and was enjoying the introductions. The unique personalities were like any other group of children, he believed.

He moved to the next child and shook hands with yet another boy who said, "Mr. President, I'm Ephrem, the fifth child, and I'm very happy to meet you. Thanks for letting us be on your team."

The President spontaneously turned to the parents and said, "You sure started with a bunch of boys."

Turning back to Ephrem, he said, "Your parents are the real ones to thank. It was all their decision. I was just happy that they agreed."

He started to turn to the next kid when Zeke blurted out, "Hi, Mr. President. I wanted to meet you so bad. I have something I've been working on to show you. I call it the triple-twisting tornado loop. It puts those Iranians to shame. Doesn't it?"

He looked from side to side as he said the last part seeking support from his siblings, but none came.

Walking down the line beside the President, Dr. Carter piped up, "Zeke is our character in the group, as you see. He keeps us in good humor. His triple-twisting tornado is something to see. I'll have him show it to you when we finish the tests."

The President shook Zeke's hand and said, "I've heard all about you. I'm glad to meet you finally. I can't wait to see your tornado trick. I bet you keep this team on their toes."

The President heard some murmurs from the scientists confirming his statement in the background.

To the right, he moved again and shook a girl's hand for only the second time.

"Mr. President, I'm very pleased to make your acquaintance. I'm Eve, the seventh child and second daughter of the Davidsons," she said. "I offer my deepest apologies for my brother Zeke's behavior."

Now the President lost a bit of composure and busted out laughing.

He said, "I have children too. They're adults now, but they were quite the handful at your age. Zeke would fit in with my boys just fine. More importantly, I'm pleased to meet your acquaintance as well. However, no need for such formality."

Eve remained stoic even after his comment, but he expected this was more trying to show good behavior than her core personality.

The next child introduced himself as the President stepped to the next in line, "Mr. President, I'm Thad. Child Eight. Pleased to meet you."

Straight and to the point as ever for the future engineer, thought his dad, listening off to the side.

The President said, not letting it pass without notice, "Nice to meet you. Short and sweet, just like my youngest son would do."

Next was Irene, who introduced herself with a subdued, "Hi. I'm Irene, the ninth of the children. It's a pleasure to meet you, Mr. President. Thank you for visiting us."

He expected this was probably more her personality than a front. There was no sense in pretending with this one.

"The pleasure is all mine," he said.

He began to move to the next in line as he realized there was no way he would remember all these names with the faces. He was great on the campaign trail but was hitting his limit.

Number ten was next.

She introduced herself by saying, "My name is Kai. In some languages, my name means 'keeper of the keys,' but I prefer the Hawaiian version, which means sea. Nice to meet you, Mr. President."

The President smiled at her and responded, "I prefer the Hawaiian, too, since it comes from one of our most beautiful states. It's a pleasure to meet you. I might call you Number Ten, though."

She smiled at his comment and gave him an enormous thumbs up.

Knowing he was nearing the end, he stepped to his right and said to the girl next in line, "And you are?"

She promptly said, "Number eleven, Mr. President. Lacey is my name, and I can't tell you what it means other than something to do with lace. I'm glad to, um, um. I mean, I'm pleased to meet you."

He also felt the children were getting tired of the introductions, but he liked that this crew had spunk. He was ready to conclude the introductions and quickly moved to the last child.

As he stepped, he said, "And you must be Marian. Number twelve. The last of them all and the one who beat the laser."

She looked over and winked at Beatrice and beamed all over again. Zeke grumbled something under his breath and figured it was best not to say something for once.

Now that the President had met the entire team, Dr. Carter was ready to do three demonstrations arranged for the President, one with the latest laser and the other two with new missiles. He told the President and Defense Secretary ahead of time that the children could defeat both, but it would give them an idea of the team's progress. Dr. Carter didn't want the failure of the two tests to come across negatively for their team and further spiral morale into the dirt.

The first test was with the laser. The team had increased the power to five times that of the laser used in the earlier tests with Zeke and Marian. The laser was installed on a high-speed, gyro-controlled targeting system to direct it at the target. The system provided pinpoint accuracy for the weapon, allowing it to slew from target to target quickly.

Dr. Stolton hoped the newest version would prove far more formidable than the predecessor.

Kai was selected to go against the weapon and put her discs in two shield layers, as Zeke and Marian had done in the previous tests. She sent her shield discs spinning, hoping Marian's technique would have the same success. Kai knew the scientists were making progress, so she was ready to race her other discs down for the attack.

The laser fired and immediately popped her front disc, and she just narrowly closed the hole when that disc blew apart.

The new laser was quite impressive and caught her off guard. She forgot to send her attack discs down range to nail the laser target. Lacey quickly adjusted by positioning a third row of discs behind the second to fortify her shield, but the laser popped through a first and second layer. She had to close both gaps quickly or suffer defeat.

The laser began moving its target location randomly, confusing her as multiple discs across her first shield began to blow apart. Finally, after closing another hole in her first layer, she recognized she never went after the target and hastily sent one of her discs down range to strike the laser target and end the demonstration.

It was still a defeat of the laser, but it was apparent that the latest laser power was getting closer to making quick pickings of the discs. Progress was very obvious to the Phoenix team. Dr. Carter wanted the make it evident to the President. He planned to show Marian's test from weeks before; then, he would replay Kai's test.

When Kai returned to the viewing room, she said, "Wow. That was a lot harder than I expected. The laser was fast, and I was worried I could keep up. Luckily I got my thinking straight and sent my discs to the surrogate target."

Dr. Carter felt some satisfaction in her comments. Her confirmation of the progress was important for all of them to hear.

The President watched the two videos along with the Defense Secretary. Both could see the progress from the earlier test, but it was hard to see that this was a weapon ready to defeat a sizeable army of Iranian warriors. With the stress of the current global situation, it was hard not to show disappointment, but he reminded himself this was a motivational meeting with the team, and he needed to commend their progress.

The President offered a conciliatory, "Clearly progress from the first. The laser was quick and kept her guessing, so the element of surprise was a critical aspect of the laser targeting. I can see the advantage of the laser if it could pop through their discs faster. Can you get more power out of the laser to make that happen?"

Appreciative of the tone of the question, Dr. Carter responded, "Mr. President, we're working to triple the laser power. If we can, the system will pop through the discs easily, and the new targeting system will be capable of slewing quickly from target to target with great accuracy. Our bigger challenge is keeping it all compact enough to integrate it into a fieldable system that can be more transportable overseas."

The President nodded that he understood, saying, "Makes sense. Do we have the right combination of power generation and laser?"

"Yes, Mr. President. This test gave us some confidence we were heading in the right direction. We have the laser I mentioned completed, and it's being integrated with a new high-performance targeting system planned for a shipboard interceptor.

We'll combine those two pieces with a new power system from another program developing an electromagnetic pulse weapon. If we can integrate them and the combined system prove capable, we'll need some resources to build production versions. Help from you and the Defense Secretary to make that happen would be greatly appreciated."

The President looked at the Defense Secretary for a response.

She said, "We'll get you everything you need. If it works, I promise you that we'll make it happen. How soon until we test this new configuration?"

Feeling the pressure, Dr. Carter said, "We'll make it happen within two weeks."

His team was uneasy about that aggressive date he threw out since they thought it was more like a month.

The President said emphatically, "Anything you need, I mean anything, we'll get it for you. You have the capabilities of this nation behind you."

"Thank you, Mr. President. I'll let the Defense Secretary know if we need anything."

Dr. Carter knew that building multiple production copies would take some resources. He knew he had laid down an aggressive timeline but sensed the President's urgency.

Shifting to the planned tests, Dr. Carter said, "Shall we do the test with the hypersonic missiles? We don't expect these to be a primary weapon, but we believe in conjunction with the laser, they could be quite effective for other aspects that we may encounter in a battle with the Iranians. The military is going to love these."

"Absolutely," said the President.

Dr. Carter had Eve head to the test range next for the first test. He warned the President and Defense Secretary not to blink as the missile and trial were fast. He told Eve to go after the missile in any manner she desired.

Unsure how to best defend the target, she set up two shield rows of discs like the others had done with the laser. She knew the missile was considerably different than the laser, but she figured it was better to be safe than sorry.

She kept the other discs flying in the air and ready for an attack on the laser. However, like Lacey, she planned to push the missile as soon as it fired. Waiting in anticipation of the firing, she concentrated on sensing the missile. Eve figured the scientists had something up their sleeve.

The missile ignited, and she pushed it to the side with her force. Unexpectedly, it resisted her push and seemed to adjust its thrust to counter her, showing no signs of crumbling. She didn't panic, sent a disc to meet the missile, and struck it hard, stopping it before reaching the target. Again she was surprised that the impact didn't destroy the missile, but the force knocked it off its path, and the missile just missed the target.

Once again, the viewers could not discern what occurred because this all transpired in less than one second. The President could see it missed the target, but the fact that Eve didn't stop the missile surprised him. He expected a far less successful demonstration.

Eve hurried back to the viewing room. She had not prepared for the missile to fight against her and push toward the target.

When she entered the viewing room, there was considerable chatter as everyone commented on the progress from the last test, and while the missile missed, it nearly got the target.

Dr. Carter showed the prior testing with the hypersonic missiles first. He wanted to demonstrate the progress in clear visual terms.

Afterward, he replayed Eve's test and said happily, "You can see here that the reinforced body of the missile stopped it from crumpling from Eve's initial attempt to push it with her force. Lacey's push on the missile caused it to crack in the previous test. Additionally, the new propulsion system in this prototype uses a more sophisticated navigational system that counters her force and her disc's strike. The missile couldn't correct enough to hit the target, but it just narrowly missed."

Dr. Carter added, "We're not sure it will ever be a primary weapon against the Iranian warriors. However, it will be one of the most powerful tools on the battlefield for standard warfare. Compliments to the hypersonics team."

The President couldn't help being impressed with the missile. The weapon just missed after being forced away and struck by a disc. He could see they were getting close to having the answer for him.

He energetically said, allowing his excitement to come through, "The missile's speed was unimaginable. Lacey, it was quite impressive since you only had a split second to deal with it. You made two decisions in that short span."

Zeke took that as an invitation to talk and shouted, "And you still haven't seen my triple spiral tornado loop. Wanna talk about something spectacular!"

The President said, not missing a beat, "And I'm not leaving until I do."

The group broke into laughter, and Zeke pushed out his chest with a bit of pride. He chose not to look at his parents or General Nunez for fear of their piercing looks.

Dr. Carter planned one last experiment using a slightly modified hypersonic missile setup that Dr. Carter chose not to share with the group.

Dr. Carter selected Thad for this test and sent him to the test range. He set up his discs just as Eve had done and waited. They took little time to fire. Instead of just one missile, though, they launched a second one.

All Thad's discs flew to the ground as the first one fired. Thad's face showed nothing but horror as the two missiles slammed into the target, one after the other, and exploded into a massive burst of flames.

Thad sat there momentarily, looking at the exploded target nailed dead-on by the missiles. He turned and looked back at the viewing room with cutting eyes, knowing exactly what had happened.

Thad set off at a blistering pace to the viewing room.

The room was abuzz with discussion amongst the scientists about what had just transpired. The children were quietly standing there, unwilling to share what they knew had occurred. Beatrice looked at Al from where she stood, not with anger but understanding.

As soon as Thad reached the door, he screamed with a deep roar, "Why did you do that, Al? Why'd you mess with my test?"

A hush fell over the room as everyone looked at Al, wondering what he had done and why.

Al started talking immediately so his parents wouldn't interrupt what he had to say.

He looked at Thad apologetically, "Thad, I'm sorry. Please know I wasn't trying to do something to hurt or embarrass you. I needed to prove a point to this team, and demonstrating it during a test was the best approach, especially with you unaware that it would happen. You would've destroyed both of those missiles. You know it, I know it, and we all know it here."

Turning to the broader group, Al said, "I did it to show this team that there is a viable way to succeed in this fight against the Iranians. As do the other children, I believe you're making significant progress with these weapons, but we also know that we children still have many options to defeat your new weapons, even with improvements. Your latest weapons have yet to test the limits of our skills.

Consider that for a moment, and then imagine the options that several Iranian warriors working together will have against our weapons. While we know you are working diligently, we Davidson children have difficulty seeing a path to success on the Phoenix Project without additional aid.

There is a simple answer. We can be that additional aid and bring our country the best chance of success. You keep improving these weapons but allow us to make them more effective.

Beatrice and I have greater capabilities than their warriors. She and I could train as a team and be a force, even fighting against large numbers of their warriors at once. The other ten can match any Iranians and defend your weapon systems.

I'm sure the argument will be that we're still children. We know that we're still technically underage, but our country sends people to war who are older but less mature than any of us twelve. Okay, maybe Zeke is a challenge to that statement, and he may talk a lot, but he is capable of great focus and has a good heart. We have discussed this and wish to participate in the fighting. Our collective future may depend on it."

Knowing she owed Al support, Beatrice added, "Mom and Dad, we want to help, and we can make a huge difference. We can nullify their warriors, and in the case of Al and I, we may be able to do much more than that."

Beatrice turned to the President and said, "I hope, Mr. President, that you'll consider our request. I'm sure it'll take your approval if our parents agree."

The entire group was stunned by the children's request, but none more than the President. The scientists knew the instant Al brought it up that D12 would be a huge factor in making the weapons more effective. For the first time, General Nunez realized what a spectacular lot of kids these were and was willing to admit that they could provide a massive boost for the weapon systems.

The President just stared at the parents. He was unsure if he would allow it, but it started with them, not him.

"Beatrice raised this with Peter and me before we agreed to bring the children on the project," said Heidi, speaking first. "We were adamant against it at that time. However, we have seen their skills grow and all blossom under the freedom to be more than some hidden-away children on a government-protected Maryland farm.

What you see before you are the miraculous result of a new way to revitalize injured children. These twelve children would have otherwise been lost to the world. As parents, we want more for our kids than to be hidden away, trapped by their uniqueness. We want them to be out in the open and experience the freedom this country offers its people. Sending all twelve of them to fight a war is not our desired first step down that path, but we recognize that if we're not successful in defending this country from an inevitable war, these kids may never enjoy the freedom they deserve.

They are, as Al says, very mature for their age, and we wrestle with the right balance of protection versus promotion when it comes to their subsequent life experiences. I ask that you give us some time to talk with the children and listen to what they have to say before we decide."

She turned and hugged her husband, who embraced her warmly back.

The President scanned the children and said, "I need to consider it myself. Your courage and bravery are unquestionable, and you are an amazing group of children. America and this team are lucky to have you. I'll wait first to hear from your parents. Can I see Zeke's triple spiral tornado loop to lighten the mood?"

Dr. Carter gave Zeke the go-ahead nod.

Zeke pumped his colossal fist in the air as he headed out the door. Zeke moved to center himself in the viewing room window so the group had the best angle to see him and his discs.

He split his discs into three groups. They went spinning upward as three separate cones whirling like tornados. He ran them up and down and all around the test range.

With the velocity he was generating, the discs created huge eddy effects that picked up the dust and debris left on the test floor and sucked them into his tornados.

Even the other kids were impressed with his display and the force he generated as they whipped around the arena. The group had seen him practice, but he was working on making it extra powerful today for the President.

Zeke brought all three tornados in front of the viewing room window to conclude his dazzling show. They could feel the pressure in the room drop as the cyclones sucked the air through the gaps in the windows. The force of the tornados rattled the door with tremendous intensity. After that final pass, Zeke slowed them all down and brought his discs back into their pyramid stack.

The young man bowed to the viewing room crowd as if playing the maestro at the show's end.

They couldn't help but clap at his outstanding performance. It measured up to the hype he had been spewing for several weeks.

You could have pinched him a thousand times, and he wouldn't have felt one of them. He glowed with complete satisfaction that he had dazzled them all.

President Schmidt, loving this kid's spunk, encouraged him to take another bow and the group to give him another round of applause. Zeke was dancing on cloud nine.

The parents and General Nunez weren't sure the President's encouragement of the young man wouldn't create an enormous monster, but they let him have his moment.

The President concluded his visit with a closed-door meeting with Dr. Carter, the Defense Secretary, and himself. He needed to ensure Dr. Carter understood the concerns about an Israeli invasion and his plan for timing a strike against Iran.

Dr. Carter was already feeling the pressure but understood the President's desire to strike when Iran's attention was elsewhere. The Phoenix Project had to bring it together, with D12 or without.

Chapter 15

Uncertainty Under Pressure

A follow-up summit in Europe was called between the Western allies. Prime Minister Carrington hosted this one in London.

The former Soviet states were halfway into Kovalyov's three months to decide their allegiance to his unification decree. So far, the planned deceit by the countries was playing out well. Western European countries offered numerous options for the former countries to visit, and their people were coming in droves.

Kovalyov kept a watchful eye over the states, ensuring there wasn't more to their delayed decision. The former republics asked Kovalyov to keep his people out of their countries out of respect for the momentous decision and allow their citizens to decide without pressure from Russian influencers.

The Russian leader reluctantly agreed, and the former states compromised by ensuring a constant flow of envoys back and forth to Moscow for discussions on the best approaches for rejoining the union. They knew Kovalyov had spies everywhere, so their deceit may quickly end as he figured out their plan.

The U.K. prime minister opened the summit with a warm welcome.

After a quick agenda review, he got down to business on the first topic by saying, "It seems like efforts to move women and children away from the front during the period are going well. Our established lines through both Finland and Italy are both working efficiently. Moreover, the ruse by the former republics is proceeding without issue with no indication that Russia is the wiser. It's likely to fall apart soon, but our intelligence tells us that the former states are eighty percent ready today."

Finnish President Lehtinen added, "We have established routes into Estonia and Latvia. Our teams have been careful because we know the Russians are patrolling by air, and they brought submarines to the Baltic to watch sea traffic. We know Kovalyov trusts no one. I give these countries a lot of credit; they still remember how to operate under the noses of their former Russian leaders."

"We also have established strong lines into Croatia and Slovenia," added the Italian Prime Minister Caponero. "The Russians don't enjoy the same proximity with our routes, but we know they use routine airborne surveillance to watch Germany. So far, it has gone quite well. We're smuggling countless women and children from the two countries into our country before the war begins."

The U.S. President stated, "We'll continue coordinating supplies with you and help in any way you need. We should break off relations immediately with the former states to help their cover story a little longer. If we appear displeased with them, Russia will take this as a huge win, which may help buy them more time. My team believes Russia is sensing that they are being played."

Prime Minister Carrington agreed and said, "Makes sense. If we push them away now, it will keep the Russians guessing. Kovalyov's ego will relish in the triumph."

French President Corbin concurred as well and then changed the subject.

He asked, "Any intelligence from anyone on the robed warriors or the discs?"

Each responded no, and the French President seemed a bit agitated.

Prime Minister Caponero said, "How's oil production going? As you know, the tightening by Iran and Russia will grow very soon."

The Norwegian Prime Minister Nilsen answered, "We continue to progress on our oil output. We're keeping up with needs in Europe, but I hope, President Schmidt, you bring some of that fracking back online and ready to produce more."

President Schmidt was happy to report, "We're making great progress. It hasn't been long since my predecessor shut most of it down, so the know-how and equipment are still available. Continued research into better ways to extract it has come a long way over the last four years. We should be in great shape in another sixty days."

Prime Minister Nilsen added, "I expect when they get resistance from their former states, Russia may accelerate the squeeze on us, figuring we were a part of the plan. Sixty days are about all you have before we need you back at full capacity."

President Schmidt responded, "We're going to be there. Undoubtedly, they will squeeze as soon as they suspect we played a part in their defiance. We suspect that Iran will soon attack Israel, and they will want to pressure us to stay out of it. Oil may be their way to do that."

He stopped there and didn't share his thoughts that this may be a good time to strike Iran. With Russia on the move, he figured the European countries would have their hands full and not likely to aid Israel.

German Chancellor Kruger spoke for the first time. He had been unusually quiet.

He asked, "What if Russia blazes through their former republics and sits on our doorsteps? We know that Kovalyov will not stop there. He desires so much more. Polish President Kaminski's chiding of me last time was well-founded. Kovalyov has made several claims about Germany. However, he won't just stop at Germany."

None doubted what he said, but the Norwegian Prime Minister responded, "I'm sure we're all preparing for the worst and hoping for the best. Our day may come when we must unite to fight Russia. When that happens, we must be ready to do our part. Beyond that, fate will decide. However, let's focus today on what sits before us."

Quiet filled the room, and the American President saw dread on all their faces as they considered what the Norwegian leader had said. He knew that none desired to enter a conflict with Russia, let alone the combination of Russia and Iran. It was also evident that Nilsen's statement constantly burned in the back of all their minds, whether or not they wanted to face it.

Still unhappy there was no response about the Iranian warriors and their discs, the French President pulled them from their dark thoughts when he asked, "Are any of you concerned with China's role? They have been eerily quiet. Could they be waiting for Russia and Iran to make their moves which will engulf our collective attention and then strike in the Pacific region?"

President Schmidt was so focused on his surprise attack that he hadn't considered China could wait for the same moment to make its move. They might be playing possum with Korea and

Japan, with a plan to strike once we become engaged with Israel and Europe.

He decided to keep his response contextually simple by saying, "Intriguing idea. Keeping our intelligence sources sharing information from the Pacific region is worthwhile. We don't have any indications about what you suggest, but it would be a smart tactic."

German Chancellor Kruger informed the group of a critical intel piece, "We had a German envoy group in China last week that picked up from numerous sources that there is unrest in the Xinjiang region. President Schmidt mentioned last time that this region and its history might never allow China to have the same relationship Russia enjoys with Iran. The Muslims in the region have been requesting Iran to free them and allow them to join United Iran. After years of persecution and reprogramming camps there by the Chinese central government, it's not surprising. Anyone else hearing this?"

The room was a sea of negative head nods and no answers.

"This is all recent," the chancellor added. "We should all keep our teams on alert for more on the situation."

The topic then shifted to Iran.

Prime Minister Carrington said, "We hear Iran is suffering through some growing pains with their new acquisitions. It's not always easy to digest your food when you overeat."

The group had a short laugh at Iran's expense but quickly changed to a more serious tone.

Norweigan Prime Minister Nilsen said, "Our sources tell us they are going into Afghanistan soon to make an example of them. They want to show the world that resistance against them means death and destruction. We also hear the Russians will support their efforts given their detailed knowledge from their years of conflict there."

The British Prime Minister confirmed they heard the same and added, "We and Russia proved how difficult it was to fight in the region. It will be interesting to see how they go with their discs. It seems Russia may have to provide much of the heavy force, which may be a much longer conflict than they intend."

President Schmidt wasn't sure that the Iranians would rely too heavily on the Russians or that Iran planned to take long. He knew from D12 that the warriors could hunt the caves with their discs as long as they could get close to the cave entrances.

To not overexpose his knowledge, he replied, "We see the Iranians seeking to make an example of Afghanistan. Their egos are bulging, and they don't like to be told no."

The meeting continued for a little longer, with good dialogue among the team members.

President Schmidt felt a little cornered when he was pulled to the side by the French President, who asked in a hushed manner, "How is your progress on finding a way to defeat the Iranians? We know America must be working on ways to counter them, and we all suspect you know more than you share. Maybe you should start providing us with more details."

The American President didn't flinch at the obvious baiting by President Corbin.

He responded dismissively, "We're all working on defeating the Iranians and making some progress, as I hope you are. As for providing more details, there may be an appropriate time to share more. However, we should be careful about our collective intentions leaking and causing these aggressors to accelerate their plans. I urge us all to be extremely cautious."

The French President wasn't satisfied with the President's response but chose not to push it further.

He couldn't help leaving the summit hoping that the former Soviet Republics would keep Russia busy for a while. Furthermore, he wanted Afghanistan to be challenging to Iran. More time, he kept telling himself, was their collective friend, and he wished for a few breaks to go his way.

The European nations, as planned, announced after the summit that they were breaking off ties with the former Soviet states. It gave the former Soviet States a few more days to hold up their ruse, but Russian spies confirmed a truth suspected from the outset that it was a ploy to delay their invasion.

Kovalyov was irate and sought wicked retribution. He launched bombing strikes on several large cities within the former states and began the immediate march of his troops. Russian troops met no large contingent of resistance forces, but they were attacked by small bands of soldiers every time they settled into a location.

Intelligence from the front in the Ukraine, Latvia, and Estonia was that the Soviets wondered where the people had scattered. Confusion turned to anger as the Russians realized their former states had masterfully played them.

They responded by torturing those resistance forces they encountered to find details of the former states' plans. The guerilla tactics, including decentralized leadership and only local knowledge about tactics and strategies, favored the former Soviet states. It also limited the intelligence the Russians could obtain from a single source.

Reports of significant blows to invading Russian troops and the heavy destruction of Russian equipment fueled hope throughout the region. Kovalyov was dismissive of the tactics in his speeches, but he showed complete disdain for their achievements in his mannerisms.

Two weeks into the Russian invasion, a pivotal event occurred for the world to see. Late one evening, Lithuanian special forces raided a Russian location where an Iranian warrior encamped with their troops.

Russia had spread the ten warriors provided by Iran across the entire front of their offensive. Russia was under strict orders to keep the Iranian warriors isolated from their troops, and their warriors were only to be commanded by accompanying Iranian soldiers. The U.S. leadership surmised that while Iran agreed to utilize their warriors to support the Russian effort, Iran hid details about the robed individuals.

As the Lithuanian special forces entered the camp, they found a tent devoid of Russian soldiers near the rear. They quietly approached the tent, where they surprisingly found one of the Iranian warriors asleep, surrounded by half a dozen Iranian soldiers standing watch but distracted in conversation.

They seized the moment as a huge opportunity to unload their weapons on the warrior and the unsuspecting soldiers. They rushed into the tent and were stunned to find a giant of a man hidden under the robes. They hurriedly captured some quick pictures of him lying dead beside two other soldiers.

Uproar broke out at the camp at the sound of gunfire, and chaos ensued. Luckily for the Lithuanians, the Russian forces were under orders not to bother the Iranians, so they checked their location last, giving the Lithuanian forces the needed time to escape with their finding.

The Lithuanian leadership posted the pictures on the internet and social media, recognizing the importance of their discovery and the value of their photos. The world was abuzz with speculation about the giant man and what this all meant. Clearly, the world understood these Iranian warriors were not indestructible for the first time.

Tales about the pictures spanned the spectrum, from those that contended Iran had created some form of monster to Iran being in cahoots with aliens to claims that the photographs were fake. One thing was abundantly clear; it renewed hope for many beyond any seen since the Iranians defeated the U.S. forces in Iraq. It also started a low-level undercurrent of doubters in the Muslim world about what Iran had at its disposal.

The American President was ecstatic about the development in Eastern Europe. It was all rolling now, and if the President was correct, the Iranians would be inclined to soon be on the move and regain their momentum. He thought luck was shining favorably at this point in his plan.

President Schmidt convened a Cabinet and national security team meeting to discuss the latest developments. As he entered the meeting room, the President saw the weeks of tireless work etched on their dedicated faces.

He chose to start the meeting with an upbeat tone. Even seasoned leaders need to hear good news when it comes.

The President began, "The plans of the former Soviet republics are proceeding well. The Russians are bombing and destroying the very cities they hope to occupy. Not because it makes military sense but because they want to show they are wreaking havoc, and Kovalyov is angry about their defiance and trickery. The Russian efforts are doing little to affect the dispersed resistance forces. Our supply lines are holding, and while this may not last, it has been very effective.

On another note, Margaret has some recent intelligence out of Tehran that I want her to share."

The National Intelligence Director took the cue and said, "We hear the Supreme Leader is devastated by losing his holy warrior in Lithuania. They are further distraught that he was shown to the world unrobed. All intelligence points to them recalling the other nine warriors from the Russian war effort due to a belief that they violated the wishes of Allah and used the warrior outside their jihad.

It won't make Russia vulnerable if they do, but it sure makes the efforts of the former states and our allies all the more important. Sources say Iran will immediately pull them back and head directly into Afghanistan. We heard Iran still holds the Russians to their agreed airlift support."

The President said, "Maybe another ray of hope for our friends in Eastern Europe, and I'm hopeful some Western Europeans grow bolder in their efforts to support them. Let's move on to Afghanistan. Margaret, give us a little more on them."

"Yes, Mr. President," she said. "Sources tell us that Iran is going into the country to destroy the Afghan resistance once and for all. They plan a seek-and-destroy effort going cave to cave with their warriors. Based on the input from the Davidsons, we now know that the warriors will be quite effective in sending their discs into the caves like an attacking swarm. It will still be a problematic hunt because of the region's vastness and the considerable elevation change of the mountains.

We've received no intelligence about the number of warriors they plan to use, so it's difficult to gauge a timeline for them to complete the invasion. We understand the invasion will start within the next two weeks."

"We hear the relationship between Moscow and Tehran has cooled immensely," the Secretary of State added. "Kovalyov is quite miffed at the loss of the warriors in his efforts. He knows that it will instill energy into the resistance."

It all was playing out as the President had hoped, but he needed the Phoenix Project to bring a solution soon. He was still waiting for a decision from the Davidsons about their children. Except for the Defense Secretary, the Cabinet was unaware of the children's request to participate in the fight.

The President wrestled with the decision constantly. It went against everything he believed in, but he knew, like the others, that these were unique times. He kept it under wraps until he heard from the Davidsons and had time to consider it more thoroughly. This decision was not one he needed or wanted input from anyone other than the Davidsons.

President Schmidt kept the meeting moving, " Our visit to Idaho went well. The Phoenix Project is making excellent progress. The demonstrations proved very informational, but we don't have a solution to defeat them. I ask you to please stay on top of any Phoenix Project requests as the top priority. If Cassandra asks, then please ensure it gets taken care of quickly. With the invasion of Afghanistan imminent, Israel will follow shortly."

"Dr. Carter would like to have a secure conference with you and me tomorrow afternoon," said the Defense Secretary.

She didn't elaborate, but the President concluded it was most likely about D12. She was coy about the topic because he had chosen moments ago to avoid it with the group.

They moved on to China, where all intelligence information showed China maintaining a subdued position across the globe. Reports continued to confirm cordial relations with Korea, Japan, and others. Nevertheless, it didn't ease the leery feelings in the region.

The President concluded the meeting with a motivational discussion about hardened pockets of resistance, like the former Soviet republics, choosing freedom over a return to rule by a dictator. He told them their efforts would prove meaningful to all nation's long-term security, including the one they were serving dutifully.

While the President was meeting with his Cabinet, the Davidsons called a family meeting in Idaho to discuss the children fighting alongside the military. Before the family meeting, the parents had difficulty coming to terms with allowing their children to go and fight. Heidi and Peter decided they would listen, but their sense was this was too much of an ask.

D12 assembled on the test range where the parents had told them to meet.

Peter had asked Dr. Carter if they could have the range to talk privately as a family. Dr. Carter, understanding the importance of the discussion, agreed without hesitation.

The parents entered the vast area and saw their twelve children huddled in the middle.

Peter Davidson started the meeting by saying, "Your mom and I love all of you so much. That has not and will not ever change. We appreciate your desire to join the military effort against Iran. You have done so much for this project and continue making us prouder daily. However, to send one of you off to fight would be difficult, but to send all of you has us at an unfathomable breaking point. We try to be rational but understand where our feelings lie and why."

Peter stopped and put his arm around his wife. The two of them had agreed to listen without giving the children a litany of reasons why not. They stood there handing the discussion to their children.

The children had selected Beatrice to represent them in the meeting.

Beatrice responded by saying, "We love you both as well. All of us, without exception and question. However, we believe nothing is more important than helping us win. Your work and our lives are unavoidably intertwined with what is happening today. We can't undo that, but we can help fix it.

All twelve of us know there is little chance the Phoenix team will devise a solution to beat one of us, let alone a group of us. When President Schmidt deploys our forces to fight Iran, they won't know how many warriors with our powers they'll face.

Our desire to participate in this fight comes down to one core element that none can deny; if we don't go with them, our future, America's future, and every other country's future are at risk.

We have no choice but to go because we know we'll make a difference. The twelve of us wish there were an alternative, but we know there isn't one. Your colleagues on this project know this as well, but they choose not to pressure you.

We're afraid of what we'll face, but that won't stop us from doing the right thing. We saw the pictures of the Iranian warrior and know we may die too, but we still choose a future of our own making. You need to let us do this and convince the President that this is right."

All twelve kids confirmed their agreement.

The parents looked at each other. They knew everything she said was true, but it didn't make it easier.

Heidi said through a muffled sob, "We love you kids so much. The joy you bring to us is endless. As the President said, you are the most courageous children, and your maturity belies your age. You twelve died once, but you came back to us as a miracle of science and a blessing to us and this world. Let your father and I discuss this alone. We'll give you a final decision tonight."

The children seemed satisfied that their message was understood. Before the family meeting, they had decided that piling on wouldn't help their parents come to terms with it, so they stopped there. Short and sweet was their best hope and best delivered by Beatrice.

The kids stood up, and the parents hugged each of them. It was a simultaneous coming-of-age moment for all twelve of them and a time when the parents were coming to terms with the fact that the children were correct; if they didn't help in the fight, there was no hope of winning.

As D12 walked inside, they saw the laser team waiting for the family meeting to conclude. Laser testing was scheduled to begin, but Dr. Carter asked them to give the family some time alone.

The new high-powered laser was about to complete integration with its new power source and fire control system. The team felt this would be their ultimate weapon, and it was time to move on to the last challenge, smoke obscurants inhibiting the laser.

The U.S. was keenly aware that the Russians and the Chinese, much like themselves, had been looking at airborne obscurants for some time, understanding that laser weapons would eventually become viable battlefield equipment.

Beatrice, who stayed back on the range while the rest of the family left, had yet to spend significant time practicing with her complete set of discs. Her duties on the Phoenix team focused primarily on evaluating what the Iranians would do with their disc sets, limiting her to the same disc set as her siblings and the Iranians. She was excited to have a little time to play and sent them into the air like an endless flock of birds.

Beatrice imagined herself battling multiple Iranians at one time and worked to establish attack techniques while playing with different shield approaches. She relished the opportunity to work with them by herself and left to her thoughts.

Nearby on the test range, the laser team was busy firing off their latest laser. Beatrice could read the team's frustration and assumed they were encountering problems from the various smokes she saw in the air, even at a distance. She watched for a while as the group became more and more exasperated.

Just as it looked like the team was planning to shut the testing down, an idea struck her, and she hurried over to Dr. Stolton, who was conversing with Dr. Carter.

Beatrice said apologetically, “Dr. Stolton, I don’t mean to interrupt, but it appears you’re having some difficulties with the various smokes.”

Dr. Stolton, clearly displaying frustration, grunted, “We can’t get through any of these smokes. Even with the new power level, it’s unable to penetrate. Our analysis showed it might ionize a path through it, but the smokes are too absorptive and, frankly speaking, too well designed by the scientists who developed them to let that happen.

If the laser could find a way to penetrate through cleanly, this weapon is the answer. With no obscurants, it blasts the discs apart immediately upon engaging them. We can't go higher in power or select a wavelength that may penetrate more easily. Several technical factors have trapped us, and the smoke is confounding the entire approach."

Happy to see that he didn't get testy at her interruption, she pressed him further, "Can you try your worst-case smoke one more time, please? I'd like to try something."

He was puzzled by her request but was willing to let her try something, so he yelled to the team, "One more time on smoke number five. It was the worst. I want to try it one more time."

A few minutes later, the group introduced smoke number five into the air on the test range and fired the laser. As they did, Beatrice took a group of her discs and created one of Zeke's tornados. She moved the tornado near the laser, and as she did that, the tornado began to scoop in the smoke.

Seeing the success, she quickly ran the tornado down the field in front of the laser, watching the smoke collected within the funnel. Within seconds, the laser burst through and blasted the target. Dr. Stolton and the laser team couldn't believe their eyes.

He hurried over to Beatrice and said, "That was ingenious. You addressed our major limitation. Phenomenal. Simply phenomenal," he uttered as he headed back to his boss, who clapped his hands to celebrate the feat.

Moments later, the two approached Beatrice, who had returned to practice.

"Beatrice," said Dr. Carter. "You are a sharp one."

She blushed and said, "I have to give the credit to Zeke. His triple spiral tornado was the real inspiration. I can tell you, but please don't let him know I said that. His ego is already challenging. If he knows he's the inspiration for the laser's success, we may never hear the end of it."

They all laughed, knowing she was spot on, until she said, "Mom and Dad are still thinking about whether we can fight. Then we have the President, who didn't seem too sure he'd allow it. If we focused our training on working with your devices, we'd discover several new ways to improve their effectiveness."

Dr. Stolton and Dr. Carter chose to stay quiet on the point. Neither of them was stepping in front of the parent's decision.

Meanwhile, back at their facility housing, the Davidson parents discussed how to respond to their request.

Heidi told her husband, "Peter, it may destroy me if we lose them again. This time it wouldn't just be Al and Beatrice. We could lose all twelve of them. I might not make it through that."

The thought of losing any of them was hard for him as well. He recognized what the kids meant to the effort, but the tug on his heart was also unbearable.

He placed his arm firmly around his wife's back and lovingly said, "I feel the same, and I would struggle too. Should the worst happen, we would need each other. Hopefully, we'll make it through together.

I won't pretend war won't take a toll on our children, even if we win and they come back unharmed. Fighting and killing someone changes a person, never in a good way. Our children are still teenagers, but they aren't just any teenagers. Maybe they came back to us for this very purpose."

Heidi looked at him intently for a few moments searching his inner thoughts. She was crying heavily.

Wiping her eyes, she said, "I know this country is in serious trouble, like many others. I know the children are right about making a difference. The new laser configuration will be a formidable solution for the Iranian warriors, but we know our kids will likely make it unbeatable. Even with that, can we send them off to war?"

Peter softly said, "I think we have to, Heidi. They are mature beyond their age, and I think they are committed to doing this. We both know that. Maybe Zeke isn't, but they feel it's their purpose. Let's grant their request."

She laughed about the Zeke comment through her crying and said, "Okay. We must work extra hard to get them the best laser possible from this project and train them full-time. Let's get them together and let them know what we'll tell the President tomorrow."

The parents quickly gathered them and shared their decision to ask the President to support their request. On the one hand, the kids were excited, yet they were overwhelmed by what it all meant on the other. They knew they better get training hard, and their parents told them they were willing, under the circumstances, to suspend their studies for a while, which was met with great enthusiasm by all except Thad, who was enjoying his second semester of calculus.

The Davidsons and Dr. Carter met with the President and Defense Secretary via secure video conference the following day. They proposed that the President grant an exception and allow the underage participation of their twelve children in the military. The President, torn like the parents over his willingness to send these children to war, remained unconvinced.

He was about to reject the idea when Heidi Davidson said, "Mr. President, I can see you disagree. I can read it all over your face. It took Peter and me quite some time to get here. I want to say something to you before you give a final answer.

Like so many others, we voted for you as President because you were a man of integrity, morals, and intellect. One who believed we were much stronger together than divided as a people. You drew a nation together when it was faltering. We believe in you and this country, even more so now that we've gotten to know you personally. We reared our kids to think and believe in the same ideals you rallied this nation to believe in again.

After Iraq, your job became more important to Americans and much of the world. We need you to lead the restoration of order around the globe. Unless you finish that, these kids' futures are likely very dark. These kids understand that and know that no other people at your disposal can do what they can do. They are our best chance, and we recommend you honor their request."

Her impassioned words moved him. The sacrifice by a parent to make the world a better place fits into his definition of the ultimate patriot. The President was uneasy about accepting this, but he knew they needed these children to lead a successful attack.

He answered, "We'll do it then. I promise to do everything to bring your children back safely and win this war. This country owes you and them a huge debt."

Chapter 16

Ultimatum and Opportunity

United Iran reclaimed their nine warriors from the Russian effort and buried its dead warrior in a religious ceremony in Mecca. They chose the burial site near some of Islam's most influential people in history. Millions of people throughout the large republic flooded the streets as they mourned the loss of Allah's gift to their cause.

The Supreme Leader broadcast an emotional speech throughout the large country. He called out their failure to heed Allah's will and the transgression of using their blessed soldier outside the jihad for which Allah had equipped them. He shared that this would not happen again, and their focus would be on the final consolidation of Allah's grand unification.

A few days after the funeral, Iran launched their attack on Afghanistan. Intelligence from the region revealed their strategy involved significant air transport support from Russia and more than one hundred Iranian warriors with their discs.

They dispersed them throughout the mountain regions. As expected by the American leadership, they sent them hunting through the maze of caves and mountain hideouts. Others were sent sweeping through the countryside, eradicating any men of fighting age with little regard for whether they supported the decision to join Iran.

Merciless was the best description of the slaughter. Iran's government pushed numerous videos and images out to the media to ensure the world witnessed what non-compliance to their will meant.

President Schmidt kept abreast of the latest developments in Afghanistan and scheduled an update with his Cabinet and national security team. Many critical events were in motion, and he wanted close coordination with his leadership during these tenuous times.

He joined the team in his situation room and immediately began with agenda item one, Afghanistan.

"Margaret, what is the latest on the fighting in Afghanistan?" he asked. "I heard the Iranians are methodically hunting the mountain regions as we expected."

The National Intelligence Director responded, "Mr. President, indeed they are. They sent a large number of warriors into Afghanistan. Intelligence from the region estimates that number to be around one hundred twenty. The large number indicates that their reserve supply of these warriors is extensive. All indications are that they are making quick work of the country. Iran is surely not trying to hide its brutality. They are using it as promotional material."

Concerned, the President said, "We weren't sure how swiftly they would cover the terrain, but looking at what you handed me, they seem to be making quick work of it. With a willingness to kill and destroy without regard for life, they make the Afghanis wish they complied. I'm not convinced that the constant media images and videos are promotional. They are a warning for us and Israel."

"Anything else before we move on to Russia," the President asked.

"No, Mr. President," replied his Intelligence Director.

He shifted to the next topic and said, "Moving on to Russia. We know Kovalyov is undoubtedly livid about the loss of the Iranian warriors, and he has to be frustrated by the effectiveness of the former states in fighting against them. His furor has been translated into him wreaking havoc in Ukraine and Poland.

I heard yesterday from Italian Prime Minister Caponero that their lines are sustaining their flow of supplies to the resistance forces. The word is that the resistance is striking solid hits on Russian troops with their tactics. He said Kovalyov had deployed Russian Special Forces to hit some critical pockets, but they didn't have the resources to be everywhere. Margaret, what intelligence do you have from the region?"

The National Intelligence Director answered, "We have from several sources that the Romanians and Polish forces have moved forward and are helping to keep the Russians from progressing deeper into the region. The common belief by the resistance is that he is destroying the cities, not as a battle tactic, but as a psychological technique to break the spirit of the opposition, typical old-school KGB stuff.

Much like Iran, Kovalyov uses the media to play out his propaganda. Reports tell us that the opposite is happening; the resistance is becoming more fortified by their successes and the exit of the Iranian warriors."

The President considered her words for a moment. He pondered that ruling a people by fear has long been the approach of tyrants. Those regimes, history shows, last for only short periods.

"Humans are an interesting breed, and poor leaders often fail to understand the needs and desires of those they try to lead or, in this case, dominate," said the President. "Fear works only in the short term and generates no loyalty. Cruelty and the heartless murder of innocent people will remain with those who experience it for as long as they live. Kovalyov's approach will never yield willing participants.

As for Iran, once the truth comes out about the true nature of its warriors, their willing subjects are going to realize they were manipulated for Iran's benefit and not for the will of Allah. Many Islamic people are caught up in this cause, much like many Germans were enthralled by Hitler. Once they understand that Iranian leaders concocted this, they will again choose to regain their freedom and rebel."

The President needed to share his decision about using the Davidson children in the attack.

"I have an announcement to make," said the President. "D12 has requested they be allowed to fight with our military. They have been working with the Phoenix Project for some time and helping them develop new weapon systems to defeat the Iranian warriors.

The team is close to having a new laser system capable of defeating the Iranians, but it remains vulnerable to a group attack by their warriors. D12 know they can defend the laser systems from those attacks and ensure the success of the weapons. Their defense of the system shifts the probability of success from low to high. The Phoenix Project believes this is unbeatable and allows us to challenge Iran.

The parents agreed with the children and convinced me to allow the exception for their underage entry into the military. I wish a better alternative existed, but this seems to be our only hope.

The children are now actively training with the Phoenix Project team. Dr. Carter is finalizing the weapons platform. They know time is short and must be ready immediately once Iran enters Israel."

The President clasped his hands at the table and looked forward in a contemplative stare. The group could tell this decision was uncomfortable and weighed heavily on his mind.

"Mr. President, I'm sure this decision was difficult," said the Vice President. "We understand the dilemma, but we also understand the difference these children will make to the effort."

"Agreed," said his Secretary of State.

Several murmurs of agreement came from around the table. These were unique times and called for difficult decisions. The entire group quietly sat there while they looked at the President, seemingly lost in thought.

The National Intelligence Director broke the silence in the room and said, "Mr. President, I would like to discuss China quickly. There is breaking news that I need to share with you. In the Xinjiang region, the Uyghurs have been actively pushing for separation from China and the part to join United Iran."

"Yes, the German chancellor mentioned they had heard something about this back at our second summit," said the President with keen interest.

"Our intelligence tells us that Iran sent a delegation to the region escorted by five of the warriors. Our sources share it was part of a demand by the Iranian Supreme Leader to cede the territory and its Muslim population to United Iran.

Accounts of what transpired are unclear and varied, but one crucial detail consistent in everything we heard is that the five

Iranian warriors disappeared. There is no trace of them, and China's government told Iran they have no idea what occurred."

"Do we have any idea what may have happened?" asked the President.

"None. We have tried to ascertain from further intelligence, satellite imagery, and information from our allies, who had some additional elements to share, but we can't figure out what occurred."

"Any chance China has some new weapon?" asked the President.

The National Intelligence Director responded, "We reviewed in detail all details and can trace the delegation's movements into the region. Once they arrived, we could detect no battle but also no departure. They just disappeared, and interestingly enough, Iran maintained their five warriors in five different locations. So, they didn't disappear by one incident, but five simultaneously."

"I don't believe they just disappeared," said the President. "Something happened there that we don't understand yet. How's Iran taking that explanation?"

"That's strange, too," said the National Intelligence Director. "All reports are that Iran was unhappy with the situation but accepted China's explanation. We heard that they were confident that no one could have taken out five of their warriors in five locations and left no evidence of a struggle or some use of a weapon, especially when others from the delegation were unharmed and located nearby. Their disappearance was no lucky Lithuanian strike. It was a surgical operation of extreme precision with a capability we don't possess. Either that or the five claimed asylum, and China is covering for them."

"What does China know that we don't?" asked the President, concerned that China could pull off something he knew they couldn't.

"Not sure," she answered. "We know Iran hasn't attempted to send other warriors back to the region, and China shows no signs they are hiding anything. Maybe the warriors did go rogue."

"I wouldn't bet on that," responded the President. "Get every detail you have to Dr. Carter and the Phoenix team and see if they can figure out what happened."

"Will do, Mr. President," said the Director. "One other item associated with China. Concern has emerged from the region as China has suddenly stepped-up military exercises. Communications and relations with other countries remain cordial; however, our allies in the region wonder if this is the first part of a similar action like Russia. We have no intelligence supporting that conclusion, but it does fit the pattern. The Chinese Ambassador informed us that this is routine and no concern. I'm not sure what action we take at this time."

The President was not dismissive of her concerns but preferred to let things play out further with China.

He said, "I saw a report on that earlier. It concerns me, but we need to monitor their actions and keep our allies closely connected. I want regular intelligence briefings to keep abreast of the latest."

"Yes, Mr. President," she responded.

The President transitioned to the topic of Israel.

He stated, "I talked with Prime Minister Yaakv two days ago. He told me that Israel figures that Iran will move on to Israel once Afghanistan is under control. He was confident, so they must have strong intelligence on the matter. The prime minister showed more concern than the last time we talked due to the large contingent of Iranian warriors reported in Afghanistan. He informed me they had new ways to defend themselves, but he seemed less assured of their prospects. Despite his lack of confidence, he still didn't ask me for military assistance. His refusal to ask has me concerned about the lengths they may go if attacked."

Once the President finished, the Vice President added, "Mr. President, I have been keeping close communications with my connection in Israel. He informs me that they have a new weapon they have successfully developed. The plan is to deploy several copies of it around the country, as we surmised. Iran's primary interest will be Jerusalem.

More specifically, it will be the Al-Aqsa Mosque, the last crown jewel, so to speak, for the united Islamic country. They expect Iran to be careful in Jerusalem and endeavor to add the final piece of their Islamic consolidation without destroying the city. To that end, Israel plans to put their defenses around major cities, but Jerusalem will be heavily fortified."

"Word from our State Department sources in Israel is that surrender will never be an option," said the Secretary of State, chiming in. "They plan to use every means necessary and will not let Iran have any part of Israel."

The Defense Secretary, hearing this information, knew Israel would be prepared to use anything and everything if the war called for it. She knew they likely had a similar approach to the U.S., but they would not hold back the same way President Schmidt chose to with alternative weapons.

She said, "Of course, we don't know what they may have developed, but we have some good guesses that it's along our lines with lasers. While Israel possesses some advanced technologies, they likely can't match what we have put together on the Phoenix Project. Our advantage is that we've tested against D12, and they have been guessing about Iran's warriors."

"We can speculate about what may happen," said the President. "Guessing what they may do is fruitless since we don't know what Israel has developed nor how they plan to use it. That information won't leave Israel until that war begins. As you know, their security is better than our own. Therefore, we need to focus on what we plan to do.

Dr. Carter informs me that two new key weapons are being readied for a final test before full production. He thinks if all goes well, he could have ten production units ready to be deployed within the next thirty days. He is integrating them into mobile platforms that will host them with a crew and two Davidson children. Six of these platforms will have to lead our attack against Iran's warriors, and we'll have four spares."

He could tell by the looks on several of their faces that they were processing images of what he had just described with D12 central to these weapons. Most had never seen the whole group of Davidson children.

He tried to calm their concerns by saying, "I share many of the same concerns running through your heads. These are the same concerns their parents had, as well. I can also assure you that Dr. Carter and his team, including the children and their parents, believe the Phoenix Project is the only way to succeed.

I have already sent thousands to their death in Iraq. So, please understand I don't do this lightly or without regard for the lives of these children. Nothing is further from the truth."

His Secretary of State, the ultimate elder statesman but one who had his differences with his boss, offered his support by saying, "Mr. President, we know the type of man you are. We wouldn't be here on this team if we didn't believe in you. I'm unaware of any other man that could have handled what you've dealt with during this presidency better than you. If you decide to do this, I support it without question, and I'll use every means to convince others of that."

"Jack, I appreciate your confidence," the President said.

He scanned the faces of the rest of them. He could see that Jack's support struck home with all of them.

The President said, "We're in a historically difficult period for this nation, and this team will lead us through the struggle. You'll be tested further as we navigate our way forward, but this will only be the first step in what will assuredly be a long war.

We expect Iran to have numerous warriors. Once we surprise them and inflict serious damage, they will regroup and adjust their tactics. We only have six platforms and can't defeat them quickly. Step one is to be ready when they attack Israel. That is our opening. I want to punch them hard enough that they need to regroup and question their dominance.

Let's break here and finish what we need before this happens. My thanks to you and your teams."

Three weeks elapsed before Iran declared complete control and assimilation of Afghanistan. After leaving carnage across the country, they moved into Kabul at the last stage.

Reports varied, but most estimates suggested that around ten million Afghani men, young and old, died in the sweeping invasion. As with the others, Iran added Afghanistan as another new province and kept a contingent of their warriors to ensure no further uprisings.

The Supreme Leader announced Iran's decisive victory and wasted no time putting forward the next step in their unification plan. He declared they were reclaiming the land given to Israel, which was stolen from Muslims by the United Nations after World War II. By taking Jerusalem, the leader said, Iran would consolidate the last Islamic holy place under the control of United Iran.

Many thought they might sweep in and destroy Israel without delay, but he announced ninety days for Israelis to flee the nation or perish. Unlike the proclamation given to Muslim countries, this decree carried the explicit ramifications of death to all Jews if they failed to comply. No exceptions for women, children, or the elderly were given.

He further proclaimed that western nations responsible for forming Israel and placing the Jewish state in the region could now come and assist with their exit. While approving them to help with the evacuation, Iran warned they would swiftly destroy any nation supporting Israel in fighting against Iran.

Using the media again to promulgate their message, Iran distributed numerous images and videos of the destruction left behind in Afghanistan to put an exclamation point on their warning. The announcement was loud and clear to the West, if you fight against Iran, you will die.

The moment the President had been waiting for arrived, he was happy to have the ninety-day deadline to finalize details. The clock was now ticking. The country's hopes rested with Dr. Carter's team and D12.

Wasting no time, President Schmidt invited the Vice President, Secretary of Defense, the Chairman of the Joint Chiefs, and Dr. Carter to the Oval Office to formalize the attack plan. He wanted every detail reviewed and tied out, leading to his sneak attack.

The meeting attendees entered the Oval Office, and the President asked them to be seated. He was all business.

President Schmidt said, "The time has come for us to pull the pieces together required to initiate the counterstrike on Iran. Israel has their mandate, and luck favored us with ninety days to operate."

Turning to Dr. Carter, he said, "Are we going to be ready? How is the training with the Davidson kids going?"

Dr. Carter, all business, said, "Mr. President, we'll be ready with our newest laser, and we're finalizing integration onto our armored mobile platforms.

Each platform will contain our latest high-powered laser with a new optical-gyro-enabled fire control system and a compact fusion power source made by Skunk Works. The fusion source and its short pulse power distribution system make this weapon system possible.

On the exterior of the platforms, we'll have specialized armor made from ultra-resilient nanofibers that we know will hold up against attacks from the discs. Each platform will house a crew of soldiers and two Davidson children who will operate their discs from an armor-protected dome on top of each side.

As for D12, we've learned much recently during training and refined our tactics. It continues to come together quite nicely. The vehicles with the children defending them are a sight to behold.

There is one drawback. The mobile platform is so large that we can't fit the vehicles on any aircraft. Our options by sea are pretty limited as well. General Nunez believes the only means is an aircraft carrier. Unfortunately, stealth or surprise is out of the question."

"Our plan is for the carrier to enter Iran from the Persian Gulf," said Admiral Lawton. "Iran will be engaged with Israel through Jordan, Saudi, and Lebanon, so we believe it's best to hit them from the other side. They will recognize we're coming to Israel's defense, but they then face a choice to either stick with their invasion of Israel or split their forces. Iran's leadership will probably consider us easy prey given Iraq, so they may only divert limited resources."

"Admiral, I understand that approach, but I would like to propose an alternative that will keep the element of surprise," said President Schmidt. "Let's send ships to the Mediterranean to transport people out of Israel. We'll need to do that, regardless, for the evacuation.

Each group of ships will include cruise ships aided by the U.S. Navy, including aircraft carrier groups. I believe we can do this without raising suspicions. It may be touchy to sell, and we may have to hang back at a distance from Israel, but that works for my plan anyways.

We'll have several weeks of activity to demonstrate our peaceful actions supporting the exodus. None of our efforts will display anything but humanitarian support. We can keep this façade to the end and inform Iran that we expect last-minute evacuations. The last exiting ships will house our new platforms and our attacking forces. What do you think?"

"Mr. President, I see you have been giving this considerable thought," said the Defense Secretary. "It has merit as long as they let us get close with the carrier group. We can keep our new weapons below deck until we launch them. We were already planning to use the USS Gerald Ford for this initiative. As you saw on your visit, the new carrier brings us better weapon systems and capabilities that may play to our advantage during the attack."

An idea occurred to the Defense Secretary. The President's scheme could be disguised further with some changes to make the supporting ships appear less threatening.

"Admiral Lawton and I can discuss creating a carrier support group that looks less like what it's and more like a humanitarian support group," she said to President Schmidt.

Turning to Dr. Carter, the Defense Secretary said, "I would like the specifications on your laser platforms. Once we have the specifics, we can look at the arrangements for the carrier. We must also consider launching these platforms once we reach our intended attack point.

The platforms are wheeled armored vehicles with dual lasers with 180-degree hemispherical coverage," said Dr. Carter. "We'll get you all the relevant dimensions and weight. The two lasers are mounted on a fire control system with a high-powered, high-speed machine gun that will follow the same aiming line as the laser. The two lasers, the vehicle itself, and the two domes made for the Davidson children are all protected with as much armor as we can afford.

We refer to the domes as the disc support stations. That's where the children will be. These stations will allow them to operate independently from any activities of the vehicle weapons with the sole intention of defending the vehicle from attack. They will also help open any blocked paths to the targets. If all goes as planned, the lasers will provide the kill shots, and the children will defend the platform.

Additionally, each vehicle has one central hypersonic missile battery. The battery will carry sixteen missiles, and the vehicle will hold two additional sets under armor. The rockets are not the primary weapon system, but they will be helpful in various battlefield situations.

Finally, to top it off, we made one platform with no lasers but identical capabilities otherwise. It will house Alan and Beatrice, who will operate the command vehicle, the name we gave to their platform. Their function is to coordinate platform defenses and organize coordinated attacks on the warriors. The five laser vehicles are very effective in their own right, but with these two providing top cover, I believe we have a sizeable advantage."

"I know your confidence is well-founded," said the President. "Once we neutralize Iranian warriors in a specific area, we can release our conventional military and press our offensive forward in measured phases. We must be careful that they don't regroup and overwhelm our forces with huge numbers of their warriors. How vulnerable will the carrier be before moving the platforms onto land?"

The Defense Secretary responded, "We'll have a contingent of support ships and some of our submarine force stealthily standing by for any surprises. We could be vulnerable if Iranian warriors and their discs somehow attacked the carrier group. We might have to call D12 into action if that occurs."

President Schmidt broke from his focused demeanor and smiled at the thought of D12 working with the naval fleet. He still hoped his decision to allow them to participate would not haunt him.

Responding to the Defense Secretary's comment, the President said, "If we have to utilize them in such an attack, we do so. Admiral Lawton, we should put that into our training plan before deploying."

"By the way," said the President. "How are the children doing now that their decision to participate has been made?"

Dr. Carter lightheartedly responded, "They are doing well. They continue to amaze me. I can't begin to portray the energy of the Phoenix Project since they started training with the lasers. Even General Nunez has swallowed his pride and is a huge fan of them. He even told me the other day during exercises on the range that we had no hope without them. The Defense Secretary and Admiral Lawton can tell you how big that change in mindset is."

"I'm glad he came around," the President said with a smile. "I need to wrap this up because Alan and I have one last item to discuss in private."

The Defense Secretary, Dr. Carter, and the admiral exited the room.

Once the door closed behind them, the President turned to the Vice President and said, "Alan, before you leave, I have a mission for you. I was hoping you could go to China to communicate our mutual interests in a peaceful world and understand what they see in this whole mess. Our intelligence organizations seem unable to get a precise bearing on their plans, so I think this requires some direct diplomacy.

I'm only trusting this vital assignment to you. Also, see if you can pick up anything on the disappearance of the five warriors in the Xinjiang region. Margaret has yet to find anything further on the incident other than it stopped Iran dead in its tracks on requesting China to cede the territory.

They may be tight-lipped and unwilling to share, but you have a good sense of people and may get an inkling about their true intentions. Worse case, we at least keep an open dialogue with them and shore up our connections."

"Absolutely, Mr. President," responded the Vice President, understanding the logic behind the visit. "I have some strong senior party members ties I have developed over the years working trade negotiations. I may get a read from some of them whether they are planning something."

"Good. Once you get it coordinated and an agenda set, let's go over how you plan to handle some specifics," responded the President.

So many details needed addressing to pull off an attack while so many other balls were in the air. The President wanted flawless execution once they initiated their plan. He knew they only got one chance; if it failed, Iran would exact their revenge on the U.S. with unimaginable consequences. The overused phrase 'Failure is Not an Option' never rang truer in American history than it did now.

Chapter 17

Training Days

As he looked across the test range witnessing the Phoenix Project's five new platforms whizzing around firing, Dr. Nicholas Carter thought this war would be like no other. The children were holed up in an armored nest to each side of the vehicle as they controlled their flock of discs whizzing around the simulated battlefield. Science fiction could not have portrayed what he was witnessing any better. Dr. Carter knew the opening battle would be crucial to establishing the offensive, and he imagined these vehicles coming face-to-face with the Iranian warriors.

The laser power was now substantial enough to blast away their discs instantly. However, the team was concerned that the warriors could still deploy tactics to protect themselves or even have other unforeseen objects available for protection. Their ace in the hole, he knew, was the team of Al and Beatrice. They would be a wrecking ball for the Iranian warriors.

Inside the armored vehicles, each laser was operated by a dedicated soldier. That soldier had a state-of-the-art infrared night-vision system to find and aim at their targets. Additionally, the vehicle carried two machine guns buried in the dome under the laser that followed the laser's line of sight. Each machine gun has a dedicated gunner.

The hypersonic missile battery rested with its independent fire control system at the vehicle's center. It possessed a retractable armor shield that opened for a split second on firing and rapidly closed. An additional soldier operated the missile fire control.

The Davidson children's turrets were positioned center-left and center-right on the vehicle. Each had a 360-degree view around the platform with a topside opening where they would reside. Their primary function was the defense of the lasers and the vehicle.

Overall, it was a masterful design, and Dr. Carter was proud of the project's solution. He reminded himself that this was a tool to combat an aggressor wielding a significant advantage, not a large-scale weapon of mass destruction like the U.S. used in World War II.

Down at the far side of the range, Al and Beatrice were training together. She was weaving her ensemble of a thousand discs in various attack patterns on a set of targets the team had built for them. She always kept her discs behind Al's as he went in first at the target and followed with her discs.

Dr. Carter suspected they planned to use Al's strength to disrupt the Iranians, then have her follow with her huge flock of discs weaving through the open spaces he might create. Her skill and his might need only give the smallest gap to score a lethal strike.

Strange, he thought, how a medical breakthrough led to this moment. Science twisted for someone to gain power they otherwise would never have achieved, resulting in children prepping to fight children. Cranio-Genesis has indeed changed the world.

Disrupted from his musings by a loud blast to his right, Dr. Carter headed over to see Hans Stolton, Kerwin Templeton, and General Nunez, who were in the midst of some tests.

"Good morning, gentlemen. How are things going?" Dr. Carter inquired.

General Nunez was the first to speak.

The general said, "The children are finding the best techniques to operate against the warriors while providing the most effective support for the vehicle's mission. The Iranian warriors have not yet been concerned with fighting other warriors, but they must change their tactics when we attack. As we've learned, fighting another warrior is quite different since they can use their powers in other ways than just controlling discs.

D12 have learned to use a variety of combinations to defeat one another's attacks or defenses. For instance, should an Iranian warrior level an attack with their discs on the platform, D12 can deflect with some of their discs or use their force to counter the incoming discs. Depending on the situation and how engaged in fighting they are, they may choose one, the other, or a combination. It's fascinating, and the training will prove a sizeable advantage when we first engage Iran.

The one risk we face, and it's a significant one, is that a large group of warriors attack a single platform. They may overpower the defenses of the two Davidsons. Our combat plan utilizes Al and Beatrice to track any activity and aid such a platform. We feel they can balance any unevenness in the fight. We hope to think of all possibilities and train for them."

Dr. Stolton added, "The children are doing a great job keeping the attacking discs from reaching any part of the vehicle. With that protection, the new high-power laser can make quick work of the Iranian warriors and their discs."

"Dr. Carter," said a contemplative General Nunez. "You know I was a huge skeptic of these children and the real might of the Iranian warriors. Even with the new laser and missiles, I see now that we would have had no fighting chance without these twelve. When I watch what they can do and how they handle themselves, I'm ashamed that I doubted them."

"Don't be so hard on yourself," responded the head of the Phoenix Project. "A skeptic plays a key role on any development team. Without one, teams move forward with all abandon and often find themselves at the end with nothing useful. Keeping the team on their toes and checking off every contingency is always the best path to success. Speaking of that, what risks do you see?"

General Nunez answered, "There are two major ones to consider. The first is an attack by a large enough group of warriors to overwhelm the twelve. We estimate it would take on the order of twenty of them attacking together at one time. Even then, their warriors must avoid our lasers during their attack.

Should more than that quantity of Iranian warriors attack our vehicles at one time, we must bring in a large-scale airborne assault to occupy the warriors. This tactic will give the lasers and the Davidsons time to reduce the Iranian advantage. It may likely result in heavy losses of our airborne assets, but it's the only tactic that will nullify their upper hand. We must hope they can't bring hundreds to one location at a time. We'll never be able to neutralize that advantage."

"We can pass that along to Defense Secretary Edgard," said Dr. Carter. "What's the second risk you see?"

"The second major risk is the failure of the lasers. Lasers are temperamental, and we accelerated the laser development and the fusion power source by several years, so, unfortunately, we have no information on their reliability. The laser team has invested numerous hours into the design and installed several redundant elements to increase its reliability. The redundancy makes me more confident it can handle the stress of deployment."

"The backups we've added should something fail significantly reduces the probability of failure by my calculations," added Dr. Stolton.

"I've looked over your designs of the lasers," said Dr. Carter. "I think you've done an excellent job minimizing the failure risks. Thanks for the update."

Looking at Al and Beatrice working off to his side, Dr. Carter said, "I'm going to chat with those two."

The siblings were on the far side of the test range, trying different formations and tactics. As Dr. Carter approached, they saw him and anticipated he was coming to see them. They recalled their discs back into their pyramid stacks just as he arrived.

"Hello, you two," he said as he neared. "Looks like you are making a heck of a team. Any breakthroughs you would like to share?"

Beatrice said, "No, nothing significant. We're working on our timing, with Al leading a hard strike to overpower their warriors and me coming in behind to penetrate their defenses and close the attack.

"We anticipate it'll take some time for the Iranian warriors to realize we have different capabilities. I plan to keep my discs grouped in sets of two hundred, so they don't realize I can control more. Likewise, it will be impossible for them to understand that Al has much greater power than them, so we continue to strategize how to use it best. We hope our superior capabilities can be used in tandem with great tactics to surprise our foes."

Al added, "We seek a delicate balance between my force and Beatrice's large flock attack. Communication between each other is proving critical. Most teams find that out at some point, but we're new at this."

"Spectacular," Dr. Carter responded with a grin. "Seems like General Nunez, Dr. Stolton, and Kerwin are quite happy with the results of the exercises."

"Even General Nunez," said Beatrice. "Never would've believed that."

Even under the current pressures, they couldn't help but smile, and Al said, "Now that General Nunez has come around, I see Zeke is constantly pestering him. Thad told me that Zeke asked the General to develop new tactics that use his tornados. General Nunez told him the only tactic they've found useful is to suck up the smoke for the laser, which made Zeke quite unhappy."

"That one will probably find something useful for his tornado," said Dr. Carter. "General Nunez probably wishes he kept his grumpy demeanor with the young man a little longer."

Dr. Carter wished them well in their practice and headed back inside. He was happy to see the progress and dedication of the teams. Things were congealing, and preparation was on track to deploy when the President needed them.

Peter and Heidi Davidson were coming out just as he was at the door.

"Hello to both of you," said Dr. Carter. "Coming out to see the exercises?"

"Actually, we were looking for you," said Peter. "We wondered if we could travel aboard the aircraft carrier when the children deploy?"

"I'm sorry, but I don't think that is possible," he responded glumly. "General Nunez says only personnel critical to the operation will be on board. He also said they are struggling to get aboard everything they need to support the attack due to the large size of the six platforms."

"We're struggling with the decision to use the kids, as you might imagine," said Heidi, holding back tears. "It's important that we go the last leg with them before this all begins. We're just two people and won't take up much space. Our service to this program should account for some special consideration."

He knew what they said was true, but he had to make them understand that the mission took precedence. Besides that, he didn't think it would be healthy for the children's psyches.

Dr. Carter said, "You have been invaluable to this project, but this crew and this carrier have an important mission. Maybe the most important in U.S. history. We don't belong in the middle of that mission, and I'm afraid your presence may create an emotional conflict for the children if things go awry."

Peter nodded and said, "We expected that answer, but we felt it necessary to ask. Would you still please ask the Defense Secretary?"

"I'll gladly do that, but please don't get your hopes up," he said as he turned and entered the door.

The next few weeks went quickly as the teams continued refining tactics and improving more subtle aspects of the vehicle and weapons operations.

General Nunez came up with the idea that resonated with the Phoenix Project team but made ten Davidson children cringe. He proposed the five laser vehicle platforms battle the team of Al and Beatrice.

The general's logic was simple: if the platforms could beat these two, they would have proved their advantage over the Iranians, and everyone would feel better about the deployment. Dr. Carter loved the general's suggestion, and they organized the test.

The Phoenix Project team set up the ground rules and simulated targets so no one would get hurt and the vehicles would avoid damage. They put extensive effort into the test to make it as realistic as possible, including using numerous military personnel armed with conventional weapons, mortars, and other munitions to attack along with the vehicles.

The test team placed targets extended outward from the vehicle to each side to give Al and Beatrice places to attack without risking damaging the platforms. Likewise, those were the locations that the other Davidson children needed to protect.

On the other end of the range, there were two posts set far to the side of Al and Beatrice to give the five platforms simulated targets to attack while Al and Beatrice defended them.

They were ready to begin the exercise with all details finalized and everyone comfortable with its safety. The first team to score a hit would be declared the winner.

Eve huddled the ten children from the vehicles together.

She said in a hushed tone, "Al is too strong for us to work alone; we have to team up to defend against him. I've been watching them practice. Beatrice likes to come behind him and strike where she senses weak spots. If he tries to overpower any of us, we need four of us to band together to counter his strength. We then need five other of us to protect against Beatrice's discs. She'll try to outmaneuver us if we provide small gaps, so watch for her trying to sneak in. That leaves one of us to attack.

So, I suggest Del, Thad, Kai, and I focus on countering Al while Ephrem, Irene, Lacey, Marian, and Gabriel defend against Beatrice sneaking through. That leaves you, Zeke, to attack.

I want you to spin those darn tornados up when we start. Keep them chaotic and wandering toward their targets but don't strike at them. Let the lasers do their work.

Zeke, when I give you the signal, you attack those targets. Everyone got it?"

They could see that Eve had picked up a lot from Beatrice about strategy, but she also picked up her bossiness. None of them minded it too much since they had no better ideas, and her logic was solid. They all nodded and headed to their vehicles.

Al asked Beatrice, "What do you suppose they're up to on the other end of the range?"

Beatrice responded, "Trying to figure out how not to let you overpower them, and then I blow one by them. You handle the shield for both our targets. Spin your discs as fast as possible, and see if we can hold off those lasers. We haven't tested your spin speed against those lasers; it may be fast enough to avoid them popping.

Let's attack together and do it one vehicle at a time. You pick whichever one you like, and I'll follow. Let's give those vehicles a run for their money."

Eve shared her strategy with the five vehicle commanders so they knew how they planned to operate. She wanted the vehicles to go after the downrange targets and let them worry about Al and Beatrice.

The test began, and Al spun his shield discs in front of their two targets. They rotated at a ridiculous speed, far greater than any of the others could, and it caught Dr. Stolton, who was watching from the viewing room, by surprise.

The lasers engaged immediately, and Al's extra rotational speed proved effective against the lasers. Comfortable they were holding, Al and Beatrice went on the attack. Al chose the closest vehicle to attack first, which happened to be Del and Lacey's.

Racing his discs at the vehicle with a crushing attack, Al was surprised when they deflected to each side of the platform, and he missed the targets by a wide margin. Beatrice brought her discs in tight behind Al's, hoping they would be distracted by his attack, but hers were also repelled.

She and Al both cut their eyes and sneered at the other children.

Al commented to his sister, "Beatrice, they're working together against us. Maybe you should veer off at the last minute and go after a second vehicle. See if the element of surprise will work. My shield seems to be holding up, so let's try that."

Beatrice responded, "Ok. Come at them again. I'll act like I'm swooping behind and then split to go after one of the others."

"By the way," she added. "What is Zeke doing with those tornados? Is he playing while the rest of us are working?"

Al shook his head and said, "I think he's just being Zeke."

Eve quickly saw them talking and announced over their communication link, "Watch for Beatrice to try something. She and Al must've figured we're working together, and they probably think we may be vulnerable on the other vehicles. Zeke, keep doing what you're doing and wait for my word."

"Aye, aye, Cap'n. Awaiting further orders on the tornado attack," said Zeke back on the commlink.

"Oh, brother!" could be heard from someone on the commlink.

Eve wasn't sure, but she believed it came from Marian.

Al started his second attack and came in with another ferocious speed. Beatrice kept her discs in hot pursuit just behind his. However, just as Al was about to engage Lacey and Del's vehicle, Beatrice split her discs into two attacks. One set attacked Gabriel and Eve's vehicle to her left, and the other jetted toward Ephrem and Irene's to her right.

Eve's plan worked again. By assigning responsibilities to specific children, each could focus on their role and protect against a surprise move. They easily deflected Al's and Beatrice's discs from their targeted vehicles.

So far, so good on Eve's tactics, but she knew Beatrice would come up with something special for them, so she contained her enthusiasm.

Just as Al and Beatrice started to regroup, Eve opened the comm link to the vehicle team.

"Concentrate all lasers on one spot on one target," she barked.

The lasers moved to the left target, concentrating their energy, and one of Al's discs popped. Then a second one. The laser combination was starting to work.

Let it go a bit longer, thought Lacey. Then I'm sending Zeke in for an attack.

Beatrice recognized their new vulnerability, "Al, send additional discs back to protect against the laser and give us a bit more time. I have an idea.

Attack again, but leave a narrow slot for a single file throng of my discs to come through. They'll think I'm going to branch off again, but as soon as you sense them pushing your discs away, stop all of them in front of the vehicle. Make sure to keep the slot. I'll come through your opening like a machine gun of discs."

"Got it," said Al.

On the other end, Eve got back on the commlink. "They'll try something new, so be ready," she bellowed. "Beatrice is the sneaky one, so pay attention to what she's doing with her discs. Remember, Al is just the muscle, but she's the assassin. Laser team, could you folks hurry up and hit their targets."

Al started the third attack wave, sensing they needed to make this one count as his shield discs were popping at a constant rate and wouldn't hold out too much longer. His discs flew down the test range toward Lacey and Del's vehicle.

Just as the defenders started to push Al's discs away from the platform, Al pulled them to a stop and formed a solid wall with a single slot in the center.

Eve screamed over the commlink, "Now, Zeke. Attack the target the lasers are after and give it everything you have."

She thought she confused them with the tactic, so Beatrice sent her discs through the slot. They looked like machine-gun fire coming out the side of Al's armored wall.

Unfortunately for Beatrice, the Ephrem, Irene, Lacey, and Gabriel team were ready for it and began pushing her rapid-fire of discs away from the vehicle.

Zeke, on the other end, went in guns-a-blazing. His tornados swept in on Al's shield and battered them while the lasers continued to blast the shield's center apart.

Just as the last of Beatrice's discs came through Al's slot, the laser broke through the shield and scored its first target hit. If they could hit the second target, the vehicle teams would win.

Al and Beatrice were stunned and tried to regroup for another attack. They knew the lasers would shift to the second target, and Zeke would be helping them, but they knew they had a bit of time before the shield would fail.

As they pulled their discs back to launch another attack, Eve barked into the commlink again, "Everyone, and I mean everyone. Combine your forces to pull Al's shield discs away. Overpower him. Even he and Beatrice aren't more powerful than the ten of us. Do it NOW!"

Al's discs migrated from their location in front of the target the second time she said it, and the lasers blasted the second target.

Zeke let out a primal howl to celebrate the moment. It surprised everyone. Proud of their accomplishment, Eve jumped in and started howling with him. Within seconds, ten of them were howling like a wolf pack.

On the other end, Al and Beatrice shrugged their shoulders at each other and joined the other ten howling to celebrate the accomplishment of the entire Phoenix Project.

After a few minutes of delightful revelry, the vehicle teams stopped near the viewing room and exited their vehicles to resounding cheers from the Phoenix team members.

The scientists were equally ecstatic to see their results performing flawlessly and came out to greet the platform teams.

While unhappy with losing, Al and Beatrice took comfort in knowing the children's participation was a difference-maker. They felt for the first time that they were ready for what they were about to do.

Dr. Carter came out last with the Davidson parents. They went to the twelve children, who were actively discussing what had happened during the test.

As they approached, Dr. Carter hollered out, "Well done. It seems our solution proved effective against some fierce competition."

The project leader turned to Al and Beatrice and smiled at them both.

"We should all feel a lot better about what transpired," he said to them.

Turning to the entire group, he loudly said, "Let's get our teams to look over the five vehicles and ensure everything checks out. I suggest we continue these drills daily until you deploy. I guess it's just a few weeks away, but continuing to train is in everyone's best interest. Any questions?"

Everyone seemed content and comfortable with his training mandate.

Dr. Carter headed over to talk with Dr. Stolton and Kerwin. The two were discussing something while looking over a vehicle.

The Davidson parents quickly joined the kids in discussing how the exercise played out. Both were impressed that each side developed strategies and tactics to combat the other. They recognized how focused they had become on the task before them. It still tugged at their hearts that these games could become life-and-death decisions of war at any moment.

Chapter 18

Fortitude Against All Odds

The Israeli evacuation received limited participation at the halfway point. Many American and European Jews were lobbying for the U.S. and European countries to join Israel in defending against the expulsion by Iran.

Unfortunately for Israel, all countries made it clear they would not participate in the fight against Iran. This stance was met with anger by numerous influential Jews pushing politicians and businesses to act. However, no country's leadership caved to the pressures under fear of Iranian retribution. Israel, it believed, was on its own.

Even though they were not yet fighting a war, Russia's efforts to retake the former Soviet republics consumed Europe. They feared this was the first step in Russia's plans to take the whole continent, so they had little interest in diverting resources toward helping Israel.

Unknown to Israel or the rest of the world, the U.S. pursued the President's plan for a sneak attack. Many Congressional leaders pushed the President to join the former Soviet states against Russia and help defend Israel.

The President used the terrible loss in Iraq to justify his lack of action in Europe and Israel. His position struck many leaders and pundits worldwide as weak-minded and overly self-protective. The President cared little about the negative chatter surrounding the U.S.'s lack of action. It played right into his scheme, as he hoped to leave no person or country the wiser about his attack.

He did not plan to ask Congress to vote on the attack this time. The prior approval to go to war in Iraq gave him the latitude to engage. He would brief them after it occurred. He knew that any discussion with Congress created a considerable risk to the secrecy of the effort.

Not approaching Congress was a political risk. Should the attack fail, it would result in his political demise. He was playing for success alone, and secrecy was a critical element.

The President scheduled a Cabinet-level meeting with his national security team. He wanted to discuss the final deployment details and the nation's many issues.

The economy was in shambles, businesses were going under, inflation had skyrocketed, and unemployment was rapidly growing. The stock market was in the toilet and showed no signs of rebounding, while the deep recession was nearing depression.

Even without any further military action since Iraq, Iran's grip on the U.S. grew as they exerted global influence to strangle the nation economically and politically. He recognized that years of U.S. sanctions on Iran were getting fed back to the country in spades. The U.S. was currently unable to combat any of it.

For Americans, this was a painful diversion from the norm. Most people in the U.S. had spent their entire lives living with few inconveniences, and most were struggling to accept the current reality.

Different pockets of the population formed various alliances. Some wanted military retribution, some cowered in fear and could not function in the new reality, and others thought we should apologize for past indiscretions and offer peace. The largest segment thought it was time for the U.S. to pull inward, close itself off, learn to operate in a self-contained manner, and forego international participation.

President Schmidt recognized that these were all driven by fear, but none resulted in sustainable peace for the world. The U.S. had to restore military balance before all hope was lost, and it was too late.

Entering his scheduled meeting, the President, attempting to ease the tension he felt as he walked in, said with a kind grin, “Good day, everyone.”

His disposition caught the group off guard. The President could tell they expected a somber discussion, but he was energized to strike back at Iran.

The President continued, “We all have a lot on our collective plates. Troubles appear around every corner, but we now have a path to pushing Iran back from its reprehensible scheme. I believe it’s an opportunity to restore global peace. It won’t come quickly, and it won’t come easily, but it will come.

Now, to the meeting’s topic, let’s discuss our planned attack. So far, our humanitarian efforts are proceeding without raising suspicions in Iran. That’s a huge checkmark.

Israel’s unwillingness to this point helps us maintain the narrative of a late mass exodus. While it helps our attack strategy to require significant evacuation efforts as the deadline nears, Israel has yet to evacuate the number of women and children we had hoped they would.

I’m concerned that their delay will result in a humanitarian catastrophe. I realize we can’t make the choices for their people, but we must encourage their leaders to make the right choices. Jack, any word from your sources in Israel?”

The Secretary of State responded, "Yes, Mr. President, our sources tell us they refuse to call it an exodus. Israel refers to those leaving as short-term evacuees while defending the country in a Great Holy War.

My people on the ground there tell me they are organizing the transport of a large contingent of children and elderly. We should expect, they say, greater use of our resources over the next few weeks. Our team keeps telling them they can't wait until the last minute for fear of the inability to move the desired quantities before the deadline. Many Israeli women are planning to stay and fight alongside their men. The evacuation focus is more on the elderly and children. They are a brave bunch, as you know."

The President acknowledged the comment with a head shake and said, "The fortitude of these people is beyond measure. I'm gravely worried that Iran will quickly slaughter large numbers of Israelis when they attack, just like elsewhere. I hope to get Prime Minister Yaakv to share details about his plans."

President Schmidt feared that the bravery of the Israeli people was so powerful that it would lead them to stay in such large numbers. He knew Iran was not merciful on any nation's resistance forces, but he feared Israel might receive even worse treatment.

"Back to our plans," the President said, "We need to get the Phoenix Project vehicles to the USS Ford in Norfolk. Cassandra, are they ready to move out?"

"Ready and prepared to go within three days from your signal," responded the Defense Secretary. "The three days should give us plenty of time to make the trek on several predetermined routes that can support the vehicle's size and not raise suspicions about what we're doing. We'll continue to train up to the last moment.

As for the travel to Norfolk, each trailer will go on one of four paths with civilian wide-load markings operated by U.S. special forces. Our trailers traveling along the same routes will be staggered to mitigate any hiccups before the next platform reaches the same point. Their size and weight make the transport difficult as we'll encounter numerous bridges and overpasses.

The Phoenix Project has designed a trailer with a large, partially exposed boat at its front. The laser vehicle will be on the trailer's back part, concealed under a protective tarp. While being transported, the trailer will give the impression that it's a set of large boats. Its disguise is quite ingenious and compelling.

The USS Ford is in Norfolk, and its crew will be briefed on their orders upon your go-ahead. The Commanding Officer will keep the crew shipboard once they've been briefed, so there's no chance of blown secrecy.

Admiral Lawton, General Nunez, Dr. Carter, and I have all agreed that details of D12 will be held in secrecy until just before they board. We have strict protocols about the children staying below deck once on board to avoid any possibility of satellite or any other surveillance picking up their presence. We plan to let them have free reign below deck. Let us know when you want us to roll on everything, and we'll put it all in motion."

"Excellent," said the President. "We can't afford any slip-ups. Please make sure each delivery is well-resourced, and they are all there when we need them. I expect that we'll move out in a few weeks.

As for the Davidsons, I suggest you let them demonstrate their abilities to the crew. Seeing is much more effective at understanding than hearing about it. Under no circumstances are details of Project Cranio-Genesis, including how D12 and the Iranian warriors came into being, to be revealed to anyone. Am I understood?"

The Defense Secretary replied, "Understood. Once you give the go-ahead, D12 and the rest of the vehicle crews will fly to Norfolk and await the arrival of the vehicles.

Just a few more details. Once the platforms arrive, we'll load them aboard the USS Ford and keep them below deck until we reach our attack location. In addition to the Davidsons, we'll keep most of the crew below deck for the trip to give the impression of using the carrier solely for evacuation support.

We have designed some top-deck shelter structures to support those appearances further. They are easily removed once the attack begins, and we need to move the vehicles and aircraft top side. The other ships that deploy in the carrier group will be minimized not to raise suspicions, but they will still carry numerous lethal capabilities. Also, we'll have a contingent of submarines following along if the Russians or Chinese are up to any antics."

President Schmidt liked the laydown. It would not appear unusual given the evacuation activities and the stealthiness of the delivery was well thought out.

"Once we begin, I want our other forces immediately brought to DEFCON 2," said the President. "We can then resource the fight with Iran quickly. There will be no looking back at that point. Also, I want the Phoenix Project to begin the production of as many of these platforms as possible. We should have them available throughout our military ASAP. I'm sure Dr. Carter thought his job was over, but I know he will understand.

Final note. I want to make it clear to Israel and any other nation that we plan to be the last ship set coming in for the evacuation. We can't afford any last-minute glitches to derail this effort. When I talk with Prime Minister Yaakv, I'll emphasize this without overplaying it and tipping our hands. I also plan to share detailed intelligence with him on the Iranian warriors. Not specifically about the Cranio-Genesis or the Phoenix Project, but enough to make him understand what they're up against when Iran attacks. He may not listen to me, but I'll try."

The Vice President nodded and said, "Absolutely, Mr. President, but you know they are determined to defend their homeland at all costs. Their determination to defend the homeland at all costs raises another question: how will we handle this group that calls themselves the Alamo Volunteers of Texas?

They want to deploy two thousand people, mostly Texans, to Israel to help fight. Israel has already said they are willing to take anyone willing to participate. The group is asking for military transports to take them so they can bring large caches of weapons with them."

"I admire their convictions," said President Schmidt. "We don't have a legal right to stop them, but I also don't want to encourage their participation, so we won't use our military transports to take them. Commercial transportation is acceptable, but they must make legal arrangements for weapons transport to Israel.

I think the actions of Russia and Iran have the whole world on edge, and many people are itching to fight. There will be plenty of time for that, so carefully choose your words in public so we diffuse tensions, not raise them. That's what good leadership does. We don't need to help ignite the powder keg of some anxious Americans."

Excited people were often spun into a frenzy resulting in stupid decisions by leaders feeding the beast. The President knew the nation's pent-up tension could explode into a disaster with a key leader's poor choice of words. He wished to avoid that.

The President wanted to clarify a critical point of his post-attack plan concerning the U.S.'s key allies. He expected that many of his team wondered when he would reveal Cranio-Genesis.

He said, "Once we launch our attack, I plan to brief many of our key allies on the basics of the Cranio-Genesis Project and the origin of the Iranian warriors. I expect significant resentment from several of them for not sharing this long ago. I'll own that. If it had leaked, Iran would have attacked us long ago to keep their secret intact. We couldn't risk that."

The Secretary of State furrowed his brow with concern and said, "Mr. President, I must have missed something in the prior meetings. You imply Iran doesn't know about the Davidson children."

The President, realizing that the topic had never been raised openly to his team, said, "Jack, I'm sorry that you were not aware of this, and I now see that we never briefed most of you on this. As it turns out, as a part of the Cranio-Genesis closeout and the decision to hide away the children, the Air Force annotated that all subjects were terminated.

We've verified that the Iranian files contained the closeout documentation, so they believe the children no longer exist. The attack on their home by Russian special forces confirmed that.

It's another element of surprise that we'll have over them in the attack."

Seeing the group pondering this news and no responses emerging, the Defense Secretary said, "Our European allies insist on sending their naval ships to support our efforts with the evacuations. We may not stop them from getting in the middle of our attack. How do you want us to handle that?"

Having already considered this, the President said, "Cassandra, I'm glad you raised that. Please inform our allies, twenty-four hours before our attack, that Iran has asked us to space out our naval support because they are uncomfortable with the concentration of military assets. Be emphatic that our carrier group will handle the last push. I'll make calls if necessary to ensure they let us do this."

Once the President finished, the Defense Secretary added, "We're using a rotation of two commercial cruise ships outfitted with navy personnel for the evacuation. They're dressed in civilian clothes and appear to be humanitarian workers. We'll rotate different carriers into the mix, so it won't raise suspicions when the Ford arrives on the last mission.

On the last group, as they're exiting Israel, we'll have the USS Ford and the rest of the carrier group break away and head full speed toward Lebanon. We won't initiate the attack until Iran goes into Israel. But once we begin our attack in Lebanon, we'll head east through Syria, then into Iraq, and ultimately into Iran, at least Iran as we knew it before their great expansion.

In Lebanon, we'll press the offensive, but we won't allow ourselves to be ambushed by a massive contingent of Iranian warriors. We need to execute our march with patience and diligence. As we clear with our laser vehicles, we'll use our conventional military force to fight their conventional forces and push their military eastward. With only six vehicles, things will progress slowly. We're now calling the effort: Operation Restoring Liberty."

The President was pleased to see the plans coming together. The next few weeks, he knew, would feel like an eternity.

"It's my pleasure to work with you," he sincerely stated. "I appreciate the hard work and dedication you have shown through one of, if not the most, trying times in this nation. Please pass my thanks to your numerous people working in the trenches. Tell them that while we live in dark times today, we'll persevere through this and that the best of this great country lies before us."

The Defense Secretary had one more concern to throw on the table.

She looked to the President and said, "Once we push back Iran into Iraq, would you consider using submarine-launched Trident missiles? We feel that over such a short distance from the coast of Lebanon, even their warriors will struggle to intercept the missile without it inflicting significant damage to them."

The President eyed her intently. He wasn't sure whether she was probing as a primary tactic or a just-in-case possibility. It didn't matter in his mind. Allies would find it difficult to support the U.S. should it happen. Many nations with leanings toward Iran would band together further. The big loser in that approach would be the United States.

He curtly responded, "Cassandra, I'm sure that has surfaced numerous times in your discussion of tactics. However, I stand firm, as I conveyed from the beginning. There will be no nuclear weapons used regardless of their perceived effectiveness."

Realizing she had delved into a touchy item, she responded ruefully, "Understood. I wasn't challenging your prior decision. I felt it important to understand our boundaries once this all begins."

The Director of National Intelligence sensed an opportunity to shift topics as dead silence choked the room.

She said, "If I may shift topics, Mr. President, can I speak on the war in Europe?"

"Margaret, this is an excellent time to move on," said the President, grinning since he knew that while her question was important, she was trying to ease the group's discomfort at the exchange.

"We have been monitoring the activities in Eastern Europe and the war with Russia," she began. "The Russians are making progress seizing cities that were more or less relegated to them. They are cutting utilities and communications as they move in to hold the people in a siege-like manner.

They are, of course, broadcasting grand claims of increasing control and battle successes. However, the factual situation is that they are making some progress, but the resistance forces expected these techniques and thus far are not discouraged by the actions.

Russia's control of the cities has allowed them to move resources more efficiently by controlling the airports and major highway arteries into the countries. The resistance forces are still doing their best to hold off the Russian troops, but the Russians are progressing westward. We expect the Russians to march into Poland, the Czech Republic, Slovakia, and Romania by next month.

If we succeed with the initial attack against Iran, it may encourage the rest of Europe to join the war against Russia. Europe should be motivated as they watch Kovalyov brutalize the resistance fighters and broadcast it across Europe, just as Iran has done elsewhere. Kovalyov seems less focused on preserving the integrity of the countries he invades and more on punishing the people for fighting against him."

"Kovalyov will make his point loud and clear for all to see," said the President with a look of concern. "His confidence, I hope, will be his downfall. He cares little for reunification. It was simply an excuse to invade, and he cares only for his grandeur.

The former Soviet Republics have put up one hell of a fight and given us the needed time. We owe them much for their courage and bravery. I know it will be different in Israel against the Iranian warriors, but I hope Israel has watched and learned a few tricks from the European resistance forces. I wish we had more to offer our European friends, but they will have to stand up and fight for themselves while we carry on the attack against Iran with Israel."

Now the Defense Secretary was the one with the concerned look. She was thinking about the U.S. having a vulnerable flank from the East.

She said, "Mr. President, we'll leave ourselves vulnerable in the Pacific when we attack Iran. If China has similar aspirations to the other two, we could quickly see the region fold. Then, they could come at us where we'll be exposed."

"I understand your concern, and it's well-founded," he responded, looking ponderously at the ceiling. "That is why I have asked the Vice President to travel to China. He leaves next week. We have kept it low profile and out of the press.

Thankfully, China has agreed to meet and keep this under the radar. I was encouraged by that and hoped we could establish some sense of their intentions."

"Mr. President, we have been working with our Chinese diplomats and our other allies in the region," said the Secretary of State. "All of them say China displays no indication of any vile plans. China could be playing them into a false sense of comfort, but even Taiwan seems to think nothing is happening."

Concluding the meeting with his final thoughts, the President said, "Right now, we take them at face value, but I want a lot of eyes on their activities. I want to hear about anything that seems out of sorts. Also, once we attack, if there is any indication they are moving to aid Iran with military forces, we may need to engage them. If China joins Russia and Iran after we attack, World War II could look like a scuffle. Let's engage them diplomatically and be ready if their posture changes."

Chapter 19

Final Preparations and Farewells

The test facility of the Phoenix Project was abuzz with final preparations for the trek to Norfolk. The Davidson children had completed numerous training exercises, with Alan and Beatrice battling the five laser platforms loaded with their siblings. While Al and Beatrice had learned a few tricks along the way, the vehicle teams were honing their skills and becoming more effective at defeating the two of them. Al and Beatrice never defeated the laser platforms.

Over the last few days, Dr. Carter switched things up and rotated Al and Beatrice into the mix. He put them in their command vehicle and had four other laser vehicles working with them. Dr. Carter chose Zeke and Marian to swap into Al and Beatrice's former roles.

With Al and Beatrice on their side, the platforms made swift strikes on the target against the highly overmatched Zeke and Marian.

Even with the quick defeats, General Nunez insisted that the platforms train this way. He told them they were still learning how to communicate with one another and coordinate their attacks with Al and Beatrice's command vehicle. General Nunez informed them that they would fall back on their training in the heat of the battle, as all soldiers tend to do.

Another benefit that General Nunez didn't mention was that the practice boosted the morale of his non-telekinetic crew members as they saw their kill rate improve immensely with Al and Beatrice on their team.

Dr. Carter planned a farewell dinner for the platform teams and Phoenix Project members. He had a special surprise for D12 during the dinner that he hoped would be well accepted by the twelve.

Over the past month, he recognized a weakness he chose to rectify. His idea and design were made possible by the Phoenix Project. He loved the resulting output and was excited to unveil it. It made him feel better about using these children to fight a war.

Dinner that night was attended by the entire project team. Dr. Carter set tables at the front for all the crews from the six platforms. He had a special table built to suit the demands of the twelve giant Davidsons and placed it front and center.

Once everyone was assembled, Dr. Carter went to the makeshift podium and opened the evening with, "My words won't effectively communicate the gratitude I have for all of you and the huge sacrifices you have made to work, day and night, on this important project."

"Your efforts have moved forward years of technology development and created an unequivocal response to the Iranian warriors, thus, completing the task President Schmidt asked of us all."

"The deployment of these men, women, and children sitting behind me was only made possible by the work of this team. We will send these six teams off to fight an enemy that destroyed more than sixty-four thousand American troops. Since then, this enemy has seized control of one billion more people worldwide while killing millions. Tomorrow, we send twelve of our telekinetic children and these men and women in vehicles you developed to fight this fearsome enemy."

The seated team members rose to applaud the laser teams sitting behind him.

Dr. Carter then called out each name on the platform teams. The Phoenix Project team members stood throughout, clapping for each of them. It was a heartwarming display that meant a lot to the deploying forces and General Nunez, who understood what these men and women would soon face.

Dr. Carter saved the last group of introductions for D12. As he called each one and they stood up, the applause roared. Each child beamed at the display.

After the final child was called, Dr. Carter asked everyone to be seated. He then motioned to his side.

Two men rolled a sizeable container beside him. He gestured quickly to the men, and they opened the container.

Dr. Carter smiled as he watched the crowd. Everyone watched in anticipation, not knowing what he was revealing.

As the sides came down, everyone caught sight of an enormous mannequin the size of one of the Davidson children. Like something out of an Iron Man movie, an armor suit covered the figure.

Dr. Carter saw the excitement on the faces of the twelve children.

He grinned and told the group, "This is the last of our platform protection system. The only people exposed outside the vehicle armor are the twelve unprotected children sitting up in their domes."

"I wasn't comfortable with that situation, so I developed a suit to protect them better. I knew the twelve children could handle wearing armor suits on their bodies because of their sheer strength. Therefore, I developed a variant of the armor plating used on the vehicles to make them each a flexible protection suit.

They're constructed from the same nano-fiber armor and tungsten carbide outer shell covering the vehicles. The small tiles which comprise the suit are interlinked in a tight mesh-like old chainmail armor. However, this suit's interconnect linkage is tighter, providing greater strength yet not compromising maneuverability. These suits exceeded my expectations and are a marvel in their own right."

"Please come down and take a look if you like. I made each suit custom fit the dimensions we took off each of you when you came aboard the Phoenix Project. You can try them out after dinner if you like. I'm having them shipped on the plane with us tomorrow night."

The twelve children and most of the Phoenix Project team rose to look at the suits. No one was up faster and to the armor than Zeke.

Upon reaching the suit, Zeke quickly turned to Dr. Carter and said, "Would it be possible for my suit to have a triple tornado emblem printed on the front? I could make up a design tonight and get it to you."

Before Dr. Carter could respond, Eve blurted out, "Zeke, we already saw you working on a design two weeks ago on the computer. Don't act like this was a fresh idea. Even without the suit, I'm sure you planned to put that design on your vehicle somewhere."

"Listen, Eve, that ain't my thang!" he retorted, mocking her with a facetious southern drawl. "I wouldn't put it on our vehicle because the vehicle isn't just mine. It's our whole team's. The triple tornado is all me."

Eve scoffed at him, and Marian chimed in, "Bull-you-know-what! Don't let him kid any of you. He asked if he could put it on our vehicle, and I emphatically told him that it would be over my dead body."

Marian looked over at Zeke and stared him down.

He ignored her cutting glare and Eve's snide comment and said, "Dr. Carter gave me a better place to put it, so that's where it's going."

He realized Dr. Carter hadn't approved the last part, so he stopped there.

General Nunez stepped in, "Troops, enough of the squabbling. I won't have that amongst my team. Your communication and coordination are paramount to this team's success. Maintain your focus on the tasks at hand."

Zeke knew better than to utter a word after the chiding by the General.

General Nunez smiled slightly at Zeke, knowing that Zeke wanted to add some more trash talk.

The General said, "Zeke, about your original request, we encourage our pilots and military personnel to personalize their aircraft, vehicles, helmets, et cetera. So as long as you can get me your desired logos within the next 24 hours, I'll expedite every one of them."

Dr. Carter appreciated General Nunez's gesture since he wasn't sure how to answer the young man or the approved protocol for Zeke's request.

The team continued touching and marveling at the suits Dr. Carter designed. A surge of pride flowed through him as they oohed and aahed at what he'd done.

A tap on his back shoulder startled him. He quickly turned around to find Peter and Heidi Davidson standing there.

Heidi Davidson reached out and grabbed Dr. Carter into an appreciative embrace. She squeezed him with such vigor that he had to gasp a bit for air.

"Thank you from the bottom of our hearts," she said, fighting back the tears. "This means so much to the both of us that you would do this for them. Putting their safety first. We're a bit ashamed that we didn't think of it."

"You two have had a lot on your minds," said Dr. Carter. "I'm glad that I was able to make it happen. It makes me feel better about what we ask them to do. I know it has to be the same for you two. I only wish there was more we could do."

Peter Davidson said, "You've done more than you can imagine. Since joining this project, our kids have grown so much, and you've had much to do with that. The way you welcomed them and brought them onto the team. Thank you very much for all that you've done for us."

"You're very welcome. How about we get this dinner rolling so everyone can get a good night's sleep because we have another big day tomorrow."

"Sounds like a great idea," said Peter, who had missed lunch and was starving.

"Can I have everyone's attention?" shouted Dr. Carter, waving his hands to signal that he needed quiet. "I want everyone to return to their seat to get this dinner underway. Remember, we have a big day tomorrow. General Nunez hosts General Jenkins,

Admiral Lawton, and the Defense Secretary for tomorrow's final briefing on the deployment plans. We'll begin promptly at zero-seven-thirty. I want everyone to get to bed at a reasonable time, which means we have to get this dinner over."

Everyone returned to their seats and enjoyed a delicious Italian pasta and chicken parmigiana dinner. All welcomed the camaraderie and the break from the intense action of the last several months of activity.

D12 was itching to try their new suits and were excited about the upcoming deployment. They hoped the dinner would move along quickly.

With the dinner progressing slowly and much of the group seemingly engaged in endless conversations, Beatrice stood and headed to the table with Dr. Carter and her parents.

"Would it be okay if we left and tried on our new suits?" she asked. "We're anxious to see how they feel and how well we can move in them."

"I have no problem with you doing that," said Dr. Carter realizing the long dinner conversations held D12 back.

Looking at the parents, he said, "If, of course, the two of you are okay with it?"

"I think it's time we start allowing them to make their own decisions," said Heidi Davidson, looking up at Beatrice. "We need to treat them like adults given what they are about to embark on."

Beatrice smiled at the remark. It was liberating for the twelve of them to experience the freedom to operate independently and make their determinations on their own. The twelve of them were not too different from any child who leaves the comforts of home for the first time, a hefty dose of enjoying the freedom mixed in with a bit of apprehension.

"We're off then, and Dr. Carter, we'll let you know what we think of your invention in the morning," she said with a wink to the project leader.

She hustled over to the other children. They read her look to say that she had received approval. The group rose in unison from the table and headed inside.

Dr. Carter rose quickly and approached the children with one of the men who brought in the mannequin version of the armor.

Dr. Carter said, "He will show you where your suits are stored. They are marked with your names, so there's no guesswork."

The line of children excitedly followed the man, eager to get hold of their armor. The man handed their suits to them one by one, and they headed back to their rooms to try them on. They were amazed at how heavy each suit was as they carried it through the corridor. Even with their size and strength, the children found the tungsten carbide armor a bit of a load.

They were about to head to their rooms when Al said, "Let's meet back here when we get them on and discuss what we each think of them."

"Good idea," said Zeke. "We can decide where our logos go."

"On your butt is where yours needs to be," said Marian. "It's what you seem to show the most."

"Knock it off," snapped Beatrice. "General Nunez wasn't kidding about what he said. All joking is over. We're headed off to our first outside exposure to the world: to fight a war. I want us to shape up from this time forward. We must have each other's back and stop the childish behavior."

"Sorry, Beatrice," said Marian. "Zeke always has a special way of getting under our skin, but you're right. On our best behavior going forward. I promise!"

Al thrust his hand forward to get the team to stack them on top of each other in a sign of unity. Enthusiastically, they all joined in.

Beatrice capped the stack and yelled, "All for one."

"And one for all," erupted from the group as they lifted their hands in unison.

"We're kinda like the Avengers," said Lacey.

"Uh, no," said Beatrice. "We're the Davidsons, D12, and let's not forget the humility that mom and dad instilled in us."

Zeke started to respond, "I sure like the sound of …."

"Don't even go there, Zeke," interrupted Al. "You won't like the outcome."

"Let's get changed and get back here," Beatrice said.

They hurried into their rooms and began to put on the armor. They were amazed at how intricate the design was and how amazingly comfortable they felt. The outside was a smooth polished metal, and the tungsten carbide created a shiny glimmer as they moved around.

While heavy, the distributed weight on their powerful frames was no hindrance. They could move and flex in any direction with more or less unlimited freedom. It was hard not to feel like a superhero in the suit, but all were afraid to mention it again and catch Beatrice's ire.

They hurried back into the corridor to look at each other in the nifty suits and share their impressions. Eve commented how they looked so sleek and impressive. Zeke said he felt fierce and indestructible. Al slammed down on the shoulders of Ephrem's suit, to which Ephrem responded that he barely felt it. Dr. Carter had outdone himself was the overall impression.

Hearing Zeke's comment about being indestructible, Beatrice felt a tinge of fear for what they were about to take on. To date, she knew, the battles had been fun and games. Starting tomorrow, they were soldiers. She wondered whether they were ready for this task. She kept her thoughts to herself and rationalized that the best thing she could do was concentrate on leading them.

"Everyone! Hello! Stop for a second!" Beatrice barked. "The uniforms are awesome! Everyone looks fantastic and feels great, but we have other work to finish. General Nunez offered to allow each of us to personalize our vehicles and our suits."

"We need to generate logos. I suggest placing the reversed American Flag on our right shoulder like American soldiers and our personal logo design on the left."

"I also suggest we wear name tags as the Greek letters that our names originated from and not our true names: Alpha-Alan, Beta-Beatrice, Gamma-Gabriel, Delta-Del, Epsilon-Ephrem, Zeta-Zeke, Eta-Eve, Theta-Thad, Iota-Irene, Kappa-Kai, Lambda-Lacey, and last but not least Mu-Marian. I think it fits nicely with these uniforms, and there is no attachment to our real names in case we get captured."

Beatrice realized she should have left the last part out. She didn't want the group to think too deeply about the horrors they may face.

"So, if everyone agrees, I'll pass it along to Dr. Carter and General Nunez in the morning," she added, figuring it best to move on quickly.

Zeke, always the first to respond to just about anything, said, "Fine by me. At least they'll know I'm not just a number. Ha-ha! Get it? I'm really a Greek letter."

He didn't need to look up since he knew that Beatrice held a sharp, piercing glare at him. They all let it drop and offered their agreement.

"Then let's get working on our logos," Beatrice said. "One last suggestion, let's work with our respective teams to develop the platform names and logos. Reach out to them and find what they would like, and we can roll them into our file for Dr. Carter."

Everyone loved that idea and headed to their rooms to work on their logos.

As they were walking back, Zeke shouted, "If anyone needs help on theirs, I'm pretty much done with mine, and I'm very good at it. So, just ask me."

Marian, avoiding a smart-remark reply and another counseling session from Beatrice, said, "For maybe the first time, what he says is true. He's actually quite good at it and will probably be a big help!"

Zeke was somewhat floored by her friendly, if maybe a bit backhanded, comment and kept his mouth shut for once.

Maybe they were all growing up, thought Beatrice, until Zeke said, "Of course, no one can use anything associated with a tornado in their design. That's been trademarked. Well, I have at least researched how I could trademark it."

"Oh, brother," said Thad. "Thank you, Marian, for having him in your vehicle and taking one for the team."

"What piece of what I said before did you people miss?" yelled Beatrice. "We go to war tomorrow. We've barely been outside our backyard until we came here, and tomorrow, we're heading to fight an enemy who's killed millions. We need to shape up before we leave and quit spending calories being immature children. Get it together. NOW!"

Al intervened, "Beatrice, chill out. Blowing off a little steam and being excited about a few things like these ultra-cool suits isn't a problem. We understand what we're facing, and each of us deals with it in our own way. So, ease up. When it comes to brass tacks, every single one of us will be ready. Including Zeke!"

He peered over at Zeke and gave him an assured nod.

"Alright, but we must stop the chatter and act as a team. I want us to behave like we know what we're doing. More importantly, I want us to know what we're doing."

"We got it, Beatrice," said Eve. "Let's work on our logos, and please, no one mention or use the flippin' tornado in theirs."

They all proceeded to work on their logos. Each of them, including Beatrice, was excited about the prospect of personalizing their uniform. While they were excited about their logos, they were also interested in seeing what the others created.

Just as they began to head out, their parents walked in. They were stunned by the impressive, armored suits the children bore. All of them looked much older and were an eerily intimidating sight. Looking at each other in disbelief, Peter shrugged as if to say, who knew?

"Wow," said the dad. "Quite the crew here. Iran doesn't know what's coming their way."

"Peter, you are doing it again," Heidi said. "Don't encourage them. We want them to be cautious and protective of one another."

"We're ready," said Beatrice. "Aren't these suits impressive? We love them, and they conform to us so well. It also allows us to maneuver easily. We're just about to head off to work on our logos and get some sleep."

"Good idea," said their dad. "By the way, the suits are impressive in their own right, but you twelve donning them is quite the sight."

"You have a busy day tomorrow with General Jenkins. He will be the commander of your mission and oversee the operation once it begins in Lebanon. General Nunez speaks highly of him."

"All of you get some sleep," said their mother. "The logos needn't take too much time."

They each worked a few hours and then got some sleep. Planning briefs the next day would be demanding. Most of them uneasily slept as Beatrice's admonishment about the seriousness of what may come next began to creep into their thoughts.

The children reviewed each other's logos early the following day at breakfast.

Al started and showed a picture he identified as Thor's hammer fighting off a stream of discs. Fitting for him, they thought.

Beatrice selected an eagle with strong talons reaching to snare its prey. Her depiction was a true reflection of her spirit, they concluded.

Gabriel picked a lion in the midst of a fierce roar.

Del selected crossed sabers which he told the group represented his commitment to defend his vehicle.

Ephrem laughed when Del showed his.

"Mine's a shield for the very same reason. Great minds think alike," Ephrem said as he high-fived Del.

Zeke's was an elaborate design with three tornados drawn with beautiful detailing. The three cyclones swirled across the ground, sucking objects into their vortexes. Now, none of them doubted Marian's comment from the night before. His was truly impressive.

Eve selected a dragon with a similar embodiment to Beatrice's eagle. Most of them believed that Beatrice shared her eagle idea with Eve and that Eve found a way to have one similar.

Thad picked a fearsome knight mounted on a mighty steed with his lance pointing ominously out.

Irene picked a griffin, which no one, except Thad, understood. She scolded the group that it was an ancient Greek symbol of strength and power they had covered in their lessons the prior year. They all shrugged off her slight and concurred that it was unique and well done.

Kai picked a horse with rippling muscles that exuded power and grace.

Lacey selected a wolf crouched to pounce with its fangs exposed.

Lastly, Marian selected an image no one recognized, including the brainiac Thad.

The design was interesting but didn't align with the other images. Marian told them it was a depiction of Mother Nature. Mother Nature, she said, could control the weather and keep tornados under control. Its subtlety was priceless but apparent to all of them except Zeke.

Zeke said, "Oh. I get it. We're heading into a storm, and she can control it. Makes sense. You all see that. Right?"

"Incorrect, my yappy teammate," Marian exclaimed. "It represents my role in controlling your behavior and those often talked about tornados of yours. Translated more clearly, I'm overseeing your insolent behavior and keeping you in check."

While not on theme with the rest, the team couldn't help loving her creativity and recognizing that she had her hands full. Zeke accepted the sentiment but wouldn't let the jab ultimately pass without a retort.

He snickered and said, "If you choose that, that's fine. But you should clean it up so it at least looks good."

"I'm going...," said Beatrice as she was interrupted mid-sentence.

"You don't need to finish," Zeke interjected. "I'm sure you're going to take her side. Maybe I should switch with you, and then Al and I can take the command vehicle while you work with Marian."

"Nope. Not happening. I'm all good," said Al shaking his head emphatically.

"Not happening anyways, Zeke," Beatrice said. "You two make a great team. One of the more formidable ones that Al and I've faced."

Beatrice knew that flattery was the best way to shut him up. Her comment left a few others wondering how she rated their teams, but none dared to raise the question with her.

"You're probably right," he said. "We're probably the best."

"Ha!" exclaimed Eve. "Zeke, we ate your lunch in every single trial. Your tornados spent their whole time trying to suck up our dust. Of course, Marian, I mean no offense to you."

"Sure, Beatrice Junior," Zeke snidely fired back. "Let's see who's on top when we get into some real action."

"You all are impossible," chided Beatrice.

Frustrated, she said, "I'm leaving to deliver our logos to Dr. Carter. Let's get headed to the briefing so we aren't late, and please, everyone, be on your best behavior. Now is the time to be one team and listen to these experienced professionals share their insights. That goes double for you, Zeke."

Everyone settled down and headed over to the briefing room. Beatrice caught Dr. Carter on his way into the meeting, handed over the designs for each logo, and explained the name selections.

"I had no idea that the origin of your names came from the first twelve Greek letters," said Dr. Carter.

"Alan and Beatrice were our actual names at birth. But our parents being scientists, chose them for that reason. Kinda geeky, but you can imagine that was their mark of creativity. When they revived the others on the Cranio-Genesis project, they continued the trend and named the other ten accordingly."

"I must say that the Davidson family is a constant set of surprises," he acknowledged. "Let's get to the meeting. Today's information will provide the vehicle teams with all the details starting with your arrival in Norfolk through the first wave of the planned attack in Lebanon."

She followed him into the room. General Nunez was actively introducing the other eleven Davidson children to General Jenkins. General Jenkins looked incredulous as he shook the hands of each of them. The general was a large, muscular man in his own right, but he looked undersized against the lineup of children, which the senior officer rarely encountered.

Seeing this, Dr. Carter imagined the crew on the USS Ford meeting these children. They were going to find their new shipmates even more fascinating as most wouldn't match the General's stature or the pre-briefing on the children he received.

Dr. Carter motioned for Beatrice to join the introductions. She walked over and joined at the end of the line behind Al.

When Al came up and shook the general's hand, General Jenkins said, "So, you are the one with the super-strength. Having seen what those Iranians accomplished, I can't fathom what power you possess."

Al responded, "General, I hope to show you and them when we arrive."

The general said, "And thank you for your service. The world and this nation need you."

Al stood a little taller at the notion of recognizing that he was now indeed in service to his country. Strange feeling, he thought to himself. A year ago, he was a kid who had never left the farm.

Beatrice stepped up to shake the general's hand next. He reached out and said, "I understand that you're the leader and star of this group. Dr. Carter and the others all gushed about your intellect and prowess. They told stories about you finding solutions to numerous problems and ways to defeat their weapons. Thank you, as well, for your service."

"Thank you, general," she said. "Dr. Carter and the others are being kind. We hope to make a difference for this country and are happy to serve."

He was impressed with her demeanor in the face of the mission they would soon take on.

The general said, "Let's get seated so we can start the briefing."

The group quickly sat down, and the general introduced Major General Ken Swift, who would give the briefing.

Major General Swift took the podium and began, "The platforms left yesterday on their ground trek to Norfolk. All of them should arrive within three days. You will be there before their arrival, so they will be the last items to board the carrier for the mission.

This evening at nineteen hundred, we'll board flights to Norfolk. Once we board these flights, all crew members will be unallowed to have any external communications. The limits on communications are a key security protocol and must be obeyed without incident as it could jeopardize the mission.

The flights will arrive in Norfolk approximately five hours after takeoff. We'll disembark at a cleared airfield, where transports will take you to the USS Ford.

Once aboard the carrier, you will remain below deck for the entirety of the trip until you reach Lebanon. Again, secrecy is paramount. We want to ensure there is no sign that anything is amiss. The carrier must appear outfitted solely for humanitarian purposes supporting the Israeli evacuation."

He paused for questions, but no hands went up.

Major General Swift continued, "The laser vehicles will be loaded upon arrival. In addition to the six vehicles, the carrier will load two spares that will remain onboard until needed, should that occur. We have crates to place around each vehicle before loading. They read 'Humanitarian Support Equipment.' As expected, concealing the vehicles hides the mission's true nature and maintains alignment with the cover story.

After the vehicles are loaded, the Commanding Officer of the carrier group will brief the ship's crew on the mission. During the briefing, the Admiral will share the purpose and nature of the platforms and their crews. Afterward, you can interact with any carrier crew freely but keep clear of all shipboard operations and follow the CO's directions without question."

The general paused again, looking for questions.

Dr. Carter raised his hand, and the general pointed to him.

"Heidi Davidson, Peter Davidson, and I have authority from the Defense Secretary to come on board with the platform teams until you provide the shipboard briefings. How long should we expect to be aboard?"

The general, without hesitation, said, "I would expect that you will be on board for about three hours. Any other questions?"

Dr. Carter knew the parents hoped for more time.

The general continued, seeing no further questions, "We'll leave Norfolk shortly after the briefing to meet the two cruise ships overseas. Both ships are being refitted for the evacuations in Naples, Italy.

In Naples, U.S. Navy personnel will staff the cruise ships. They will maintain all appearances as a civilian crew for the entire voyage. We feel it's necessary to have the military crew should something happen as we launch our attack.

We'll meet the cruise ships in the Mediterranean and then head to Israel. These two cruise ships will make up the last evacuations before the deadline. The refitted cruise ships will be able to take on fifteen thousand evacuees. A Red Cross ship will also travel with the two cruise lines there and back. We have been unable to change this element for fear that Iran will become suspicious."

A laser scientist from the Phoenix Project raised his hand. The General asked, "Do you have a question?"

"Yes, what happens if more than fifteen thousand people need evacuation at the last minute?"

"Unfortunately, we can't address that problem," replied the general. "There is considerable coordination between Israel and several nations, including ours, to ensure we don't have chaos at the deadline. Our envoys have made it clear that this will be the last naval group and our limitations. We pray Israel is heeding these warnings and we don't have a bigger humanitarian issue. Regardless of that concern, our mission must go as planned. There can be no deviations."

The gentleman seemed satisfied and sat down.

Seeing no more hands raised, General Swift continued, "The carrier group will consist of a scaled-down version of what a typical carrier group would support. The smaller version is being done to minimize the appearance of a military threat. We'll still have ample firepower, an anti-submarine destroyer, two frigates, and an air defense cruiser traveling with the group.

We have successfully used identical groups with some evacuations to date so that nothing will appear out of the ordinary. Consistency is a critical element of the plan. Everything must look routine."

The general reached under the podium and picked up a water bottle. Taking a drink, he scanned the audience for questions. None emerged.

Setting the bottle back down, he continued, "As we travel toward Israel, the approach will be identical to the prior ones, with the cruise ships breaking off and heading into the Israeli ports alone. The carrier group will remain offshore, awaiting their return. Once loaded, the cruise ships will reunite with the carrier group and head to Naples.

The speed coming out of Israel will be slow by design. Once again, to avoid suspicion, we have asked some evacuation groups over the following weeks to deploy similar tactics so that nothing will appear out of sorts.

The last cruise ship will leave two hours before the Iranian deadline to allow plenty of separation from the Israeli port if Iran attacks immediately after the deadline. Satellite images show they have been massing troops for several weeks in preparation for the deadline, so we foresee no reason for them to delay."

General Nunez raised his hand and asked, "What happens if they, for some reason, delay their invasion, and the carrier group is forced to travel much further toward Italy than anticipated?"

"It's a legitimate concern we've considered," answered General Swift. "One of the cruise ships will broadcast an engine issue and need to slow down for some maintenance. This can buy us a little time without generating concern with Iran, but we can't stall for several hours.

Once we exhaust that ploy, we must proceed from the region toward Naples. Depending on how long they delay an attack, we could have to make the entire trek back from Naples. This scenario would leave us having to travel twenty-four hours at full speed in open water to return to Lebanon.

Our route will demonstrate we're heading back to the region and alert them to our attack. Unfortunately, this scenario gives Iran time to have their invasion underway for a full day in Israel and numerous hours to respond to our coming. There's no alternative to this, so we hope for a bit of luck that this scenario never materializes.

We're concerned the Russians may play a crucial part in alerting them to our change of direction. They are indeed active with their submarine fleet keeping an eye on us. It's a vulnerability we can't overlook, but at the same time, we can't avoid it."

General Nunez understood their difficult position.

"Should that occur, I propose you put D12 up on deck with their discs," suggested General Nunez. "Let them be ready to deal with anything coming your way. I can't convey how much they may help your chances of making it safely to Lebanon should you encounter enemy forces.

We're trying to keep their existence and participation a secret, but if you, for some reason, face their warriors, I assure you that you will be happy to have them up there."

"You think it would make that much difference?" asked General Jenkins.

"Without question," he answered. "After we finish the briefing, let me take you to the test range and have these twelve give you a demonstration. If you don't walk away taking my advice, I'll be shocked."

General Jenkins said to Major General Swift, "Let's take a look. It would give us another element of protection as a last resort."

General Jenkins then signaled for him to continue the briefing.

"Once we reach Beirut, Lebanon, we'll establish a clear entry point and unload the six platforms and two thousand marines. All aircraft on the carrier will be readied for air support once air superiority is ensured by the six vehicles.

Additionally, the marines will come in behind the platforms sweeping through and eliminating Iran's conventional military in the region.

One element of risk at the beginning of the attack is that the naval carrier group will be the lone defense support. The limited air support will last for a brief period until we can bring in additional forces from the Army and aircraft from the Air Force. We expect this period to be less than three hours.

As we press the front inland in Lebanon in the initial attack, we'll establish an operating base. The initial attack will proceed for twelve hours. We expect you to push to the east as far as possible before halting. Central Command will reassess and deliver further plans depending on our progress and Iran's resistance, including our effectiveness against any telekinetic warriors we encounter. Any questions?"

Dr. Carter raised his hand.

The General pointed to Dr. Carter, who said, "The only significant risk to the effectiveness of these laser vehicles is if the platforms are overwhelmed by a large contingent of Iranian warriors. We briefed our recommendations about how to respond should this occur to the President and Defense Secretary when they last visited the Phoenix Project.

I recommended, at that time, that we use numerous conventional air attacks provided by jets and drones to rain fire on the warriors. The tactic will force the Iranian warriors to combat the aircraft and its weapons. It will help neutralize the advantage of their large numbers and give the laser vehicles better odds of success. My question is: given that we'll only have air support from the carrier group initially, will we have the assets at the onset to accomplish that if needed?"

He looked over at Heidi and Peter Davidson as he asked the question, knowing the general's response would be important to them.

"We'll have more airborne assets approximately three hours after the attack begins, but for obvious reasons, we must keep assets out of the region. Until they arrive, the platforms have to survive with limited support.

Don't underestimate what the carrier alone will have for firepower. Depending on their numbers, we could face some risk. We have clarified to the carrier group that protecting the laser vehicles is priority number one, even above their own."

The general's response put no one at ease about the risk for the first few hours, but his last line made the Davidson parents feel better about the military's priorities.

As for the Davidson children, his response initiated the inevitable knots in their stomachs. The dreadful reality of what they may be up against sent shivers down their spines.

The general moved to the next slide in his presentation. He glanced at the screen to recall his place in the briefing.

After a momentary pause, he said, "The vehicle crews will stay onboard the carrier until they disembark in Lebanon. We anticipate that we'll be required to fight our way into the port there when we reach Lebanon. So, you should expect to be on alert sometime before that. The Admiral will make the decision when and direct you accordingly.

Once on alert, the laser vehicle teams will be readied to leave at a moment's notice, and they should also anticipate enemy fire and likely Iranian warriors. That wraps up the overview of the attack launch.

Onboard during the trip, you will stay below deck. You will have assigned living quarters, and they will be cramped. Welcome to travel, Navy style. We ask that you make yourselves comfortable within that space and avoid disrupting normal shipboard operations. You can engage with the crew but be sensitive to their duties. We expect the crew to be curious, especially of the Davidsons, and please feel free to discuss things freely as you deem acceptable.

Located on the carrier, Read Admiral Leighton will be the Commanding Officer of the entire carrier group, and you will follow his directions. Captain Ed Callaghan will be the commanding officer of the carrier itself.

The deploying forces will be under Army Colonel Mark Lee. Once launched, Colonel Lee will operate from the command vehicle, supported by Alan and Beatrice Davidson. Colonel Lee will also direct operations for the deployed Marines, who Lieutenant Colonel Sam Williams will lead.

Please follow the chain of command and obey all our established security protocols throughout the mission. Godspeed and good luck! That concludes my presentation. Any other questions?"

Zeke's hand shot up. Heidi and Peter Davidson raised their eyebrows, and the other eleven Davidson children sat there in shock. Had the kid not listened to anything they told him during the last twenty-four hours? They all wondered what was going to come from his mouth.

The General said, "Go ahead, young man. What can I answer for you?"

"I was wondering ...," Zeke said.

Here it comes, thought the other children. Probably something about his ridiculous infatuation with those tornados once again.

"Our appearance always seems to come as a bit of shock for most people," Zeke started. "Our capabilities seem to create a level of discomfort. We saw this with the scientists on the Phoenix Project when we first came aboard; many are more open-minded than your typical person, at least what we've seen on TV and in the movies. We haven't spent time out in public. Oh, never mind that.

My question is - can the twelve of us do something to set the crew at ease so they can focus on their mission and not be afraid of twelve giants with superpowers riding along with them?"

The child shocked the entire Davidson family and the Phoenix Project team. Not because he said something offhand or smart-aleck like usual, but because he asked a well-thought-out question eloquently that showed deep thinking. Wow, they thought. Did Zeke demonstrate a mature moment?

The General responded, "That is a good question. I'm not sure how to answer that. I'll share your concern with Admiral Leighton and have him take it up with Colonel Lee when you get onboard. Admiral Leighton understands his crew best and something we need to take up with him. If there are no further questions, we have some items to close out with the Phoenix Project leadership and prepare for the evening flight."

The group dispersed, and D12 headed to their rooms, where they still needed to finish packing. They were each given two large duffle bags and asked to put all clothing and other belongings they required into them. Space would be tight.

They mused about the journey ahead and what they expected to face with the Iranian warriors as they packed. They shuffled in and out of each other's rooms. The camaraderie was evident. They stayed busy, which helped them avoid too much idle time thinking about the perils ahead. That time would come aboard the carrier when they would find few things to do and much time to reflect.

Beatrice had surmised that the trip would be difficult and boring. She shared her concerns with Al and solicited his help to keep the group engaged in activities to take their minds off things. Beatrice wanted to avoid prolonged periods where the children were left to their thoughts. She knew this would be unhealthy for all of them, including herself. He agreed to help her and told her he would consider it.

When Beatrice talked to Al, he knew her concerns were well-founded. He had already gone down a tortuous path himself, wondering how he would deal with killing someone. Al recognized that this must be what every new military person must face on their first venture into war. So, he was all in when Beatrice discussed finding ways to keep their minds on something else.

The evening came quickly, and soon it was time for them to board the aircraft. The Phoenix Project team gathered in a line to shake the hand of each crew member of the laser vehicles.

Colonel Lee asked his team to allow the twelve Davidson children to be last in line. Probably a request by Dr. Carter.

As the twelve children moved through the line, handshakes turned to hugs and crying for most of the scientists. The display overwhelmed the children, and most of them started crying. Zeke stood there blubbering the most. It was a solemn display but completely sincere.

General Nunez was the last Phoenix team member to shake hands with the laser vehicles team. He told each crew member that they were fine soldiers. When the Davidson children reached him, he told them they had each earned a new title, American Warrior.

It was a gesture that only General Nunez could have made. He initially doubted the children and their importance but now was bestowing them a particular rank of honor. The pep in the twelve children's steps grew tenfold as they paraded onto the plane headed to Norfolk.

The aircraft accommodations for the children were first class. There were huge, cushioned seats with plenty of legroom accommodating their size. The seats were custom-made for them, compliments of Dr. Carter. The arrangement was three groups of four, organized front to back, with two seats facing two others. In addition to being comfortable, the arrangement allowed four of them to converse on the five-hour flight.

The first part of the flight was smooth, and the conversation was light. Most of the children either slept or listened to music.

About halfway into the flight, Irene stood up from her seat and came over to Beatrice's seat.

"Are you scared, Beatrice?" she asked. "I've been thinking a lot about all this for the last couple of hours, and I feel my anxiety level rising."

Beatrice looked over at Al, sitting across from her, and moved her eyebrows as if to say, see what I was worried about happening.

Beatrice calmly answered, "Irene, we feel the same way. It's perfectly normal. The best thing we can do is keep our wits about ourselves, intently listen to directions, and be prepared to work as a team. Al and I are there to have your backs. For now, the best thing to do is keep yourself occupied. Therefore, Al is going to get us all doing something."

"I had Dr. Carter load us up with card decks and chips for this occasion," he said. "We'll run three games of Texas Hold'Em simultaneously, one game for each group of four chairs. The top four chip winners from the first round will play in the champions' game. The other eight will play in two consolation games. Irene, let's you and I get the cards out and set up the chips."

Al and Irene talked to the rest of them, and everyone was happy to participate. Flying was new to them. They had each only taken one helicopter flight after the Russians attacked their home and their flight out to Idaho. None of them felt any queasiness about flying, but they were bored.

The first round proceeded, and the four highest chip winners were Thad, Ephrem, Irene, and Zeke. During the champions' game, the last hand came down to Thad going all in, which dragged Irene and Zeke in as well.

Thad threw down with a confident sling of his two-hole cards. Three jacks was his call, ace high.

Irene also had three of a kind, but her three of a kind were only fives.

After Irene's laydown, Zeke stood up from his seat, tossed his two hole cards of a jack and a five, and said, "Full house! Read 'em and weep! Tornado Man, the king of the American Warriors, has destroyed you!"

For the other eleven, there could have been no worse outcome. Zeke needed zero confidence boost or ammunition to feed his incessant boastfulness. He started making shushing noises like a strong wind and spinning his fingers in an eddy-like rotation.

"Swept up in the storm that I bring," he piled on.

"Don't let the title, given by General Nunez, get to your head," snapped Beatrice. "It was a complimentary distinction he gave us, and better not be abused by you again."

"And don't make me bring out Mother Nature and squash that little twister of yours," said Marian with an air of finality supported by a deadly look from Beatrice.

Zeke was about to let something else fly from his mouth when 'Prepare for landing' came over the plane's loudspeaker. 'Please take your seats and fasten your safety belts. We'll be on the ground in Norfolk shortly.'

After the announcement, Peter Davidson got up and headed back to the children. Before landing, he wanted to check on them and find out what the hoopla was that just went on.

"Zeke just won our poker tournament, which was about as bad as it gets," said Gabriel. "At least Marian deflated him nicely and turned his obnoxious tornado into a wispy cloud of nothingness."

"Good to see your spirits are fine and your spunk has not withered," said their dad. "See you all when we're ready to deplane. They will have a special canopy to cover us from prying eyes in the sky. General Jenkins told us it might take a few moments for them to get it all in place. He also informed me that the President and Defense Secretary had secretly come down from Washington and would meet us on board the USS Ford. The President insisted on seeing the twelve of you off."

"Should we put on our new armor suits for him?" questioned Zeke. "I can introduce him to Tornado Man."

"Sorry, Zeke," said the dad. "Dr. Carter told me they are still being outfitted with your logos and name tags. He flew them earlier today to Norfolk. He said it would be tight getting them completed before the vehicles arrive and you have to leave. I better get seated. See you all in a bit."

The plane landed, and they waited for about fifteen minutes while they erected a large cover. A fleet of vehicles lined up under the canopy to take the group to the carrier. As the crews deplaned, they loaded into military escort vehicles. The last two vehicles were tall Mercedes sprinter vans outfitted with large seats to accommodate six Davidson children each. Once loaded, they proceeded directly to the carrier and unloaded under a similar canopy.

Rear Admiral Leighton greeted the platform crews as they boarded the carrier. He had been pre-briefed on his newest arrivals and didn't flinch as the immense Davidson children came aboard.

"Pleasure to have you aboard," said the admiral to the children. "We'll have some logistics to discuss with you after getting underway, which should be very soon. My aide will take you below to your quarters, where you can stow your belongings. You will be informed when we're ready to assemble for the briefing.

We'll meet below deck in a ward area near your quarters. Please familiarize yourselves with the guidelines pamphlet on each of your bunks. We made some special modifications to the bunks for the twelve of you. The passageways are doorways that will prove challenging, but according to details from General Nunez, you should fit through them."

The admiral's aide showed the children and the rest of the platform teams below deck. The young officer seemed intimidated as he escorted the group, constantly peering over at the Davidson children, scanning their huge frames, as he explained many of the ship's areas as they passed through.

After reflecting on Zeke's astute question from the day before, the children expected the treatment. They figured this was just the beginning, given the carrier crew and marines would total six thousand curious personnel aboard.

The quarters and makeshift wardroom configured for them were better accommodations than D12 had expected. General Nunez warned them to expect things to be tight for them onboard. Given the constraints, the carrier crew tried to make the space comfortable. Being young, D12 were more adaptable than most, even at their size, and happy it exceeded their expectations.

"Just got word that we'll meet in thirty minutes," said the admiral's aid when he returned. "The President and Defense Secretary are on board with Dr. Carter, your parents, and some other senior officers."

Before the meeting, the children began familiarizing themselves with their quarters and wardroom. They were impressed by the ship, having never been on one before. Its enormity matched their own.

They arrived for the meeting and saw their parents standing toward the front. They decided to stand in the back next to General Nunez, who stood beside General Jenkins. They had no problem seeing what was happening up front at their height. President Schmidt and Defense Secretary Edgard stood at the front with Admiral Leighton.

The President stepped forward to address the group.

President Schmidt began, "I'm a man who believes that most people, regardless of where they live, their religious beliefs, their upbringing, or what government leads them, prefer to live a peaceful life. Today, the critical element of world peace is a balance of power amongst the strongest nations and tight alliances between countries with similar ideals. In my last statement, the word 'peace' is misleading because it's not actually peace in its true meaning but is more appropriately contained and muted aggression. As such, peace is always fragile and vulnerable to the ebbs and flows of military superiority.

World War II was the last war that consumed the world's most powerful nations. Since that war, a global balance of power has led to growing economies, prolific international trade, and an intertwined existence of all countries.

Other wars, skirmishes, and terrorist activities have blotted post-World War II history, but none have yanked the leading nations into head-to-head warfare. That held until about a year ago when Iran, having established unfathomable might, goaded us into a war, then went on a multi-country acquisition binge. They haven't finished, but we'll disrupt those plans."

The President paused, carefully considering his words.

After collecting his thoughts, he continued, "A top-secret program, run years ago by the U.S. Air Force, with intentions of helping humanity, resulted in the revival of severely injured children. The children, unintentionally affected by the electromagnetic radiation they were exposed to, experienced a mutation that created a different growth pattern and led to unique capabilities.

Standing in the back are the twelve children revived under that program. They are a miracle of modern science, all once brain-dead from severe injuries but now thriving individuals. I can also attest from personal experience that they are a joy to behold and share the same hopes and dreams as the rest of us.

Some scientific discoveries, unfortunately, which yield untold benefits, can be seized by some and used for evil purposes. The leaders of Iran did that exact thing. They stole the secret information by cyber extraction and created an army of telekinetic warriors. They revived children with a stimulation technique we developed. Its purpose was to save children, yet they grew them into deadly telekinetic warriors.

While they built the army, they hid them for years, training with a villainous purpose until they had such a significant force that no country could challenge them. They then baited us into a war and spun the Islamic world into a religious fervor claiming this came about as a gift from Allah.

Their twisted plan soon demanded the Islamic world bow to them and unite under their leadership or perish from the wrath of their warriors. Many Islamic people became enthralled in their greatness and followed as many Germans did behind Hitler.

As I mentioned initially, I believe most Muslims, like most people, wish for a peaceful life. Iranian leaders falsely lured Islamic people into servitude under the guise that it was a gift from Allah. We know it's manipulation by Iranian leaders who sought to increase their power, money, and influence on the backs of these Iranian children turned warriors based on nothing but a lie."

Shaking his head and emphatically clenching his hand, he said, "It's the purpose of this mission to begin restoring the global balance of power. Iran must be stopped, starting with your mission which is the first wave of Operation Restoring Liberty.

If we can demonstrate an ability to fight these warriors, our allies sitting today on the sidelines will join the fight and work with us in what could be a brutal war. Once we eradicate the telekinetic Iranians, we can again use our conventional military forces and nuclear deterrent to restore the balance of power with other nations.

I believe so strongly in this that I'm willing to commit twelve children, born from a secret program and who volunteered to help a country that hid them away for a decade, to the task. America and the World need you to succeed!"

The President stared at the men and women. He scanned the group slowly, catching many of them in his gaze so they could see his conviction. Feeling the enormity of the moment, he breathed deeply.

"Finally, I say this last part so that you better understand my purpose in all this," he said. "It's time to hold the Iranian leadership accountable for their great lie and actions. Once we open the attack, I'll share the true origin of their telekinetic warriors with the world, and Iran will no longer hold a grasp on the Islamic world. I say it's time for the Phoenix to rise! I thank each of you for your service to this nation. We'll forever be in your debt. God Bless each of you, and God Bless America."

The President had only come aboard to deliver his final address and wish them well. He shook hands with every crew member. He saved his last goodbyes for the Davidson children and made Beatrice the last of them.

"I wish you well," he said to her. "There is no doubt that you're the leader of the twelve of you. As that leader, I'm counting on you to bring them home safely. Am I understood?"

He said the last part with a smile.

"Yes, sir, Mr. President," she said with a smile. "I promise to try my best."

"This is America," he fired back at her. "We don't try. We do!"

As he left, the President patted her on her shoulder, knowing they were in the best hands possible.

Dr. Carter, Heidi, and Peter Davidson were the last to leave the ship. They remained as long as Admiral Leighton allowed them. The parents stayed with the children while Dr. Carter had last-minute discussions with the platform and carrier crew.

The Davidsons chatted. The parents kept the discussions calm and unemotional. They wanted to part ways with the twelve of them on a positive note and with a keen sense of encouragement. Like any parent watching their child head off to war, they could see the perils that lay ahead tugging at their psyche. They knew what the children were experiencing was normal and wished they could bear the burden themselves. However, this journey was their own.

"You will face difficult choices on this mission," said their father.

He knew they didn't want to stir up doubts before they had to part with the children, but some important things had to be said.

"Some choices may involve life and death. Others may be to save your own life or the life of others. You may need to hurt or kill many people to accomplish what must be done in this mission.

It's often difficult to come to terms with this afterward, but I hope you can all remain strong and rely on each other for support. Your mom and I hope you can maintain the perspective that the people you protect come at the expense of those you must defeat. Standing up to evil and being willing to risk your life to save others is as noble as it gets.

Always keep in mind how proud of you we are. Work together, fight as a team, find success, comfort each other, and please come home together. Remember, you are the mighty D12. We'll be here waiting for you when you return."

Tears welled, leaving not one dry eye among them. These children were experiencing a colossal shift in their lives. Going from hidden away teens experiencing little of the world to now being the hope of their nation and off to fight a war. Movies would surely be made of this tale.

Heidi Davidson, swimming in tears and uncontrollably weeping, couldn't get a sentence out. She had told herself not to do this, but the moment overwhelmed her. She grabbed them and hugged them, one by one, with all her might.

As Peter reached for her hand so they could leave, she squeaked out, "We love you with all our hearts, and we want you to know that no matter what happens, your life has brought magic to ours."

She realized she better not stay any longer, or leaving might be impossible. Holding Peter's hand, she turned as he put his arm around her, and they left.

As they reached the door, the children yelled in unison, "We love you more!"

After the emotional farewell, the children settled down and kept to themselves.

Later, the vehicle teams were briefed on the protocols during their journey, escorted for a tour of the ship below deck, and provided a daily schedule before reaching their final destination in Lebanon.

Exhausted from the flight and activities of the long day, the Davidsons headed to their quarters for some needed sleep.

Chapter 20

The Element of Surprise

The first ten days of the trip on the carrier passed without issue for the vehicles teams harbored below deck. The carrier group met the cruise ships outside Naples as planned. They were now on their way toward Israel.

The daily routine and cramped quarters made D12 claustrophobic and a tad cranky. Whenever there is irritability around, there is no one like Zeke to make matters worse.

The twelve sat in the wardroom, bored with their afternoon and with little to do, when Zeke said, "Do you think they will make a movie about me? Probably call it Tornadoman, kinda like Ironman? Maybe even Cycloneman. That has a better ring to it."

"Probably call it Braindeadman," said Thad. "Get it? You were braindead."

"That's a pretty good one, Thad," said Irene. "And you whipped it out so quickly. You haven't been thinking about that one for a while, have you?"

Giving him a wink as she asked that.

"Joking about our prior condition is not funny," said Zeke, sneering at Thad. "Anyways, Thad, they surely won't do a movie called Knightman. Don't be jealous that my chosen name will make Hollywood come knocking as soon as we get back."

"If you don't knock it off, I'll have Al take you on deck, lift you into the air, and drop you into the ocean, never to return," said Beatrice. "Then you'll be known as Dunkedman."

"Nice try," Zeke retorted. "We're not allowed on deck, so that can't happen."

"I wish we could at least play with our discs for a while, but they have them stowed with the vehicles," said Eve wishing to quell the boredom. "They tell us we should be there within a week, but it seems like an eternity."

"Okay," said Al, who Beatrice had challenged to manage the boredom.

He had been remiss in his duties.

"We have limited space and things to play with, but surely we can develop a game to play and keep ourselves occupied. They tell us we have one week to kill before we meet with the cruise ships coming out of Israel. We should shoot for something that fills that week."

"Too bad we left the cards and poker chips on the plane," mused Gabriel. "We could have held a bigger tournament, which would give us a rematch against Zeke."

"I saw a game once in a movie that maybe we could play," chimed in an excited Ephrem. "I think I can remember how to play it. They folded a piece of notebook paper into a small triangle. They called it Paper Football. The object, as I recall, was for two competitors to push the triangle around a tabletop, alternating turns.

You score a touchdown when the triangle stays on the table and hangs over your opponent's edge. After the touchdown, you have to flick the triangle vertically to complete the extra point. We could set a time limit and create a full schedule to play one another before the top ones compete in the playoffs. Are you interested?"

The boredom was so bad that they would have agreed to just about anything, so they all consented. Al set a schedule, time limit, and rules, and the group spent a few hours rotating and practicing the game. Beatrice decided they would use their telekinetic powers rather than their fingers to help them practice their fine control.

There were no objections, so they set out to play their matches. The schedule, including the playoff, was set to last the week and take them to their anticipated launch into Lebanon. The games were raucous, as one would expect, and they quickly learned more finesse than they ever required before with their powers. The competition consumed them and was healthy for their mental state.

Likewise, they began to familiarize themselves with several carrier crew members. Many were familiar with paper football and enjoyed watching the games themselves. It was an excellent icebreaker for developing camaraderie and a wonderful outlet for the crew when they were off duty.

Soon, the match schedule became known around the ship. Huge groups showed up for the games, maybe even doing a bit of gambling on them, but that was all kept hush-hush.

One afternoon, one of the sailors approached Al and said, "I hear you have greater strength than the others. The word all over the ship is that it's some crazy amount of weight you can lift. My buddy and I have a bet that you can't lift this one container we have down in the storage area. It says three thousand pounds on the side. Do you think you can show us?"

"I think I can manage that amount," said a confident Al, hoping to win the young man some money. "Take me to the space, and I'll show you both."

"We're coming too," said Del and Zeke.

They went to a storage area down from their quarters. The sailor grabbed his friend along the way, excited that Al accepted.

When they reached the space, they saw the enormous metal cargo container. The '3000lb' marking was indeed on the side. The Davidson trio smiled to themselves, knowing Al, or any of them, for that matter, would not have a problem lifting that much.

The sailor told Al to proceed when he was ready.

Al, appearing theatrical, waved his hands back and forth. He feigned exerting mental concentration on the object. Zeke and Del enjoyed the theatrics, which they knew was just showmanship.

The sailor who asked Al to come to the cargo seemed happy about Al's lack of progress. He began gloating about easy money, and Al realized that the man who summoned him was actually betting against him.

"I knew they were exaggerating about your strength," said the sailor. "Those Iranians were only flinging around two hundred discs. Whoopee. That's nothing. They probably weigh a pound each."

"Quite the contrary," explained Del. "Each disc weighs seventy-five pounds. They're made of tungsten carbide, denser than lead and harder than steel. Two hundred discs multiplied by that weight means they are whizzing around fifteen thousand pounds simultaneously. Al is three times stronger than they are."

Color evaporated from the sailor's face as his confidence in his bet went to zero.

Taking Del's explanation as a cue to get on with it, Al changed his theatrics and held out only two fingers as if that was all it took to lift it. The cargo container rose from the storage deck. Unsure of the content's value, Al brought it up only six inches before letting it settle back down again.

He bowed as if finishing a performance and walked over to the sailor that bet for him. Al put out his hand, and the sailor seemed intimidated by the size of his hand. Not sure he wanted to deny the gesture from the kid, the sailor put his hand in Al's.

Al shook it and said, "smart bet, my friend. A pleasure to help you out today. Come watch my Paper Football match against Beatrice when I show her who's the boss."

"Thanks for the invite," said the sailor. "But I probably won't bet on that game. I hear she is unbeatable."

"Ha," rebuffed Al. "I just got a little too aggressive in our first match. This time, I'm going all Tom Brady on her."

Word of Al's feat reached every corner of the carrier within an hour. The visits to the Davidsons by crew members became more frequent and numerous.

Zeke took every opportunity to tell any of them about his triple tornado, but it was hard for the crew to visualize it fully. Unfortunately for Zeke, most of the focus was on Al for his might and Beatrice's Paper Football prowess.

By week's end, the Superbowl of Paper Football came down to Eve and Beatrice, or as Gabriel liked to say, Beatrice and Beatrice Junior. The carrier had stopped just outside Israel for a day. The deadline set by Iran was only twenty-four hours away.

Once they hit the deadline, they would move to high alert, waiting for Iran to initiate the attack.

Interest in the Superbowl had grown throughout the week. The wardroom was packed like a can of sardines.

Eve and Beatrice had developed tremendous finesse over the week of play, and each scored on most opportunities. Most figured that Beatrice would win since she hadn't lost the whole week. Eve, though, had improved her skills such that she was going to give Beatrice a run for her money.

The Superbowl came down to the last few seconds, and they were all tied.

Eve kicked off to Beatrice. Beatrice had time for only one flick to score, or time would expire, and they would move to overtime. Chants broke out from the crew members, rooting for the two players. Both had developed large fan bases over the week.

Beatrice studied her position carefully and gave her final mental flick with time expiring. The paper triangle slid toward Eve's edge, spinning across the table. As the triangle settled near the table's end, the final corner stopped with its tip pointing at Eve, who sat there disbelieving that the triangle's tip lay just beyond the table's edge.

The crowd erupted into chants of "Beatrice, Beatrice, Beatrice." She smiled and shook hands with Eve, who acted like the gracious loser.

"I got lucky," Beatrice told her.

Eve was happy she kept it that close since Beatrice had crushed most of her opponents throughout the games and had beaten Eve twice in their previous matches.

Not ashamed of the loss, Eve said, “It’s never a problem to lose to the best. I would have died if I’d lost to Zeke.”

To which Zeke responded, “Ha! You just said you didn’t have a problem losing to the best, so how could you EVER be upset losing to me? Since I’m the best.”

“Not today,” said one of the sailors who’d been chanting for Beatrice. “You’re junior varsity compared to these two.”

Colonel Lee came in as the crowd dispersed. He needed to meet with D12.

In a serious tone, he said, “We’re back underway, as you’ve recognized. The carrier group with the two cruise ships is heading away from Israel toward Naples. Our closest location to Lebanon will be in about two hours. We hope to make our move at that time.”

“We’ve been placed on high alert by Admiral Leighton. It’s showtime, so get prepared. As briefed, you must be in your armor and vehicle as soon as we turn toward Lebanon. I’ll let you know as soon as that happens.”

Two hours passed, then another two hours, and then another. Iran had failed to attack at the deadline. Admiral Leighton speculated that Iran might have been concerned about the U.S. carrier group being so close and wanted to wait for it to be farther offshore.

Unsure of when the attack may take place, Colonel Lee told D12 to turn in and get some rest.

In the middle of the night, Colonel Lee woke the children.

He disappointingly said, “We have traveled fourteen hours, and Iran has yet to launch their attack. Under our backup plan, cruise ship one has feigned issues with its propulsion, and the group has stopped its progress toward Naples while they tend to their supposed issues.

The admiral tells me that we'll do this for a few hours. After that, the group will have to restart, but we can probably limp along slower than we were moving. Each minute we spend going the wrong way will cause us additional time to return to Lebanon. Unfortunately, where we sit now, we already have about four times as much distance to cover to get back to Lebanon as we hoped. Additional distance is additional risk, as you know."

"Thanks for the update," said Beatrice. "Is there anything we can do right now?"

"Get some more rest," he said. "It's going to be exhausting once we hit land. You may not get to sleep for days depending on the situation there. I'll keep you updated if I hear more."

The colonel hurried out the door and headed toward his quarters.

"Get some sleep," Beatrice echoed to the other eleven kids. "You heard the colonel."

They awoke again when the carrier got underway again. They could tell the speed was slower than before and surmised that Iran was still holding off their attack on Israel.

Into their room popped Colonel Lee.

"You can see that it's still no dice on the attack," he said. "We're continuing to move forward at half our prior speed. They're still telling us to be ready at any moment."

He shrugged his shoulders and darted away again.

D12 decided to get cleaned up, grab some breakfast and be ready to go immediately.

A ship alert came over the intercom as they were finishing their breakfast.

The intercom blared, "Iran has begun its attack on Israel. We'll head to Beirut and arrive in approximately seven hours. At that time, we'll offload the laser vehicles. Our course reversal will likely signal our military advance, so we're beginning flight operations immediately."

Colonel Lee hurried into the room, "you just heard that we're up. You all ready?"

"We're," Beatrice said.

Colonel Lee read the deep concern on the kid's faces.

"Remember your training," he said in a calming tone. "Keep tight communications and focus on doing your job. Don't panic, and don't try to do more than your job. If you have a question, ask. If we execute as we trained, then we have this."

"They're saying seven hours to get there. I want us holed up together in the cargo space two hours from now. We can talk through our plans again. Any questions?"

He saw the concerns grow a bit and recognized that newbie look. They reminded him of his first deployment to Iraq. He was terrified after leaving the states for his deployment. Nothing ever prepares you for the real thing.

"We'll be there," was Beatrice's short response.

The Davidsons met at their designated time in the cargo space. The sound of jets taking off and periodically landing issued another dose of reality. The teams killed time by discussing logistics and how the vehicles would disembark. They studied maps, and Colonel Lee reviewed their intended route once on land. Unsure of what resistance they would face with their current voyage, most likely known by the enemy now, he told them to be ready on a moment's notice to adjust their plans and follow any orders given without hesitation.

About two hours offshore from Lebanon, the carrier experienced an abrupt slowdown. Alarms were going off all over the ship, and sailors were racing in every direction. Admiral Leighton burst into the cargo area and approached Colonel Lee.

"We have a major problem," growled the Admiral. "Our nuclear propulsion system had another damn failure, and we can't proceed. I've been riding Naval Reactors' asses about this for a year. They can't seem to fix these problems.

Unfortunately, because of Iran's delay in attacking Israel, we had to head back at top speed and push it more than we had hoped. Our pushing at full speed exacerbated the issue and caused the failure. Now we can only limp along.

To make matters worse, our F-15s just picked up a contingent of Iranian naval ships heading our way. The crews said the vessels had dozens of Iranian warriors on them. Their discs just took down both jets. I'm awaiting orders on how we're supposed to proceed. Colonel Lee, stand by and have your people stay in place until we figure out what we're doing."

"Aye, sir," answered Colonel Lee.

"What're we going to do with those ships coming at us?" inquired Beatrice. "If they have dozens of warriors together, we've got to get up on deck and help them fight. We should get the laser platforms up there as well."

"The laser vehicles will create issues with the flight operations," he told her. "Let's wait for our orders."

The twelve kids felt a sense of impending doom. The one high-risk element to their attack was several warriors attacking them simultaneously. They were dead in the water with a large group of Iranian warriors heading straight for them. If the Iranians reached the carrier, it was unclear how the Davidsons would fight them without the laser vehicles. Unfortunately, this situation was never considered.

Thirty minutes elapsed with very few words spoken amongst the vehicle teams. They waited to hear from the Admiral on the plan or for the aircraft carrier to recover its propulsion capability. The bustle of people moving in all directions continued, which they took as a bad sign.

After another fifteen minutes, a junior officer approached them and addressed the team.

"The Admiral received orders," he said. "I need D12 on the top deck with me ASAP."

"What about the others on the platform teams?" asked Colonel Lee. "Are we planning to bring the vehicles up on deck?

"My orders are only to bring the Davidsons up on deck, sir," the officer responded. "The Admiral said nothing about doing anything with the vehicles."

Turning to the twelve Davidsons standing together, he said, "Come with me, please."

The children filed in behind him and climbed to the top deck. The admiral was standing there waiting for them to arrive.

"I've been told to get you twelve to safety," the admiral said firmly. "We're going to evacuate you immediately."

"How?" asked Beatrice looking around.

"You'll see in a moment," he shot back. "I understand you can lift each other and move yourselves from one spot to the next?"

"Yes, sir," she acknowledged. "But why do you ask?"

"You're going to need to do that," he said as an American nuclear submarine surfaced on their port side. "We're sending you back to the states aboard that. It's the only way we can ensure your safe return given the circumstances."

"We can't leave you here," Beatrice said emphatically. "Our team is still below deck. You'll be destroyed without us fighting alongside you against those Iranian warriors. You need us!"

"We're not sure you will survive if you stay," he said. "You're to be protected by order of the President. We must get you moving now. Your delay is putting the sub crew and you at risk. Please comply."

As they peered down at the sub, a few crew members on the sail eagerly motioned for them to get going.

Beatrice turned to the group and said, "We have to follow orders. We all agreed to that when we signed up to do this. Eve and I'll go first, then bring two more. Al, lift everyone else over, and I'll bring you over last. Let's do this."

"Get going," screamed the Admiral. He then trotted back toward the ship's observation deck.

Al sent Beatrice and Eve over. Beatrice directed Eve down into the sub while Beatrice stayed on the sail's deck.

Al then sent Gabriel and Lacey next, followed by Kai and Marian.

A Russian submarine surfaced on the carrier's starboard side just as he was about to send Ephrem and Irene over. The Russian submarine's hatch opened on its sail, followed by several missile tubes. Iranian warriors began to pour out onto the Russian sub's platform. One of the Iranian warriors started to lift the others over to the carrier deck, and their discs began to stream from the Russian missile tubes. First, one Iranian moved to the carrier, then two, four, six, and eight.

Al began to panic.

Zeke suddenly said something to Al that Al didn't understand, and Zeke sprinted away, back below deck.

Al was stunned. What the hell was Zeke doing, he wondered. Panicking and unable to focus on Zeke, Al hustled Ephrem and Irene over just as Al saw two more Iranian warriors land on the deck. He now faced ten Iranian warriors and still had to get three more of them to the sub.

Uncertain about what to do, Al looked around for the heaviest item on the flight deck and spotted a large cargo container near the starboard edge of the carrier. Lacking any better solution to stop the flow of Iranian warriors onto the carrier, he lifted the cargo container into the air. He then sent it hurling over the side deck onto the Russian submarine.

The massive weight of the falling container crushed the sail and sent the submarine listing sideways. Al intended to ensure they couldn't get more Iranian warriors on the deck. Ten was more than Al thought he and Beatrice could handle.

The Iranian warriors paused at Al's maneuver, unsure of what they saw. Iran didn't know that the twelve Davidsons existed, so the warriors were unsure how to proceed, especially since the force he had just used was more substantial than theirs. The Iranians regrouped and decided to attack the three Davidsons up on deck.

"Where is Zeke?" asked Thad. "Where did he go?"

"I'm not sure, but we have to move," Al yelled. "I'll move you two over and wait for Zeke."

He sent Del and Thad flying over to the submarine's sail deck.

A few Iranian warriors sent discs after them, but Beatrice, sensing the discs, deflected them."

As Del and Thad landed, she demanded, "What the hell is going on up there?"

"The Russians just surfaced a submarine on the other side," answered Thad. "They had Iranian warriors on the sub with their discs. Ten made it onto the carrier deck before Al cratered their sub with a huge cargo container. Zeke ran below deck for some reason, and Al is waiting for him."

"Damn that kid," she shouted. "I'll try to help Al."

After Al successfully sent the two over, the Iranians focused on him. They sent barrage after barrage against them. He struggled to contain their ten sets of discs, even with Beatrice's help from the sub's deck.

The Iranians were hitting him shot after shot. Beatrice could tell they were periodically striking his body hard. Al crouched to minimize his vulnerability, but their attack was relentless. He writhed in pain as the discs came in, one after another. He and Beatrice tried to hold off the swarm of two thousand Iranian discs, but there were too many.

Suddenly their attack waned, and Al stumbled and fell forward onto his knees. He was severely hurt and bleeding from his head and left arm. The battering had injured Al badly, and he was losing consciousness.

Glancing back up and wondering why they stopped their attack, Al noticed the entire group of Iranian warriors looking to their right. He peered over to see what grabbed their attention and saw Zeke sprinting from below deck, dressed in his armored suit, followed by a stream of his discs. That was Al's last sight as he fell into a ball unconscious on the deck.

Zeke saw Al on the deck, bent over and bloodied. He started to run toward him, but the Iranians changed their attack to focus on him. With Beatrice's help, Zeke began fighting off the discs as he approached Al. The suit withstood the pummeling at the moment, but he and Al needed to get over to the sub immediately.

Zeke yelled, "How badly are you hurt?"

He received no answer from Al.

An incoming barrage struck Zeke hard on his shoulder as he rolled Al onto his back. Zeke's suit was holding up well against the numerous Iranian discs bludgeoning him, but he knew Al needed protection.

Knowing he wasn't enough to even the odds and fight them off, Zeke bunched Al into a ball and draped his armored body over his unresponsive brother while bringing his flock of discs in tightly around the two of them as a protective shield. If he couldn't fight them off, he could at least shield Al.

The Iranian warriors fumed and concentrated their brutal attack on Zeke's cocoon of discs. They pounded away from every angle seeking points to penetrate the shield, more than a thousand hammers smashing away on a single nail.

Beatrice tried to deflect as many discs as possible, but ten warriors were too many for her and Al. So she and Zeke were surely no match. She couldn't tell how much damage the repeated barrage was hurting them below Zeke's shield.

Beatrice realized she needed to do something or feared they would finish the two of them off. She tried to lift them using her force, but the Iranian warriors countered her move and held them in check.

Beatrice yelled something down below to someone on the submarine. She hoped they understood what she said.

Looking back up, she saw the battering continuing, the protective shield weakening, and the Iranians finding penetration points. She could sense that Zeke was still working with her to deflect the discs, but she wasn't sure of Al's condition.

A considerable noise emanated from the carrier deck. Behind Al and Zeke emerged one laser vehicle and then another. The lasers began blasting away at the warriors. They were popping the Iranian discs like popcorn in a microwave, one after another. The Iranian warriors maintained their focus on Al and Zeke until a laser finally took out one of the warriors. The warrior slumped to the deck, blasted by the laser.

Recognizing their peril, a few of the Iranians began targeting the vehicles. The vehicles were vulnerable without any Davidson children on board to protect them.

Beatrice focused on helping Zeke and Al as the lasers fired away.

A loud bang and shattered glass shot in all directions as an Iranian disc shattered one of the vehicle's laser apertures.

The three remaining lasers, however, kept blasting away.

They had already cut the number of Iranian discs by a third as the second Iranian warrior met his demise. As Beatrice hoped, the lasers were starting to even the odds.

She hoped Al and Zeke were hanging on under the reduced barrage.

A laser blast took out another Iranian warrior, and their supply of discs continued to evaporate under the high-powered laser fire. With three warriors eliminated, they were approaching the odds for which Beatrice knew she might handle the rest alone.

Unfortunately for the Davidson children, another successful strike by an Iranian disc took out a second laser just after it took out another Iranian warrior.

The remaining two lasers continued to fire away at the six Iranian warriors left.

The six warriors focused their discs on the two lasers, recognizing they were the real threat.

A laser blast took out a fifth Iranian, and the warrior crumpled to the ground. However, the focused barrage of discs took out the third and fourth lasers in a one-two strike.

Five Iranians left was a better than fair fight for her, Beatrice thought. But as she looked to the deck, she saw Zeke, no longer protected by the discs. Below him was Al lying on the deck, unresponsive. Beatrice could see blood all over Zeke's suit, but Zeke seemed unhurt. She then realized it must be from Al.

The two were now exposed to the five warriors' discs. They took the remaining three hundred discs between them and regrouped them to focus on Al and Zeke.

Another screeching noise erupted on the carrier deck as the command vehicle with Colonel Lee standing in Beatrice's dome rose from the weapons elevator. He held up one of her discs and pointed to the back of the vehicle.

She understood immediately.

Up in the air rose her flock of a thousand discs. She spun them ferociously in a giant whirlwind that sucked in the wind across the carrier's deck.

The Iranians, unsure what they were facing, cowered at the sight.

Beatrice let her anger consume her as she swept her spinning discs toward the remaining five.

As discs neared them, the first warrior was pulled inside the twister and spun upward into the swirl of discs. She moved the cyclone toward another Iranian, who was promptly swept in. Then a third, a fourth, and finally, the last of the five.

The Iranians spun viciously inside the twister with reckless abandon, unable to escape the eddy forces.

Knowing she had them trapped, Beatrice lifted the twister high into the air and swiftly slammed it onto the carrier deck, leaving the last five Iranian warriors heaped in a pile.

Beatrice yelled to Zeke to bring her over to the carrier.

Zeke lifted her over immediately.

Beatrice ran to Zeke, who was holding Al in his arms.

"Are you ok?" she cried with concern.

"I took a lot of hits, but this suit's amazing," he said as blood spurted from his lip.

Looking at Al, Zeke said, "He's injured pretty badly. He needs medical attention now. We must get him to the sub now or risk another attack."

The Admiral came running over.

"Does he need medical attention?" he asked.

"He's hurt pretty bad," said Beatrice.

"I'll let the sub's commanding officer know. They'll give him medical attention there," he said sympathetically. "You have to get over there now. The Iranian ships are only twenty minutes out."

"By the way," the admiral said to Zeke. "You're a brave young man. You saved his life."

As he picked up Al in his arms, Zeke said, "He would have done the same for me."

"You have to go," said the admiral once more.

Beatrice lifted Zeke, who was carrying Al, to the sub's deck.

"I'm sorry we can't stay to help you against what's coming," said Beatrice to the admiral. "You saw what ten of them did against us. It'll be a bloodbath if they have dozens like your recon told you."

Ignoring her warning, the admiral responded, "I'm sorry we didn't get you to your destination and allow your team to complete their objective. I understand the criticality of this mission."

"This wasn't your fault. I hope this doesn't make matters worse for our country," Beatrice lamented. "The President was so adamant that the success of this attack was critical to protecting our country."

"Nevertheless, I'm responsible," the admiral said. "I did witness the potential of these laser vehicles. They're quite impressive against the Iranians, and if you twelve were protecting them, they would've put up one hell of a fight in Lebanon. I plan to get the others on deck to help us when the Iranian ships arrive. With those lasers and our submarines, we may surprise those Iranian ships. Don't underestimate the United States Navy."

"You're probably right," Beatrice said. "Good luck, and give them hell."

"Same to you," he said as Beatrice motioned to Zeke.

Zeke lifted her over to the sub while giving the admiral a salute.

Beatrice scurried below deck. A sailor closed the hatch, and the submarine submerged into the sea below.

Chapter 21

Chaos and Consequences

Turmoil in Washington ensued as news agencies worldwide reported an attempted attack by the U.S. against Iran shortly after the invasion of Israel.

The Iranian government, who leaked the information, promptly confirmed the unprovoked attack and announced that they had quickly quelled it.

People filled the streets across United Iran, screaming hatred against America, burning the U.S. flag, and praising Allah for their Iranian warriors who continued to thwart the infidels. They begged their government to act against America in retaliation. Iran conveniently forgot to mention the demise of ten warriors and the disappearance of many more at the hand of the U.S. Navy.

Meanwhile, the Iranian government celebrated its early successes against Israel and announced that Jerusalem would soon be theirs. Their news outlets reported that their invasion was going as planned, even with America aiding Israel.

Iran officially declared war against the United States in response to the American attack. It added that any other country coming to the aid of Israel would receive a similar fate.

Furthermore, due to the damage done to the Russian submarine in the failed attack, Russia declared it would join the war against Israel and the United States. Furthermore, Russia, supported by Iran, announced it was also declaring war against

Europe. As feared by Europe, Alexei Kovalyov said it was time to free the European people from the bonds of capitalism, an excuse many knew he continued as justification for his greedy desires.

The world expectantly waited for China to announce similar intentions in the Pacific. China, however, issued no proclamation, and the U.S., along with other western nations, breathed a sigh of relief.

President Schmidt, distraught by the failure of the USS Ford, knew the U.S. should expect a terrifying reprisal from Iran with the help of Russia. He also realized that his European allies were now overtly in the crosshairs of Kovalyov due to his failed attack.

The President had hoped that a successful attack on Iran would show the world that Iran was not indestructible and get other nations to join the war. Now he faced a dire situation, unsure how Iran would proceed. The entire U.S. sensed the resulting threat, and the President struggled to maintain his command of a failing nation.

He scheduled an emergency meeting with the Vice President, Secretary of State, and Secretary of Defense. The President needed options and a game plan. He wasn't sure when or how, but the U.S. needed its defenses ready for whatever may come.

They convened in the Oval Office for the meeting. The President had not slept since the failed attack. He was frustrated and angry at what had occurred. Answers were required to update the nation and Congress, who knew nothing of his secret attack before it broke in the international news. Ire from every part of America erupted about the failed effort, and there was going to be political hell to pay.

"Damn it, Cassandra," the President yelled, uncharacteristically letting the pressure get to him. "We had this all lined out. So much work and planning went into this, and the carrier propulsion system fails? The Defense Department has to be better than this. We need accountability."

"Understood, Mr. President," she said. "It's already being addressed."

"What's the current status with the carrier group?" he questioned, not hiding his continued angst.

"The carrier and the cruiser survived the attack. Unfortunately, we lost twelve hundred men and women, two frigates, and they took out four helicopters and six F-15s.

Two of our submarines finally sank the five Iranian ships, and none of their crews or telekinetic warriors survived. We learned in the battle that these telekinetic warriors aren't as lethal in the water. They still can use their powers, but the discs are far less agile and damaging moving through water.

Admiral Leighton brought the laser platforms on the carrier's deck and told us that the Phoenix Project vehicles were instrumental in the fight. He used them to take out Iranian warriors trying to get on the carrier deck during the battle.

As for the carrier's propulsion, Naval Reactors flew an engineering crew to the carrier with replacement hardware. They were able to get the propulsion system back up and running. The carrier needs some additional repairs, and we were hoping to get them in Naples, but Italy is refusing to let them into their ports now."

"And what about the Davidson children?" he asked, losing some of his ire. "What's their current status?"

"The submarine that rescued them was met by a Navy helicopter after passing through the Strait of Gibraltar," said the Defense Secretary. "They are being flown back, as we speak, from the naval air station in Spain to Andrews. We expect them to land within the hour. Two of the children were injured, as you know. Zeke's injuries were minor and treated on the sub. His armor suit proved the difference.

On the other hand, Alan sustained serious injuries before Zeke protected him. Alan was unconscious, last we knew, but stable. He will need surgery immediately when he arrives."

"I'm glad they made it out alive," said the President. "See to it that Alan gets the best medical care available. At least I don't have their lives on my hands. We've already lost too many people again."

The President put his head in his hands, rubbing his temples. The backlash for what occurred was going to be immense.

Unsure of how to proceed, he said, "We have several difficult discussions ahead. Congress, the American people, and our allies are furious that they had no clue we were launching this attack. Now seeing it failed, they will blame us for the careless move and the resulting wrath of Iran they hoped to avoid. Where should we start, and what's our message?"

His question was rhetorical, to which none of them responded. He calmed himself and tried to focus.

President Schmidt added after several seconds, "At his request, I have an urgent call with Israeli President Yaakv in thirty minutes. I'll come clean on our plan and tell him this is not over, and we're all in. I'm unsure what he urgently wishes to share with me, but I'll know soon enough. Folks, I ask that you get your teams together and figure out how we can prepare for what's coming our way."

"I would like to reach out to China, Mr. President," said his Vice President. "I developed a solid rapport with a few key leaders during my visit, and I would like to gauge their concerns and gather any insight they would be willing to share. Are you comfortable with that?"

"Absolutely," he answered without hesitation. "Do it, and let me know what you find out.

Jack, I need you to contact Prime Minister Caponero in Italy and get him to let that damn carrier into port. Tell him that now is not the time to play politics and that war is upon all of us. Remind him that there may be a day soon when they want our help with Russia."

"Yes, Mr. President," said his Secretary of State. "If you are comfortable with me contacting some ministers in France and the U.K., I would like to do that. I know you must call President Corbin and Prime Minister Carrington, but I can get a sense of the political landscape before those calls."

"Always thinking ahead for me," the President said with a strained smile.

"Cassandra, I need a war plan immediately," said the President. "We have two of the four most powerful countries globally having declared war on us in the last six hours. I need something concrete in the morning. I have to address the nation today, but I must get to Congress first. They are demanding answers. My own party is abandoning me."

"You'll have it by zero-seven hundred, Mr. President," the Defense Secretary answered with conviction.

Into the Oval Office burst the President's assistant. "Mr. President, you need to turn on the national news," she screamed. "We're under attack in New York and Boston."

"What do you mean?" he said with fear draining further hope from his face. "Get it on now."

As the screen came on, they heard the news anchor say, "This footage just came in from New York."

The video clip showed two Iranian warriors with discs walking the streets of Manhattan. The discs were shattering the windows of buildings and striking people walking the streets. People ran in all directions and scrambled out of high-rises from every exit as discs pursued them.

'Somehow, Iran got two warriors into New York,' said the anchor. 'Horrific images, I have to say. Wait, new video coming in from Dallas, Texas.'

A video came up with similar images: two Iranian warriors were walking the streets of downtown Dallas, brutalizing people with their discs, smashing vehicles, and taking out the inter-city train.

'We have confirmed that the Iranians are also in Seattle, Houston, Philadelphia, and Atlanta,' said the stunned anchor. 'The attack is massive. Hold on; something is just coming in on my earpiece. Oh God, they are in the nation's capital as well. I just confirmed two of them are operating near Dupont Circle, near the White House. Capitol Hill, the White House, and the Pentagon are likely headed for lockdowns. What we're witnessing is a full-scale invasion.'

"We need to get moving now," barked the President to the Defense Secretary. "Get the military deployed. We have to do our best to defend against these warriors."

The Defense Secretary darted out of his office on her way to the Pentagon. The other two stayed behind, watching the television.

Distraught, the news anchor said, 'We now have confirmation of attacks ongoing in forty-three cities across the nation. America is once again under attack on its soil. This attack is far larger than Pearl Harbor. Reports rolling in are consistently providing details of cold-blooded massacres.'

"We unleashed a serpent into our den," said the President.

His words he meant for no one. He was talking to himself.

"I'm not sure how we defend ourselves against this," he muttered, thinking of what he learned during the Phoenix Project about their capabilities.

The President's assistant hustled into the office once again. Her eyes wide with fear, she said, "Mr. President, the President of Iran is on the phone demanding to speak with you."

President Schmidt mirrored her fear. The pit in his already nauseous gut wrenched.

He muttered, "Put him through."

The President picked up the phone and said, "President Schmidt."

A snarl came through on the other end.

Speaking in English, the Iranian President said, "You dare launch an attack on our country. Did you think you could slip by our watchful eyes and we not catch you sneaking into our waters? You think we're fools and underestimate our sophistication. Furthermore, you failed to recognize that the United States is no longer a world leader, free to take action without consequences. Allah has designated Iran the world's new leader, and we bring his might. You made a terrible mistake, and now your people pay the price with their lives. I'm calling to give you a simple opportunity to save many of your people."

Breathing heavily on the phone and most likely working through the English in his prepared speech, he continued, "Before I give you the proposition, I need you to understand your current situation so that you may make the best decision for your people.

We have placed two holy warriors in each of your fifty largest metropolitan areas. They are now sweeping the streets, killing everyone in sight and wreaking havoc on everything around them. I have unleashed them to kill and destroy at will. They will continue to do so until I give them the order to cease.

That order will come after our discussion should this call meet my approval. Otherwise, they will continue until we have washed your people from all the land, carried away in their blood.

Understand this; an unwillingness to accept my proposition will cause me to continue the destruction of your cities and force me to bring more of our warriors to sweep through the rest of your land."

The evil in his voice shook the President.

"We won't stand for this. How did you get your telekinetic warriors into our country?" demanded the President.

"Still now, you don't realize how puny you have become. No one fears the United States anymore. You ask me how I got my warriors in when you know that your porous borders allow drug dealers, criminals, spies, and our glorious warriors to slide easily in and out of your country. So pitiful how you choose to operate your government and ignore the very things that make you vulnerable.

President Schmidt, your nation came into existence such a short time ago, and now it will be gone in the blink of an eye, only remembered as a tiny scourge on the history of man.

In contrast, our people have persisted for nine thousand years, far before the Romans and the Greeks. While our existence has ebbed and flowed during those millennia, we have never truly broken as a people. Only a year ago, the Great American Empire was feared by many and beloved by many others. Yet now, it has fallen and sits at the mercy of Iran. Our time to reign supreme is now. You will bow to us, and you will do so soon."

"Get to your point," the President demanded assertively.

Laughing, the Iranian President said, "Still trying to tell your new master what to do. You Americans never learn, but I understand. Being subservient is not what you are used to, but you and your people will soon learn. I've had enough of this idle chatter. Here is my proposition, and you need to understand that there is no negotiation. Accept what I'm about to tell you, or you and your people will all die. We'll erase you from the face of this planet if need be."

"I'm listening," said the President in a more docile tone, recognizing that his military would have little success against one hundred of their warriors. He also realized that the threat of Iran sending more warriors was not idle, as their supply seemed somewhat endless after a decade of build-up.

"President Schmidt, within the next twenty-four hours, you will go on television, in front of your people and the world, and unconditionally surrender the United States of America to the United Islamic Republic of Iran. After this call, I'll cease my one hundred warriors' slaughter of your people until that deadline.

You must tell your people, police, and military to give our warriors a keep-out area of one mile in radius in all directions around them or perish within that circle.

I recognize that our warriors in Washington, D.C., are within a mile of your White House. We'll make an exception for you, but the Supreme Leader will keep a watchful eye on you with our two best warriors. Our warriors there will allow travel as necessary from the White House, the Capitol, and your Pentagon so you can adequately coordinate your surrender.

Any other movements toward our warriors will result in the death of those who violate the keep-out. If your military attempts to attack our warriors in any city, I'll have our warriors in Washington march directly to your home. Do you understand my demands and your situation?"

"I do," came out from the President.

"Then I'll stand them down. Get the word out quickly to your people. Tell them they must stand down, or there will be many more deaths. We look forward to your surrender tomorrow night. I know there is no way you will do so before that time as you will wait until the deadline hoping for a solution to your dilemma. None will come.

Everyone will tell you there are alternatives. You will even think about nuclear strikes or unleashing some contagion you have developed. They won't work. We have studied these techniques. We'll handily defeat them and then make you choke on them at your death for trying them against us."

"You will hear from me in twenty-four hours," the President assured him, not wishing to prolong the call.

"I know that I will. Hopefully, America's pride doesn't overcome its inevitability. When I hang up the phone, Iran will notify the global media of everything we discussed. Good day to you, President Schmidt."

The President hung up and was momentarily mortified by the message. What struck him hardest was that he couldn't see a way out. After months with the Phoenix Project, he knew there was no available protection for the people. The military was no match for the warriors, and the civilian organizations were even less.

Lost in his thoughts, the President forgot the Vice President and Secretary of State were still in the room. They could tell by his mannerisms that what just transpired was horrible.

"What did he say?" asked the Vice President.

"He told me that we have twenty-four hours to proclaim our unconditional surrender," said the President, turning more ashen with each word forming on his lips. "And to keep our people away from their warriors until that time. Anyone or anything that approaches within one mile will be quickly destroyed.

Should we not accept the surrender by then, they will sweep their warriors through our fifty most populated cities first and send reinforcements to finish the rest of the country, wiping us from the planet. I believe he meant every word of it."

"How will we respond, Paul?" asked the Secretary of State.

The use of the President's first name seemed appropriate for the moment.

"How can we help?" added the Vice President.

"Thank you, Jack and Alan," responded the President, looking uncertain. "I think we need to call an immediate meeting of the full Cabinet, key Congressional leaders, and heads within the military. The discussion we need to have can only happen with these organizations represented. We can discuss our options then."

"On it," exclaimed the Vice President.

Alan and Jack urgently left together to round up the leaders.

The news channel was still on in the room. Across the bottom banner, below the anchor, read 'Breaking News: Truce called by Iranian Leadership Under the Condition that the U.S. Unconditionally Surrender in the Next 24 Hours.'

It's already out there. There will be no time to ponder anything. The crisis had just become a catastrophe. The President had two commitments to take care of before the leadership would get to the White House.

He opened his door, and sitting outside was Heidi and Peter Davidson. A million things were on his mind, but he knew it was essential to speak with them, albeit quickly. He owed them that.

"Please come in," said the anxious President.

"Is everything okay?" asked Peter seeing the troubled looks on the Vice President and Secretary of State who had just bolted out of his office and a prominent pained expression on the President. "It seems like they left in a panic."

"We have a delicate situation at hand, and I need to make this quick," he answered without details.

The Davidsons had been sitting outside his office for an hour and hadn't heard what was occurring.

"I wanted to update you on your children," said the President. "We informed you that we got them off the carrier and onto a submarine for transport back to the U.S., but you received no other details. Here is the laydown. They were in a battle on the carrier before they escaped. A Russian sub brought Iranian warriors to the carrier, and a fight ensued.

Right now, the twelve of your children are on a jet that will soon land at Andrews. Alan is severely injured and will require emergency medical attention at Walter Reed when he lands. Per our last update, he is in stable condition, but his injuries are significant. Zeke has minor injuries, and they treated him on the sub. I suggest you get to Andrews and head to the hospital with Alan."

He dreaded telling them this, but he knew this news was much better than it could have been if they hadn't gotten them out.

"Thank you for letting us know," said Peter. "We'll get over there immediately. What happened in the attack?"

"I'll let them debrief you at Andrews," said the President. "I have an emergency meeting any minute now, and I need to prepare. My assistant will escort you out. We have transportation ready to take you to Andrews.

I'm sorry, but important matters need my immediate attention. Be aware that there is going to be chaos when you leave. The U.S. is under attack across the country by Iran."

"We didn't know," said Heidi, shocked by the news but eager to get to Andrews and see her children. "Thank you for taking the time. We won't hold you up a second longer."

He showed them out, and his assistant handed the Davidsons off to the security team waiting to transport them to the Air Force Base.

"You have the call with Prime Minister Yaakv to take," said his assistant. "We're about five minutes late in doing so. I rang their side, and they are on hold, waiting for you to finish with the Davidsons."

The President was pressed for time but needed to take this call. People would arrive soon, so he hurried and picked up the call.

"Prime Minister Yaakv, sorry for the delay," said the American leader. "I'm sure you have seen the news announcements. I have an emergency meeting, but I promised you the call."

"President Schmidt, I saw the news," replied the Israeli. "I know you must have a great deal going on. I promise to be prompt. My call has two purposes. The first is to thank you for attempting the attack on Iran and attempting a surprise second front to the war with Iran.

I'm unsure why you didn't bother sharing this with me in advance, but we Israelis understand secrecy is often essential, even with allies."

"I'm glad you understand, and I'm sorry we were unsuccessful," responded the President.

Prime Minister Yaakv didn't linger on the last point.

"The second reason I have called you is to inform you of the actual situation in Israel. News sources are non-existent in Israel right now. The information Iran is leaking is skewed for their purposes, as you might suspect.

In the beginning, Iran destroyed most of our communications links to control coverage of the war. We're now speaking on a special network we developed for this purpose years ago. You need to know the facts and what we have done before making your decision in America.

I know what Iran has done to you and their demands. I warned your predecessor to control your borders. I even offered to provide our technology. Nevertheless, I'm not here to lecture you. The circumstances in Israel is that Iran has already killed more than two million Israelis since the start."

"I'm surprised it's not worse," muttered the President, letting it slip.

"We're using guerilla tactics like the resistance forces fighting in Eastern Europe supported by the new laser cannons we developed. They have done well, but after a short period of operation, their warriors understand their location and destroy them.

Our military placed a heavy concentration of lasers around Tel Aviv and Jerusalem and dispersed many others along our borders. We've removed dozens of their warriors, but they seem to have endless supplies.

To quickly get to the second purpose of my call, I wish to inform you that we'll soon execute a military operation we've designated Operation Tav. We'll detonate one nuclear bomb in the West Bank along the border with Jordan during the operation, which will start soon.

The bomb is only meant to demonstrate our commitment to Operation Tav. We'll inform Iran, which sits outside our cities and fights as we speak, that we'll begin detonating other nuclear bombs in succession if they continue their invasion. We'll not tell them where or when, or how many we have placed throughout the country.

The ploy is simple, and we hope effective. Jerusalem will never be theirs, nor will any of the lands of Israel. If they insist on continuing their invasion, we'll leave them only a barren, toxic wasteland that will blow into their glorious united lands through the winds, poisoning them for decades.

Our evacuees and other Jews spread worldwide will carry our lineage forward from their dispersed positions and keep our people and spirit alive. We who have stayed behind will perish, but we'll not let Iran win. We'll only give them the Tav."

Sorrowfully, the President responded, "Your path Orem is one where no one wins. I know your options are limited. I have nothing to offer you regarding options, but please consider other alternatives."

"We already have Paul," he gloomily answered. "This is our final stand. You will soon consider these same options, my friend. I need to make final preparations before we initiate this. I don't envy your position. I hope you discover a better option. Thank you for the call."

The Israeli Prime Minister hung up, and the President set the handset down.

The President felt the entire world was collapsing simultaneously. He wondered if this was the best humanity was able to cobble together. He didn't have time to dwell on it as he had to get moving.

People everywhere were glued to the television or online news sources. Reports of significant casualties rolled in from across the country at the hands of the Iranian warriors. Grotesque images of mangled bodies, smashed cars, and shattered buildings flowed into news services nationwide.

Network traffic was so high many providers were unable to support the activity, and connectivity was lost. Panic followed as people assumed it was the result of the ongoing attacks. Cell service and over-the-air television became mainstream outlets for people to find that the attacks had ceased.

Cumulative estimations already tallied in the hundreds of thousands of dead after only minutes of Iranian warrior action.

Most news channels cut in with the breaking news of the Iranian President's demand for the U.S. President to surrender.

President Schmidt waited until all the called key leaders reached the White House or connected by video conference. He had to clear his head and consider his options, but there was no time.

Upon notification that those he requested to attend were ready, he headed into the meeting.

The assembled group included the Cabinet, the Joint Chiefs, the National Intelligence Director, and the two top leaders representing both parties in the senate and the house. He also asked Dr. Carter to join them for his expertise on the capabilities of the Iranian warriors and the Phoenix Project.

The President wasn't sure what to say to them. He knew the moment demanded more than he could muster, but he didn't try to fake any grandeur.

"It's with grave concern that you are all called here today," he started. "You have already heard, I'm sure, of the demands from Iran, so I won't take time to rehash them."

House Minority Leader, Barnaby Blankenship from Alabama, fumed in his seat.

The President ignored his obvious displeasure.

Waiting only for the President to hesitate a second, the Alabama Congressman seized the moment.

He exclaimed, "What in damnation do you think you are doing initiating an unprovoked attack on Iran without the approval of Congress? You put the United States in one hell of a pickle."

"It wasn't possible to obtain approval and ensure the security that we needed to pull off the attack," said the President, unwilling to play politics at such a crucial moment. "Approval from Congress equals an announcement to the world, a risk I couldn't take."

"But you failed with a poorly executed plan," the Congressman fired back. "We follow security protocols. It wouldn't have gotten out. Don't hide under cover of secrecy. This move is typical of what we've gotten from this presidency."

"Not the time to play politics," the President snapped back. "We need real leadership discussions here."

"I think we should start by you resigning so we can get some better leadership in place," groused the Congressman, not relenting on his pressing of the President.

"That's enough, Barnaby," said the Senate Majority Leader, Texas Senator Art Schram, to his fellow party member.

Senator Schram was a senior, four-term Senator and a big burly man that looked like everything you might believe a former Texas soldier might be.

"I spent twenty-six years in the Army and have followed the President's every step throughout his presidency with great interest. In my opinion, which comes from many deployments, he has done everything he should have militarily. His attack, while it failed, could have been a huge blow to Iran. As the President said, let's drop the political bullshit and focus on what we must do."

The Alabama Congressman didn't appreciate getting dressed down openly and squirmed in his seat. He was about to continue but saw the whole group eyeing him and seemingly agreeing with the Texas Senator.

"Thank you, Art," said the President, appreciating the Senator's support.

"I need to bring many of you up to speed on important matters that feed into the attempted attack we were launching," the President started again.

Many sitting around the table with the President knew nothing about the Cranio-Genesis Project or that it was the origin of the Iranian warriors. For that matter, they didn't even know of the Phoenix Project. He needed to share this with them, understanding that if they were angry before about the secrecy of the attack, they would be livid about this.

"I kept other elements from you due to security concerns," said President Schmidt, resuming. "The origin of the Iranian warriors comes not from Allah, as Iranian leadership has spewed, but from a top-secret U.S. military program called Cranio-Genesis."

The President saw the same looks of dismay when he first heard about it from the Defense Secretary.

"We don't have time to go into the details, but you have a brief in front of you that contains all the key elements. The bottom line is that the project resulted in individuals with telekinetic capabilities. Iran stole this information over a decade ago after we shut down Cranio-Genesis. Iranian leaders then proliferated it secretly for years, hidden from the world, and turned it into a large army of these warriors."

Again, the President recognized the churning thoughts and the light bulbs about the Iranian warriors going off in their heads.

Unwilling to let another interruption come, he continued, "Studying the powers and capabilities of these warriors, Iran created tungsten carbide discs for these telekinetic warriors to use as highly lethal weapons. While there are still questions in the public view about how the discs and the warriors play together,

I'm here to tell you that the warriors are the technology. The discs are ultra-durable, reusable ammunition. It's like having a gun with huge bullets that never runs out."

He stopped and gave them time to digest what he had just told them. He could see the Alabama Congressman squirming, but he held his tongue this time. He also realized that the Defense Secretary had never read her Joint Chiefs, except Admiral Lawton, into either project. She had taken his directive literally, as she should have.

"If we developed this, do we have warriors?" asked the Army Chief.

"We have twelve," answered the President. "They were on the carrier and were going to be a key part of the attack."

"And where are they now?" said New York Senator Darren Cameron, the Senate Minority Leader.

"They just landed back at Andrews. One is severely injured and headed to Walter Reed for medical attention as we speak."

"What went wrong with the attack?" asked Speaker of the House Lillian Tellini.

"The carrier encountered a major propulsion failure and was stranded about two hours outside Lebanon, where we planned to go ashore and initiate the attack."

"Iran sent ships, loaded with their warriors, out to meet the carrier group. Given the inability to carry out the mission, we decided to extract our twelve telekinetic warriors. To do so, we surfaced one of our submarines to take them safely back to the states. However, a Russian submarine surfaced beside our carrier before the Iranian ships arrived and dispatched ten Iranian warriors and their discs onto our carrier's deck.

One of our telekinetic warriors damaged the submarine, and a U.S. frigate subsequently sunk the Russian sub."

The President could see each of them linking the version in the press to what occurred. Iranian news sources failed to mention that the Russian sub played a role in attacking the U.S. carrier group. Their news sources stated it was another unprovoked U.S. attack on Russia.

The President clarified for the group, adding, "Yes, Russia aided the attack."

The President knew the group deserved an explanation of the events but didn't want to get bogged down in too many details. There was still a lot to discuss.

"Our warriors and new laser weapons, critical elements of our planned attack, took care of the ten Iranians in a fierce battle on the carrier's deck. After evacuating the twelve warriors, two of our submarines destroyed the approaching Iranian ships and dozens of their warriors, but that battle was also fierce.

Shortly afterward, the carrier reestablished propulsion, and the group left the region. Unfortunately, our allies will not allow the carrier group into their ports."

"How many of these warriors does Iran have?" asked the Speaker.

"Hundreds, maybe many more," said the President grimly.

"You have hidden much from us," sputtered the Alabama Congressman. "Are there any other vital details you failed to share for supposed secrecy reasons?"

He dribbled out the last word with a callous tone.

"Just one more," said the President, unflinching at the Congressman's lack of respect. "Their warriors and ours are all teens or even younger possibly, in the case of the Iranians."

They were stunned, and pure disbelief screamed from their faces.

"So, you sent children to lead an attack, which you purposely hid from us, and we're now under attack on U.S. soil because of it," screamed the Alabama Congressman, standing and pointing his finger at the President. "You damn fool. I'll accept nothing other than your resignation as a good start to cleaning up this whole mess."

"Sit down, Congressman," shouted the Texas Senator. "The President isn't a fool, but you're coming across as one. He knows what he's doing. Use your head; many of the people in this room knew everything that's happened, and there no imbeciles either. I know him well enough to recognize that he must have done it for the right reasons. If you can't be helpful in these discussions, I'll kick your ass out of here myself."

The President was surprised by the sharp tone from the Texas Senator against one of his closest party allies. He recognized that a man who served his country for so many years knew that certain military decisions utilize the best information at the time and require calculated risks along with tightly held secrecy.

President Schmidt appreciated the support as he had little tolerance for the Congressman's antics, given the need to be productive in the current situation.

"Let's proceed," was the President's succinct response.

He understood that this predicament strummed those chords of human nature to find blame, but playing that game derailed their ability to focus.

"Please, let's just concentrate on the difficult situation at hand," he said, encouraging proactive discourse.

"Our subs took out the Iranian ships even with their warriors on board. Do we have a distinct Naval advantage?" inquired Admiral Simpson, the Chief of Naval Operations.

"We appear to, but now with Russia on their side, they will be a force to deal with," answered the President. "Iran will choose to leave the sea fighting to Russia and engage us in the air and on land. Their warriors have the advantage there. We should expect them to adjust after what happened in the Mediterranean and change their tactics."

"And what about China?" asked the CNO.

"We have not seen any formal military engagement from China, but many have felt they were waiting for the right time. That time may be upon us. There were no indications they were involved in the carrier group incident or the attacks on Israel."

"Should we deploy nuclear weapons?" asked Senator Schram. "I know it's a dangerous move, but if we can't beat them with conventional weapons, then it may be necessary."

"Before I address your question, Senator, everyone needs to hear one last item. Before starting this meeting, I had an urgent call with Israeli Prime Minister Yaakv Israel is about to initiate a plan he referred to as Operation Tav.

Tav is the last letter of the Hebrew alphabet. My interpretation is they mean the end.

Israel will soon set off a nuclear bomb in the West Bank along the border with Jordan. He shared that they are prepared to do the same in numerous locations throughout their country, including Tel Aviv and Jerusalem. Israel plans to leave nothing for Iran to take. He will demand Iran either back away or lose everything, including Jerusalem. The fallout and radiation, he hopes, will take to the wind and poison Iran for ages and leave a toxic wasteland in the region."

"That's not a plan. That's doomsday," said the Texas Senator.

"I concurred and told him as much, but I don't think I changed his mind in the slightest," said the President. "Unfortunately, our situation is no different. Iran is going to wipe us out if we don't comply. At least Israel has a prized Islamic religious asset in Jerusalem and, thus, a bargaining chip. We possess nothing they desire, and Iranian President Kazemi confirmed that point in our brief discussion.

But back to your question, Senator. I've made it clear that I'll not subject the world to the use of chemical, biological, and nuclear weapons. That approach will result in harsh retaliation and lead to mutual destruction. No country wins that war.

We also know that the Iranian warriors can intercept dropped or launched weapons with their discs at remarkably high altitudes and stop them from reaching their target. We suspect they have specific warriors positioned for this purpose.

Could we slip something into their country and detonate it? Likely we could, but they would strike back with a force of a hundred times greater, and they have Russia's support in that endeavor. If anyone would win that exchange, it would likely be them."

"Maybe we can hit them with chemical or biological weapons in their current locations in our cities?" suggested Air Force Chief Antony. "Low blast zone, small kill zone, but nothing survives within its reach. Eradicate them before they can do any more harm. We'll have some time to initiate that before the deadline."

"Let me share something else with you. I secretly created an effort, the Phoenix Project, to assess and develop counter-weapons against the Iranians," said the President, waiting for another outburst from the Alabama Congressman about yet another hidden item.

None came, so he continued, "The capability of these warriors is not just in their telekinetic powers but also their sensory abilities. The gentleman on the video screen in the center, Dr. Nicholas Carter, headed the project for me. He can share many of the findings from the project at some other time, but we know that if we attempt to get close or launch something at them, they will sense and destroy it.

For this reason, we may find it challenging to strike at them, but it may be an option with them corralled in a tight space."

"General Antony's proposal may be a good start to fighting back," offered the Alabama Congressman, looking at his Texan counterpart to assess whether his statement was okay.

"That could be one element of an attack that might work," said the Secretary of Defense, resonating with the idea. "I know you said no nuclear, chemical, or biological weapons, but these are desperate conditions."

She offered the last piece hesitantly due to the angry response she received from the President the last time she inquired about their use.

"It could be a possibility," replied the President if we decide to fight. "Know that they could inflict considerable damage without leaving their one-mile radius. Their powers extend quite a distance, so we have to hit them swiftly before they wreak havoc. They may suspect we have planted some traps if we don't surrender. I think it deserves further discussion. But realize that while we may eliminate these hundred, they will soon send more with great vengeance. The Iranian President coldly referenced that in our discussion if we fail to surrender."

"We'll NOT SURRENDER," blasted the Alabama Congressman. "That shouldn't even be up for discussion. We need to blast them damn Iranians to kingdom come."

"That's not your decision, Congressman," said the President calmly. "That power rests with me and me alone. We have millions of American lives to consider, and we can't just do something because we're angry. We're responsible for doing what's right for the nation as a whole."

Anguish, futility, and dread clouded their minds. It was not in the mindset of Americans to think the United States of America would ever consider surrendering.

"I'm not inclined to surrender nor risk the lives of hundreds of millions of Americans, including my own family, but I don't have an answer," declared the President.

"I understand your earlier point, Mr. President, but I'm not sure the people of America will follow you if you issue a surrender," said the Texas Senator. "You may do it, but no American has to follow that directive upon you doing so. You will never be able to police that decision. Many, maybe even most, will still choose to fight, and many are well armed."

"I agree with that statement," grumbled the Alabama Congressman.

"As do I," said the Speaker.

She understood the dilemma and difficult situation, but she also knew large pockets all over America would fight for years if they had to.

"And they will die horrible deaths!" came from the video screen.

For those on the video, Dr. Carter approached the camera on his end so they could see his face better.

As he got close to the camera, so they could better see his face, he said, "My team has been studying their capabilities for the last several months. Our scientists have been testing our telekinetic children to assess the whole gamut of their powers so we better understand the Iranian army we now face.

You don't understand how formidable these warriors are. Recall Iraq, Afghanistan, Saudi Arabia, and the swift Turkish defeat. They can sweep through and wipe out with speed and ease using their discs or anything less than a few thousand pounds they choose to propel.

They now sit within our borders in all our major metropolitan areas. It's not that the beasts can only kill you easily; they are sitting on top of us with our throats in their maws, begging us to make them bite.

Americans don't need you to act boldly. They need you to act in their best interest. Iran baited us once into a battle in Iraq, and they destroyed us in minutes. Don't underestimate this foe."

"What he says is spot on," interjected Admiral Lawton. "The Defense Secretary and I have been tightly coupled with the Phoenix Project. You are underestimating their warriors."

"So then, why did you initiate an attack?" asked Senator Cameron. "If they're so indestructible, why attack?"

"We found a way to defeat them by using our twelve children to counteract their powers and use laser weapons recently developed by the Phoenix Project to take them and their discs out," said Dr. Carter. "The laser vehicles were intended to sweep in and eliminate their warriors so our other conventional military could come in behind without fear and drive Iran back. Ultimately, we believed we could use the technique to defeat them."

The President added, "At a minimum, we hoped to restore a balance of power and seek a peaceful end. According to my discussion with the Israeli Prime Minister, Israel uses similar lasers. He says they are having success, but their issue is as soon as they use a laser to kill, the Iranian warriors know its location and sweep in and destroy it.

Our approach used the twelve telekinetic children to protect the lasers. Based on significant testing on the Phoenix Project, we demonstrated a clear military advantage against the Iranian warriors. That is why we launched the attack. Hit them on their home soil before they could bring the fight to us."

"So why not use the lasers here, now that they are on our homeland?" asked Admiral Simpson.

"We could, but we only have a few additional vehicles currently in Idaho or another eight on an aircraft carrier that's days away," responded the President. "Aircraft can't transport them due to their size, so we required the aircraft carrier to deliver them to Lebanon. We won't have them for a few weeks at best. The ones in Idaho are not where we need them either. They would be, at best, a day away from a few of the cities under attack."

"There is one additional major vulnerability should we say no," said the Defense Secretary, who still felt many in the room didn't comprehend the severity of the situation. "We know Iran is nuclear-capable, and Russia is always extremely dangerous with their nuclear arsenal. Neither of them cares for the U.S. and could launch their nuclear strike against us. Their likelihood of success is far greater than our own, especially with the Iranian warriors. I understand that surrendering is not in the American vocabulary, but it's time you start recognizing that we teeter on a dangerous high wire."

"The dramatics are not necessary. We do get it. So, what would you have us do?" asked the Speaker.

"I'm sorry, but we don't have a solution," answered the Defense Secretary. "All options are horrific."

"Let me be clear again. I don't want to surrender either," said the President, taking back control of the conversation. "Life as we Americans know it will end. The choice is loss of life or loss of freedom. On one side, sending most Americans to their death is not leadership; it's insanity. While on the other hand, surrendering this nation and its people to Iran is unreasonable."

"Can we create a multi-pronged strategy that will at least kick Iran back on its haunches," asked Admiral Lawton with a contemplative stare.

"What do you have in mind?" asked the President, looking for ideas.

"If we go down, then we go down fighting," replied the admiral. "I don't believe we have a choice. All options result in the death of many Americans, so let's play out the option where we fight.

So, we think they can take out our nuclear missiles, but I'm not convinced they believe that with complete assuredness. They don't understand all our capabilities, even with Russia on their side. Why send their warriors here into our cities if they weren't afraid of our abilities? Iran needed to put their hands around our throats to ensure we didn't do something like that.

Let's bluff them. Boldly deny the surrender Iran so eagerly craves. Let's eliminate their hundred warriors and pump our chests out like we have something they need to be afraid of engaging. Something so powerful and effective that we remain confident in facing them.

They know we're not stupid, so they will question their supremacy and proceed cautiously. Iran and Russia will hold back from a nuclear attack, unsure that our retaliation won't destroy them. Mutually assured destruction will exist heavily in Iran's mind, particularly if we boldly reject them. Their grand unification means nothing if it creates a holy mess on Earth. It will give us time to regroup and give America a fighting chance."

"I follow your logic," said President Schmidt. "Please continue."

"Let's deploy a multi-pronged attack. Start with our airspace within our borders. We need to control that to accomplish anything. So, step one is to eliminate their warriors. We have the means to do that, but we must scramble to get them to all the locations and deployed before the deadline. That will be tricky but doable."

"Ok, so we take our airspace back by stopping their warriors," followed the President. "Many people will likely die before we accomplish that, but I see where you are going."

"Yes, and step two, we deploy the Davidsons with the laser vehicles in Idaho to wherever we need them most," continued the admiral. "There is little coverage with just six vehicles, but we know they are highly effective if any of their warriors appear. Our best scenario would be to spread them across the U.S. in our most densely populated areas.

Next, we enlist key industry partners and build lasers as fast as possible and as many as possible. These lasers will be without the protection of the Davidsons, but we can use them like Israel. According to what you said, Mr. President, they were effective briefly until destroyed. Maybe we can even find ways to protect them better with some creative thoughts from the Phoenix Project team.

After that, we seal everything: our ports, coasts, and borders. We can't allow for another breach with their warriors. Not easy, but critical to our safety, and our people will be motivated to help secure it.

Finally, we get as much of the Navy on the open sea and control the oceans the best we can. We keep our nuclear submarines prepared to launch at a moment's notice, and we fight.

Once our homeland is secure, we can assess how we use the Army, Navy, Marines, and Air Force.

Then you, Mr. President, try to enlist our European allies into the bigger fight. Russia is coming for them now, and they can't continue to run from it. We all stand up and take these enemies head-on. The worst-case scenario is that we live to fight another day and keep looking for ways to win this thing."

"I agree with the Admiral," said the Texas Senator. "If you surrender, many won't follow that decision, as I said. They will fight in far more hopeless manners than we can if we stand and fight. We still have numerous assets that sit at your disposal. I think the admiral has it correct, but you have to lead us down that path. I, for one, will support you in that decision."

"You know, I sure as hell agree," the Alabama Congressman yelled.

"I agree with them as well," said his Secretary of State. "Mr. President, you are the one man who can lead this nation down this path. We need you to do this."

"Not to throw cold water on the admiral's statements or the others," said the Defense Secretary. "But if China joins them, they may create a far greater overmatch than we can handle."

"Cassandra, I picked you for many reasons, but reasoning like that was the main one," said the President, appreciative of her concern about other risks and not drawn into the patriotic zeal. "If China comes to the party, then we fight them. I need a plan drawn up ASAP to cover all elements of what we'll do, and you have the go-ahead to implement any time-sensitive piece. The clock is ticking. And thank you, everyone, for your counsel. Let's get this rolling. I know what I have to do."

Chapter 22

One Nation Unwilling to Grovel

The time was passing quickly, and the deadline was racing toward them. There were so many moving parts that the Pentagon, the White House, and the President's team scrambled to tie them all down. The Executive Order by the President for people to stay away from the keep-out zones was not going well. As the Texas Senator had suggested, people across the nation were not accepting of the Iranian warriors attacking their cities.

Hundreds of New York City police teamed with their fellow fire department colleagues and launched a strike on the two warriors in Manhattan. They used numerous fire trucks and SWAT vehicles to carry out the attack. As the vehicles, police, and firefighters entered the keep-out zone, the Iranian warriors launched a fervent counterassault. The officers and firefighters hardly breached the keep-out zone before the Iranian warriors made quick work of them, leaving smoke-filled streets and dead men and women strewn around the area.

In Chicago, several street gangs attempted to reach the Iranian warriors in the Windy City. The gangs found themselves unable to approach the warriors as their first wave of attack was met by a grotesque hammering by the warriors. The brutal slaughter of their members enraged the groups leading to a series of additional coordinated attacks, none more successful than the first.

In Dallas, five hundred Texans, loaded with military-grade weapons and supported by a National Guard group, attempted to infiltrate the city's keep-out zone. They decided to try guerilla tactics and infiltrate the area using numerous spread-out groups slowly entering it. As each group entered, the Iranian warriors used their discs to eliminate them. As another entered, they found a similar fate.

One last attack in Dallas came with the remaining groups storming into the zone from all directions. They even attempted to send two single-engine planes loaded with bomb material in a suicide attack. The Iranian warriors unleashed their discs simultaneously in all directions. The discs took care of the two planes well above the city buildings, and the warriors easily dispelled the broad attack.

In Los Angeles, a tragic occurrence resulted in the loss of nearly five hundred homeless people. Intrigued by the events unfolding near where they lived on the streets, the homeless innocently came in droves into the keep-out area, unknowing an order to stay out was issued. The scene unfolded on national television and was gut-wrenching as the unsuspecting people continued to run into the keep-out area, only to be viciously destroyed by the warriors' flying discs.

Each city had numerous incidents where groups tried to band together and fight. The Iranian President was not kidding when he told the President that anyone who entered the space would be promptly destroyed. After a few hours, most cities began barricading the keep-out areas. Many states deployed the National Guard to manage the sites to inhibit militia attempts.

Meanwhile, many cities nationwide saw protests for and against the surrender. Many of the demonstrations became extremely violent as the two sides clashed. President Schmidt went on television briefly to demand the protesters stand down and let the government determine the path forward. It helped calm a few of the protests, but several still raged. The President hated seeing Americans waste their energy but wanted to keep his defiance until the last moment. He knew the military needed time to put things in place.

At the White House, the President organized last-minute details and kept abreast of what was occurring nationwide. The head of the Secret Service asked for a moment of the President's time, and the President asked him into his office.

"We want you in the air aboard Air Force One as soon as you finish on television today," said the head of the Secret Service. "They can't know your whereabouts. Your entire family will be with you."

"I'm not sure you will be able to get me to Andrews and fly out of there, given our current plans," said the President.

"We won't fly out of there," said his security head. "We have moved it to an undisclosed remote location. We'll get your family there ahead of time. We have a discrete exit plan for you, coordinated with the Pentagon. The military will have secured the air space by then, but we still choose to put you out of a remote location."

"Understood. I'm not sure I feel right about leaving, but I understand the protocol," the President reluctantly said.

"We'll fill you in on the details of our flight plan when we depart from here."

"And you will inform my family?" inquired the President. "My wife knows, but my children and their families only know bits and pieces. I asked her to share very little with them, so this will be a surprise."

"We'll handle it, Mr. President. They understand the gravity of the situation and are aware of the protocols. One more thing, if you could keep the speech short, it will give the Iranians less time to react and improve our ability to get you out of there safely."

"Are you saying I can be a little long-winded?" cracked the President. "I think I can manage to make it short. This speech is one where less is more."

The President escorted him out of the office and asked his assistant when the Vice President would arrive.

"He should be here any moment," she responded.

"Thank you. Send Alan in when he arrives," the President said.

The President had a slew of updates waiting for him to read. Things were happening worldwide that he needed to be informed on. It was too much to keep up with in real-time, so he had a constant set of short briefings generated for his quick perusal when he had available moments.

The first one he picked up was an update on Israel. The nuclear blast in the West Bank rocked the region, he read. An open declaration by Israeli Prime Minister Yaakv of Operation Tav followed it. The report said the strategy had partially worked, as Iran held Tel Aviv and Jerusalem under siege but was not pushing to enter those cities. Iran had tried to continue its move across other parts of Israel, but Israel detonated a second bomb near Haifa in response to that and once again rocked the nation. Yaakv wasn't bluffing, thought the President.

He picked up the second brief on the war in Europe. Russian President Kovalyov stepped up the war efforts in Europe. He was attacking with abandon across Eastern Europe and had successfully executed a strike on Riga, Latvia, and Kaunos, Lithuania. He read that the European nations were still deciding on their path forward. The President suspected they were still avoiding stoking Iran's ire as the U.S. had. His report went on to say that several U.S. intelligence sources in Europe were reporting that there was about to be a unified declaration of war against Russia by the entire European bloc. He wondered if they had finally come to the same realization that the U.S. had. This world war was unavoidable.

The third brief discussed the latest across U.S. cities. Many cities were still experiencing attempts to go at the Iranian warriors, even by blowing through barricaded sections placed by police and National Guard. Americans, he knew, were going to be a stubborn foe.

As he flipped the briefing page, he caught sight of the label on the briefing below. In bold letters, he saw 'CHINA.'

He quickly shifted his papers to that brief to see the latest. The brief discussed the considerable risk that China posed to the West. He was stunned to read further that China had begun substantial military exercises in their country and sizeable naval exercises in the Pacific region. God, the President thought, we don't need another heavyweight in the ring with us.

He gulped at the thought, reflecting again on the risks of defying the surrender.

He was just about to return to the brief on U.S. activities when a knock at the door, followed by a head peeking in, caused him to put the papers down.

"Come on in, Alan," said the President. "I'm just catching up on the recent news. These briefs have been helpful."

"Have you seen the latest in Israel?" asked the Vice President.

"Something more recent than what I just read?" inquired the President, realizing that Alan's tone suggested something new may have happened.

"Just moments ago. So, I bet so. Iran and Israel announced a one-week cease-fire just after Israel detonated a third nuclear bomb north of Nazareth along the border with Lebanon. Israel, only moments before that, launched three nuclear missiles into Syria.

The Iranian warriors intercepted all three, but Israel successfully detonated them as they were hit by the discs and rained nuclear fallout over a large swath. The intended target of the missiles appeared to be Damascus. The region is quickly becoming a toxic waste dump, as Yaakv suggested. Iran has agreed to discuss further the prospects of war. You have to hand it to Israel."

"There is no doubt that Israel plans to have the last say in all this," said the President. "They are going to make Iran earn whatever they take there. It plays in our favor as well. Iran is seeing their first real look at what a real enemy will do. Have you seen the latest on China and the war exercises? It looks like they are going to join this damn war."

"I saw that earlier today," said the Vice President shaking his head in disbelief. "When you sent me there to meet with their leadership, I didn't get any of that from them. I would have almost guaranteed they wouldn't become a part of this. They played me well."

"They played us all well," countered the President.

The final moments were approaching, and the Vice President knew the President had to be anxious about what was about to go down.

The Vice President asked, "Have you worked out your speech yet?"

"I only know one element so far," said the President with a smirk. "It will be short, per direction from the head of the Secret Service. They plan to whisk me off to a remote location and get me aboard Air Force One. I understand that you and your family will go to the bunker."

"Yes," the Vice President answered. "Is Cassandra on her way to with the final details?"

"She is supposed to be here in thirty minutes. You have some time if you want to attend to some other details."

"I might do that," answered the Vice President as he headed to the door.

As he opened it, the President's assistant said to the President, "I have a call from Europe for you."

"Which leader is it?" the President curiously asked.

"Several of them," she responded. "They are on a multi-line connection."

Curious about a call from multiple leaders, he motioned for the Vice President to stay and went over and picked up the phone.

As he lifted the receiver, Prime Minister Carrington, hearing the click of him picking up, said, "Is that you, President Schmidt?"

"Indeed, it is, Prime Minister," he responded. "How may I help you?"

"I have a group of us on the call," he answered. "Corbin, Caponero, Nilsen, Kruger, and Lehtinen are all on. We called to implore you to fight and not surrender. We know your predicament is far worse than ours, but that won't be true for long. Those scoundrels will be on us soon enough. Our friends in the former Soviet states and Israel are glorious reminders that freedom is worth the fight. Please tell us that you don't plan to surrender."

"We're still assessing the situation," answered the President, careful not to announce the U.S. intentions prematurely. "You know they sit inside our fifty largest cities waiting to exterminate us if I say no. I'll make a final decision after receiving an update from my Defense Secretary just before I take the stage."

"Don't do it," yelled French President Corbin. "We must fight, and we're here to join you. Russia and Iran are now one enemy, and we ask America to join us."

"I'm sorry, but too much is at stake," reiterated the President, unsure how to tactfully tell them they needed to wait until he went on television. "I can't decide until I have all available information, which I don't possess now."

"We know the weight you carry in this decision, and we shall press you no further," announced Italian Prime Minister Caponero. "I'm sorry for denying you port access with your naval ships, but like you, we had to make certain decisions before acting."

"I appreciate that, prime minister," said the President, genuinely appreciative of him sharing that it wasn't personal but just a bureaucratic issue. "I hope to be able to communicate with all of you shortly after my announcement, but please understand there is tremendous uncertainty about what occurs once I make that announcement."

"Understood," said the British Prime Minister. "One reason for our call was to inform you that we'll make a joint announcement declaring war against Russia. The announcement will include most of Europe. Only a few will withhold their commitment.

We'll not mention Iran unless you tell us now that you will join us in this broader declaration of war. We know that avoiding the mention of Iran in our announcement will do little to prevent their wrath in the long term, but it made no sense to kick the bear. We sincerely hope you will join us in this effort after your announcement. At that time, we also hope you will share the inner workings of your Cranio-Genesis Project with us."

President Schmidt couldn't believe his ears. How did they know? He couldn't believe that this had escaped his multi-layered security. Even under rigorous controls, the escape is why he was so careful because he knew that word always seemed to slip somewhere when it came to people.

"How do you know of that?" he embarrassingly asked.

"France discovered it. While reviewing their prior intelligence associated with Iran," the Prime Minister said. "After the battle in Iraq, President Corbin ordered a review of all Iranian intelligence. His team discovered data recovered from a former Iranian sleeper cell that had worked with a known Russian hacker. The entire group was killed, including the Russian. France was happy to see the cell eliminated and the troubles that came with it, so they didn't use many resources to figure out why.

At the time, the conclusion was the Russian hacker was being used to steal money to fund their activities. The second review found something they missed. The Russian hacker had secretly embedded an encrypted message, probably meant for his Russian comrades, but they never found it. The coded message read: The United States has developed telekinetic capabilities – find out about their Cranio-Genesis Project. No further details were included in the message, so we don't know how you did it. Just that you did."

"How long have you known?" asked President Schmidt, feeling like a heel.

"Since our first meeting in Italy. President Corbin shared it with us before you arrived. We hoped you would come clean. I assume that you had your reasons for not doing so."

"I did," he said without elaborating.

He figured it would take a while to explain his logic. It wasn't necessary at the moment.

"When we meet next, I'll share my reasons."

"Good luck to you," came from the group across the Atlantic. "We look forward to hearing from you shortly that you are an ally in this fight."

The phone clicked, and the President was happy to hear they had united to fight. The U.S. would need them, but he was embarrassed that they knew about Cranio-Genesis and didn't trust them enough to share the details months ago.

"You look like you saw a ghost," said the Vice President with concern.

"They knew since the beginning that we created telekinetic capabilities under a program called Cranio-Genesis. How we did it, they don't know. Just that we did."

"You had good reasons for holding back from them," said his Vice President, understanding the President was ashamed.

"I'm not going to dwell on it. A broad European alliance is about to declare war against Russia. They will wait to mention Iran unless we join the war."

"I take that as good news, given what you are about to do," said the Vice President.

"I think you're right. Go take care of what you need to do," said the President hoping to have a few moments for his thoughts before the Defense Secretary showed up.

"Will do," he responded, recognizing the President needed a moment alone.

Once again, the President faced addressing the nation at a horrible moment, frankly, the worst in American history. He planned to do as he had always done, be honest, be straightforward, and tell them like it was. He mentally ran through the possibilities again but came up with the same option. They had to fight!

The Defense Secretary soon arrived at the White House from the Pentagon. She met up with the Vice President on her way to the Oval Office. As they arrived outside the President's office, his assistant informed them he was ready.

They entered and saw the President staring blankly at his desk, lost in thought. A lone year under these pressures had aged him immensely, but they also saw a man of grit. If they had any chance at winning this fight, Paul Schmidt was as good as it gets to lead it.

"Please take a seat," said the President softly. "Just trying to gather my thoughts and formulate my speech for the announcement. It's going to be quick and to the point. The moment it happens, we better be ready to roll. We need our A-game, Cassandra."

"We've accomplished a lot in a short period, Mr. President," said his Defense Secretary. "Our troops have chemical cluster bombs placed around the warriors in thirty-seven of our cities. They don't have the time to install them at the others, so we've installed some other traditional bombs at those locations.

It may not take them out, but it will slow them down, and they have to wonder where they move next because something may come up and bite them. In your speech, you must make it clear for everyone in our cities to stay back. It's going to get ugly quickly."

"Are we sure the chemical weapons will work?" asked the President. "What about collateral damage?"

"The weapons are very potent against anyone in a sizeable swath," she answered. "Larger than the mile radius, so there will be collateral damage, unfortunately. But, if we don't make it overkill and get these warriors, their destruction will grossly outweigh the damage these will cause."

"I need to have a call to arms of all citizens," said the President recognizing the dangers in that statement. "Not to actively engage this enemy. But if any or all of this fails, I want them to defend themselves if they can. Maybe some get lucky and get in a lick like those Lithuanian special forces."

"They were special forces, Mr. President," said his Defense Secretary. "Not your average Joe."

"You grew up in New York City, Cassandra," responded the President. "From where I'm from, people hunted all their lives and can be some capable militia."

"As can some of those who lived in the city's tough parts, Mr. President," she retorted.

"Touché," he relented.

"On the naval side, we're actively energizing as much of the fleet as possible without raising suspicions. More will leave port once you make the announcement. We'll have excellent coverage in the Atlantic and can move numerous assets to Iran from the Mediterranean and the Arabian Sea. However, we'll be short on assets to protect against large-scale action from China.

The naval fleet will carry a large contingent of Marines ready to go wherever we need them."

"Next up is the Air Force, ready to deploy Operation Communikaze," she continued. "I think you were briefed on this at the beginning of your presidency."

"Yes, we plan to disable communication satellites of targeted countries."

"Indeed, it's," she said, knowing this man didn't miss much. "We'll target known Iranian and Russian assets, but we should expect a reprisal from Russia as we know they have some similar tricks up their sleeve."

"How do you want to handle China, Mr. President? Should we target them as well? If we're wrong about them, we could drag them into this if they consider this an act of war."

"Hold off. We can't take a chance starting something neither of us wanted," he said, unwilling to risk encouraging the Chinese to join the war.

"Will do," she said. "Next, we have several EMP weapons ready to launch over Russia and much of Iran. They may intercept them over Iran, but even if they do, the pulse will still create an electric firestorm that will damage numerous electronics around the intercept point.

Between these and the satellites, there will be a massive loss of connectivity for both countries. We have no planned launches of

EMP weapons in China. Do you want us to hold off on this as well? Our resources will be strained to pull that off, but we can hit some of their main locations."

"Let's hold off on that," said the President. "But be ready to launch both if they enter the fray."

"Understood," she answered. "Additionally, the Air Force will be on alert, with numerous recon and support roles awaiting to see where they're needed. As for the Army, they will deploy as we deem necessary."

"As soon as this goes down, I want you on the phone finding out how we can support the Europeans and Israelis," he ordered his Defense Secretary. "We'll be spread thin, but we have to find ways to help each other mutually, and they may bring something to the table we can leverage and vice versa."

"We'll need all the allies we can muster," she responded. "If nothing else, we still have a lot that needs to be tied down, so I need to head back to the Pentagon. Good luck with your speech."

"I'll be in touch from Air Force One just after this starts," he said reassuringly to her. "Alan will be available from the bunker, as well."

"Any specifics for me, Mr. President?" said his Vice President.

"I want you to phone your Chinese contacts and see if you can intervene and stave any actions from them at the start," said the President hoping to inhibit an escalation if at all possible. "They may tell you to stick it, but we must try."

"Soon as I'm secured into the bunker, I'll make the call," confirmed his Vice President.

"I have to get working on my final notes for the speech. I only have thirty minutes. Cassandra, good luck and stay safe. Alan, I'll see you in the press room in about twenty-five minutes."

The Vice President and Defense Secretary left the room. Cassandra hurried back to the Pentagon, and his Vice President closed out some final details for his post-announcement arrangements.

The President enjoyed a quiet moment and reflected on his campaign and short tenure. His hopes and dreams for the country never materialized. He had accomplished little of what he had promised. The unifying spirit he hoped to bring to the American people had turned into despair, devastation, and the brink of collapse.

Gathering his wits, he decided it was useless to dwell on that. He reminded himself of his father's old saying; nothing is ever accomplished by wallowing about what could have been, only by doing what needs to be done.

With that, he composed his short speech for the American people.

As he finished the end, he lost himself in the speech and was startled by a rap on the office door. He looked up to see the door opening and a look of anguish on the face of his assistant.

"Mr. President. Iran's President is on the phone and demanding to speak with you again," she said, trembling.

Fright and uncertainty tore through him as he said, "Put him through."

"President Schmidt," said the American President, hesitantly picking up the line.

"President Schmidt, you surprise me with your actions," the Iranian President said, seething again. "I take that back. You

Americans never surprise me. Did you think I would let you try to encapsulate my warriors in your wretched snares? Of course, you did. That is why you have moved to circle them so that once you deny me the surrender, you can move to eliminate them. Iran is not that foolish.

I forgot to inform you that I placed another warrior in each city, hidden from you, that will secure the release of my other warriors while swiftly destroying everything along their way. In our game of chess, President Schmidt, I call checkmate.

You have about fifteen minutes until the deadline. I suggest you rethink your plan and offer the surrender or perish with millions of other Americans. I look forward to your answer momentarily."

The phone hung up on the Iranian President's end, and Paul Schmidt stood there, unsure what to do now.

Had things changed with this revelation, he wondered? He knew the answer to that was yes. There was no way to reestablish control of our airspace with other warriors hidden. Even if they could get to some of the Iranian warriors before the hidden ones came to their aid, the U.S. forces would be more or less powerless to stop their slaughter alone.

He needed to talk with the Vice President. He couldn't see another choice than to surrender.

"Get the Vice President in here, immediately," yelled the President to his assistant as he stood at his doorway. "I need him here now!"

"Mr. President, he is in an impromptu meeting," she said, hesitating because she could tell the President was in no mood to deal with anything but compliance.

"Get him out of it and over here," he barked.

"He was urgently called into the meeting by Chinese Ambassador Chen, Mr. President," she hesitantly answered. "He said he needed to find out what he wanted."

"What in the hell?" yelled the wide-eyed President. "I hope they aren't going to stick it to us in our final moments. Get him out of it and get him over here now."

Just as he yelled the last part, the Vice President came around the corner with the Chinese Ambassador in tow.

"Mr. President, I know you know Ambassador Chen," said the Vice President while still approaching. "We need a moment of your time."

"Alan, I have only a few moments left, and I just received some urgent news that we need to discuss," he impatiently said. "Just you and I."

The President was frustrated with his Vice President's insistence at such a critical time, and his tone reflected that.

"Mr. President, stop for a second," said his Vice President calmly. "You need to hear what he has to say now!"

"It better be important," said the President, ushering the two into his office.

"President Schmidt, I know your time is short," started the Chinese Ambassador. "Let me be quick and brief. China is keenly aware of your Cranio-Genesis Project and the discovery of your two scientists, Drs. Heidi and Peter Davidson.

Our cyber teams monitor many outlets of worldwide network traffic. Often, we follow in behind hackers that we find trying to infiltrate any number of things. Interestingly, we have found that hackers are trying to cover their tracks and hide from those they are infiltrating but very often pay little attention to those sliding behind them on their coattails. We have made great use of this technique over the years."

"Get to your point," warned the President, unwilling to delay his discussion with the Vice President to hear some Chinese gloating.

"We followed behind the notorious Russian hacker that took your secret documents for Iran. We obtained the information without anyone knowing we were ever there.

We were awestruck by the results of your project. We have historically operated a program to limit the number of Chinese children born to a family in China. With our large population, you know that we often have to end the life of many children, especially when there are multiple births at one time. We selectively used some of these children to try out your Cranio-Genesis excitations. We didn't believe it inhumane since they were designated for termination already.

Our scientists were able to replicate the results of your project. However, we took it another step further. With so many births annually, China experiences multiple sets of identical children in any given year. It's simple probability. Thus, we tried the excitation on two identical children.

The electromagnetic pulse sequence revived the twins just as it had with the other children, but a fascinating discovery emerged. Due to their identical structure, the children experienced a form of telekinetic resonance.

When operating together, each twin became twice as powerful and could control twice the number of objects. Thus, if you follow my math, two identical twins are stronger than four individual warriors. Our scientists pushed it farther with triplets, quadruplets, and finally, a set of quintuplets. All experienced the same resonance, and their powers multiplied by the number of telekinetic children."

"You have telekinetic groups that are all identical?" asked the President, stunned by the revelation.

"We do. The identical groups, like the Iranians, have been secretly training for years, hidden from the world," he responded. "We never considered using children to conquer others, but we considered them a critical part of our defense strategy. We have many sets of twins, dozens of triplets, five quadruplets, and one extremely capable set of five, the Chang quintuplets."

"Why are you sharing this with us now?" inquired the President.

"We wish to be your ally in the war that will soon escalate?" he adamantly said.

"China has been no ally to the United States," said the President furiously. "You've worked with Iran and Russia to cripple us and allow Iran to emerge as the leading power globally."

"President Schmidt, I'm sure you are familiar with the saying 'Keep your friends close and your enemies closer,'" said the Ambassador.

"Of course, it's an often-used phrase in our country," the President responded.

"Americans think it originated from Michael Corleone in 'The Godfather II,' but it, in fact, it came from China," replied the Ambassador. "It was a key tenet of Sun Tzu in his famous book, 'The Art of War.'

We have always been suspicious of Iran and untrusting of Russia. We allied ourselves to ensure we understood the limits of the force, their leaders' honor, and their specific plans.

While China and the United States often do not see eye to eye on many things, we respect that you are, more or less, an honorable country. China believes that the U.S. is an ally it needs and can trust. Specifically, we trust you, President Schmidt."

"Iran is only a few minutes from wiping my people out," said the President realizing he had only moments to get on the television. "The Iranian President just called to tell me that he hid another warrior in each of our cities to safeguard against a trap and carry out their plan if we successfully stop the others. So, each city now has three warriors to contend with."

"If you accept China as your ally, we start this battle right here in the U.S., President Schmidt," said the Ambassador. "China has brought fifty-one sets of warriors to the United States overnight. Our warriors are in your cities and will eliminate the Iranian warriors threatening you. Please tell your forces to stand down and let us engage them."

"Can I trust you?" asked the President looking for any hint of deception.

"I give you my word that China is honorable in its intentions," answered the Ambassador.

"What about Russia?" the President asked.

"Kovalyov is not a man of honor," he answered with a hint of a sneer. "We'll join you, Europe, and Israel in the fight for the soul of the world."

"You said fifty-one groups?" asked the Vice President.

"Yes, the last one is our most prolific group, the Chang quintuplets," he answered. "Unknown to you, Iran also placed another set of twenty warriors outside the home of your Davidsons. Iran learned that the Davidsons had returned to their home and that their children from the project were still alive. If you do not surrender, Iran will order twenty warriors to execute the entire Davidson family. The Chang quintuplets will ensure that doesn't take place."

"Can your warriors stop them?" asked the President.

"I'm sure you heard of the incident in the Xinjiang region where five of Iran's warriors mysteriously disappeared," responded the ambassador.

"Yes, we did," answered the President.

"The Chang quintuplets at their best," the ambassador said, smiling broadly.

"Is there anything else? I need to get on television," asked the President hurriedly.

"Just know that China is not a savior for the world in this. We have many warriors, but we learned that Iran has a few thousand in its control. Our force does not nearly match that number. We can help you escape your current predicament, similar to how we swiftly defeated the five warriors they sent to Xinjiang.

But know this; it will be a long war. We'll require a lot of coordination amongst many allies to win this. Please go tell the world that we fight together."

"Thank you, and tell President Li that we'll coordinate once we get things in order here and are sure the Iranians are dealt with," offered the President. "Alan, get with Cassandra and tell her to stand down. Let her know what happened and have her teams ready for an updated game plan when things settle down."

"Will do, and the Chinese Ambassador needs to give the go-ahead," he said, rushing out with the Chinese Ambassador.

The President's mind spun in a thousand directions. He was out of time and had to get into the briefing room. He knew the world was anxiously watching as most figured the Great American Empire had fallen. He was about to inform them otherwise.

He took the podium, invigorated by a better fighting chance. Their plan had changed, and success would be earned from this point forward, but the balance shifted. He knew today would be a historic date in an epic world war.

He looked at the array of cameras as he entered the press room. So many global news agencies were peering in to see his answer for the world.

He momentarily hesitated as he took the podium and said, "My fellow Americans and friends to this nation, it's with great distress that I address you this evening. America has been attacked on its own soil by an enemy with a formidable new technology that has granted them an unmatched edge against the rest of the world.

Iran has placed three of its warriors in our fifty largest cities. Their warriors, using their discs, inflicted death and destruction in those cities upon their arrival. We've estimated that two million people were lost in the streets of these cities during the short period since their initial attack."

He paused and touched his forehead lightly. He was exhausted and wanted to ensure his words were clear.

He said, "I received a call twenty-four hours ago from the President of Iran, under the direction of their Supreme Leader, demanding that we unconditionally surrender. Should we not, he informed me that Iran would wipe our people out as they have done in numerous other countries across the world.

I had to consider the options I had in front of me as Commander in Chief and leader of this great nation. All choices result in the significant loss of American lives, but surrender means losing American freedoms that we treasure and protect."

Lights from the numerous camera crews were causing him to sweat profusely, and he reached up to wipe his brow. Anger grew in him as he considered the billions of people sitting on the other side of those camera connections waiting to see how the ugly position of the U.S. turned out. He dispelled those thoughts and regained his composure.

He continued, "Our nation is established on the principles of freedom. We've made grave mistakes, and we're far from perfect. However, when I awake each day, I endeavor to push this country one step forward toward making this a better place for all people, not just here but across the world. If I can string those days together, I'll soon be making significant progress. This approach was an important lesson instilled in me by my wonderful parents.

Furthermore, in America, we're a nation that prides itself on hard work, invention, competing, and winning. Other countries see that and interpret our combination of attributes as arrogance. It's not. It's better categorized as a unique blend of optimism and determination that we call the American Dream."

The last piece was critical, so he hesitated to consider his words. He couldn't use what he had prepared at his desk as the conversations with the Iranian President and the Chinese ambassador changed everything and destroyed its usefulness.

"Unconditional surrender of the United States was the demand from Iran," he began again. "We're a great country, but we're not arrogant enough to believe that we exist in this world alone, without friends or enemies. Our nation did not blossom by itself but on the backs of numerous friends, partners, and allies. We've always welcomed support from those with shared beliefs and the guts to help.

America, no, that is not appropriate for me to say. It's not America. I failed to consider the support and alliance of others and the complimentary trust of ideas and intelligence to address common causes and solve problems. As such, I have brought peril to the doorstep of America. For that, I'm deeply sorry."

It was time to deliver the punch. Anger roiled through him again as he considered his final words. This time he let it burn inside him.

Red-faced and steely-eyed, the President said, "I'll fix that now, for you need to know that the United States of America created the telekinetic capabilities used by the Iranian warriors. Allah didn't bring that capability to Iran; we did. They acquired it from us by way of a thieving Russian cyber pirate.

Free people of the world, we must stand up and unite because today, the United States of America defies the zealotry of Iran and the militancy of Russia. Today, we ally ourselves with the great nations throughout Europe, Israel, and China to defeat your aggression. We'll never surrender! You have awakened the eagle for which you will forever be sorry."

Thank you for selecting my novel. I hope you enjoyed the first installment of the Cranio-Genesis Project. My second novel in the series, The Cranio-Genesis Project: Days of Reckoning, is out.

If you are so inclined, I would appreciate you leaving a review on Amazon. Reviews are a critical piece of Amazon's search and ranking. As an independent author, they help us compete with large-scale publishing machines.

About the Author

My writing focuses on the scientific plausibility of a concept that grabs the reader, then whisks them on a journey.

After an adventurous career in the tech industry, I settled down to create stories born from my background.

I live in Georgia with my lovely wife, Tracey, while I pursue my passion for writing these entertaining tales.

Made in United States
Orlando, FL
07 May 2023

32902931R00233